PENGUIN  CLASSICS

EGIL'S SAGA

SVANHILDUR ÓSK... ...degree in Iceland and pursued further ...ies ...the universities of Toronto, Copenhagen and London where she was awarded a Ph.D. for her thesis on a medieval chronicle in the Icelandic manuscript AM 764 4to. She was Lecturer in Icelandic at University College London for six years before taking up a research post at the Árni Magnússon Institute in Reykjavík. She has published on Icelandic literature, medieval and modern, and contributed to literary programmes on radio and television. In 2003 she received the Young Scholar of the Year Award from the Icelandic Research Council.

BERNARD SCUDDER was born in Canterbury, Kent, and studied English at the University of York and Icelandic at the University of Iceland. Since 1977 he has lived in Reykjavík, where he is a full-time translator. Including more than a dozen published works, his translations from Icelandic encompass sagas, ancient and modern poetry, and leading contemporary novels and plays. He translated two major sagas for *The Complete Sagas of Icelanders* (1997) and edited most of the poetry in that collection. In 1998 two novels in his translation were shortlisted for the European Union's Aristeon Literary Prize.

Egil's Saga

Translated by
BERNARD SCUDDER
Edited with an Introduction and Notes by
SVANHILDUR ÓSKARSDÓTTIR

PENGUIN BOOKS

PENGUIN BOOKS

Published by the Penguin Group
Penguin Books Ltd, 80 Strand, London WC2R ORL, England
Penguin Group (USA) Inc., 375 Hudson Street, New York, New York 10014, USA
Penguin Books Australia Ltd, 250 Camberwell Road, Camberwell, Victoria 3124, Australia
Penguin Books Canada Ltd, 10 Alcorn Avenue, Toronto, Ontario, Canada M4V 3B2
Penguin Books India (P) Ltd, 11 Community Centre, Panchsheel Park, New Delhi – 110 017, India
Penguin Group (NZ), Cnr Airborne and Rosedale Roads, Albany, Auckland 1310, New Zealand
Penguin Books (South Africa) (Pty) Ltd, 24 Sturdee Avenue, Rosebank 2196, South Africa

Penguin Books Ltd, Registered Offices: 80 Strand, London WC2R ORL, England

www.penguin.com

Translations first published in *The Complete Sagas of Icelanders (Including 49 Tales)*, I and II,
edited by Viðar Hreinsson (General Editor), Robert Cook, Terry Gunnell, Keneva Kunz
and Bernard Scudder. Leifur Eiríksson Publishing Ltd, Iceland 1997
First published by Penguin Classics 2002

5

Translation copyright © Leifur Eiríksson, 1997
Editorial matter copyright © Svanhildur Óskarsdóttir, 2004
All rights reserved

The moral right of the translator and of the editor has been asserted

Leifur Eiríksson Publishing Ltd gratefully acknowledges the support of the
Nordic Cultural Fund, Ariane Programme of the European Union, UNESCO,
Icelandair and others.

Set in 10.25/12.25 pt PostScript Adobe Sabon
Typeset by Rowland Phototypesetting Ltd, Bury St Edmunds, Suffolk
Printed in England by Clays Ltd, St Ives plc

ISBN-13: 978-0-14-044770-5

www.greenpenguin.co.uk

Penguin Books is committed to a sustainable future
for our business, our readers and our planet.
The book in your hands is made from paper
certified by the Forest Stewardship Council.

Contents

Acknowledgements

Help and advice from many individuals – too numerous to mention in full – is gratefully acknowledged. Bernard Scudder would particularly like to thank Örnólfur Thorsson; Fredric Heinemann for his critical reading of the original translation; Don Brandt for his proofreading; the late Bjarni Einarsson for graciously allowing the use of his unpublished revised readings of source manuscripts of the saga; and Finnbogi Guðmundsson for his perspicacious suggestions of improvements to the verse translations. Svanhildur Óskarsdóttir would like to thank, among others, Bergljót S. Kristjánsdóttir, Peter Foote, Helgi Þorláksson, Orri Vésteinsson, Sverrir Tómasson, Torfi Tulinius and Úlfhildur Dagsdóttir for their constructive advice, comments and inspiration.

The editor and translator jointly thank Jóhann Sigurðsson, publisher of *The Complete Sagas of Icelanders*, Viðar Hreinsson, editor, and Jean-Pierre Biard, who produced the maps, on the Icelandic side of this project, and Hilary Laurie, Lindeth Vasey, Emma Horton, Laura Barber and others at Penguin.

Introduction

The world that forms the stage for the events in *Egil's Saga* is that of the Vikings. It is a vast world, even in the eyes of the modern traveller. In the period AD 800–1100 those Scandinavian seafarers left their mark in regions as far east as Novgorod and Kiev, as far south as Constantinople and Baghdad, as far west as Greenland and the eastern shores of North America. Their impact was mixed and multifaceted. They conducted lucrative trade in furs, slaves, walrus ivory, amber and honey; some served as mercenaries for foreign kings and rulers; they sacked monasteries and burned villages; they settled new lands and left a lasting legacy in ornamented artefacts and in their poetry.

Egil Skallagrimsson, the main protagonist of *Egil's Saga*, is a precocious Viking – and a poet. He composes his first verse at the age of three, slays his first victim at seven and soon thereafter sets off on his first Viking raids. The saga catalogues his many journeys and his struggle to uphold what he perceives as his rights against those who seek to infringe them, the kings of Norway in particular. In this he is helped by his kinsmen and his loyal friend Arinbjorn, but his foes are many and their means often foul. Throughout his life Egil uses his poetry to reflect upon his experiences; his thoughts never stray far from himself, his feelings, his skills and his interests – Egil Skallagrimsson is as much at the centre of the poems attributed to him as of the saga that bears his name.

The saga was written in the thirteenth century, some three hundred years after the historical Egil is thought to have roamed the seas around Britain, Iceland and Scandinavia. It has long ranked with the most popular sagas of Icelanders, thanks largely, no doubt, to the attraction readers continue to feel towards its controversial hero. Egil is no ordinary individual and his story is marked by contradictions. His life is dominated by his quest for justice, but the justice he metes out to his victims is questionable. He seems at times to be clouded with rage and frustration, yet he produces poetry of intricate beauty. He comes across, initially, as some sort of juvenile delinquent on a monstrous scale, but towards the end of the saga we see him as the respected leader of his community in Iceland. Such are the proportions of this character, and the saga so richly undercut with irony, that it is difficult for the reader to jump to any conclusion about Egil and the events he becomes embroiled in.

Through this complexity of Egil's character and his long and, at times, chequered career, the saga explores issues as diverse as loyalty and the value of friendship, the power of poetry with its link to the occult, the social and hereditary status of illegitimate offspring, the frictions between generations of the same family and the complicated relationship between two brothers who love the same woman – as well as entertaining the reader with scenes that range from violent splatter to intimate illustrations of sorrow and grief.

Kings and commoners

Although the saga brings together many different issues, its overarching theme is the struggle of independent farmers against overbearing kings. This theme takes on added significance when it is borne in mind that Icelandic society in the first centuries after its settlement – that is, in the time when *Egil's Saga* is set – was a society without a sovereign ruler; it had no governmental executive in the person and retinue of a king. Instead, legislative and judicial power was in the hands of a large group of chieftains, the godis, whose social and political status was not vastly different from that of the ordinary farmer. This changed in the thirteenth century when, after a tumultuous period where several leading families fought each other to gain power in the country, Icelanders accepted the authority of the Norwegian king. *Egil's Saga*, in the form we know it, is the product of this troubled century. It glorifies the powerful farmer who is ready to defend his honour and that of his family against anyone who seeks to diminish it, be it a fellow countryman or a foreign king. This picture of the proud chieftain may be all the more clearly presented because the author and his contemporaries were aware that such individuals were now becoming figures of the past. There was no room for them in the changing economic and political milieu of thirteenth-century Iceland – no room, that is, except in stories. We can detect in *Egil's Saga* a certain nostalgia for the times when an Icelandic farmer was able to hold his own against powerful rulers of other countries. At the same time, Egil is portrayed as a man of such overgrown dimensions that it is hard to see him inhabiting the world of Icelandic farmers at the time when the saga was written. He is out of their league and hardly a role model for young men seeking to establish themselves in thirteenth-century Iceland or pursuing a career at the court of the Norwegian king. Skuli Thorsteinsson, the man we see in the closing lines of the saga, is much nearer their reality in this respect. He is Egil's grandson, but achieves his fame through fighting alongside a successful contender to the Norwegian throne rather than challenging the royal authority: the farmer no longer gains his glory by opposing the king but by supporting him.

The situation is very different at the beginning of the saga where we meet Egil's ancestors in north Norway and witness the struggle of his grandfather, Kveldulf, to hold his own against the royal ambitions of Harald Fair-hair. These events take place in the late ninth century when Norway was made up of several small kingdoms and tensions between the many rulers were rife. *Egil's Saga* describes how Harald, who ruled lands in the south of the country, fights to become the first sovereign king of Norway; he gradually moves northwards, crushing all opposition on the way. Thorolf, one of Kveldulf's two sons, allies himself with Harald, against his father's advice. The story follows the escalating friction between the king and the family of Kveldulf, which leads to the family emigrating to Iceland following the death of Thorolf at the hands of the king. Kveldulf dies at sea, but his remaining son, Grim (nicknamed Skallagrim), settles in the Borgarfjord district of Iceland where his wife, Bera, gives birth to several children, among them the sons Thorolf and Egil. The saga describes the settlement where Skallagrim assumes local leadership, a role that Egil inherits and retains almost to his death. One thread of the story is therefore concerned with events in Iceland, although most of its action takes place in other countries, mainly in Norway and England, with kings among the cast.

Despite the family's relocation to Iceland, Kveldulf's descendants continue to spar with royalty. Thorolf Skallagrimsson takes after his uncle and namesake in that he actively seeks the friendship and favours of kings, whereas Egil is both warier and more belligerent. Egil's main adversaries are Harald's son, King Eirik Bloodaxe, and his queen, Gunnhild. On his first trip to Norway, Egil manages to get on the wrong side of the royal couple and later, when he lays claims to his wife's inheritance in Norway, Gunnhild, in particular, does everything in her power to thwart him. But when Eirik's brother, Hakon, assumes power in Norway, Eirik and Gunnhild flee to Britain. It is at their court in York that we see the struggle between Egil and Eirik, commoner and king, reach its climax (chapters 60–62): Egil receives the gift of his own head – a grudging royal pardon – in return for a poem in praise of the king, and thus narrowly escapes the fate of his uncle Thorolf. The incident marks the end of Egil's dealings with Eirik, but he continues to press for justice in Norway, now ruled by King Hakon. The inheritance dispute is finally settled, but Hakon, mindful of Egil's obstinacy towards Eirik, does not wish to maintain any relationship with Kveldulf's descendants. Egil does not cease to intervene in the dealings between Hakon and his subjects, and helps his Norwegian friend, Thorstein, by undertaking on his behalf to collect tribute for the king. Hakon suspects Thorstein of disloyalty and threatens him with expulsion, but, thanks to Egil, Thorstein keeps his honour and his lands in Norway.

King Hakon had been fostered by King Athelstan of England, who adds an extra dimension to the saga's portrayal of kings and their relationship with their subjects. Athelstan is shown in

many ways as a benevolent and generous king, the antithesis of
Eirik. He is brought into the story when the raiding brothers,
Thorolf and Egil, decide to go to England and join the king's
forces (chapter 50). They fight on Athelstan's behalf in the battle
of Wen Heath, where Thorolf is killed. The saga's portrayal of
political events in England is no more historically accurate than
its depiction of Norwegian affairs, although in both cases the
narrative is built into a historical framework. The saga mentions
correctly that Alfred became the first sole ruler over England
(excluding the Danelaw from 900–1100) and was succeeded by
his son Edward, who was in turn succeeded by Athelstan in 924,
but its account of events leading up to and including Athelstan's
battle with the Scottish king Olaf differs in many ways from
that given in English sources. According to *The Anglo-Saxon
Chronicle*, the kingdom Athelstan inherited did not include
Northumbria, but he struck up an alliance with its ruler, King
Sihtric, upon whose death in 927 he invaded it and assumed
the throne, driving out Sihtric's son Anlaf. In the aftermath,
Athelstan subjugated the other kings in the British Isles, including King Constantine of Scotland. *The Anglo-Saxon Chronicle*
mentions that Athelstan 'went into Scotland with both a land
force and a naval force' in 934 'and ravaged much of it',[1] but
the motive is not given. Three years later Athelstan fought a
bloody battle at Brunanburh against Constantine and an army
of Norsemen led by a king called Olaf (possibly the son of
Guthfrith, Sihtric's brother) and emerged victorious. The battle
of Brunanburh offers the closest historical parallel to the battle
of Wen Heath described in *Egil's Saga*. The saga makes Olaf,
who is said to be descended from Scots and Norsemen, king of
the Scots and intent on reclaiming Northumbria from Athelstan.
In this he succeeds, but only temporarily until Athelstan retali-
ates by fighting at Wen Heath where Olaf and his earls, Hring
and Adils, are killed by the heroes of the saga. Later, when Eirik
Bloodaxe is banished from Norway he sails west and raids
England. According to the saga, Athelstan rides out to fight him,
but a truce is brokered whereby Eirik becomes Athelstan's liege
lord in Northumbria, where Athelstan's power was still in-
secure, and establishes himself in York. Contrary to the saga's

description, Athelstan and King Eirik Bloodaxe were not contemporaries. Athelstan died in 939 and *The Anglo-Saxon
Chronicle* mentions that King Eric (the saga's Eirik) was received
by the Northumbrians in 952, but driven out two years later in
favour of Eadred. In the saga, the time-span is cleverly con-
densed and Athelstan brought into Eirik's affairs to fit the plot.

Although the action of the saga revolves around the dealings
between members of Kveldulf's family and various kings, and
therefore mostly takes place in Norway and Britain, the settings
are wider. The Viking raids by the brothers Thorolf and Egil
take them not only to the British Isles but also to other parts of
the Viking world. They raid to the east on the Baltic coast all
the way to the region named Courland (approximately where
Latvia is today), and they sail south to Denmark and Frisia.
Early in the story the reader had been given a taste of the Far
North, as the first part is mostly set in northern Scandinavia;
Thorolf, Kveldulf's son, travels north into Lapland and east
towards Karelia to collect tribute for King Harald. And before
he is driven from Norway, King Eirik raids in the east and fights
a battle at the river Dvina in Permia, now northern Russia. Some
parts of the saga, most notably the last dozen chapters, are
played out in Iceland. The reader is thus repeatedly introduced
to new regions and different scenery, and the sheer geographical
scope of *Egil's Saga* gives it an edge over most other works of
the genre, where the action, typically, is centred around a single
district in Iceland and involves disputes between farmers, rather
than what might be described as one man's crusade against the
Norwegian dynasty.

Crafting a saga

Egil's Saga was probably composed in the first half of the
thirteenth century – it may be among the first sagas of Icelanders
to acquire written form. In crafting the saga, its author drew on
information preserved in other written sources, such as *The
Book of Settlements*, and he must also have relied on oral
accounts of some of the events he depicted. The verses which
he incorporated into the saga would have been considered a

trustworthy source by his audience. Much of the poetry is thought to date back to the tenth century and could well have been composed by the historical Egil, although there is much scope for disagreement on this matter and some scholars argue that most – if not all – of the poetry should be attributed to the author of the saga.[2] The oldest surviving manuscript fragments of the saga are dated to the second half of the thirteenth century, but the oldest complete text is in the codex known as *Möðru-vallabók* (AM 132 fol.), dated to *c*.1330–70, which contains ten other sagas. *Egil's Saga* does not identify its author, nor do the manuscripts divulge his name. Scholars have advanced the hypothesis that the historian Snorri Sturluson (1178/9–1241) could have been responsible for its composition: he was descended from Egil, lived in Borgarfjord and was no doubt knowledgeable about the history of the district. Snorri was also a learned scholar of poetics and a connoisseur of verse. He is thought to be the author of the treatise on Old Norse poetry and poetic diction often referred to as the *Prose Edda*, as well as the compilation of sagas of Norwegian kings named *Heims-kringla*.

Leaving aside the identity of the author, it is clear that he must have been erudite and well versed in the art of narrative composition. He shows great skill in weaving the various strands of the narrative together, linking events in the life of one genera-tion to those of the next, developing two threads of narrative simultaneously, and so on. Like many medieval authors he divides his story into two main parts: in the first the action is built up around Thorolf Kveldulfsson, while in the second, much longer part, Egil dominates the action.

The structure of the saga is characterized by parallels and contrasts which are evident in small episodes as well as in the larger scheme of the story. There are many parallels between events in the two parts and also between episodes within each one. Thorolf Kveldulfsson's struggle against his lord, King Harald, in the first part is mirrored by the battles that Egil, who is not one of the king's men, wages with Harald's descendants. Both Thorolf and Egil become involved in disputes over inherit-ance which have a similar root, namely an unlawful (or at least not fully legitimate) marriage: the claim of Hildirid's sons against Thorolf for Bard Brynjolfsson's inheritance (chapter 9), and Egil's claim to the inheritance of his father-in-law, Bjorn, Asgerd's father.

Sometimes the two parts are linked together through striking similarities in scene-setting. For example, the ways in which Skallagrim's visit to King Harald (chapter 25) and Egil's visit to King Eirik (chapter 60) are depicted. Both men arrive in a company of twelve; they wait outside while the mediator is fetched. When they enter the king's hall both Grim and Egil attract the king's attention because they are a full head taller than their companions, and a bitter conversation ensues. But these parallels also serve to highlight the differences between the scenes. Skallagrim's meeting takes place before he avenges his brother, Thorolf, by killing King Harald's kinsmen and supporters and flees the country, never to meet the king again. Egil has already exacted a cruel revenge on Eirik, by killing many of his men, including his son, before he turns up at his court in York. When he departs, he does not have to flee, he has the king's leave, but, as in the case of Grim, this is their last exchange. Parallels of this kind knit the story more closely together while at the same time demonstrating that events in the past repeat themselves in the present, although their outcome may be different.

The skilful use of parallels and contrasts often invites the reader to compare men's motives and view their actions from more than one perspective. For example, in the first part of the saga where the descriptions of Thorolf's conduct are pitched against the version of his actions that Hildirid's sons give to the king. On the one hand, Thorolf is shown as an ambitious but popular vassal who is loyal to his lord, collecting taxes and delivering them faithfully. But the 'hearsay' version pictures him as a man too proud for his own good, who amasses a fortune with the aim of overthrowing the king's power in the region. It is left to the reader to evaluate these accounts and to judge Thorolf's intentions. And in the crucial scene in which Egil meets King Eirik at York, Egil, Arinbjorn, Eirik and Gunnhild are all given the opportunity to voice their contrasting views, giving the reader a clear picture of what is at stake when Egil goes off to compose the poem that will decide his fate. Although the saga often seems to support Egil's property claims and to condemn the way King Eirik and his men thwart the process of law, the author's sympathy does not lie exclusively with Egil; the issues are far too complex for that. The reader is given another opportunity to speculate on the nature of justice towards the end when Egil acts as an arbitrator in the dispute between his son, Thorstein, and Thorstein's neighbour, Steinar Sjonason, over grazing rights (chapter 85). How does this man, whom the saga has repeatedly portrayed as the wronged party in his quest for justice in Norway, acquit himself in the role of judge? Egil's verdict will seem surprisingly harsh to most readers – he has Steinar's land confiscated and banishes him from the district.

This play with contrasts also extends to the more technical aspects of the narrative, such as the way the author uses different points of view to masterful effect. One example is the episode after Egil has been outlawed in Norway, when he seeks out Berg-Onund (his opponent in the inheritance dispute) on the island of Fenring. In this scene the point of view switches effortlessly between Onund, Egil and Onund's men, Hadd and Frodi. It adds to the suspense, but also creates comic relief, when Onund and his men assume they are pursuing a real bear:

> Berg-Onund ran up to the shrubs. He was wearing a helmet, carried a shield in one hand and a spear in the other, and was girded with a sword. But it was Egil, not a bear, that was hiding in the shrubs, and when he saw Berg-Onund he drew his sword. There was a strap on the hilt which he pulled over his hand to let the sword hang there. Taking his spear, he rushed towards Berg-Onund. When Berg-Onund saw this he quickened his pace and put the shield in front of him, and before they clashed they threw their spears at each other . . . Hadd and Frodi ran over to Berg-Onund when they saw he had been felled. Egil turned to face them. (chapter 58)

Another characteristic is the way the action is delayed by descriptions of the weapons and the movements of the men. The effect is similar to that of slow motion in films, and the frequent shifts between Egil's point of view and Onund's are also reminiscent of cinematic montage. A similar technique of retardation and shifting viewpoints is used with great skill elsewhere in the saga, for example in the episode describing Egil's journey to England and his meeting with King Eirik in York (chapters 60–62). Egil's shipwreck and his subsequent deliberations are used to slacken the pace of the narrative temporarily and to create suspense by delaying the moment Egil comes face to face with the king.

Descriptions of weather and nature are often cleverly placed before violent episodes, as if to set the scene for the events and create a contrast between the initial stillness and the subsequent storm of bloody action. This 'lull before the storm' is nowhere as marked as in the description before Egil's frenzied attacks on King Eirik's men at Fenring and at the fishing camp at Herdla where Rognvald, the king's son, is among his victims (chapter 58). When the breeze gets up and Egil finally attacks, the calm sea and peaceful nights that preceded the violence linger in the mind of the reader in vivid contrast to the subsequent slaughter.

The author uses anticipation and repetition to heighten the reader's expectation. Kveldulf's foreboding (chapters 5–6) about his son Thorolf and King Harald turns out to have been accurate, and Bera likewise proves prophetic when she pronounces the young Egil to have the makings of a true Viking (chapter 40). The repetition of events at different points in the saga also serves as a build-up to a climax. Egil's melancholy, for instance, is a theme that is repeated with increasing intensity, until he is prepared to die after the loss of his son Bodvar (chapter 79). And the repeated references to Egil's head form a thread that runs through his story, from his childhood, where he is described as a talkative child with a gift for words (a talking head of sorts), to the penultimate chapter of the story where his skull is unearthed and proves unbreakable. The head becomes a symbol for Egil's hard-headedness, but also for his gift with words. There are at least two sides to that gift: Egil is a remarkable poet and saves his head with its product – a poem – but his powers extend beyond that. With words carved in wood he is able to heal a sick girl and also to invoke the spirits of the land in a powerful curse against King Eirik. These magic powers and the poetic skills go hand in hand with his ability to assume a wolf-like identity (see 'Characters' below). Egil's head is referred to repeatedly in the saga, in the prose and, to a greater extent, in his poetry, and offers a good example of how verse and prose echo each other. It has also been argued that the saga plays on the idea of the king as the head of his subjects, in which case the heads of Kveldulf, Skallagrim and Egil, emphatically described as standing out above the crowd, may be seen as raised in constant challenge to the authority of the king.[3]

Although the saga is marked by dramatic scenes and, at times, horrific events, it is also full of humour, albeit often of a grotesque kind. For example, the doubtful identity of the creature in the shrubs at Fenring adds a humorous twist to the scene. The stories of Egil as a child who is 'enough trouble when . . . sober' likewise have a comic if somewhat discomforting quality to them. And Egil's plan in his old age, to take his chests of silver to the Althing and strew their contents among the people to start a fight, is another instance of black humour, compounded by the irony that most of his own life has been taken up by disputes over property.

Poetry and prose

Verse may serve several different purposes in the sagas of Icelanders: to emphasize events and sentiments expressed in the prose, but also to add an extra dimension to the text, to its structure and to the portrayal of character. In *Egil's Saga*, the saga of a poet, the verse is of exceptional importance; it is an integral part of dialogues, narrative sequences and characterizations, and it is hard to see how the many facets of Egil's character could be shown so effectively were it not for the poems he recites – from boastful stanzas and others filled with rage to poems in praise of kings and elegies on the deaths of relatives.

There are sixty single stanzas, more than fifty of them spoken by Egil, often as replies or as comments having a similar function to the monologue in drama. The stanzas are thus linked directly to the prose; the narrative flows seamlessly from one form into the other as can be seen in chapter 65 when Egil fights the berserk Ljot the Pale, or in his exchange with the earl's daughter in chapter 48. Although the poetry advances the plot just as much as the prose, it also enables the saga writer (and the reader) to delve deeper into some aspects of the story and the feelings of its characters: the very first verse is an expression of Kveldulf's grief at the death of his son Thorolf, which is matched later by the sorrow Egil expresses after the younger Thorolf, his brother, is killed in battle. The tenderness of such stanzas creates an effective contrast to the brutal actions described in the prose.

This contemplative element which may be seen as intrinsic to the verse form can also be used to delay the plot and create suspense in the story, such as when Egil speaks a verse immediately before killing Bard in Atley (chapter 44). And sometimes the stanzas carry some premonition of events which are yet to unfold, as when Skallagrim examines the axe which King Eirik sends him:

> Many flaws lie in the edge
> of the fearsome wound-biter,
> I own a feeble tree-feller,
> there is vile treachery in this axe . . . (v. 6)

The weapon becomes a symbol for the advancement Skallagrim's sons may expect from the king – Thorolf's friendship with Eirik proves every bit as useless to the brothers as the axe to Skallagrim. In contrast to this stanza, with its sense of foreboding, there are verses in which the main purpose is the celebration of victory or other heroic deeds performed by kings – or the poet himself. Egil is never slow to sing his own praises and claims in his first poem that his grandfather would be hard put to find a three year old better versed in poetry (v. 4).

In addition to the single stanzas, the saga contains three long poems attributed to Egil: 'The Loss of My Sons', a eulogy on his friend Arinbjorn, and 'Head-Ransom'. The latter is not included in the saga in some manuscripts and may well be a later addition. Its authorship is also disputed and it has been argued, on linguistic and metrical grounds, that it is a twelfth-

century creation, i.e. composed some two hundred years after
Egil allegedly went to York. But even if some scholars have
doubted that a poet named Egil ever recited 'Head-Ransom', it
has had a central role in the transmission of *Egil's Saga* and is
included in this translation. The other two poems are more
firmly (though not indubitably) associated with the historical
Egil and they also reveal new sides to the saga character Egil.
Incorporated into two late chapters, these poems appear to
provide an overview of Egil's life when he has put behind him
his violent Viking past and returned to the mundane existence
of a farmer in Iceland. The deep sense of grief expressed in
'The Loss of My Sons' marks a stark contrast to the incessant,
unyielding aggressiveness celebrated in Egil's earlier poetry
where, true to tradition, he boasts of his actions. Egil's triumphs
are seen against the loss of his kinsmen, his parents, his brother
and his sons – the family whose honour and interests the many
(and sometimes questionable) actions of the hero were meant
to advance. The 'Ode to Arinbjorn' is likewise retrospective,
albeit on a lighter note. It begins by replaying the incident at
York and praising Arinbjorn's role as a friend and intercessor
between Egil and King Eirik, with the remainder devoted to
warm praise of Arinbjorn's qualities.

The poetry in *Egil's Saga* belongs to the genre of skaldic verse,
characterized by extensive use of *kennings*, a special type of
metaphor often based on references to mythology. These metaphors commonly denote battles, warriors, ships and swords, but
in *Egil's Saga* the technique is also frequently used to describe the
poet himself and to allude to his gift with words which he
receives from Odin, the god of wisdom, magic and poetry. Egil
displays a mastery of the balanced stanza in which the second
half is frequently a restatement of the content of the first using
different imagery with new connotations, not unlike the way
Shakespeare elaborates the arguments and scene-painting in his
sonnets with extended metaphor.

The poetry, characterized by its ornate language and often
complicated syntax, creates a powerful contrast to the style of
the prose which is generally straightforward, based on short
sentences with few subclauses, in which the narrative voice is

not prominent; it gives an impression of objectivity which the poetry is meant to enhance, since the poems are presented as sources contemporaneous with the events of the saga. The storyteller generally refrains from commenting directly on men and their actions, but occasionally alludes to general opinion with phrases such as 'people claimed that . . .' or 'x was said to be . . .', distancing himself in that way from the action and seeking to blend in with his audience. Despite the seemingly plain style of the prose it is never dull. Stylistic devices such as repetition, ambiguity and understatement all add to the dimensions of the text, not least in speeches. One example is Skallagrim's speech at King Harald's court: 'Everyone knows that Thorolf was much more able than I am in all respects, but he lacked the good fortune to serve you properly. I will not take that course. I will not serve you, because I know I lack the good fortune to serve you the way I would like and that you deserve. I imagine I would lack many of Thorolf's qualities' (chapter 25). The ambiguity here hinges on the kind of service the king deserves, and the repeated words and phrases enhance the effect of the understatement contained in Skallagrim's words: the service he wants to render the king is to kill him.

Whether casting their words in regular metre or flowing prose the members of the Kveldulf family are portrayed as men with the gift of language. This is also true of the writer of their saga who forged poetry and prose with great skill and a vivid understanding of the qualities each element brings to the overall structure of the saga.

Characters

Character development of the kind that is seen in modern novels is alien to the sagas of Icelanders and *Egil's Saga* is no exception. The characters are described matter-of-factly with seeming objectivity, although the author occasionally adds an evaluative comment, usually when introducing characters for the first time:

> Grim was swarthy and ugly, resembling his father in both appearance and character. He turned out to be an active man; he was

gifted at working in wood and iron, and grew to be a great craftsman. (chapter 1)

Harek and Hraerek . . . grew up to be handsome men, small but clever, like their mother's side of the family. (chapter 7)

These examples also illustrate the tendency of the author to trace characteristics from one generation to another. This is especially evident in the descriptions of Egil and his family. The descendants of Kveldulf can be divided into two groups, as is stated expressly in the closing chapter of the saga: handsome men, fair in complexion, and dark, ugly characters, shape-shifters who in appearance and in conduct are reminiscent of wolves. Some names draw attention to their lupine nature: Kveldulf means 'Night Wolf', while his father's name, Bjalfi, means a hide or skin, hinting at an animal within. Bjalfi and Kveldulf are descended from half-trolls and berserks. Berserks (the word may have signified wearing the skins of animals) were famous for being able to work themselves into a frenzy in battles. The saga describes how Kveldulf grows so bad-tempered towards evening that people dare not address him. His double nature has echoes in the folklore tradition about werewolves, humans that can change into wolves at will. For the people of northern Europe the wolf must have ranked among the most dangerous beasts – said to be strong and cunning animals, and above all greedy. Their strength and sense of self-preservation gives them an advantage over their adversaries, reinforcing the belief that they could live to a great age. Men who drew strength from bestial nature by assuming a wolf's shape showed an ability to transcend human limitations and the shape-shifters were often associated with other forms of magic. Kveldulf and those of his descendants who take after him display a wolf-like strength, wariness and resilience. But their human side is also apparent, for example they are resourceful farmers – and much is made of Skallagrim's skill as a carpenter and blacksmith.

The sunnier character traits associated with the descendants of Kveldulf, such as generosity and cheerfulness, come from Salbjorg, Kveldulf's wife, and her family. Thorolf Kveldulfsson is said to be 'an attractive and highly accomplished man ... a cheerful, generous man, energetic and very eager to prove his worth. He was popular with everyone' (chapter 1). Unlike Skallagrim, Thorolf does not find fulfilment in working on the farm, his ambition takes him out into the world and to the court of King Harald. His nephew, the younger Thorolf, takes after him, in appearance as well as in character, and the two serve as an antithesis to the darker characters of Kveldulf, Skallagrim and Egil. But although Thorolf is graced with pleasant qualities from his maternal side, it should not be forgotten that Salbjorg's father, Kari, was a berserk and that the wolf is hidden in the name Thor(w)olf, as if to make us wary of drawing absolute conclusions.

Egil himself combines many of the characteristics of his ancestors on both sides, although those of his father and grandfather are more apparent, as his physical appearance suggests:

> Egil had very distinctive features, with a wide forehead, bushy brows and a nose that was not long but extremely broad. His upper jaw was broad and long, and his chin and jawbones were exceptionally wide. With his thick neck and stout shoulders, he stood out from other men. When he was angry, his face grew harsh and fierce. He was well built and taller than other men, with thick wolf-grey hair, although he had gone bald at an early age. When he was sitting in this particular scene, he wrinkled one eyebrow right down on to his cheek and raised the other up to the roots of his hair. Egil had dark eyes and was swarthy.
> (chapter 55)

Egil also seems to take after his father and his grandfather in his ability to change shapes – most memorably during his duel with Atli the Short, whom he bites through the throat (chapter 66).

But along with the wolf-nature inherited from Kveldulf and Skallagrim comes the gift of poetry. Egil composes his first verse at the age of three and receives remuneration in the form of three shells and a duck's egg. From then on, poetry and the wolfish head that fosters it become increasingly important, and

intertwined, elements in the story. When Egil is finally incapacitated by old age, his ability to compose verse remains intact –
he leaves the story as he enters it, making memorable stanzas,
with himself as the main subject, before killing for the last time.
The reader gets a final glimpse of Egil's head when his remains
are exhumed and people marvel at the size and the thickness of
the poet's skull.

However, it is characteristic of the sagas that the reader rarely
gets a chance to follow what happens inside the skull. People's
thoughts are not described, nor are their feelings revealed apart
from what might be gleaned from the their behaviour and
utterances. There is a significant scene in *Egil's Saga* where this
rule is broken, leading up to Egil's fateful encounter with King
Eirik in York:

> After he had found out all this news, Egil made his plans. He did
> not feel he had much chance of getting away even if he were to
> try to hide and keep under cover all the way back out of Eirik's
> kingdom. Anyone who saw him would recognize him. Consider-
> ing it unmanly to be caught fleeing like that, he steeled himself
> and decided the very night that they arrived, to get a horse and
> ride to York. (chapter 60)

This description of Egil's deliberation fits in well with the pre-
occupation in this saga with its protagonist and the egocentrism
of his poetry. While characters in sagas often convey their
feelings through verse, Egil is exceptional in that he seizes every
opportunity to make himself and his actions the subject of a
verse.

On the occasions when he remains silent, Egil's feelings can
be gauged from his appearance, as in the description above
where he sits opposite King Athelstan after Thorolf has been
killed in battle. His looks would have revealed a great deal about
his character to a medieval audience who believed that the
balance of the four cardinal humours in a man's body determined his temperament, and had their parallels in the four
elements. A man whose constitution was dominated by blood
was sanguine, he was like the air, warm and light, i.e. friendly

and cheerful, his complexion fair. Conversely, a man whose dominant humour was black choler resembled the earth, cold and dry: he had a dark complexion, was prone to depression, taciturn by nature, mean, devious and bad-tempered. Egil displays many of these dark characteristics, which are intricately bound up with his poetic temperament. His melancholy manifests itself on many occasions: in the scene in King Athelstan's hall he is unable to speak, but merely wrinkles his eyebrows until the king soothes his temper with gifts. Similarly, Egil's love for Asgerd makes him sit 'with his head bowed into his cloak'. The grief that strikes him at the loss of his sons surpasses all his previous bouts of depression, and it is only by breaking his silence and composing a poem that he is able to overcome it. But it is not only his feelings for his loved ones that bring on Egil's melancholy. His spirits are similarly subdued when he feels he has been wronged, although on such occasions melancholy frequently gives way to ill temper – or blind fury, resulting in horrendous deeds.

It is Arinbjorn who, more than anyone, is able to stem the aggressiveness of his friend Egil. Arinbjorn is his opposite in many ways, a man adorned with the classical virtues of wisdom, fortitude, temperance and justice. These stand him – and Egil – in good stead during the testing episode in York where Arinbjorn acts as a go-between for Egil and King Eirik, with the result that Egil is allowed to keep his head while Arinbjorn remains on good terms with the king. It has been argued that *Egil's Saga* is, above all, a story about friendship between equals and how a king's man may reconcile that friendship with his allegiance to his lord.[4] The friendship between Thorolf Kveldulfsson and Olvir Hump in the first part of the story introduces this theme and prefigures the later events involving Egil and Arinbjorn. Olvir is one of King Harald's men and talks Thorolf into joining the court against Kveldulf's advice. Olvir defends Thorolf against the slander of Hildirid's sons, but in the showdown he follows his lord in the attack on Thorolf and witnesses the death of his friend. He attempts to bring about reconciliation between Harald and Thorolf's family, but when that fails he shows his loyalty to his dead friend by helping Skallagrim get away from

the court and by hindering the king's men from pursuing him
(chapter 25). It is not said what happened to Olvir after this
incident – the silence suggests that he may not have managed to
salvage his good relationship with the king. The friendship
between Thorolf Skallagrimsson and Bjorn Brynjolfsson also
creates a parallel to the relationship between Egil and Arinbjorn.
In a way similar to Olvir's and Arinbjorn's mediation between
their friends and their kings, Thorolf stands by Bjorn against
his father, Skallagrim, when the latter becomes enraged by
Bjorn's elopement with Thora, the daughter of Thorir, Skallagrim's friend (chapter 34). The reader witnesses a variety of
perspectives of the bonds of friendship between two men, and
the dilemmas these may create.

Other pairs of friends or kinsmen serve a different purpose.
The lesser adversaries of the Kveldulf family often come in pairs
– Hildirid's sons have been mentioned along with the decisive
role they play in Thorolf's downfall, but there are also Hallvard
and Sigtrygg, who pursue him without success (chapters 21–
22), and Alf and Eyvind, who are sent by their sister, Queen
Gunnhild, to kill the brothers Egil and Thorolf Skallagrimsson
(chapter 49). The pictures painted of some of these pairs border
on caricature. This is perhaps especially true of Hallvard and
Sigtrygg, who are brought into the story mainly to cast a more
splendid glow over Thorolf Kveldulfsson and his heroic death:
they are overconfident, as indeed the king warns them, in their
plans to take on Thorolf, and their mission fails miserably.
When they are killed as a consequence, the reader feels little
sympathy for them and may rather be inclined to laugh at their
fate.

The pairs of men are also sometimes brothers, such as
Hallvard and Sigtrygg, and Alf and Eyvind. The relationship
between Thorolf and Egil is central to the story, as in the
earlier, parallel relationship between Thorolf Kveldulfsson and
Skallagrim. There is an inbuilt tension which springs from the
brothers' different characters and temperaments. The two
Thorolfs seek advancement and honour through royal service,
whereas their brothers are wary of kings and their promises.
The respective dark, ugly brothers stand in the shadow of the

handsome and older ones, but emerge to seek revenge or compensation for the death of their kinsmen, and to reaffirm their independence and resilience in the face of royal power. It is necessary to point out, however, that Egil's relationship with kings is more complicated than that of his father and grandfather. Although he takes after his forebears in his stubbornness and self-reliance, he does not lack the ambition to court the favour of kings. And whereas Kveldulf and Skallagrim seek to establish themselves outside the royal realm, Egil is repeatedly drawn into it.

There is a clear element of competition between Thorolf and Egil, and the latter shows from an early age that he is loath to be counted second best. This is made clear when he refuses to be left behind on the occasion of the feast given by his grandfather, Yngvar (chapter 31). He likewise insists on accompanying Thorolf abroad with Asgerd (chapter 40), although Thorolf does not want him on account of his temper, but is forced to give in after Egil sabotages his ship. Egil's insistence on joining Thorolf on the voyage may reflect his anxiety over Thorolf's intentions with regard to Asgerd, another cause for envy on Egil's part. When the party arrives in Norway, Thorolf does indeed ask for Asgerd's hand in marriage, to which Egil reacts violently although he does not direct his anger at his brother and his bride. When the wedding feast approaches, Egil takes to his bed, albeit not for long. The saga becomes here a masterpiece of implied contrasts. While the newly-weds spend their first night together outside the narrative, the reader follows Egil on a grotesque mission to the island of Atloy where he finds King Eirik and Queen Gunnhild feasting. There the host, Bard, helped by the queen, poisons Egil's drink and the climax is reached, amid spilled drink and much vomit, in Egil's stabbing of Bard (an incident which may be seen as taking on sexual significance).[5] It has been argued that the tension between Egil and Thorolf reflects developments in thirteenth-century society which placed increasing emphasis on the right of primogeniture.[6] The brothers love the same woman, but it is Thorolf, the elder (and fairer) brother who wins her. The rivalry and its roots are never brought out explicitly in the saga, which gives the reader a wide scope for interpreting it. It is only after Thorolf's death that Egil's feelings for Asgerd are revealed, when Arinbjorn enquires after the reasons for his melancholy, but even then Egil answers cryptically, hiding Asgerd's name in a verse. Arinbjorn is here, as ever, the trusted friend and secures the bride for Egil.

The reader receives little information about Asgerd's view of marrying Egil. She is understandably upset at her husband's death and answers Egil's offer to provide for her by playing 'the matter down' (chapter 56). When Egil makes a proper proposal she refers the matter to her father and to Arinbjorn, her kins-man. Asgerd adheres to the codes and conventions of society, but the scant references to her reactions invite the reader to speculate on her motives. The author of *Egil's Saga*, in general, pays little attention to women and their situation, which reflects the fact that women in thirteenth-century Scandinavia had little control over their lives. Nothing is implied about Hildirid's feelings when an old man, Bjorgolf, weds her in haste in order to have her immediately, nor do we know what Sigrid in Sandnes, wife of Thorolf Skallagrimsson, and Asgerd thought of the men they married. Marriages were arranged on behalf of women by their male relatives, although legal codes from the thirteenth century stipulate that a widow could make her own arrangements. That is how Sigrid at Sandnes proceeds when she enters on her third marriage, but the reader cannot but wonder what thoughts may have crossed her mind when the suitor arrived, sent by the king: 'Then Eyvind produced the king's tokens and message to Sigrid, and he proposed to her, saying the king had ordered that he should be granted this match. Given what had happened, Sigrid felt she had no choice but to accept the king's will' (chapter 22).

Nonetheless, women play an important role in *Egil's Saga*. We have seen how liaisons between men and women and resulting disputes fuel the plot – again one could mention the part played by Hildirid's sons in Thorolf's downfall, and Egil's repeated attempts to claim Asgerd's inheritance in Norway. But women also take a direct part in the action and show themselves to be the equals of the men. The saga says of Thorgerd Brak, who fostered Egil, that she 'was an imposing woman, as strong as a man and well versed in the magic arts' (chapter 40). She saves Egil's life when his father attacks him in a frenzy. Towards the end of the saga, another Thorgerd, Egil's daughter, is the only one who dares to intervene when her father appears to be succumbing to melancholy. And Egil's most formidable opponent – his only match in cunning and ruthlessness – is Queen Gunnhild. She enters the saga at about the same time as Egil and the story of the struggles between the two stretches over nearly thirty chapters. Gunnhild thus, theoretically, dogs Egil for the best part of his career. It is not until Egil has finally won his battles over Asgerd's inheritance in Norway (chapter 66) that King Eirik is killed in England. This forces Gunnhild to leave England for Denmark, which marks her exit from the saga. The queen threatens to outshine the king: 'Gunnhild was outstandingly attractive and wise, and well-versed in the magic arts' (chapter 37). She is even more bloodthirsty than her husband and not prepared to spare a man on account of an old friendship. Thorolf and Gunnhild strike up a close liaison during Thorolf's time at the court, but Egil and Gunnhild, on the other hand, seem to take an immediate dislike to one another. In consequence, Thorolf is banished from the queen's favours (it may also be significant that Thorolf is by this time no longer unattached), and after Egil kills Bard at Atloy she sends men out to kill either or both of the brothers. From then on Gunnhild uses her considerable cunning and power to break Egil, and he has to draw on all his abilities to resist her.

The tension between Egil and Gunnhild turns on the fact that they are two of a kind. Their magic powers, closely bound up with the power of words and poetry, manifest themselves in their ability to call on supernatural forces (the queen performs magic rites in order to entice Egil to England). Gunnhild is also a shape-changer like the dark poets in Egil's family, and she attempts to use that ability at a crucial moment to silence the poet, to prevent him from drawing strength from his verbal skills. Her failure to do this signals a turning point in the story, and Egil emerges victorious, his head and his powers intact.

Egil's Saga brims with colourful characters, suspense-filled episodes and dramatic confrontations. It has enjoyed much popularity in Iceland throughout the centuries, as witnessed by the large number of manuscript copies that have survived. The allure of the saga lies not least in the way it defies one-sided descriptions and black and white interpretations. It can be read as a tale of friendship, but it is also a story of unquenchable hatred; it describes the struggle of commoners against a ruler and at the same time traces the history of a family that uproots itself to settle in another country; it shows Vikings at their most violent and simultaneously paints a picture of a poet who turns the world into metaphors. Above all, it is the story of a man of extraordinary proportions who elicits (not always in equal measures) disgust and admiration from his fellow men – and from the readers of his saga.

NOTES

1. *The Anglo-Saxon Chronicle*, ed. by Dorothy Whitelock et al. (London: Eyre and Spottiswode, 1961), p. 69.

2. See *Egil's Saga*, ed. Bjarni Einarsson (London: Viking Society for Northern Research, 2003), pp. 185–9.

3. See Bergljót S. Kristjánsdóttir, 'Primum caput. Um höfuð Egils Skalla-Grímssonar, John frá Salisbury o.fl.', *Skáldskaparmál* 4 (1997), pp. 74–96.

4. This is the view taken by Baldur Hafstað in his doctoral dissertation *Die Egils saga und ihr Verhältnis zu anderen Werken des nordischen Mittelalters* (Reykjavík, 1995).

5. The behaviour of Egil on his visit to Atley has been brilliantly analysed by Jón Karl Helgason in his article 'Rjóðum spjöll í dreyra.' Óhugnaður, úrkast og erótík í Egils sögu', *Skáldskaparmál* 2 (1992), pp. 60–76.

6. See Torfi H. Tulinius, *The Matter of the North: The Rise of Literary Fiction in Thirteenth-Century Iceland*, (Odense: Odense University Press, 2001), pp. 234–89.

Further Reading

PRIMARY SOURCES IN TRANSLATION

Book of Settlements, The, trans. Hermann Pálsson and Paul Edwards (Winnipeg: University of Manitoba Press, 1972).

Complete Sagas of Icelanders, The, including 49 Tales, ed. Viðar Hreinsson, 5 vols (Reykjavík: Leifur Eiríksson Publishing, 1997).

[*Grágás*] *Laws of Early Iceland: Grágás* I–II, trans. Andrew Dennis, Peter Foote and Richard Perkins (Winnipeg: University of Manitoba Press, 1980–2000).

Snorri Sturluson, Edda [*Prose Edda*], trans. Anthony Faulkes (London: Dent, 1987).

Snorri Sturluson, Heimskringla, trans. Lee M. Hollander (Austin: American-Scandinavian Foundation/University of Texas Press, 1964).

Sturlunga Saga, trans. Julia McGrew and R. George Thomas (New York: Twayne/American-Scandinavian Foundation, 1970–74).

STUDIES OF EGIL'S SAGA

Byock, Jesse L., 'The Skull and Bones in *Egil's Saga*: A Viking, a Grave and Paget's Disease', *Viator* 24 (1993), pp. 23–50.

Clunies Ross, Margaret, 'The Art of Poetry and the Figure of the Poet in *Egils saga*'. In *Sagas of the Icelanders,* ed. John Tucker (New York: Garland, 1989), pp. 126–49.

De Looze, Laurence, 'Poet, Poem and Poetic Process in Egils

Saga Skalla-Grímssonar', *Arkiv för nordisk filologi* 104 (1989), pp. 123–42.

Finlay, Alison, '*Egils saga* and other poets' sagas'. In *Introductory Essays on Egils saga and Njáls saga*, eds. John Hines and Desmond Slay (London: Viking Society for Northern Research, 1992), pp. 33–48.

Fjalldal, Magnús, 'A Farmer in the Court of King Athelstan. Historical and Literary Considerations in the Vinheidr Episode of Egils Saga', *English Studies* 77 (1996), pp. 15–31.

Grimstad, Kaaren, 'The Giant as a Heroic Model: the Case of Egill and Starkaðr', *Scandinavian Studies* 48 (1976), pp. 284–98.

Hines, John, 'Egill's *Hǫfuðlausn* in Time and Place', *Saga-Book of the Viking Society* 24 (1995) pp. 83–104.

Hines, John, 'Kingship in *Egils saga*'. In *Introductory Essays on* Egils saga *and* Njáls saga, eds. John Hines and Desmond Slay (London: Viking Society for Northern Research, 1992), pp. 15–32.

Kries, Susanne and Thomas Krömmelbein, '"From the Hall of Laughter": Egil Skalla-Grímsson's "Hǫfuðlausn" and its Epodium in Context', *Scandinavian Studies* 24 (2002), pp. 111–136.

Larrington, Carolyne, 'Egill's longer poems: *Arinbjarnarkviða* and *Sonatorrek*'. In *Introductory Essays on* Egils saga *and* Njáls saga, eds. John Hines and Desmond Slay (London: Viking Society for Northern Research, 1992), pp. 49–63.

Ólason, Vésteinn, 'Jorvik Revisited – with Egil Skalla-Grimsson', *Northern Studies* 27 (1990), pp. 64–76.

Sayers, William, 'Poetry and Social Agency in Egils saga Skalla-Grímssonar', *Scripta Islandica* 46 (1995), pp. 29–62.

Sørensen, Preben Meulengracht, 'Starkadr, Loki and Egill Skallagrimsson'. In *Sagas of the Icelanders*, ed. John Tucker (New York: Garland, 1989), pp. 146–59.

Tulinius, Torfi H., 'The Prosimetrum Form 2: Verses as an Influence in Saga Composition and Interpretation'. In *Skaldsagas: Text, Vocation, and Desire in the Icelandic Sagas of Poets*, ed. Russell Poole (Berlin/New York: Walter de Gruyter, 2001), pp. 191–217.

THE SAGAS OF ICELANDERS, LITERARY
AND CULTURAL BACKGROUND

Byock, Jesse L., *Viking Age Iceland* (London: Penguin, 2001).

Clover, Carol J. and John Lindow, *Old Norse-Icelandic Literature: A Critical Guide* (Cornell University Press, Ithaca, 1985). Contains full bibliographies.

Clunies Ross, Margaret, ed., *Old Icelandic Literature and Society* (Cambridge: Cambridge University Press, 2000). Essays by 13 scholars on the major genres.

Einarsson, Bjarni, 'On the rôle of verse in saga-literature', *Mediaeval Scandinavia* 7 (1974), pp. 118–25.

Foote, Peter and David M. Wilson, *The Viking Achievement*. (London: Sidgwick and Jackson, 1970).

Frank, Roberta, *Old Norse Court Poetry: The* Dróttkvætt *Stanza* (Ithaca: Cornell University Press, 1978).

Jesch, Judith, *Women in the Viking Age* (Woodbridge: The Boydell Press, 1991).

Jochens, Jenny, *Women in Old Norse Society* (Ithaca: Cornell University Press, 1995).

Jóhannesson, Jón, *A History of the Old Icelandic Commonwealth*, trans. Haraldur Bessason (Winnipeg: University of Manitoba Press, 1974).

Kristjánsson, Jónas, *Edda and Saga: Iceland's Medieval Literature*, trans. Peter Foote, 3rd edition, (Reykjavík: Hið íslenska bókmenntafélag, 1997).

Miller, William Ian, *Bloodtaking and Peacemaking: Feud, Law, and Society in Saga Iceland* (Chicago: University of Chicago Press, 1990).

Nordal, Guðrún, *Tools of Literacy: The Role of Skaldic Verse in Icelandic Textual Culture of the Twelfth and Thirteenth Centuries (Toronto: University of Toronto Press, 2001).

Ólason, Vésteinn, *Dialogues with the Viking Age: Narration and Representation in the Sagas of the Icelanders*, trans. Andrew Wawn (Reykjavík: Heimskringla, 1998).

Schach, Paul, *Icelandic Sagas* (Boston: Twayne, 1984).

Sørensen, Preben Meulengracht, *Saga and Society*: *An Intro-duction to Old Norse Literature*, trans. John Tucker (Odense: Odense University Press, 1993).

Turville-Petre, E. O. G., *Myth and Religion of the North* (London: Weidenfeld and Nicolson, 1964).

Note on the Translation

The text in this edition of *Egil's Saga* is reprinted with minor revisions from Bernard Scudder's translation as originally published in the *Complete Sagas of Icelanders* (Leifur Eiríksson Publishing, 1997) and later in *The Sagas of Icelanders* (Penguin, 2000). The saga is translated from the version printed in *Íslendinga sögur, vol. I* (Reykjavík 1987), and incorporates a number of emendations based on the late Bjarni Einarsson's unpublished rereading of Möðruvallabók, the most important vellum (AM 132 fol., dated 1330–70), and of paper manuscripts deriving from it.

Whether or not we assign the authorship of *Egil's Saga* to Snorri Sturluson (see Introduction), its concise and deceptively straightforward style is typical of the classical era in which he lived. The present translation aims to capture something of both the poise and immediacy of the original, but 'takes the liberty' of not attempting to reflect religiously the syntax of the original when this would introduce repetitions or woodenness from which the Icelandic text is blissfully free.

Like that of everyone engaged in the *Complete Sagas of Icelanders* project, the translator's aim has been above all to strike a balance between faithfulness to the original text and appeal to the modern reader. The *Complete Sagas* project as a whole also sought to reflect the homogeneity of the world of the sagas of Icelanders, by aiming for consistency in the translation of certain essential vocabulary, for example terms relating to legal, social and religious practices, farm layouts or types of ships. The translation of *Egil's Saga* is therefore a rendition not only of an independent literary work, but also of a single element from a much wider tradition.

As is common in translations from Old Icelandic, the spelling of proper nouns has been simplified, both by the elimination of non-English letters and by the reduction of inflections. Thus 'Egill' becomes 'Egil', 'Þórólfur' becomes 'Thorolf' and 'Ásgerður' becomes 'Asgerd'. The reader will soon grasp that '-dóttir' means 'daughter of' and '-son' means 'son of'. Place names have been rendered in a similar way, often with an English identifier of the landscape feature in question (e.g. 'Hvitá river,' in which 'Hvít-' means 'white' and '-á' means 'river'). A translation is given in parentheses at the first occurrence of place-names when the context requires this: 'Nearby is a small bay jutting into the land, and because they found many ducks there, they named it Andakil (Ducks' Inlet)' (chapter 28). Skallagrim's entire land-claim in this chapter, in fact, is almost incomprehensible if this is not done. For place-names outside Scandinavia, the common English equivalent is used if such exists; otherwise the Icelandic form has been transliterated. Nicknames are translated where their meanings are reasonably certain.

In keeping with the ethos behind the *Complete Sagas of Icelanders* project, the present translation opts to emphasize the fluidity and rich imagery of the verse and only hint at or vaguely echo the metrics, with the overriding aim of producing English verses that are comprehensible and poetically satisfying.

EGIL'S SAGA

1 | There was a man named Ulf, the son of Bjalfi[1] and of
Hallbera, the daughter of Ulf the Fearless. She was the
sister of Hallbjorn Half-troll[2] from Hrafnista, the father of Ketil
Haeng.[3] Ulf was so big and strong that no man was a match for
him; and he was still only a youth when he became a Viking and
went raiding. His companion was Kari from Berle,[4] a man of
high birth who had the strength and courage to perform great
deeds. Kari was a berserk. He and Ulf shared all they owned
and were close friends.

When they gave up plundering, Kari returned to his farm on
Berle, a very wealthy man. Kari had three children, two sons
called Eyvind Lamb and Olvir Hump, and a daughter named
Salbjorg. She was a beautiful woman of firm character. Ulf
married her, then he too returned to his farm. He was rich in
both lands and possessions. He became a landholder[5] like his
ancestors and was a powerful figure.

Ulf is said to have been a very clever farmer. He made a habit
of getting up early to inspect what his farmhands or craftsmen
were doing and to keep an eye on his cattle and cornfields.
Sometimes he would talk to people who were in need of his
advice, for he was shrewd and always ready to make useful
suggestions. But every day towards evening he would grow so
bad-tempered that few people dared even address him. He
always went to sleep early in the evening and woke up early in
the morning. People claimed he was a shape-shifter and they
called him Kveldulf (Night Wolf).

Kveldulf and his wife had two sons. The elder one was named
Thorolf and the younger one Grim, and they both grew up to

be big, strong men like their father. Thorolf was an attractive
and highly accomplished man. He took after his mother's side
of the family, a cheerful, generous man, energetic and very eager
to prove his worth. He was popular with everyone. Grim was
swarthy and ugly, resembling his father in both appearance and
character. He turned out to be an active man; he was gifted at
working in wood and iron, and grew to be a great craftsman. In
winter he would often set off on a fishing boat to lay nets for
herring, taking many farmhands with him.

When Thorolf was twenty, he made ready to go raiding, and
Kveldulf gave him a longship. Kari's sons Eyvind and Olvir
joined him, with a large band of men and another longship. In
the summer they went raiding and took plenty of booty which
they shared out among themselves. They went raiding for several
summers, spending the winters at home with their fathers.
Thorolf brought many precious things back to give to his
parents, for in those days it was easy to win both wealth and
renown. Kveldulf was very old by then, and his sons had reached
full manhood.

2 | Audbjorn was king of Fjordane at this time. One of his
   | earls was Hroald, who had a son named Thorir.

Atli the Slender, another earl, lived at Gaular and had three
sons, Hallstein, Holmstein and Herstein, and a daughter called
Solveig the Fair.

One autumn when there was a great gathering at Gaular for
the autumn feast, Olvir Hump saw Solveig and began courting
her. Later he asked for her hand, but the earl, not considering
him worthy enough, would not marry her to him. Afterwards,
Olvir composed many love poems and grew so obsessed with
her that he gave up raiding, leaving Thorolf and Eyvind to go
by themselves.

3 | King Harald inherited the titles of his father Halfdan the Black and swore an oath not to cut or comb his hair until he had become sole king of Norway. He was called Harald Tangle-hair.[6] He did battle with the neighbouring kings and defeated them, as is told in long accounts. Afterwards he took over Oppland, and proceeded northwards to Trondheim where he fought many battles before gaining full control of all Trondheim district.

After that he intended to go north to Naumdal and take on the brothers Herlaug and Hrollaug, who were kings there, but when they heard that he was on his way, Herlaug and eleven of his men went into the mound they had spent the past three years building, and had it closed upon them. Hrollaug tumbled from power and took the title of earl instead, then submitted to Harald and handed over his kingdom. King Harald thereby took over Naumdal province and Halogaland and appointed men to govern there in his name.

Leaving Trondheim with his fleet of ships, he went south to More where he won a battle against King Hunthjof, who was killed there. Then Harald took over North More and Romsdal.

Meanwhile, Hunthjof's son Solvi Chopper, who had escaped, went to King Arnvid in South More and asked for his help.

'Although this misfortune has befallen us now,' he said, 'it will not be very long before the same happens to you, because I think Harald will be here soon, once he has brought slavery and suffering to everyone he chooses in North More and Romsdal. You will face the same choice we had: either to defend your property and freedom by staking all the men you can hope to muster – and I will provide my forces too against such aggression and injustice – or to follow the course taken by the people of Naumdal who voluntarily entered servitude and became Harald's slaves. My father felt it an honour to die nobly as king of his own realm rather than become subservient to another king in his old age. I think you will feel the same, and so will any other stalwarts who want to prove their worth.'

Persuaded by such words, the king resolved to muster forces and defend his land. He and Solvi swore an alliance and sent

word to King Audbjorn, who ruled Fjordane province, to join
forces with them. When the messengers delivered this message
to King Audbjorn he discussed it with his friends, all of whom
advised him to gather forces and join the people of More as he
had been asked. King Audbjorn sent around an arrow of war
as a signal to call men to arms throughout his kingdom and
dispatched messengers to powerful men asking them to meet
him.

But when the messengers told Kveldulf that the king wanted
him to bring all the men on his farm to join him, he replied,
'The king would consider it my duty to go with him if he had to
defend his land and battles had to be fought in Fjordane province. But I don't think it's any duty of mine to go up north to
More and fight there to defend other people's land. Tell your
king straight out when you meet him, that while he rushes off
to battle Kveldulf will be staying at home, and will not muster
any forces or set off to fight Harald Tangle-hair. I have a feeling
Harald has plenty of good fortune in store for him, but our king
doesn't have enough to fill the palm of his hand.'

The messengers went back to the king and told him how their
errand had turned out, and Kveldulf stayed at home on his farm.

4 | King Audbjorn took the band of men he had gathered and
    | went north to More, where he met King Arnvid and Solvi
Chopper, and together they amassed great forces. By then, King
Harald had arrived from the north with his forces, and the two
sides clashed on the fjord near Solskjel Island. A fierce battle
ensued, with heavy losses on both sides. On Harald's side, the
two earls Asgaut and Asbjorn were killed, along with two of
Earl Hakon of Lade's sons, Grjotgard and Herlaug, and many
other great men, while King Arnvid and King Audbjorn were
killed on the side from More. Solvi Chopper escaped by fleeing
and became a great Viking, and often raided in Harald's kingdom, which was how he earned his nickname. Afterwards, King
Harald conquered South More.

King Audbjorn's brother Vemund kept control of Fjordane
province and became its king. This happened late in autumn,

and King Harald's men advised him not to head south past Stad at that time, so Harald appointed Earl Rognvald[7] to rule North and South More and Romsdal, and returned to Trondheim, keeping a large band of men with him.

The same autumn, Earl Atli's sons attacked Olvir Hump's farm, intending to kill him. They had far too many men for Olvir to fend off, so he fled. He went to More, met King Harald and became one of his men, then went north to Trondheim with the king that autumn and became close friends with him. He stayed with the king for a long time and became his poet.

That winter, Earl Rognvald travelled inland across lake Eidesjo and south to Fjordane, and received word about King Vemund's movements. Rognvald turned up one night at a place called Naustdal where Vemund was at a feast. He stormed the house and burned the king and ninety men inside. Kari from Berle joined Earl Rognvald with a fully manned longship and they went to More together. Rognvald took the ship that King Vemund had owned, and all the possessions he could manage. Then Kari travelled north to Trondheim to meet King Harald, and entered his service.

The following spring King Harald sailed southwards along the coast with his fleet, conquering the Fjordane and Fjaler provinces and appointing his own men to rule them. He put Earl Hroald in charge of Fjordane province.

Once King Harald had taken over the kingdoms he had recently won, he kept a close watch on the landholders and powerful farmers and everyone else he suspected would be likely to rebel, and gave them the options of entering his service or leaving the country, or a third choice of suffering hardship or paying with their lives; some had their arms and legs maimed. In each province King Harald took over all the estates and all the land, habited or uninhabited, and even the sea and lakes. All the farmers were made his tenants, and everyone who worked the forests and dried salt, or hunted on land or at sea, was made to pay tribute to him.

Many people fled the country to escape this tyranny and settled various uninhabited parts of many places, to the east in Jamtland and Halsingland, and to the west in the Hebrides, the shire of Dublin, Ireland, Normandy in France, Caithness in Scotland, the Orkney Isles and Shetland Isles, and the Faroe Islands. And at this time, Iceland was discovered.

5 | King Harald stayed with his army in Fjordane, and sent out messengers through the countryside to meet the people that he felt he had reason to contact but who had not joined him.

The king's messengers went to Kveldulf's and received a warm welcome.

They told him their business, saying that the king wanted Kveldulf to go to see him: 'He has heard that you are a man of high birth and standing,' they said. 'You have the chance to receive great honour from the king, because he is eager to be joined by people who are renowned for their strength of body and heart.'

Kveldulf replied that he was too old for going on fighting ships: 'So I will stay at home now and give up serving kings.'

'Then let your son go to see the king,' the messenger said. 'He's a big and brave man. The king will make you a landholder if you serve him.'

'I don't want to be a landholder while my father is still alive,' Grim said, 'because he is my superior for as long as he lives.'

The messengers departed, and when they reached the king they told him everything Kveldulf had said to them. The king grew surly, remarking that these must be arrogant people, and he could not tell what their motivation was.

Olvir Hump was present then and asked the king not to be angry.

'I will go and see Kveldulf,' he said, 'and he will want to meet you when he knows how important it is to you.'

So Olvir went to see Kveldulf and, after describing the king's rage, told him he had no choice but to go to the king or send his son in his place, and that they would be shown great honour if they obeyed. He spoke at length, and rightly so, about how well the king repaid his men with both wealth and status.

Kveldulf said he had an intuition that 'this king will not bring my family much good fortune. I won't go to meet him, but if Thorolf comes home this summer it will be easy to persuade him to go and become one of the king's men. So tell the king that I will be friendly towards him and encourage everyone who sets store by my words to do the same. As far as acting on his behalf goes, I will maintain the same arrangement I had under the previous king, if that is what he wants, and then see how the two of us get along together.'

Olvir returned to the king and told him that Kveldulf would send him one of his sons, but that the more suitable one was not at home at that time. The king let the matter rest there. In the summer he crossed Sognefjord, and when autumn came he prepared to go north to Trondheim.

6 | Kveldulf's son Thorolf and Eyvind Lamb returned from their Viking expedition that autumn, and Thorolf went to stay with his father.

When they were talking together, Thorolf asked about the business of Harald's messengers. Kveldulf told him that the king had sent word ordering him or one of his sons to join him.

'What did you tell them?' asked Thorolf.

'I said what I was thinking, that I would never join King Harald, nor would you or your brother, if I had any say in the matter. I think we will end up losing our lives because of that king.'

'That is quite different from what I foresee,' said Thorolf, 'because I feel I will earn great honour from him. I'm determined to go and see the king and join him, for I know for a fact that there are nothing but men of valour among his followers. Joining their ranks sounds a very attractive proposition, if they will take me. They live a much better life than anyone else in this country. And I'm told that the king is very generous to his men and no less liberal in granting advancement and power to people he thinks worthy of it. I've also heard about all the people who turn their backs on him and spurn his friendship, and they never become great men – some of them are forced to flee the country, and others are made his tenants. It strikes me as odd for such a wise and ambitious man as you, Father, not to be grateful to accept the honour that the king offered you. But if you claim to have an intuition that this king will cause us misfortune and want to become our enemy, why didn't you join the one you had sworn allegiance to, and do battle against him? Being neither his friend nor his enemy seems to me the most dishonourable course of all.'

'My foreboding that no one would triumph in battle against Harald Tangle-hair in More came true,' replied Kveldulf. 'And likewise it is true that Harald will do great harm to my kinsmen. But you decide what you want to do for yourself, Thorolf. I have no worries about your not being accepted as their equal if you join King Harald's men, or being a match for the best of them in the face of any danger. Just avoid aiming too high or contending with stronger men than yourself, but never give way to them either.'

When Thorolf was making ready to leave, Kveldulf accompanied him down to his ship, embraced him and wished him farewell, saying they should meet in good health again. Then Thorolf went north to meet the king.

7 | There was a man named Bjorgolf who lived on Torgar Island in Halogaland, a powerful and wealthy landholder who was descended from a mountain giant, as his strength and size bore witness. His son, Brynjolf, resembled him closely. In his old age, when his wife had died, Bjorgolf handed over all control of his affairs to his son and found him a wife. Brynjolf married Helga, daughter of Ketil Haeng from Hrafnista. Their son Bard turned out to be tall and handsome at an early age and became a man of great accomplishments.

One autumn Bjorgolf and his son invited a lot of people to a feast, and they were the most noble of all those present. According to custom they cast lots every evening to decide which pairs would sit together and share the drinking horns. One of the guests was a man named Hogni who had a farm at Leka. He was wealthy, outstandingly handsome and wise, but came from an ordinary family and had achieved his position through his own efforts alone. He had an attractive daughter named Hildirid, who was allotted a seat next to Bjorgolf. They talked together at length that evening and he thought the girl was beautiful. A short while later the feast ended.

The same autumn old Bjorgolf set off from home on a boat that he owned, with a crew of thirty men. When they reached Leka, twenty of them went up to the farm, leaving the other ten behind to guard the boat. Hogni came out to meet him at the farmhouse and greeted him warmly, inviting him and his men to stay there. Bjorgolf accepted the offer and they went into the main room. After they had changed their sailing clothes for tunics, Hogni had vats of ale brought in and his daughter served the guests.

Bjorgolf called Hogni over and said, 'The reason I have come here is to take your daughter home with me and I will celebrate our wedding[8] here now.'

Hogni saw he had no other choice than to let Bjorgolf have his way. Bjorgolf paid an ounce of gold[9] for Hildirid and he shared a bed with her afterwards. She went home with him to Torgar, but his son Brynjolf disapproved of the whole business.

Bjorgolf and Hildirid had two sons, Harek and Hraerek.

Then Bjorgolf died, and when he had been buried, Brynjolf made Hildirid and her two sons leave Torgar, and she returned to her father's farm at Leka where she brought them up. They grew up to be handsome men, small but clever, like their mother's side of the family. Everyone called them Hildirid's sons. Brynjolf held them in low regard and did not let them have any of their inheritance. Hildirid was Hogni's heir, and she and her sons inherited the farm at Leka where they lived in plenty. Brynjolf's son Bard and Hildirid's sons were about the same age.

For a long time, Brynjolf and his father Bjorgolf had travelled to Finnmark collecting tribute.

In the north, in Halogaland, there is a large, fine island in Vefsna fjord called Alost, with a farm on it called Sandnes. A wise landholder named Sigurd lived there, the richest man in that part of the north. His daughter Sigrid was considered the finest match in Halogaland; as his only child, she was his heir.

Brynjolf's son Bard set off from home on a boat with a crew of thirty men, and sailed north to Alost where he visited Sigurd at Sandnes. Bard announced that his business was to ask for Sigrid's hand in marriage. His proposal was answered favourably and Bard was promised her for his bride. The wedding was set for the following summer, when Bard was to go back north to fetch his bride.

8 | That summer King Harald sent word to the powerful men in Halogaland and summoned all those who had not yet been to meet him. Brynjolf decided to go and took his son Bard with him, and in the autumn they went south to Trondheim and met the king. He welcomed them and made Brynjolf a landholder, granting him revenues in addition to those he already had, as well as the right to collect tribute and trade in Finnmark[10] and collect taxes in the mountain regions. Afterwards Brynjolf returned to his land, leaving Bard behind with the king's men.

Of all his followers, the king held his poets in highest regard, and let them sit on the bench opposite his high seat.[11] Farthest inside sat Audun the Uninspired, who was the oldest and had been poet to King Harald's father, Halfdan the Black. Next to him sat Thorbjorn Raven, and then Olvir Hump. Bard was given the seat next to him and was nicknamed Bard the White or Bard the Strong. He was popular with everyone and become a close companion of Olvir's.

The same autumn, Kveldulf's son Thorolf and Eyvind Lamb, son of Kari from Berle, came to the king and were well received by him. They arrived with a good crew on a twenty-seater swift warship that they had used on Viking raids, and were given a place to stay in the guests' quarters with their men.

After staying for what they thought was a suitable length of time, they decided to go to see the king. Kari and Olvir Hump accompanied them and they greeted the king.

Olvir told the king that Kveldulf's son was there: 'I told you in the summer that Kveldulf would send him to you. He will stand by all his promises to you, and you may now see as a clear token of his desire for full friendship with you that he has sent his son to serve you, a fine figure of a man as you can see for yourself. Kveldulf and all of us implore you to receive Thorolf with the honour he is due and allow him to become a great man in your service.'

The king answered his request favourably and said he would do so, 'if Thorolf proves to be as accomplished as his brave looks promise'.

Then Thorolf swore allegiance to the king and joined his followers, while Kari and his son Eyvind Lamb went back south on the ship that Thorolf had arrived on. Kari went back to his land, and Eyvind too.

Thorolf stayed with the king, who gave him a seat between Olvir Hump and Bard, and they all became close companions.

Everyone agreed that Thorolf and Bard were equals in terms of looks, physique, strength and all accomplishments. Thorolf stayed there with the king, who was very well disposed to him and also to Bard.

When winter passed and summer came round, Bard asked the king's leave to go to fetch the bride to whom he had been betrothed the previous summer. Once the king became aware of Bard's obligation, he gave him leave to return home. When his leave had been granted, Bard asked Thorolf to go north with him, rightly pointing out that Thorolf might meet many kinsmen of high rank there whom he had never seen or heard of before. Thorolf thought this was a good idea, so they both got leave from the king, prepared a fine ship and crew for the journey, and set off when they were ready. When they reached Torgar island they sent men to tell Sigurd that Bard had arrived to claim the marriage they had arranged the previous summer. Sigurd replied he would keep every part of the bargain they had made, and they set the date for the wedding, which Bard and his men would go to Sandnes to attend. When the time came round, Brynjolf and Bard set off, taking a great number of important people with them, their relatives by birth and marriage. As Bard had said, Thorolf met many of his kinsmen there that he had never seen before. They went on their way until they reached Sandnes where a splendid feast was held. At the end of it Bard took his wife home and stayed there for the summer, and Thorolf was with him. In the autumn they went south to stay with the king and spent another winter with him.

That winter Brynjolf died. When Bard heard he had come into an inheritance, he asked for leave to go home, which the king granted him. Before they parted, Bard was made a landholder, as his father had been, and the king granted him all the revenues his father had held. Bard went home to his land and soon became an important figure, while Hildirid's sons received no inheritance, no more than they had before. Bard and his wife had a son named Grim. Thorolf stayed with the king in great honour.

9 | King Harald mounted a massive expedition, assembling a fleet of warships and gathering troops from all over the country, then left Trondheim and headed south. He had heard that a great army had been gathered in Agder and Rogaland and Hordaland, mustered far and wide from the inland regions and Vik, with which many men of rank intended to defend their land against him.

The king moved his forces down from the north, sailing in his own ship. Thorolf, son of Kveldulf, Bard the White, and Olvir Hump and Eyvind Lamb, the sons of Kari from Berle, were at the prow, while the king's twelve berserks manned the gunwales. They clashed in Havsfjord in Rogaland, in the greatest battle King Harald ever fought,[12] and there were heavy losses on both sides. The king kept his ship to the fore in the thick of battle. Eventually, King Harald won the battle. Thorir Long-chin, king of Agder, was killed there, and Kjotvi the Wealthy fled with all the men he had left who had not already surrendered. After the battle, when King Harald's troops were checked, many of them had been killed and others seriously wounded. Thorolf was badly injured, and Bard even worse, and none of the men from the fore of the ship came through unscathed apart from the berserks, whom iron could not bite. The king had his men's wounds treated, thanked them for the courage they had shown and presented them with gifts, singling out for praise the men whom he felt deserved it and promising them greater honour. He mentioned the skippers of the ships, and then the men in the prows and others who had been aforeships.

This was the last battle King Harald fought in Norway, for he met no resistance afterwards and gained control of the whole country. Those of his men who had a chance of living had their wounds treated, while the dead were prepared for burial according to the custom of that time.

Thorolf and Bard were laid up with their wounds. Thorolf's wounds gradually healed, but Bard's proved fatal.

He had the king called in and told him, 'If I should die of these wounds, I ask your leave to allow me to dispose of my bequest myself.'

Once the king had agreed, he continued: 'I want my kinsman and companion Thorolf to inherit everything, my lands and my goods, and I also want to place my wife and son in his care, for I trust him best of all men for that task.'

With the king's permission he sealed this arrangement as the law prescribed. After that he died and was prepared for burial, and was greatly mourned. Thorolf recovered from his wounds and accompanied the king that summer, and earned great renown.

When the king went north to Trondheim in the autumn, Thorolf asked his leave to go to Halogaland to take charge of the bequest which he had received in the summer from his kinsman Bard. The king granted him leave, giving him a message stating that Thorolf should take over everything Bard had left to him, with the king's consent and will, and gave his tokens as proof. Then the king made Thorolf a landholder and granted him all the revenues that Bard had previously held, and the right to collect tribute from the Lapps on the same terms. He gave Thorolf a fine, fully rigged longship and sent him on his journey as well equipped as he could be. Then Thorolf set off on his journey and he and the king parted in great friendship.

Thorolf was given a warm welcome when he reached Torgar Island. He told the people there how Bard had died and bequeathed his lands and goods and wife to him, stated the king's message and offered his tokens as proof.

Sigrid heard the news and took her husband's death as a great loss, but since she was already well acquainted with Thorolf and knew him to be a man of distinction and a good match for her, and since the king had ordered it, she and her friends decided that she should marry Thorolf if her father did not oppose the idea. After that, Thorolf took over all the duties there, including the king's tax-collecting.

Thorolf prepared to leave and had a longship with a crew of almost sixty men. When he was ready to sail he set off along the coast to the north, arriving at Alost on Sandnes one evening. They put into harbour, and when they had put up the awnings and got themselves ready, Thorolf went up to the farm with a band of twenty men. Sigurd greeted him warmly and invited him to stay, because they had been close acquaintances ever since Bard had married into his family. Thorolf and his men went into the main room of the farm and stayed there.

Sigurd sat down to talk with Thorolf and asked him if there was any news. Thorolf told him about the battle that had been fought in the south of Norway that summer and that many people Sigurd knew had been killed. He also told him how his son-in-law Bard had died from the wounds he had received in battle, and they agreed it was an enormous loss. Then Thorolf told Sigurd about the arrangement Bard had made with him before he died, repeating the king's message of consent and producing his tokens to prove it. Then Thorolf asked Sigurd for his daughter's hand in marriage. Sigurd took his proposal well, saying there were many points in its favour: it was the king's will, and also what Bard had requested, besides which he knew Thorolf well and considered him a fine match for his daughter. Sigurd consented readily, the couple were betrothed and the wedding was set to take place on Torgar Island that autumn.

Then Thorolf went back to his farm with his men and arranged a great feast there, and invited many people, including many of his high-ranking kinsmen. Sigurd arrived from the north, bringing a large longship and plenty of leading men with him. It was a huge gathering.

It soon became obvious what a generous and great man Thorolf was. He kept a large band of men which soon proved costly to maintain and was difficult to provide for, but the farming was good and it was easy to obtain everything that was needed.

That winter Sigurd from Sandnes died and Thorolf inherited everything from him, a large fortune.

Hildirid's sons went to see Thorolf and told him of their claim to their father Bjorgolf's inheritance.

'I knew Brynjolf well, and Bard even better,' Thorolf answered. 'They were men of such integrity that they would have given you the share of Bjorgolf's inheritance that they knew was yours by rights. I heard you make this same claim with Bard, and he did not sound as if he thought there was any justification for it. He said you were bastards.'

Harek said they could produce witnesses that their father had paid a bride-price for their mother: 'It's true that we did not approach our brother Brynjolf about the matter first, because that was still in the family. We expected nothing but honourable treatment from Bard, but our dealings with him did not last long. But now that the inheritance has passed on to people outside our family, we cannot completely ignore what we have lost. Our low standing might prove a handicap yet again, and prevent us from winning justice against you too, if you refuse to hear the witnesses we can produce to testify to our noble birth.'

'I don't even consider that you have any birthright,' Thorolf replied, testily, 'because I am told that your mother was taken by force and carried off to your father's house.'

At this point, they broke off the discussion.

10 | That winter Thorolf went up to the mountains and took a large band of men with him, no fewer than ninety in number. Previously the king's agents used to take thirty men with them, or sometimes fewer. He also took a great quantity of goods to sell, soon arranged a meeting with the Lapps, collected their taxes and traded with them. All their dealings were cordial and friendly, partly because the Lapps feared them.

Thorolf travelled at large through the forests, and when he reached the mountains farther east he heard that the Kylfing people[13] had been trading with the Lapps there, and plundering too. He posted some Lapps to spy on the Kylfings' movements, then went off to seek them out. In one place he found thirty and killed them all without anyone escaping, then found a group of fifteen or twenty more. In all they killed almost one hundred men and took enormous amounts of booty before returning in the spring. Thorolf went back to his farm at Sandnes and stayed there for some time. That spring he also had a great longship built with a dragon head on the prow, equipped it lavishly and sailed it from the north.

Thorolf harvested large amounts of provisions for himself in Halogaland, sending his men to catch herring and cod. There were also good seal hunting and plenty of eggs to be gathered, all of which he had brought to him. Thorolf never had less than one hundred free-born men at his farm. He was generous and lavish with gifts and made friends with all the local men of rank. He grew very powerful and set special store by equipping himself with the finest ships and weapons.

11 | King Harald went to Halogaland that summer and was welcomed with feasts that were held both on his own lands and by landholders and important farmers.

Thorolf threw a feast to welcome the king and spared no expense. Once the date of the king's arrival had been decided, Thorolf invited a large number of guests, including all the leading men. The king arrived for the feast with a party of almost three hundred men, and Thorolf had five hundred. There was a large barn that Thorolf had fitted out with benches so that the drink could be served there, because he did not have a room large enough to accommodate that number of people. Shields were mounted all around the building.

The king sat in the high seat, and when the upper and lower benches were both filled he looked around, very red in the face. He did not speak a word, but it seemed obvious he was angry. Although it was a splendid feast with all the finest provisions available, the king remained sullen. He stayed there for three days, as had been planned.

On the day the king was due to leave, Thorolf approached him and asked him to come down to the shore. The king agreed. Offshore lay the dragon-prowed ship that Thorolf had had made, with its awnings up and fully rigged. Thorolf gave the ship to the king, asking him to respect his intention in having so many men at the feast simply as a gesture of honour towards him, not as a challenge. The king took this well and grew friendly and cheerful. Many people rightly added words of praise for the splendid feast and noble gift that the king was given on departing, and the great strength that he enjoyed in such men. They parted in friendship.

The king went to Halogaland as he had planned, then back to the south as the summer progressed. He attended other feasts that were held for him.

12 | Hildirid's sons went to see the king and invited him to a feast lasting three nights. The king accepted the invitation and named the date, and when it came around he arrived with his men. There were not many other people there, but the feast went very well and the king was in high spirits. Harek started talking to him and brought the subject round to his travels that summer. The king answered his questions, describing how well he had been welcomed by people everywhere as their means allowed.

'The feast at Torgar must have been in a class of its own,' Harek said, 'with more people there than anywhere else.'

The king said this was right.

'That was only to be expected,' Harek went on, 'because more was lavished on that feast than anywhere else too. But you were very fortunate that it turned out that you did not find your life in danger. Of course, someone as outstandingly wise and fortunate as you was likely to suspect a plot when you saw the great crowd that was gathered there. I'm told you either had all your men fully armed or that you kept a safe watch both day and night.'

The king looked at him and said, 'What are you suggesting, Harek? What can you tell me about it?'

'May I have your leave to talk as I please, King?' Harek asked.

'Speak on,' said the king.

'I cannot imagine that you would be pleased to hear everybody, when they are free to speak their minds at home, accusing you of imposing tyranny on them,' Harek said. 'But to tell the truth, the only thing that prevents the common people from rising up against you is lack of courage and leadership. And it is not surprising that people like Thorolf regard themselves as superior. He has strength and elegance in plenty, and keeps followers about him like a king. He would be enormously wealthy anyway, even if he made do with what is his own without disposing of other people's belongings as if they were his own too. And he was set to repay you badly for the large revenues you have granted him. To tell the truth, when people here heard that you had gone north to Halogaland with no more than three hundred men, they decided to gather forces and kill you, King, and all your men. Thorolf was the architect of that plan, because he had been offered the kingship of the provinces of Halogaland and Naumdal. He travelled back and forth through every fjord and visited all the islands gathering all the men and weapons he could, and made no secret of his plan to send the army into battle against King Harald. But it is also true that even though you would have had a smaller force when your armies met, those farmers were terrified when they saw you sailing up. They decided on another plan, to welcome you and invite you to a feast. The plan then was that if you all got drunk and fell asleep, they would attack you with fire and arms. To prove it, you were all housed in a barn, if I've been told the truth, and that was because Thorolf did not want to burn down his own fine new house. As further proof, every room was full of weapons and armour. But when all their trickery failed to work on you, they opted for the best alternative, which was to hush up the whole scheme. I imagine they will all keep the plot hidden, because I don't think many of them can honestly claim their innocence if the truth gets out. My advice to you now, King, is to take Thorolf into your company, make him your standard-bearer and station him in the prow of your ship; that's a task he is eminently suited for. But if you want him to be a landholder, then you should grant him revenues from lands down south in Fjordane, where his family comes from, so that you will be able to see to it that he does not grow too powerful. Then you can entrust your agencies here in Halogaland to less extravagant people who will serve you loyally, people whose families come from here and whose kinsmen have performed these tasks before. My brother and I are prepared and willing to do anything you wish to use us for. Our father was the king's tax-collector here for a long time and discharged his duties well. You need to take care in appointing people to manage your affairs here, King, since you visit here so rarely. This is not an important enough place for you to station an army here, but you should not visit with a small force because there are many untrustworthy people here.'

The king was furious at hearing these words, but spoke calmly as he always did when hearing important news. He asked whether Thorolf was at home on Torgar Island.

Harek said that was unlikely – 'Thorolf is clever enough to know he should avoid meeting your forces, King, because he cannot expect everyone to guard the secret so closely that you would never find out about it. He went to Alost when he heard that you were moving north.'

The king scarcely mentioned the matter to other people but it was obvious that he firmly believed what he had been told. When he proceeded on his way, Hildirid's sons sent him off respectfully, with gifts, and he promised them his friendship. The brothers found a pretext for visiting Naumdal and made detours so that they kept meeting the king, who was always friendly to them when they greeted him.

13 | There was a man called Thorgils Boomer whom Thorolf regarded most highly among all the members of his household. He had been on Viking raids with Thorolf as his standard-bearer and sat in the prow of his boat. At the battle of Havsfjord he fought on King Harald's side, steering the ship Thorolf had

used on his Viking raids. He was a man of great might and courage, and after the battle the king presented him with gifts and promised him his friendship. Thorgils looked after Thorolf's farm at Torgar in his absence and handled his affairs.

Before Thorolf went away, he had handed over to Thorgils all the tribute he had collected for the king on his voyages in the mountain regions, and told him to give it to the king if he did not return before the king travelled down from the north. Thorgils fitted out a great and fine cargo vessel belonging to Thorolf, loaded the tribute into it and took a crew of almost twenty men with him. He sailed south and met the king in Naumdal.

When Thorgils went to see the king he passed on a greeting from Thorolf and told him this was the tribute he had sent him.

The king noticed him there but said nothing, and it was obvious he was angry.

Thorgils went away, intending to choose a more suitable time to talk to the king. He went to see Olvir Hump, told him everything that had happened and asked if he had any explanation.

'I don't know,' Olvir said, 'but I have noticed that the king falls silent every time Thorolf is mentioned, ever since we were at Leka together, which makes me suspect that people have been slandering him. I know Hildirid's sons talk at great length with the king in private, and it's obvious from the things they say that they are Thorolf's enemies. I will find out from the king himself.'

Olvir went to see the king and said, 'Your friend Thorgils Boomer has arrived with the tribute due to you from Finnmark, much more than ever before and much better quality goods as well. He is eager to carry out his task properly, so please go and take a look, because such fine skins have never been seen before.'

Without saying anything, the king went to where the ship was moored. Thorgils immediately took out the goods and showed them to the king. When the king saw it was true that the tribute was much greater and better than before, his brow lifted somewhat and Thorgils was able to talk to him. Thorgils gave the king several beaver skins that Thorolf had sent along, and other precious things he had acquired in the mountains. The king grew happier and asked what had happened on their voyage, and Thorgils gave him a thorough account of everything.

Then the king said, 'Such a shame that Thorolf seems to be disloyal and to want to kill me.'

Many people who were present answered this comment, and were unanimous. They said that whatever the king had been told was slander put around by evil men, and Thorolf was innocent of such accusations. Eventually the king said he was inclined to believe them. He was cheerful when he spoke with Thorgils after that, and they parted on good terms.

When Thorgils met Thorolf, he told him everything that had happened between him and the king.

14 | That winter Thorolf went to Finnmark again, taking almost a hundred men with him. Once again he traded with the Lapps and travelled widely through Finnmark.

As he advanced farther east and word about his travels got around, the Kven people[14] came and told him that they had been sent to him by their king, Faravid. They told Thorolf how the Karelians[15] had been raiding their land and gave him a message from the king to come there and give him support. Thorolf was offered an equal share of the spoils with the king, and each of his men got the same as three Kven.

It was a law among the Kven people that their king received a third of his men's plunder, but reserved all the beaver skins, sables and squirrels for himself.

Thorolf put the proposition to his men and gave them the option of going or not. Most of them chose to take the challenge because of the large amount of wealth at stake, so they decided to set off eastwards with the messengers.

Finnmark is a vast territory, bordered by the sea to the west and the north, and all the way to the east with great fjords, while Norway lies to the south of it. It extends as far south along the mountains as Halogaland does down the coast. East of Naumdal lies Jamtland, then Halsingland, Kvenland, Finland

and Karelia. Finnmark lies beyond all these countries, and there are mountain settlements in many parts, some in valleys and others by the lakes. In Finnmark there are incredibly large lakes with great forests all around, while a high mountain range named Kjolen extends from one end of the territory to the other.

When Thorolf reached Kvenland he met King Faravid, and they prepared to set off, with three hundred Kven and a hundred Norwegians. They took the highland route through Finnmark and reached the part of the mountain where the Karelians were who had been raiding the Kven. When they realized an attack was pending, the Karelians joined ranks and advanced towards them, expecting another victory. But when the battle started, the Norwegians attacked fiercely, having stronger shields than the Kven. This time it was the turn of the Karelians to suffer casualties; many were killed, and others fled. King Faravid and Thorolf won a huge amount of booty and returned to Kvenland. Thorolf continued on to Finnmark with his men, parting with the king in great friendship.

Thorolf descended the mountain at Vefsna and called at his farm at Sandnes, spending some time there before travelling south to Torgar Island in the spring. When he arrived there, he was told that Hildirid's sons had spent the winter in Trondheim with King Harald and did not miss any opportunity to slander him to the king. Thorolf heard many accounts of the slanders they had put around against him.

'The king will not believe such lies even if he is told them, because I have no reason to want to betray him,' said Thorolf. 'He has treated me grandly in plenty of ways, and never badly. It is nonsense to claim that I would ever do him harm, even if I had the chance. I would rather be his landholder than have the title of king in the same country as another man who could make me his slave whenever he wanted.'

15 | Hildirid's sons had spent the winter with King Harald, taking the men from their farm and their neighbours with them. There were twelve men there in all. The brothers spoke a lot to the king, always presenting Thorolf in the same light.

'Were you pleased with the tribute from the Lapps that Thorolf sent you?' Harek asked the king.

'Very pleased,' replied the king.

'You would have been even more impressed if you had received everything due to you,' Harek said, 'but it turned out quite differently. Thorolf kept a much larger share for himself. He sent you a gift of three beaver skins, but I know for certain that he kept thirty for himself that were rightfully yours, and I think the same happened with other items. It's quite true that my brother and I would bring you much more wealth if you entrust collection of the tribute to us.'

Their companions corroborated everything they said about Thorolf, and in the end, the king was furious with him.

16 | In the summer Thorolf went to Trondheim to see King Harald, taking all the tribute with him and much more wealth besides, along with a band of ninety men, all well equipped. When he reached the king, they were shown into the guests' quarters and lavishly provided for.

Later that day Olvir Hump went to talk with his kinsman Thorolf. Olvir told Thorolf that heavy slanders had been put around against him, and that the king had listened to these accusations.

Thorolf asked Olvir to speak to the king on his behalf, 'because I will not be granted a very long audience with the king if he prefers to believe the slanders of evil men instead of the truth and honesty which he will hear from me'.

The next day Olvir met Thorolf and told him he had discussed his affairs with the king.

'I am hardly the wiser now about what sort of a mood he is in,' he said.

'Then I will go to him myself,' Thorolf said.

He did so; he went to see the king when he was at the dinner table and greeted him when he entered. The king returned his greeting and ordered someone to fetch Thorolf something to drink.

Thorolf told the king that he had brought him his tribute

from Finnmark, 'and I have brought you even more things to honour you. I know that whatever I do in gratitude towards you is always in my best interest.'

The king said that he expected nothing but good from Thorolf, 'because I deserve no less. But there are conflicting stories about how careful you are about pleasing me.'

'If anyone says I have shown you disloyalty, then I have been wronged,' said Thorolf. 'I think people who make such claims to you are less your friends than I am. It is obvious that they aim to be my greatest enemies. But they can also expect to pay dearly for it if we clash.'

Then Thorolf went away again, and the next day he handed over the tribute in the king's presence. When it had all been made over, Thorolf produced several beaver skins and sables, saying that he wanted to give them to the king.

Many of the people there said this was a noble gesture, well deserving to be repaid with friendship. The king said that Thorolf had already taken his reward for himself.

Thorolf answered that he had loyally done everything he could to please the king: 'There is nothing I can do about it if he is still not satisfied. The king knew the way I treated him when I was staying with him as one of his men, and it strikes me as strange if he considers me a different character now from the one I proved to be then.'

'You dispatched yourself well when you were with me, Thorolf,' said the king. 'I think the best course is for you to join my men. Serve as my standard-bearer and defend yourself against the other men of mine, and no one will slander you if I can see for myself, day and night, the way you conduct yourself.'

Thorolf looked to either side where his own men were standing.

'I am reluctant to relinquish this band of men,' he said. 'You will decide my title and the privileges you grant me, King, but I will not hand over my band of men for as long as I can provide for them, even if I have to live by my own resources alone. I want you, I implore you, to visit me and hear the testimony given about me by people whom you trust, and then do what you feel is appropriate.'

The king replied that he would never again accept Thorolf's hospitality. Thorolf went away and prepared to travel home.

When he had left, the king granted Hildirid's sons the agencies in Halogaland that Thorolf had previously held, and collection of tribute from the Lapps. The king seized possession of the farm on Torgar Island and all Brynjolf's former property, and entrusted it all to Hildirid's sons.

The king sent messengers to Thorolf with his tokens, to inform him about the arrangements he had made. Thorolf took the ships that he owned and filled them with all the possessions he could, and took all his men, slaves and freed slaves alike, and went north to his farm in Sandnes, where he lived just as lavishly with just as large a household as before.

17 | Hildirid's sons took charge of the king's tax-collection in Halogaland. For fear of the king's power, no one spoke out against the changeover, although many of Thorolf's kinsmen and friends disapproved strongly. In the winter the brothers went up into the mountains, taking thirty men with them. The Lapps were far less impressed by these agents of the king's than they had been by Thorolf, and the tribute they were supposed to pay proved much more difficult to collect.

The same winter, Thorolf went to the mountains with a hundred men, and straight to Kvenland to meet King Faravid. They made their plans and decided to go up into the mountains as they had the previous winter, with four hundred men, and they came down in Karelia, where they attacked settlements that they felt they had sufficient numbers to handle. After raiding there and winning much booty, they returned to Finnmark as winter progressed.

Thorolf went home to his farm in the spring, sending men to Vagen to fish cod and others to catch herring, and he stocked up with all manner of provisions.

Thorolf owned a big ocean-going ship, which was lavishly equipped, richly painted above the plumbline and fitted with a black-and-red striped sail. All the riggings were well designed. Thorolf had the ship made ready to sail and sent his men to look after it, loading it with stockfish, hides and ermine, and a great quantity of squirrel skins and other furs from his expedition to the mountains, a very valuable cargo. He told Thorgils Boomer to take the ship to England to buy cloth and other goods that he needed. They skirted the coast to the south, then put out to sea and landed in England, where they did plenty of trading. After that they loaded the ship with wheat, honey, wine and cloth, and set off for Norway again in the autumn. They had favourable winds and landed at Hordaland.

The same autumn Hildirid's sons went with the tribute to hand it over to the king. He watched as they did so.

'Have you handed over all the tribute you took in Finnmark, then?' he asked.

'That's right,' they said.

'This tribute is both much less and much poorer than Thorolf used to collect. And you told me that he managed it badly.'

'It's a good thing you have considered how much tribute usually comes from Finnmark, King,' said Harek, 'because then you have a clear idea how much you will lose if Thorolf ruins it for you entirely. There were thirty of us in Finnmark last winter, as has been the custom among tribute collectors. Then Thorolf arrived with a hundred men. We heard he had said he was planning to kill my brother and me and all the men with us, on the grounds that you, the king, had granted to us the office he wanted for himself. We saw no option but to avoid a confrontation with him and leave, which is why we only went up into the mountains a short way from the settlements, while Thorolf travelled over the whole territory with his band of men. He took all the trade there and the Finns paid him tribute, and he gave them a guarantee that your collectors wouldn't enter the territory. He intends to proclaim himself king of the northern territories, both Finnmark and Halogaland, and it is astonishing that you let him get away with everything he does. As outright proof of the riches Thorolf has taken away from the mountain regions: the largest knorr in Halogaland was loaded at Sandnes this spring and Thorolf was said to be sole owner of all the cargo on board. I think it was more or less full of skins and there were more beaver and sable skins there than Thorolf let you have.

Thorgils Boomer took the ship and I would guess he sailed it to England. If you want to find out the truth, you should spy on Thorgils' movements when he comes back, because I can't imagine that so rich a cargo has ever been loaded on any trading ship in our day. I think, if the truth is told, every penny on board was yours.'

Harek's companions corroborated that every word he had said was true, and there was no one there to speak out against him.

18 | There were two brothers called Sigtrygg Travel-quick and Hallvard Travel-hard, who came from Vik and were among King Harald's men. Their mother's family came from Vestfold and they were related to the king. Their father had relatives on both sides of the river Gota. He had been a wealthy farmer in Hising,[16] and they had inherited from him. In all there were four brothers, and the younger two, Thord and Thorgeir, stayed at home and looked after the farm. Sigtrygg and Hallvard handled all the king's missions, both in Norway and outside it, and had made many dangerous voyages, both to execute people and confiscate property from people whose homes the king had ordered to be attacked. They took a large band of men with them everywhere and were not popular among the common people, but the king respected them highly. They were outstanding runners and skiers, capable of outsailing other men, and strong and shrewd in most respects.

They were with the king when all this happened. In the autumn he went to some feasts in Hordaland.

One day he had the brothers Hallvard and Sigtrygg called in, and when they came he told them to take their band of men and spy on the ship that Thorgils Boomer was sailing: 'He took the ship over to England in the summer. Bring it and everything on board to me, except the crew. Let them go in peace if they do not try to defend their ship.'

The brothers readily agreed and took a longship each, then went to look for Thorgils and his men. They heard that he had returned from England and had sailed northwards along the coast. The brothers set off north in pursuit of Thorgils and his men, and came across them in Fura Sound. Recognizing the ship, they attacked its seaward side, while some of their men went ashore and boarded it from the gangways. Thorgils and his men were not expecting trouble and had not mounted a guard. Before they knew it, there were fully armed men all over their ship, and they were all captured there and taken ashore, where they were left with no weapons and only the clothes they were wearing. Hallvard and his men threw the gangways off the ship, undid the moorings and towed it out to sea, then veered south until they reached the king. They presented him with the ship and everything in it.

When the cargo was unloaded, the king saw that it was very valuable, and that Harek had not been lying.

Thorgils and his companions found transport for themselves and went to see Kveldulf and Grim, whom they told of their ordeal. They were given a warm welcome all the same.

Kveldulf said everything was turning out as he had predicted: Thorolf would not enjoy the good fortune of the king's friendship indefinitely.

'And I would not bother much about the loss that Thorolf has just sustained, if there were not more to follow,' he said. 'I suspect once again that Thorolf will fail to realize his limitations in the face of the overwhelming force he has to deal with.'

He asked Thorgils to tell Thorolf that 'my only advice is to leave the country, because he may be able to do better for himself serving the king of England or Denmark or Sweden'.

Then he gave Thorgils a fully rigged boat, and tents and provisions and everything they needed for their journey. They set off without stopping until they reached Thorolf in the north and told him what had happened.

Thorolf took his loss well, saying that he would not go short of money: 'It's good to have a king to share your money with.'

Then Thorolf bought some meal and malt and other provisions he needed to keep his men, and said his farmhands would not be dressed as smartly as he had planned for a while.

Thorolf sold some of his lands and mortgaged others, but

maintained the same style of living as before. He had no fewer men with him than the previous winters – rather more, in fact – and he was more extravagant in feasts and invitations to his friends. He spent all the winter at home.

19 | Once spring arrived and the snow and ice melted, Thorolf had a great longship that he owned brought out, and had it prepared to sail and manned with more than one hundred of his men in all, an impressive and well-armed band.

When the wind was favourable, Thorolf sailed the ship south hugging the shore, then when he reached Byrda they headed out to sea beyond all the islands, sometimes so far that they could only see the top half of the mountains. They continued south and did not hear any news of anybody until they arrived in Vik. There they were told that the king was in Vik and would be going to Oppland in the summer. No one on land knew of Thorolf's whereabouts. With a favourable wind in his sails, he headed for Denmark, and from there into the Baltic, where he plundered during the summer without gaining much booty.

In the autumn he headed back to Denmark, around the time that the big Norwegian fleet pulled out from Oyr, after being stationed there as usual during the summer. Thorolf let them all sail past without being noticed, then sailed to Mostrarsund one evening. A large knorr had called there on its way from Oyr, skippered by Thorir Thruma, one of King Harald's agents. He was in charge of the king's land at Thruma, a large estate where the king spent much time when he was in Vik. Since a lot of provisions were needed for that estate, Thorir had gone to Oyr to buy cargo, malt and flour and honey, and spent a great amount of the king's money on it.

Thorolf and his men attacked the ship and gave Thorir's crew the option of defending it, but lacking the manpower to keep such a large force at bay, Thorir surrendered. Thorolf seized the ship and all its cargo, and put Thorir ashore, then sailed both ships north along the coast.

On reaching the river Gota they anchored and waited for nightfall. When it was dark they rowed the longship up the river and attacked the farm which Hallvard and Sigtrygg owned there. They arrived before daybreak, surrounded the farmhouse and shouted a war-cry. The people inside woke up and snatched up their weapons. Thorgeir fled out of the sleeping quarters, ran to the wooden fence surrounding the farm, grabbed one of the posts and vaulted over it. Thorgils Boomer, standing nearby, swung his sword at Thorgeir and chopped off the hand that was holding on to the post. Thorgeir ran off into the woods, while his brother Thord was killed and more than twenty men with him. Afterwards, the raiders took all the valuables and burned the farmhouse, then went back down the river to the sea, where they sailed on to Vik with a favourable wind. Once again they encountered a large ship owned by people from Vik, loaded with malt and meal. Thorolf and his band attacked the ship, and the crew surrendered, feeling that they had no chance of warding off the assault. They went ashore with nothing, while Thorolf and his men took the ship and its cargo and continued on their way. So Thorolf had three ships when he sailed into Fold from the east. He and his men followed the main sailing route to Lindesnes, travelling as quickly as possible but coming ashore at the headlands to plunder where they could. On the route north from Lindesnes they kept farther out to sea, but plundered where they went ashore.

North of Fjordane, Thorolf headed for land and went to see his father Kveldulf, who welcomed him. Thorolf told his father what happened on his travels in the summer. He spent a short time there, and his father and brother accompanied him back to his ship.

Before they parted, Thorolf and his father spoke together.

Kveldulf said, 'What I told you when you went to join King Harald's men was not wide of the mark: that the way things would turn out for you would not bring good fortune to any of us. Now you have taken the course that I cautioned you against most of all, by challenging King Harald. For all your prowess and accomplishments, you lack the good fortune to prove a match for King Harald. No one else has managed that in this country, whatever their power and force of numbers. I have an intuition that this will be our last meeting. Considering our ages, you should be destined to live longer, but I feel it will not turn out that way.'

Then Thorolf boarded his ship and continued on his way. Nothing eventful is said to have happened on his voyage until he arrived home at Sandnes, had all the booty he had taken carried up to his farmhouse and laid up the ships. He had no lack of provisions to keep his men through that winter. Thorolf remained at home all the time and kept no fewer men than the previous winters.

20 | There was a powerful and wealthy man named Yngvar, who had been a landholder under the earlier kings. When Harald came to power, Yngvar stayed at home and did not serve him. Yngvar was married and had a daughter named Bera. He lived in Fjordane. Bera was his only child and heir.

Grim, Kveldulf's son, asked for Bera's hand in marriage, and a match was made. Grim and Bera were married the winter after he and Thorolf parted. He was twenty-five years old, but already bald, so he was nicknamed Skallagrim (Bald Grim). He was in charge of running the entire farm where he lived with his father, and looked after all the provisions, although Kveldulf was still fit and healthy. They had many freed slaves with them, and many people in their household who had grown up there and were of a similar age to Skallagrim. Many of them were men of great strength, because Kveldulf and his sons chose very strong men to join them and matched them to their own temperament.

Skallagrim took after his father in terms of physique and strength, and also in complexion and character.

21 | King Harald had been in Vik when Thorolf went raiding, then went to Oppland in the autumn, and north from there to Trondheim, where he spent the winter with a large party of men.

Sigtrygg and Hallvard, who were with the king, heard how Thorolf had treated their quarters in Hising, and about the casualties and damage he had inflicted there. They continually reminded the king of this episode, and also that Thorolf had robbed him and his subjects and raided in his country. The brothers asked the king's permission to set off to attack Thorolf with the band of men they customarily had with them.

'You may think there are grounds for taking Thorolf's life, but I feel you badly lack the good fortune to perform that deed,' the king answered them. 'Thorolf is more than a match for you, even though you consider yourselves men of strength and accomplishment.'

The brothers said that this would soon be put to the test, if the king would grant them leave, adding that they had often taken heavy risks against people they had less reason to take vengeance upon, and had generally come off the better.

When spring arrived and everybody prepared to leave, Hallvard and his brother broached the subject with the king once again.

This time he gave them his permission to kill Thorolf, 'and I know that you will bring me back his head, with many valuables. But some people claim,' the king added, 'that if you sail north, you'll need to use your oars and sails as well on the way back.'

They prepared for their journey immediately, taking two ships and a hundred and fifty men. When they were ready, they sailed out of the fjord into a north-easterly wind, which was against them as they headed northwards along the coast.

22 | King Harald stayed at Lade until Hallvard and his brother
    | left, then as soon as they had gone he prepared to leave as well. He and his men boarded his ships and rowed towards land on the Skarnssund Sound, then across Beitsjo to the spit at Eldueid. Leaving his ships there, he headed across the spit to Naumdal, where he took a longship owned by the local farmers and put his men on it. He had his own men and almost three hundred men with him besides, and five or six ships, all of them large. They ran into a strong headwind and rowed night and day, as hard as they could; it was bright enough to travel by night then.

Reaching Sandnes at night after sunset, they saw a great

longship floating off the farm with its awnings down, which they recognized as belonging to Thorolf. He had equipped it to sail abroad, and was drinking a toast to his journey. The king ordered all his men to leave their ships, and had his standard raised. It was a short walk to the farm where Thorolf's guards were sitting inside drinking. There was no guard, no one was outside and everyone was sitting indoors drinking.

The king had his men surround the house, then they sounded a war-cry, and trumpets sounded the call to battle. When Thorolf and his men heard that, they ran for their weapons that each kept above his bed. One of the king's men called out to the house and ordered the women, children, old people, slaves and bondsmen to leave.

Sigrid, Thorolf's wife, went out with the women who had been inside and the others who had been allowed to go out. She asked if the sons of Kari from Berle were there and they stepped forward to ask what she wanted of them.

'Take me to the king,' she said.

They did so, and she went up to the king and asked, 'Is it any use to seek a reconciliation between you and Thorolf, my lord?'

'If Thorolf is prepared to surrender and put himself at my power and mercy,' the king answered, 'then his life and limbs will be spared, but his men will be punished as they deserve.'

Olvir Hump went into the farmhouse and called Thorolf to talk to him, to tell him the option the king had given.

Thorolf replied, 'I will not accept any settlement that the king tries to force on me. Ask him to allow us to leave, and we will let fate take its own course.'

Olvir went back to the king and informed him of Thorolf's request.

'Set fire to the house,' the king ordered. 'I do not want to do battle with them and lose my men. I know that Thorolf will inflict heavy casualties upon us if we attack him outside. It will be tough enough to defeat him when he is inside, even though he has fewer men than we do.'

Then the house was set on fire and the flames rapidly engulfed it, because the timber was dry and had been tarred, and the beams were covered with bark. Thorolf ordered his men to break down the wall between the main room of the house and the entrance, which was easily done. When they had removed the beam from it, as many of them as could get a grip took hold of it and drove the end against one corner of the room so hard that the joints split on the outside and the walls came apart, giving them an easy way out. Thorolf went out first, followed by Thorgils Boomer, then the rest one by one.

Battle ensued then, and for a while the farm shielded Thorolf and his men from behind, but when it started to burn, the fire closed in on them, and many of them were killed. Thorolf ran forward, hewing to both sides, towards the king's standard. Then Thorgils Boomer was killed. When Thorolf reached the wall of shields around the king, he thrust his sword through the standard-bearer.

Thorolf said, 'I took three steps too few here.'

He was attacked with both swords and spears, and the king himself delivered the mortal blow, and Thorolf fell at his feet. The king called out, ordering his men not to kill any more, and they stopped fighting.

Then he ordered his men down to the ship. He said to Olvir and his brother, 'Take your kinsman Thorolf and prepare him for a fitting burial, along with the other dead; then bury them. Tend to the wounded who have a chance of living. There will be no plundering here, because all this wealth belongs to me anyway.'

After that the king went down to his ships with most of his men, and on board they began tending to their wounds.

The king walked around the ship, inspecting the men's wounds, and saw one man bandaging a skin wound he had received.

The king said Thorolf had not dealt that wound, 'for his weapons bit in a completely different way. I do not think many people will be bandaging the wounds he delivered. Such men leave a great loss behind them.'

In the morning the king ordered the sails to be hoisted, and they sailed straight south. In the course of the day the king and his men noticed many rowboats in every sound between the islands. Their crews were on their way to see Thorolf, because he had planted spies all the way to Naumdal and in many islands, and they had noticed Hallvard and his brother heading north with a large army to attack him. The brothers had met a steady headwind and been forced to stay in various harbours. Word had got around higher up on land and reached Thorolf's spies, which was the reason they were sailing in convoy to join him.

The king had favourable winds until he reached Naumdal, where he left his ships and crossed to Trondheim overland. There he rejoined the ships he had left behind, and the party set off for Lade. News of the battle soon spread. Hallvard and his brother heard about it where they had moored, and returned to join the king after what was thought to be a rather humiliating expedition.

Olvir Hump and his brother Eyvind Lamb remained at Sandnes for a while and administered to the battle-dead. Thorolf's body was prepared according to the prevailing custom for men of high birth, and they raised a burial stone in his memory. They had the injured nursed back to health, and helped Sigrid to put the farm back in order. All the property remained intact; most of the furniture, tableware and clothing had burned inside.

When Olvir and his brother were ready they set off from the north and went to see King Harald when he was in Trondheim. They stayed with him, kept a low profile and spoke little to other people.

One day the brothers called on the king, and Olvir said, 'My brother and I would like to ask your leave to return to our farms, because after these recent events we are not in the mood to sit and drink with the assailants of our kinsman Thorolf.'

The king looked at him and answered somewhat curtly, 'That I will not grant to you; stay here with me.'

The brothers left and returned to their seats.

The next day, the king had Olvir and his brother called in to him in his chamber.

'Now you will know the answer to the matter you raised when you asked my leave to go home,' the king said. 'You have been here with me for some while and conducted yourselves in a civilized fashion. You have consistently served me well, and I have thought well of you in all ways. Now I want you, Eyvind, to go north to Halogaland and marry Sigrid from Sandnes, Thorolf's widow. I will give you all the wealth that belonged to Thorolf, and you will have my friendship too, if you know how to look after such things. Olvir will stay with me; I do not want to let him go, on account of his skills in poetry.'

The brothers thanked the king for the honour he had shown them, saying they would readily accept it. Eyvind prepared to leave and procured a good, suitable ship. The king gave him tokens to prove his mission. Eyvind had a smooth journey and arrived in Alost at Sandnes, where Sigrid gave him and his men a warm welcome. Then Eyvind produced the king's tokens and message to Sigrid, and he proposed to her, saying the king had ordered that he should be granted this match. Given what had happened, Sigrid felt she had no choice but to accept the king's will. The marriage was arranged and Eyvind took Sigrid as his wife. He took charge of the farm at Sandnes and all the property that had belonged to Thorolf. Eyvind was a man of high birth. His children with Sigrid were Finn the Squinter, who was the father of Eyvind the Plagiarist,[17] and Geirlaug, whose husband was Sighvat the Red. Finn the Squinter married Gunnhild. Her father was Earl Halfdan and her mother was Ingibjorg, the daughter of King Harald Fair-hair.

Eyvind Lamb and the king remained friends for the rest of their lives.

23 | There was a man called Ketil Haeng, whose parents were Earl Thorkel of Naumdal and Hrafnhild, daughter of Ketil Haeng from Hrafnista. Haeng was a man of good reputation and noble birth; he had been a great friend of Thorolf Kveldulfsson, who was his kinsman. He had taken part in the call to arms when forces were mustered in Halogaland to support Thorolf, as was written above. When King Harald left the north and it became known that Thorolf had been killed, the forces disbanded. Haeng turned back with sixty men and went to Torgar, where they encountered Hildirid's sons, who had only a small

force with them. On reaching the farm, Haeng attacked them. Hildirid's sons were killed there, along with most of the others, and Haeng and his men seized all the booty they could take.

Afterwards Haeng took the two largest knorrs he was able to find and loaded them with all the belongings he could manage to take with him. He put on board his wife and children and all the men who had taken part in his deeds. Baug, Haeng's foster-brother, a wealthy man of good family, was at the helm of one of the knorrs. When they were ready to sail and the wind was favourable, they put out to sea.

A few years previously Ingolf and Hjorleif [18] had gone to settle in Iceland. Their voyage was much talked about and people said there was plenty of good land available.

Haeng sailed westwards in search of Iceland, and he and his men sighted land when they were off the south coast. But because of the stormy weather and heavy waves breaking on the shores and the poor harbours, they sailed westwards along the Icelandic coast, past the sands. When the storm began to lull and the seas calmed, they came to a large estuary into which they sailed their ships and moored off the eastern shore. This river is now called Thjorsa and was much narrower and deeper then. They unloaded their ships and set off to explore the land east of the river, moving their livestock there afterwards. Haeng wintered on the west side of the Outer Ranga river, and when spring came he explored the land to the east, claiming the territory between the Thjorsa and Markarfljot rivers, from mountain to shore, and built a farmstead at Hof by East Ranga.

In the spring of their first year in Iceland, Ketil Haeng's wife Ingunn gave birth to a boy they called Hrafn, and after they took down the buildings there the place became known as Hrafntoftir (Hrafn's Toft).

Haeng gave Baug the land in Fljotshlid from the Merkia river down to the river west of Breidabolstad. Baug lived at Hlidarendi and the large family in that district is descended from him. Haeng gave land to some of his ship's crew and sold land for a low price to others, and they are also considered among the original settlers.

One of Haeng's sons, Storolf, owned the land at Hvol and

Storolfshvol; he was the father of Orm the Strong.[19] Another of
his sons, Herjolf, owned the land in Fljotshlid bordering on
Baug's, out to the brook at Hvolslaek. He lived at the foot of
the slopes at Brekkur, and was the father of Sumarlidi, whose
son was Veturlidi the Poet.[20] Haeng had a third son, Helgi, who
lived at Vellir and owned the land there as far as the boundary
of his brothers' farms by the East Ranga river. Vestar, Haeng's
fourth son, owned the land east of Ranga, between that river
and Thvera, and the lower part of Storolfshvol. His wife was
Moeid, the daughter of Hildir from Hildisey, and they had a
daughter called Asny, who married Ofeig Grettir.[21] Vestar lived
at Moeidarhvol. Hrafn, Haeng's fifth son, became the first
Lawspeaker in Iceland. He lived at Hof after his father died.
Thorlaug, Hrafn's daughter, married Jorund the Godi, and their
son was Valgard from Hof. Hrafn was the most prominent of
Haeng's sons.

24 | When Kveldulf heard about the death of his son Thorolf,
     | he was so saddened by the news that he took to his bed,
overcome by grief and old age.

Skallagrim went to see him regularly and tried to talk him
round. He told him to take heart, saying that nothing was less
becoming to him than to be bedridden.

'A more suitable course would be for us to take vengeance
for Thorolf,' he said. 'There is a chance that we will come within
reach of some of the men who were responsible for Thorolf's
death. If not, there are men we can take that would not be to
the king's liking.'

Then Kveldulf spoke a verse:

1.   The spinner of fate is grim to me:
     I hear that Thorolf has met his end
     on a northern isle; too early
     the Thunderer chose the swinger of swords.   *Thunderer*: Thund, a
     The hag of old age who once wrestled with   name of Odin; *chose*:
          Thor   i.e. for Valhalla, by
                                                     letting him be killed

has left me unprepared to join
the Valkyries' clash of steel. Urge as my spirit
may, my revenge will not be swift.

That summer King Harald went to Oppland, and in the autumn he headed westwards to Valdres all the way to Voss. Olvir was with the king and often suggested to him that he should consider making compensation for Thorolf, by offering Kveldulf and Skallagrim money or some honour they would accept. The king did not rule out the possibility entirely, if Kveldulf and his son would come to see him.

Then Olvir set off northwards for Fjordane, not stopping until he reached Kveldulf and his son one evening. They were grateful to him for his visit, and he spent some time there.

Kveldulf asked Olvir about the entire incident at Sandnes when Thorolf was killed, about the worthy deeds he had done in battle before his death, and who had struck him down, where his worst wounds were and how he had died. Olvir told him everything he asked, mentioning that King Harald had dealt him a blow that by itself would have sufficed to kill a man, and that Thorolf had dropped face down at the king's feet.

Kveldulf said, 'You have spoken well, because old men have said that a man's death would be avenged if he dropped face down, and vengeance taken on the man at whose feet he fell; but it is unlikely that we will enjoy the good fortune to do so.'

Olvir told Kveldulf and his son that he expected the king to show them great honour if they would go to see him and seek recompense. Speaking at great length, he asked them to take the risk.

Kveldulf said that he would not go anywhere on account of his old age.

'I will stay at home,' he said.

'Do you want to go, Grim?' asked Olvir.

'I do not feel I have any reason to,' said Grim. 'The king will not be impressed by my eloquence, and I do not think I would spend much time asking him for recompense.'

Olvir said he would not need to anyway – 'We will say everything on your behalf, as well as we can.'

Olvir was so insistent that Grim eventually promised to go when he felt ready. When the two of them had settled the time Grim was to meet the king, Olvir left and went back to him.

25 | Skallagrim prepared for this journey and chose the strongest and boldest of his men and neighbours to go with him. There was a man named Ani, a wealthy farmer; another called Grani, and Grimolf and his brother Grim, who lived on Skallagrim's farm, and the brothers Thorbjorn Hunchback and Thord Hobbler. They were known as Thorarna's sons – she lived near Skallagrim and was a sorceress. Hobbler was a coal-biter.[22] Other men in the band were Thorir the Giant and his brother Thorgeir Earth-long, a hermit called Odd and a freedman named Gris.

In all there were twelve in the party, all outstandingly powerful men, and many of them were shape-shifters.

Taking an oared ferry that Skallagrim owned, they followed the shore southwards and put down anchor in Osterfjord, then went overland to Voss, to the lake that had to be crossed on the route they had chosen. They procured a suitable oared ship there and rowed across the lake to a place not far from where the king was attending a feast. Grim and his men arrived when the king was sitting at table. They met some people in the yard, spoke to them and asked if there was any news. When they had been told what was going on, Grim asked someone to call out Olvir to speak to him.

The man went into the room to where Olvir was sitting and told him, 'A party of twelve men has turned up, if men is the right word. But they are more like giants than human beings in size and appearance.'

Olvir stood up immediately and went outside, guessing who it was who had arrived. He welcomed his kinsman Grim and invited him to join him in the room.

Grim said to his companions, 'It is said to be the custom here to meet the king unarmed. Six of us will go inside, and the other six stay outside and look after our weapons.'

Then they went inside. Olvir went up to the king and Skalla-grim was standing behind him.

'Grim, Kveldulf's son, is here now,' Olvir announced. 'We would be grateful if you make his journey here worthwhile, as we are sure you will. Many people receive great honour from you who are less worthy of it than he is, and nowhere near as accomplished in most of his skills. You could do what matters more than any other thing to me, King, if you feel it is important.'

Olvir spoke at length and cleverly, because he was an eloquent man. Many friends of Olvir's approached the king and put the matter to him as well.

The king looked around, and saw a man standing behind Olvir, a whole head taller than all the others, and bald.

'Is that great man Skallagrim?' he asked. Grim said the king had recognized him.

'If you are seeking compensation for Thorolf,' said the king, 'I want you to become one of my men, join their company and enter my service. I may be pleased enough with your service to give you compensation for your brother Thorolf or no less honour than I showed him. But you should be sure to act more carefully than he did, if I make you a man of his stature.'

Skallagrim answered, 'Everyone knows that Thorolf was much more able than I am in all respects, but he lacked the good fortune to serve you properly. I will not take that course. I will not serve you, because I know I lack the good fortune to serve you the way I would like and that you deserve. I imagine I would lack many of Thorolf's qualities.'

The king fell silent and his face turned blood-red. Olvir turned away immediately and asked Grim and his men to leave. They did so, left and took their weapons, and Olvir told them to get away as quickly as they could. Olvir accompanied them to the lake, with a large band of men.

Before he parted company with Skallagrim, Olvir said to him, 'Your visit to the king turned out differently from what I would have wished, kinsman. I urged you to come here, but now I must ask you to go home as quickly as you can, and also not to go to see King Harald unless you two are on better terms than you seem to be now. Keep on your guard against the king and his men.'

Then Grim and his men crossed the lake, while Olvir's men went to where the ships were beached and hacked away at them until they were unseaworthy, because they had seen a large band of men leaving the king's quarters, heavily armed and moving at great speed. King Harald had sent them after Grim, to kill him.

Shortly after Grim and his men had left, the king had begun to speak: 'I can see that huge bald man is as vicious as a wolf and will do harm to men over whose loss I would grieve, if he gets hold of them. That bald character cannot be expected to spare any of you, the people he claims have done him wrong, if he has the chance. Go after him now and kill him.'

Then they left and went to the lake but could not find any seaworthy ships. They returned to tell the king what had happened, saying that Grim and his men would have made it across the lake by then.

Skallagrim proceeded on his way with his companions until he reached home, and he told Kveldulf about the outcome of their journey. Kveldulf was pleased that Grim had not gone to the king in order to enter his service and repeated that they would receive nothing but harm from the king, and no reparation.

Kveldulf and Skallagrim discussed over and again what to do and were in complete agreement that they could not stay in the country, any more than other people who were engaged in disputes with the king. Their only alternative was to leave Norway, and they were attracted by the idea of going to Iceland, where they had heard of the fine land that was available. Their friends and acquaintances, Ingolf Arnarson and his companions, had already gone to Iceland to claim land and settle there, and had found land for the taking and were free to choose wherever they wanted to live. The outcome of their deliberations was to abandon their farm and leave the country.

Thorir Hroaldsson had been brought up as Kveldulf's foster-son when he was very young, and was the same age as Skallagrim. They were close friends as well as foster-brothers. Thorir was one of the king's landholders at the time this all happened, but he and Skallagrim remained constant friends.

Early in the spring, Kveldulf and his men prepared their ships. They had many fine ships and manned two large knorrs with thirty able men on each, not counting women and children. They took all the possessions they could, but no one dared to buy their land from them, for fear of the king's power.

When they were ready, they set sail and headed for the Solund Islands, where there are so many big islands with bays and coves that few people are said to know of all the harbours there.

26 | There was a man named Guttorm, who was King Harald's maternal uncle, the son of Sigurd Hart.[23] He had been Harald's foster-father and had acted as regent because the king was still a child when he came to the throne. Guttorm was in charge of Harald's armies when he conquered the territories in Norway and had taken part in all the king's battles during his campaign to win control of the country. When Harald had become sole ruler of Norway and ceased his warfare, he gave his uncle the territories of Vestfold and East Agder and Ringerike and all the land that his father Halfdan the Black had owned. Guttorm had two sons, Sigurd and Ragnar, and two daughters, Ragnhild and Aslaug.

Guttorm fell ill, and when his death was drawing near, he sent messengers to ask King Harald to take care of his children and lands. Shortly afterwards he died.

When the king heard news of his death, he called Hallvard Travel-hard and his brother to meet him, and told them they should undertake a mission on his behalf to Vik. The king was in Trondheim then.

The brothers equipped themselves lavishly for the expedition, choosing troops and taking the best ship they could procure. They took the ship that had belonged to Thorolf, Kveldulf's son, and had been seized from Thorgils Boomer. When they were ready to leave, the king ordered them to go east to Tunsberg. There was a town there, where Guttorm had lived.

'Bring Guttorm's sons to me,' said the king, 'but leave his daughters to grow up there until I give them away in marriage. I will appoint people to safeguard his realm and foster the girls.'

Once the brothers were ready they set off, and had a favourable wind. They reached Vik in the spring and headed to Tunsberg and stated their business, and Hallvard and his brother took Guttorm's sons and a large amount of money. Having done so, they set off to go back, but made much slower progress because of the winds. Nothing eventful happened on their journey until they sailed north into Sognefjord, on a good wind and in fine weather, and they were in high spirits.

27 | Kveldulf, Skallagrim and their men kept a constant watch over the main sailing route during the summer. Skallagrim, who was extremely sharp-sighted, saw Hallvard's party sailing up and recognized the ship, because he had once seen Thorgils in command of it. Skallagrim kept watch on their movements and noted where they moored for the night, then returned to his men and told Kveldulf what he had seen. He told him he recognized the ship that had belonged to Thorolf and that Hallvard had seized from Thorgils, and that a number of men who would make a fine catch must be on board.

Then they prepared and equipped their boats, with twenty men on each. Kveldulf commanded one, and Skallagrim the other. They rowed off in search of the ship, and when they reached the place where it was moored, they put in to shore.

Hallvard and his men had covered the ship with awnings and gone to sleep, but when Kveldulf and his men reached them, the watchmen who had been sitting by the gangway at the prow leapt up and called out to the ship, telling the crew to get up because they were about to be attacked. Hallvard and his men rushed for their weapons.

When Kveldulf and the others came to the jetty, he went on to the gangway, while Skallagrim headed for the prow. Kveldulf had a gigantic double-bladed axe in his hand. Once he was on board, he told his men to go along the gunwale and cut the awnings from the pegs, while he stormed off back to the after-guard, where he is said to have become frenzied like a wild animal. Some other men of his went into a frenzy too, killing everyone they came across, and so did Skallagrim when he ran around the ship. Kveldulf and his son did not stop until the ship had been completely cleared. When Kveldulf went back to the afterguard, he wielded his axe and struck Hallvard right through his helmet and head, sinking the weapon in right up to the shaft. Then he tugged it back with such force that he swung Hallvard up into the air and slung him over the side. Skallagrim swept the prow clean and killed Sigtrygg. Many of the crew threw themselves into the water, but Skallagrim's men took the boat they had come on and rowed over to them, killing everyone in the water.

More than fifty of Hallvard's men were killed there, and Skallagrim took the ship that they had sailed there and all the riches on it.

They captured two or three of the most paltry men, spared their lives and asked them who had been on the ship and what their mission had been. When they found out the truth, they examined the carnage on the ship and had the impression that more of the crew had jumped over the side and lost their lives there than had died on board. Guttorm's sons had jumped overboard and perished; one of them was twelve years old then and the other ten, both very promising lads.

Then Skallagrim released the men whose lives he had spared, telling them to go to King Harald and give him a detailed account of what had happened and who had been at work.

'You will also recite this verse to the king,' he added:

2.   The warrior's revenge
     is repaid to the king,
     wolf and eagle stalk
     over the king's sons;
     Hallvard's corpse flew
     in pieces into the sea,
     the grey eagle tears
     at Travel-quick's wounds.

Skallagrim and Kveldulf sailed the ship and its cargo out to their own ships. They changed ships, loaded up the one they had taken and cleared their own, which was smaller, then filled it with rocks, knocked holes in it and sank it. Then they headed out to the ocean when a favourable wind got up.

It is said that people who could take on the character of animals, or went berserk, became so strong in this state that no one was a match for them, but also that just after it wore off they were left weaker than usual. Kveldulf was the same, so that when his frenzy wore off he felt exhausted by the effort he had made, and was rendered completely powerless and had to lie down and rest.

A favourable wind carried them out to the open sea, and Kveldulf commanded the ship they had taken from Hallvard and Sigtrygg. They had an easy passage and kept their ships together so that each knew of the other's whereabouts for most of the time. But as they moved farther out to sea, Kveldulf succumbed to an illness. When it had brought him close to death, he called his men and told them he thought he would probably soon be parting ways with them.

'I have not been prone to illness,' he said, 'but if it happens, as I think it probably will, that I die, make a coffin for me and put me overboard. Things will not turn out as I imagined, if I do not reach Iceland and settle there. Give my greetings to my son Grim, when you see him, and tell him too that if he reaches Iceland and, unlikely as it seems, I am there already, to make himself a home as close as possible to the place where I have come ashore.'

Shortly afterwards Kveldulf died. The crew did as he had told them, put him in a coffin and cast it overboard.

There was a man called Grim,[24] a wealthy man of great family; his father was Thorir, the son of Ketil Keel-farer. Grim was one of Kveldulf's crew. He was an old friend of Kveldulf and his son, and had voyaged with them and Thorolf, incurring the king's anger. He took charge of the ship when Kveldulf died.

When they approached Iceland, they sailed towards land from the south, then along the coast to the west, where they had heard that Ingolf had settled. When they rounded Reykjanes and saw the fjord open up, they sailed both the ships into it. A storm got up, with heavy rain and fog, and the ships lost sight of each other. Grim the Halogalander's crew sailed along Borgarfjord beyond the skerries, then cast anchor until the storm died down and the weather brightened up. There they waited for the tide to come in, and floated their ship into the estuary of the river called Gufua (Steam river). After pulling the ship as far upstream as they could, they unloaded their cargo and spent their first winter there.

They explored the land along the coast, both up the mountains and towards the sea, and after travelling a short distance they found a bay where Kveldulf's coffin had been washed ashore. They carried the coffin out to the headland, laid it down and piled rocks over it.

28 | Skallagrim reached land where a huge peninsula juts out into the sea, with a narrow spit below it. He and his men unloaded their cargo there and called the site Knarrarnes (Knorr ness).

Then Skallagrim explored the land, which stretched a long way from the shore to the mountains and had a great marshland and wide woods, and plenty of seals to hunt and good fishing. When he and his men explored the shore to the south they came to a great fjord, and they skirted it without stopping until they found their companions, Grim the Halogalander and his companions. It was a joyful reunion. They told Skallagrim about his father's death and that Kveldulf's body had come ashore and they had buried it, then accompanied him to the place, which Skallagrim felt was not far from a good site to build a farm.

Grim went back to his men, and each group wintered where it had reached land.

Skallagrim took the land from mountain to shore, all of the Myrar marshland out to Selalon (Seal lagoon) and the land up to the Borgarhraun lava field, and south to the Hafnarfjoll mountains, and all the land crossed by the rivers down to the sea. The following spring he brought his ship south into the bay closest to where Kveldulf had been washed ashore, built a farmstead there and called it Borg. He called the fjord Borgarfjord, and they named the entire district after it.

To Grim the Halogalander he gave a plot of land south of Borgarfjord, called Hvanneyri (Angelica spit). Nearby is a small bay jutting into the land, and because they found many ducks there, they named it Andakil (Ducks' inlet), and called the river that entered the sea there Andakilsa. Grim owned the land between that river and inland to another river known as Grimsa.

In the spring, when Skallagrim was driving his livestock from out along the shore, they came upon a little promontory where they caught some swans, and called it Alftanes (Swans' ness).

Skallagrim gave land to the members of his crew. Ani was given the land between the Langa and Hafslaek rivers, and lived at Anabrekka; his son was Onund Sjoni (Keen-sighted). Grimolf first lived at Grimolfsstadir; both Grimolfsfit and Grimolfslaek are named after him. His son Grim lived to the south of the fjord, the father of Grimar, who lived at Grimarsstadir and was the subject of the quarrel between Thorstein and Tungu-Odd. Grani settled at Granastadir on Digranes. Thorbjorn Hunchback and Thord Hobbler were given the uplands beyond Gufua. Hunchback lived at Krumsholar (Hunchback's hills), and Thord at Beigaldi (Hobbler). Thorir the Giant and his brothers were given the land above Einkunnir and towards the sea along the bank of the river Langa. Thorir Giant lived at Thursstadir (Giant-Stead). His daughter was Thordis Stick, who later lived at Stangarholt (Stick-Holt). Thorgeir settled at Jardlangsstadir.

Skallagrim explored the uplands of the district, travelling along Borgarfjord until he reached the head of the fjord, then following the western bank of the river which he named Hvita (White river), because he and his companions had never seen water from a glacier before and thought it had a peculiar colour. They went up Hvita until they reached the river that flows from the mountains from the north. They named it Nordura (North river) and followed it until they reached yet another river with little water in it. Crossing that, they continued to trace Nordura and soon saw that the small river fell through a chasm, so they called it Gljufura (Chasm river). Then they crossed Nordura and returned to Hvita, and followed that upstream. Once again they soon came across another river that intersected their path and entered Hvita, and they named it Thvera (Cross river). They noticed that every river was full of fish; and then they returned to Borg.

29 | Skallagrim was an industrious man. He always kept many men with him and gathered all the resources that were available for subsistence, since at first they had little in the way of livestock to support such a large number of people. Such livestock as there was grazed free in the woodland all year round. Skallagrim was a great shipbuilder and there was no lack of driftwood west of Myrar. He had a farmstead built on Alftanes and ran another farm there, and rowed out from it to catch fish and cull seals and gather eggs, all of which were there in great abundance. There was plenty of driftwood to take back to his farm. Whales beached, too, in great numbers, and there was wildlife for the taking at this hunting post; the animals were not used to men and would never flee. He owned a third farm by the sea on the western part of Myrar. This was an even better place to gather driftwood, and he planted crops there and named it Akrar (Fields). The islands offshore were called Hvalseyjar (Whale islands), because whales congregated there. Skallagrim also sent his men upriver to catch salmon. He sent Odd the Hermit by Gljufura to take care of the salmon fishery there; Odd lived at the foot of Einbuabrekkur (Hermit's slopes), and the promontory Einbuanes is named after him. There was a man called Sigmund who was sent by Skallagrim to Nordura and lived at Sigmundarstadir, now known as Haugar. Sigmundarnes is named after him. He later moved his home to Munadarnes, a better place for catching salmon.

When Skallagrim's livestock grew in number, they were allowed to roam mountain pastures for the whole summer. Noticing how much better and fatter the animals were that ranged on the heath, and also that the sheep which could not be brought down for the winter survived in the mountain valleys, he had a farmstead built up on the mountain, and ran a farm there where his sheep were kept. The farm was run by Gris, after whom the tongue of land called Grisartunga is named. In this way, Skallagrim put his livelihood on many footings.

Shortly after Skallagrim arrived in Iceland, a ship made land in Borgarfjord. It was owned by Oleif Hjalti, who had brought his wife, children and relatives with the aim of finding a place to live in Iceland. He was a rich, wise man of good family. Skallagrim invited Oleif and all his people to stay with him. Oleif accepted the offer and spent his first winter in Iceland there.

The following summer Skallagrim offered him land south of the river Hvita, between the rivers Grimsa and Flokadalsa. Oleif accepted it and moved there, building a farmstead at the brook called Varmalaek. He was a man of high birth. His sons were Ragi from Laugardal, and Thorarin, who succeeded Hrafn Haengsson as Lawspeaker. Thorarin lived at Varmalaek and married Thordis, who was the daughter of Olaf Feilan[25] and sister of Thord Bellower.

30 | King Harald Fair-hair confiscated all the lands left behind in Norway by Kveldulf and Skallagrim, and any other possessions of theirs he could come by. He also searched for everyone who had been in league with Skallagrim and his men, or had even been implicated with them or had helped them in all the deeds they did before Skallagrim left the country. The king's animosity towards Kveldulf and his son grew so fierce that he hated all their relatives or others close to them, or anyone he knew had been fairly close friends. He dealt out punishment to some of them, and many fled to seek sanctuary elsewhere in Norway, or left the country completely.

Yngvar, Skallagrim's father-in-law, was one of these people. He opted to sell all the belongings he could, procure an ocean-going vessel, man it and sail to Iceland, where he had heard that Skallagrim had settled and had plenty of land available. When his crew were ready to sail and a favourable wind got up, he sailed out to the open sea and had a smooth crossing. He approached Iceland from the south and sailed into Borgarfjord and entered the river Langa, all the way to the waterfall, where they unloaded the ship.

Hearing of Yngvar's arrival, Skallagrim went straight to meet him and invited him to stay with him, along with as many of his party as he desired. Yngvar accepted the offer, beached his ship and went to Borg with his men to spend the winter with Skallagrim. In the spring, Skallagrim offered him land, giving him the farm he owned at Alftanes and the land as far inland as the brook at Leirulaek and along the coast to Straumfjord. Yngvar went to that outlying farm and took it over, and turned out to be a highly capable man, and grew wealthy. Then Skallagrim set up a farm in Knarrarnes which he ran for a long time afterwards.

Skallagrim was a great blacksmith and worked large amounts of bog-iron[26] during the winter. He had a forge built by the sea a long way off from Borg, at the place called Raufarnes, where he did not think the woods were too far away. But since he could not find any stone suitably hard or smooth to forge iron against – because there was nothing but pebbles there, and small sands along the shore – Skallagrim put out to sea one evening in one of his eight-oared boats, when everyone else had gone to bed, and rowed out to the Midfjord islands. There he cast his stone anchor off the prow of his boat, stepped overboard, dived and brought up a rock which he put into his boat. Then he climbed into the boat, rowed ashore, carried the rock to his forge, put it down by the door and always forged his iron on it. That rock is still there with a pile of slag beside it, and its top is marked from being hammered upon. It has been worn by waves and is different from the other rocks there; four men today could not lift it.

Skallagrim worked zealously in his forge, but his farmhands complained about having to get up so early. It was then that Skallagrim made this verse:

3.   The wielder of iron must rise
     early to earn wealth from his bellows,
     from that sack that sucks in
     the sea's brother, the wind.

I let my hammer ring down
on precious metal of fire,
the hot iron, while the bag
wheezes greedy for wind.

31 | Skallagrim and Bera had many children, but the first ones
     | all died. Then they had a son who was sprinkled with
water and given the name Thorolf. He was big and handsome from an early age, and everyone said he closely resembled
Kveldulf's son Thorolf, after whom he had been named. Thorolf
far excelled boys of his age in strength, and when he grew up he
became accomplished in most of the skills that it was customary
for gifted men to practise. He was a cheerful character and so
powerful in his youth that he was considered just as able-bodied
as any grown man. He was popular with everyone, and his
father and mother were very fond of him.

Skallagrim and Bera had two daughters, Saeunn and
Thorunn, who were also promising children.

Skallagrim and his wife had another son who was sprinkled
with water and named Egil. As he grew up, it soon became clear
he would turn out very ugly and resemble his father, with black
hair. When he was three years old, he was as big and strong as
a boy of six or seven. He became talkative at an early age and
had a gift for words, but tended to be difficult to deal with in
his games with other children.

That spring Yngvar visited Borg to invite Skallagrim out to a
feast at his farm, saying that his daughter Bera and her son
Thorolf should join them as well, together with anyone else that
she and Skallagrim wanted to bring along. Once Skallagrim had
promised to go, Yngvar returned home to prepare the feast and
brew the ale.

When the time came for Skallagrim and Bera to go to the
feast, Thorolf and the farmhands got ready as well; there were
fifteen in the party in all.

Egil told his father that he wanted to go with them.

'They're just as much my relatives as Thorolf's,' he said.

'You're not going,' said Skallagrim, 'because you don't know how to behave where there's heavy drinking. You're enough trouble when you're sober.'

So Skallagrim mounted his horse and rode away, leaving Egil behind disgruntled. Egil went out of the farmyard and found one of Skallagrim's pack-horses, mounted it and rode after them. He had trouble negotiating the marshland because he was unfamiliar with the way, but he could often see where Skallagrim and the others were riding when the view was not obscured by knolls or trees. His journey ended late in the evening when he arrived at Alftanes. Everyone was sitting around drinking when he entered the room. When Yngvar saw Egil he welcomed him and asked why he had come so late. Egil told him about his conversation with his father. Yngvar seated Egil beside him, facing Skallagrim and Thorolf. All the men were entertaining themselves by making up verses while they were drinking the ale. Then Egil spoke this verse:

4.   I have come in fine fettle to the hearth
     of Yngvar, who gives men gold from the glowing
     curled serpent's bed of heather;   *serpent's bed of*
     I was eager to meet him.   *heather*: i.e. the hoard
     Shedder of gold rings bright and twisted   of treasure it guards
     from the serpent's realm, you'll never
     find a better craftsman of poems
     three winters old than me.

Yngvar repeated the verse and thanked Egil for it. The next day Yngvar rewarded Egil for his verse by giving him three shells and a duck's egg. While they were drinking that day, Egil recited another verse, about the reward for his poem:

5.   The skilful hardener of weapons   *hardener*: wielder or
     that peck wounds gave eloquent   maker
     Egil in reward three shells
     that rear up ever-silent in the surf.
     That upright horseman of the field   *field where ships race*:
     where ships race knew how to please Egil;   sea; its *horseman*: sailor

> he gave him a fourth gift,
> the brook-warbler's favourite bed.   *brook-warbler*: duck; its *bed*:
>
>   egg

Egil's poetry was widely acclaimed. Nothing else of note happened during that journey, and Egil went home with Skallagrim.

32 | There was a powerful hersir in Sognefjord called Bjorn, who lived at Aurland; his son Brynjolf inherited everything from him. Brynjolf had two sons, Bjorn and Thord, who were quite young when this episode took place. Bjorn was a great traveller and a most accomplished man, sometimes going on Viking raids and sometimes trading.

One summer, Bjorn happened to be in Fjordane at a well-attended feast, when he saw a beautiful girl whom he felt very attracted to. He asked about her family background, and was told she was the sister of Thorir Hroaldsson the Hersir, and was called Thora of the Embroidered Hand. Bjorn asked for Thora's hand in marriage, but Thorir refused him, and they parted company.

That same autumn, Bjorn gathered a large enough band of men to fill a boat, set off north to Fjordane and arrived at Thorir's farm when he was not at home. Bjorn took Thora away and carried her back home to Aurland. They were there for the winter, and Bjorn wanted to hold a wedding ceremony. His father Brynjolf disapproved of what Bjorn had done and regarded it as a disgrace to his long friendship with Thorir.

'Rather than your marrying Thora here in my house without the permission of her brother Thorir,' Brynjolf said to Bjorn, 'she will be treated exactly as if she were my own daughter, and your sister.'

And what Brynjolf ordered in his own home had to be obeyed, whether Bjorn liked it or not.

Brynjolf sent messengers to Thorir to offer him reconciliation and compensation for the journey Bjorn had made. Thorir asked Brynjolf to send Thora home, saying that otherwise there would be no reconciliation. But Bjorn absolutely refused to return her, however much Brynjolf asked; and the winter passed in this way.

One day when spring was drawing near, Brynjolf and Bjorn discussed their plans. Brynjolf asked him what he intended to do.

Bjorn said it was most likely that he would go abroad.

'Most of all,' he said, 'I would like you to let me have a longship and crew so that I can go raiding.'

'You cannot expect me to let you have a warship and big crew of men,' said Brynjolf, 'because for all I know you might turn up where I would least prefer you to. You have caused enough trouble as it is. I will let you have a trading ship and cargo. Go to Dublin, which is the most illustrious journey anyone can make at present. I will arrange a good crew to go with you.'

Bjorn said that he would have to accept what Brynjolf wanted. He had a good trading ship made ready and manned it. Then Bjorn prepared for the journey, taking plenty of time about it.

When Bjorn had completed his preparations and a favourable wind got up, he boarded a boat with twelve other men and rowed to Aurland. They went up to the farm, to his mother's room. She was sitting in there with a lot of other women. Thora was one of them. Bjorn said that Thora should go with him. They led her away, while Bjorn's mother asked the women not to be so rash as to let the people know in the other part of the farmhouse, because Brynjolf would react badly if he found out and serious trouble would develop between the father and son. Thora's clothing and belongings were all laid out ready for her, and Bjorn and his men took these with them. Then they went off to their ship at night, hoisted sail and sailed out through Sognefjord and to the open sea.

The sailing weather was unfavourable, with a strong head-wind, and they were tossed about at sea for a long time, because they were determined to keep as far away from Norway as possible. One day as they sailed from the east towards Shetland in a gale, they damaged their ship when making land at Mousa. They unloaded the cargo and went to the fort there, taking all their goods with them, then beached their ship and repaired the damage.

33 | Just before winter, a ship arrived in Shetland from the Orkneys. The crew reported that a longship had landed in the isles that autumn, manned by emissaries of King Harald who had been sent to inform Earl Sigurd that the king wanted Bjorn Brynjolfsson killed wherever he might be caught. Similar messages were delivered in the Hebrides and all the way to Dublin. As soon as Bjorn arrived in the Shetlands he married Thora, and they spent the winter in the fort of Mousa.[27]

In the spring, when the seas became calmer, Bjorn launched his ship and prepared it for sailing in great haste. When he was ready to set out and a favourable wind got up, he sailed out to the open sea. Driven by a powerful gale, they were only at sea for a short while before they neared the south of Iceland. The wind was blowing from the land and carried them west of Iceland and back out to sea. When a favourable wind got up again they sailed towards land. None of the men on board had ever been to Iceland before.

They sailed into an incredibly large fjord and were carried towards its western shore. Nothing could be seen in the direction of land but reefs and harbourless coast. Then they followed the land on a due east tack until they reached another fjord, which they entered and sailed right up until there were no more skerries and surf. They lay to at a promontory which was separated by a deep channel from an island offshore, and moored their ship there. There was a bay on the western side of the promontory, with a huge cliff towering above it.

Bjorn set off in a boat with some men. He told his companions to be careful not to say anything about their voyage which could cause them trouble. Bjorn and his men rowed to the farmstead and spoke to some people there. The first thing they asked was where they had made land. They were told that it was called Borgarfjord, the farm there was Borg and the farmer's name was Skallagrim. Bjorn realized at once who he was and went to see him, and they talked together. Skallagrim asked who these

people were. Bjorn told him his name and his father's; Skallagrim was well acquainted with Brynjolf and offered to provide
Bjorn with all the assistance he needed. Bjorn took the offer
readily. Then Skallagrim asked who else of importance was on
board, and Bjorn said that Thora was, the daughter of Hroald
and sister of Thorir the Hersir, and that she was his wife.
Skallagrim was pleased to hear this and said it was his duty and
privilege to grant the sister of his foster-brother Thorir with
such assistance as she needed or he had the means to provide,
and he invited her and Bjorn to stay with him, along with all
the crew. Bjorn accepted the offer. Then the cargo was unloaded
from the ship and carried into the hayfield at Borg. They set up
camp there and the ship was hauled up the stream that flows
past the farm. The place where Bjorn made camp is called
Bjarnartodur (Bjorn's Fields).

Bjorn and all his crew went to stay with Skallagrim. He never
had fewer than sixty armed men with him.

34 | That autumn when ships arrived in Iceland from Norway,
     | a rumour began to spread that Bjorn had run away with
Thora, without her kinsmen's consent. For this offence, the king
had outlawed him from Norway.

When this news reached Skallagrim, he called Bjorn in and
asked about his marriage, whether it had been made with her
kinsmen's consent.

'I did not expect that Brynjolf's son would not tell me the
truth,' he said.

Bjorn replied, 'I have only told you the truth, Grim; you
should not criticize me for not telling you more than you asked.
But I admit that it is true what you have heard: this match was
not made with her brother Thorir's approval.'

Then Skallagrim said, very angrily, 'Why did you have the
audacity to come to me? Didn't you know how close my friendship with Thorir was?'

Bjorn replied, 'I knew that you were foster-brothers and dear
friends. But the reason I visited you was that my ship was
brought ashore here and I knew there was no point in trying to

avoid you. My lot is now in your hands, but I expect fair treatment as a guest in your home.'

Then Thorolf, Skallagrim's son, came forward and made a long speech imploring his father not to hold this against Bjorn, after welcoming him to his home. Many other people put in a word for him.

In the end Skallagrim calmed down and said that it was up to Thorolf to decide – 'You can take care of Bjorn, if you wish, treat him as well as you please.'

35 | Thora gave birth to a daughter that summer. The girl was sprinkled with water and given the name Asgerd. Bera assigned a woman to look after her.

Bjorn and all his crew spent the winter with Skallagrim. Thorolf sought Bjorn's friendship and followed him around everywhere.

One day early in spring, Thorolf spoke to his father and asked him what he planned to do for his winter guest Bjorn, and what help he would provide for him. Skallagrim asked Thorolf what he had in mind.

'I think Bjorn would want to go to Norway above all else,' said Thorolf, 'if he could be at peace there. The best course of action would seem to be if you sent messengers to Norway and offered a settlement on Bjorn's behalf. Thorir will hold your words in great respect.'

Thorolf was so persuasive that Skallagrim gave in and found men to go abroad that summer. They brought messages and tokens to Thorir Hroaldsson and sought a settlement between him and Bjorn. When Brynjolf heard the message they had brought, he set his mind on offering compensation for his son Bjorn. The matter ended with Thorir accepting a settlement for Bjorn, because he realized that Bjorn had nothing to fear from him under the circumstances. Brynjolf accepted the settlement on Bjorn's behalf, and Skallagrim's messengers stayed for the winter with Thorir, while Bjorn spent the winter with Skallagrim.

The following summer, Skallagrim's messengers set off back

to Iceland. When they returned in the autumn, they reported that a reconciliation had been made for Bjorn in Norway. Bjorn stayed a third winter with Skallagrim, and the following spring he prepared to leave, along with the band of men who had been with him.

When Bjorn was ready to set off, Bera said that she wanted her foster-daughter Asgerd to remain behind. Bjorn and his wife agreed, and the girl stayed there and was brought up with Skallagrim's family.

Thorolf joined Bjorn on the voyage, and Skallagrim equipped him for the journey. He left with Bjorn that summer. They had a smooth passage and left the open sea at Sognefjord. Bjorn sailed into Sognefjord and went to visit his father. Thorolf went with him, and Brynjolf received them warmly.

Then word was sent to Thorir. He and Brynjolf arranged a meeting, which Bjorn attended too, and they clinched their settlement. Thorir paid the money he had been keeping for Thora, and he and Bjorn became friends as well as kinsmen-in-law. Bjorn stayed at Aurland with Brynjolf, and Thorolf stayed with them too and was well treated.

36 | For the most part, King Harald had his residence at Hordaland or Rogaland, on the estates he owned there at Utsten, Avaldsnes, Fitjar, Aarstad, Lygra or Seim. That particular winter, however, the king was in the north. After spending the winter and spring in Norway, Bjorn and Thorolf prepared their ship, mustered a crew and set off for the summer on Viking raids in the Baltic, coming back in the autumn with great wealth. On their return they heard that King Harald was at Rogaland and would be wintering there. King Harald was growing very old by this time, and many of his sons were fully grown men.

Eirik, Harald's son, who was nicknamed Blood-axe, was still young then.[28] He was being fostered by Thorir the Hersir. The king loved Eirik the most of all his sons, and Thorir was on the best of terms with the king.

Bjorn, Thorolf and their men went to Aurland first after returning to Norway, then set off north to visit Thorir the Hersir in Fjordane. They had a warship which they had acquired while raiding that summer, rowed by twelve or thirteen oarsmen on each side, with almost thirty men on board. It was richly painted above the plumbline, and exceptionally beautiful. When they arrived, Thorir gave them a good welcome and they spent some time there, leaving their ship at anchor with its awnings up, near the farm.

One day Thorolf and Bjorn went down from the farm to the ship. They could see Eirik, the king's son, repeatedly boarding the ship, and then going back to land to admire it from there.

Then Bjorn said to Thorolf, 'The king's son seems fascinated by the ship. Ask him to accept it as a gift from you, because I know it will be a great boon to us if Eirik is our spokesman. I have heard that the king is ill-disposed towards you on account of your father.'

Thorolf said this was a good plan.

Then they went down to the ship and Thorolf said, 'You're looking at the ship very closely, Prince. What do you think of it?'

'I like it,' he replied. 'It is a very beautiful ship.'

'Then I would like to give you the ship,' said Thorolf, 'if you will accept it.'

'I will accept it,' said Eirik. 'You will not think the pledge of my friendship much of a reward for it, but that is likely to be worth more, the longer I live.'

Thorolf said that he thought such a reward much more valuable than the ship. They parted, and afterwards the prince was very warm towards them.

Bjorn and Thorolf approached Thorir about whether he thought it was true that the king was ill-disposed towards Thorolf. Thorir did not conceal the fact that he had heard such a thing.

'Then I would like you to go and see the king,' said Bjorn, 'and put Thorolf's case to him, because Thorolf and I will always meet the same fate. That is the way he treated me when I was in Iceland.'

In the end Thorir promised to visit the king and asked them to try to persuade Eirik to go with him. When Bjorn and Thorolf discussed the matter with Eirik, he promised his assistance in dealing with his father.

Then Thorolf and Bjorn went on their way to Sognefjord, while Thorir and Prince Eirik manned the warship he had recently been given, and went south to meet the king in Hordaland. He welcomed them warmly. They stayed there for some while, waiting for an opportunity to approach the king when he was in a good mood.

Then they broached the subject with him, and told him that a man had arrived by the name of Thorolf, Skallagrim's son: 'We wanted to ask the king to remember all the good that his kinsmen have rendered to you, but not to make him suffer for what his father did in avenging his brother.'

Although Thorir spoke diplomatically, the king was somewhat curt in his replies, saying that Kveldulf and his sons posed a great threat to them and he expected this Thorolf to have a similar temperament to his kinsmen.

'All of them are so overbearing they never know when to stop,' he said, 'and they pay no heed to whom it is they are dealing with.'

Then Eirik spoke up and told him how Thorolf had made friends with him and given him a fine present, the ship that they had brought with them: 'I have promised him my absolute friendship. Few people will make friends with me if this counts for nothing. Surely you would not let this happen, Father, to the first man who has given me something precious.'

In the end the king promised to leave Thorolf in peace.

'But I do not want him to come to see me,' he said. 'You may hold him as dear to you as you wish, Eirik, or any of his kinsmen, but either they will treat you more gently than they have me, or you will regret this favour you ask of me, especially if you allow them to remain with you for any length of time.'

Then Eirik Blood-axe and Thorir and his men went back to Fjordane, and sent a message to Thorolf about the outcome of their meeting with the king.

Thorolf and Bjorn spent the winter with Brynjolf. They spent many summers on Viking raids, staying with Brynjolf for some winters and with Thorir for the others.

37 | Eirik Blood-axe came to power and ruled Hordaland and
     | Fjordane. He took men into his service and kept them with
him.

One spring Eirik Blood-axe made preparations for a journey
to Permia and chose his men carefully for the expedition.
Thorolf joined Eirik and served as his standard-bearer at the
prow of his ship. Just like his father had been, Thorolf was
outstandingly large and strong.

Many things of note took place on that journey. Eirik fought
a great battle by the river Dvina in Permia[29] and emerged the
victor, as the poems about him relate; and on the same journey
he married Gunnhild, daughter of Ozur Snout, and brought her
back home with him. Gunnhild was outstandingly attractive
and wise, and well versed in the magic arts. Thorolf and
Gunnhild struck up a close friendship. Thorolf would spend the
winters with Eirik, and go on Viking raids in the summer.

The next thing that happened was that Bjorn's wife, Thora,
fell ill and died. A short time later Bjorn took another wife,
Olof, daughter of Erling the Wealthy from Ostero. Bjorn and
Olof had a daughter called Gunnhild.

There was a man called Thorgeir Thorn-foot who lived at
Fenring in Hordaland, at the place called Ask. He had three
sons; one was named Hadd, another Berg-Onund, and the third
Atli the Short. Berg-Onund was uncommonly strong, pushy
and troublesome. Atli was short, squarely built and powerful.
Thorgeir was very wealthy, made many sacrifices to the gods
and was well versed in the magic arts. Hadd went on Viking
raids and was rarely at home.

38 | One summer, Thorolf Skallagrimsson made ready to go
     | trading. He planned to go to Iceland and see his father,
and did so. He had been away for a long time, and took a great
amount of wealth and many precious things with him.

When he was ready to leave, he went to see King Eirik. At
their parting, Eirik presented Thorolf with an axe, saying he
wanted Skallagrim to have it. The axe was crescent-shaped,

large and inlaid with gold, and its shaft was plated with silver, a splendid piece of work.

Thorolf set off when his ship was ready, and he had a smooth journey, arriving in Borgarfjord where he went straight to his father's house. It was a joyful reunion. Skallagrim went with Thorolf to the ship and had it brought ashore, then Thorolf and eleven of his men went to Borg.

When he was in Skallagrim's house he passed on King Eirik's greeting and presented him with the axe that the king had sent. Skallagrim took the axe, held it up and inspected it for a while without speaking, then hung it up above his bed.

At Borg one day in the autumn, Skallagrim had a large number of oxen driven to his farm to be slaughtered. He had two of them tethered up against the wall, with their heads together, and took a large slab of rock and placed it under their necks. Then he went up to them with his axe King's Gift and struck one blow at both oxen. It chopped off their heads, but it went right through and struck the stone, and the mount broke completely and the blade shattered. Skallagrim inspected the edge without saying a word, then went into the fire-room, climbed up on a bench and put the axe on the rafters above the door, where it was left that winter.

In the spring, Thorolf announced that he planned to go abroad that summer.

Skallagrim tried to discourage him, reminding him that '"it is better to ride a whole wagon home". Certainly you have made an illustrious journey,' he said, 'but there's a saying, "the more journeys you make, the more directions they take". You can have as much wealth from here as you think you need to show your stature.'

Thorolf replied that he still wanted to make a journey, 'and I have some pressing reasons for going. When I come to Iceland for a second time, I will settle down here. Asgerd, your foster-daughter, will go with me to meet her father. He asked me to arrange this when I was leaving Norway.'

Skallagrim said it was up to him to decide, 'but I have an intuition that if we part now we will never meet again.'

Then Thorolf went to his ship and made it ready. When he

was fully prepared, they moved the ship out to Digranes and lay there waiting for a favourable wind. Asgerd went on the ship with him.

Before Thorolf left Borg, Skallagrim went up and took down the axe, the gift from the king, from the rafters above the door. The shaft was black with soot and the axe had gone rusty. Skallagrim inspected the edge, then handed it to Thorolf, speaking this verse:

6.   Many flaws lie in the edge
       of the fearsome wound-biter,   *wound-biter*: axe
       I own a feeble tree-feller,
       there is vile treachery in this axe.
       Hand this blunt crescent back
       with its sooty shaft;
       I had no use for it,
       such was the gift from the king.

39 | One summer while Thorolf was abroad and Skallagrim lived at Borg, a trading ship arrived in Borgarfjord from Norway. Trading ships would be given shore-berths then in many places: in rivers or the mouths of streams, or in channels. There was a man named Ketil, whose nickname was Ketil Blund (Snooze),[30] who owned the ship. He was a Norwegian, of a great family and wealthy. His son, Geir, had come of age by then and was on the ship with him. Ketil intended to settle in Iceland; he arrived late in the summer. Skallagrim knew all about his background, and invited Ketil to stay with him, together with all his travelling companions. Ketil accepted the offer, and spent the winter with Skallagrim.

That winter, Ketil's son Geir asked for the hand of Thorunn, Skallagrim's daughter, and the match was settled; he married her. The following spring Skallagrim offered Ketil some land to settle on up from where Oleif had settled, along the river Hvita between the Flokadal and Reykjadal estuaries and all the tongue of land between them as far as Raudsgil, and all the head of Flokadal valley. Ketil lived at Thrandarholt, while Geir lived at

Geirshlid and had another farm at Upper Reykir; he was called Geir the Wealthy. His sons were named Blund-Ketil, Thorgeir Blund and Thorodd Hrisablund, who lived at Hrisar.

40 | Skallagrim took a great delight in trials of strength and games, and liked talking about them. Ball games were common in those days, and there were plenty of strong men in the district at this time. None of them could match Skallagrim in strength, even though he was fairly advanced in age by then.

Thord, Grani's son from Granastadir, was a promising young man, and was very fond of Egil Skallagrimsson. Egil was a keen wrestler; he was impetuous and quick-tempered, and everyone was aware that they had to teach their sons to give in to him.

A ball game was arranged early in winter on the plains by the river Hvita, and crowds of people came to it from all over the district. Many of Skallagrim's men attended, and Thord Granason was their leader. Egil asked Thord if he could go to the game with him; he was in his seventh year then. Thord let him, and seated Egil behind him when he rode there.

When they reached the games meeting, the players were divided up into teams. A lot of small boys were there as well, and they formed teams to play their own games.

Egil was paired against a boy called Grim, the son of Hegg from Heggsstadir. Grim was ten or eleven years old, and strong for his age. When they started playing the game, Egil proved to be weaker than Grim, who showed off his strength as much as he could. Egil lost his temper, wielded the bat and struck Grim, who seized him and dashed him to the ground roughly, warning him that he would suffer for it if he did not learn how to behave. When Egil got back on his feet he left the game, and the boys jeered at him.

Egil went to see Thord Granason and told him what had happened.

Thord said, 'I'll go with you and we'll take our revenge.'

Thord handed Egil an axe he had been holding, a common type of weapon in those days. They walked over to where the boys were playing their game. Grim had caught the ball and was running with the other boys chasing him. Egil ran up to Grim and drove the axe into his head, right through to the brain. Then Egil and Thord walked away to their people. The people from Myrar seized their weapons, and so did the others. Oleif Hjalti rushed to join the people from Borg with his men. Theirs was a much larger group, and at that the two sides parted.

As a result, a quarrel developed between Oleif and Hegg. They fought a battle at Laxfit by the river Grimsa, where seven men were killed. Hegg received a fatal wound and his brother Kvig died in the battle.

When Egil returned home, Skallagrim seemed indifferent to what had happened, but Bera said he had the makings of a true Viking when he was old enough to be put in command of warships. Then Egil spoke this verse:

7.   My mother said
       I would be bought
       a boat with fine oars,
       set off with Vikings,
       stand up on the prow,
       command the precious craft,
       then enter port,
       kill a man and another.

When Egil was twelve, he was so big that few grown men were big and strong enough that he could not beat them at games. In the year that he was twelve, he spent a lot of time taking part in games. Thord Granason was in his twentieth year then, and strong too. That winter Egil and Thord often took sides together in games against Skallagrim.

Once during the winter there was a ball game at Borg, in Sandvik to the south. Egil and Thord played against Skallagrim, who grew tired and they came off better. But that evening after sunset, Egil and Thord began losing. Skallagrim was filled with such strength that he seized Thord and dashed him to the ground so fiercely that he was crushed by the blow and died on the spot. Then he seized Egil.

Skallagrim had a servant woman named Thorgerd Brak,[31]

who had fostered Egil when he was a child. She was an imposing woman, as strong as a man and well versed in the magic arts.

Brak said, 'You're attacking your own son like a mad beast, Skallagrim.'

Skallagrim let Egil go, but went for her instead. She fled, with Skallagrim in pursuit. They came to the shore at the end of Digranes, and she ran off the edge of the cliff and swam away. Skallagrim threw a huge boulder after her which struck her between the shoulder blades. Neither the woman nor the boulder ever came up afterwards. That spot is now called Brakarsund (Brak's Sound).

Later that evening, when they returned to Borg, Egil was furious. By the time Skallagrim and the other members of the household sat down at the table, Egil had not come to his seat. Then he walked into the room and went over to Skallagrim's favourite, a man who was in charge of the workers and ran the farm with him. Egil killed him with a single blow, then went to his seat. Skallagrim did not mention the matter and it was let rest afterwards, but father and son did not speak to each other, neither kind nor unkind words, and so it remained through the winter.

The next summer Thorolf returned, as was recounted earlier. After spending the winter in Iceland, he prepared his ship in Brakarsund in the spring.

One day when Thorolf was on the point of setting sail, Egil went to see his father and asked him to equip him for a journey.

'I want to go abroad with Thorolf,' he said.

Skallagrim asked if he had discussed the matter with Thorolf. Egil said he had not, so Skallagrim told him to do so first of all.

When Egil raised the subject, Thorolf said there was no chance that 'I would take you away with me. If your own father doesn't feel he can manage you in his house, I can't feel confident about taking you abroad with me, because you won't get away with acting there the way you do here.'

'In that case,' said Egil, 'perhaps neither of us will go.'

That night, a fierce storm broke out, a south-westerly gale. When it was dark and the tide was at its highest, Egil went down to where the ship lay, went aboard and walked around the

awnings. He chopped through all the anchor ropes on the seaward side of the ship. Then he rushed to the gangway, pushed
it out to sea and cut the moorings fastening the ship to land.
The ship drifted out into the fjord. When Thorolf and his men
realized that the ship was adrift, they jumped in a boat,[32] but it
was much too windy for them to be able to do anything. The
ship drifted over to Andakil and on to the spits there, while Egil
went back to Borg.

When it became known, most people condemned the trick
that Egil had played. But he answered that he would not hesitate
to cause Thorolf more trouble and damage if he refused to take
him away. Other people intervened in their quarrel, and in the
end Thorolf took Egil abroad with him that summer.

On reaching his ship, Thorolf took the axe that Skallagrim
had given to him, and threw it overboard into deep water, so
that it never came up again.

Thorolf set off that summer and had a smooth passage,
making land at Hordaland and heading north to Sognefjord.
There, they heard the news that Brynjolf had died from an
illness during the winter, and that his sons had shared out his
inheritance among them. Thord had taken Aurland, the farm
where his father had lived. He had sworn allegiance to the king
and taken charge of his lands on his behalf.

Thord had a daughter named Rannveig, whose children were
Thord and Helgi. Thord the younger also had a daughter named
Rannveig, the mother of Ingirid whom King Olaf[33] married.
Helgi's son was Brynjolf, the father of Serk from Sognefjord and
Svein.

41 | Bjorn received another farm, a good and valuable one, and
     | because he did not swear allegiance to the king, people
called him Bjorn the Landowner. He was a man of considerable
wealth and power.

After Thorolf landed, he went straight to see Bjorn, bringing
his daughter Asgerd to the house with him. It was a joyful
reunion. Asgerd was a fine and accomplished woman, wise
and knowledgeable.

Thorolf went to see King Eirik. When they met, Thorolf delivered a greeting to him from Skallagrim, saying that he had been grateful for the gift the king had sent him, and presented him with a longship sail that he told him Skallagrim had sent. King Eirik was pleased with the gift, and asked Thorolf to stay with him for the winter.

Thorolf thanked the king for his offer, 'but I must go and see Thorir first. I have some pressing business to attend to with him.'

Then Thorolf went to see Thorir as he had said, and was warmly received there. Thorir asked Thorolf to stay with him.

Thorolf told him he would accept the offer: 'And there is a man with me who will stay wherever I do. He is my brother and has never been away from home before, so he needs me to keep an eye on him.'

Thorir said that Thorolf was free to have more men with him if he wanted – 'We regard it as an asset to have your brother, if he's anything like you.'

Thorolf went to his ship and had it pulled ashore and taken care of, then he and Egil went to stay with Thorir.

Thorir had a son named Arinbjorn, who was somewhat older than Egil. Arinbjorn was already an assertive character at an early age, and highly accomplished. Egil sought Arinbjorn's friendship and followed him around everywhere, but relations between the two brothers Thorolf and Egil were rather strained.

42 | Thorolf Skallagrimsson asked Thorir what he would think if he asked for the hand of his niece Asgerd in marriage. Thorir answered favourably and said he would support him. Then Thorolf went north to Sognefjord, with a fine band of men, and reached Bjorn's house. He was welcomed warmly there and Bjorn invited him to stay as long as he wanted. Thorolf soon raised the matter with Bjorn and asked to marry his daughter Asgerd. Bjorn took the proposal favourably and it was easily settled, with the result that the pledges were made then and there and the date was set for the wedding, which was to be held at Bjorn's farm in the autumn. Thorolf went back to

Thorir and told him the news of his journey. Thorir was pleased that the marriage had been arranged.

When the date came round for Thorolf to attend the wedding feast, he asked people to join him, inviting Thorir and Arinbjorn first, with their farmhands and more prominent tenants, a large party of worthy men. Just before the date when Thorolf was supposed to leave home, when his party had already arrived to accompany him, Egil fell ill and was unable to join them. Thorolf and his men had a large, well-equipped longship, and proceeded on their journey as planned.

43 | There was a man called Olvir who worked for Thorir, managing his farm and the farmhands. He also collected debts and looked after his money. He was no longer young, but very active.

Olvir happened to have to go away to collect the rents that had been owing to Thorir since the spring. He went on a rowboat with twelve of Thorir's farmhands. By this time, Egil was recovering from his illness and was back on his feet. Feeling bored there after everyone had left, he approached Olvir and said he wanted to go with him. Olvir thought there was plenty of room on board for such a fine man to join them, so Egil went along too. Egil took his weapons, a sword, halberd and buckler. Once their ship was ready they set off, but encountered rough weather with strong, unfavourable winds. All the same, they proceeded vigorously, rowing when they needed to, and were drenched.

They happened to arrive at Atloy island in the evening and moored there. Just up from the shore was a large farm which King Eirik owned. It was run by a man called Atloy-Bard, who was industrious and served the king well. He was not of a great family, but was highly thought of by King Eirik and Queen Gunnhild.

Olvir and his men hauled their ship up above the shoreline and went to the farm where they met Bard. They told him what their business was and asked to stay there for the night. Seeing how drenched they were, Bard led them into a fire-room which stood away from the other buildings. He had a large fire made up for them to dry their clothes.

When they had put their clothes back on, Bard returned.

'Now we will lay the table here,' said Bard. 'I know that you must feel like going to bed. You must be exhausted after that soaking you had.'

Olvir was pleased at the idea. A table was laid and they were given bread and butter, and large bowls of curds.

Bard said, 'It's a great shame there is no ale in the house to give you the welcome I would have preferred. You must get by with what there is.'

Olvir and his men were very thirsty and drank the curds. Afterwards Bard had whey served, and they drank that as well.

'I would gladly give you something better to drink if I had anything,' Bard said.

There were plenty of mattresses in the room, and he invited them to lie down and go to sleep.

44 | King Eirik and Gunnhild arrived in Atloy the same night. Bard had prepared a feast for him, because a sacrifice was being made to the disir.[34] It was a splendid feast, with plenty to drink in the main room.

The king asked where Bard was.

'I can't see him anywhere,' he said.

'Bard is outside,' someone told him, 'serving his guests.'

'Who are these guests that he feels more obliged to attend to than to be in here with us?' asked the king.

The man told him that Thorir the Hersir's men were there.

'Go to them immediately and call them in here,' the king said.

This was done, and they were told the king wanted to meet them.

When they entered, the king welcomed Olvir, offering him a place at table opposite him in the high seat, with his men further down. They took their seats, and Egil sat next to Olvir.

Then the ale was served. Many toasts were drunk, each involving a whole ale-horn. As the night wore on, many of Olvir's companions became incapacitated; some of them vomited inside the main room, while others made it through the door. Bard insisted on serving them more drink.

Egil took the drinking-horn that Bard had given to Olvir and finished it off. Saying that Egil was clearly very thirsty, Bard gave him another full horn at once and asked him to drink that too. Egil took the horn and spoke a verse:

8.   You told the trollwomen's foe   *trollwomen's foe*: noble man
      you were short of feast-drink
      when appeasing the goddesses:
      you deceived us, despoiler of graves.
      You hid your plotting thoughts
      from men you did not know
      for sheer spite, Bard:
      you have played a bad trick on us.

Bard told Egil to stop mocking him and get on with his drinking. Egil drank every draught that was handed to him, and those meant for Olvir too.

Then Bard went up to the queen and told her that this man was bringing shame on them, always claiming to be thirsty no matter how much he drank. The queen and Bard mixed poison into the drink and brought it in. Bard made a sign over the draught and handed it to the serving woman, who took it to Egil and offered him a drink. Egil took out his knife and stabbed the palm of his hand with it, then took the drinking-horn, carved runes on it and smeared them with blood. He spoke a verse:

9.   I carve runes on this horn,
      redden words with my blood,
      I choose words for the trees
      of the wild beast's ear-roots;   *ear-roots*: part of the head;
      drink as we wish this mead   their *trees*: horns
      brought by merry serving-maids,
      let us find out how we fare
      from the ale that Bard blessed.

The horn shattered and the drink spilled on to the straw. Olvir was on the verge of passing out, so Egil got up and led him over to the door. He swung his cloak over his shoulder and gripped his sword underneath it. When they reached the door, Bard went after them with a full horn and asked Olvir to drink a farewell toast. Egil stood in the doorway and spoke this verse:

10. I'm feeling drunk, and the ale
    has left Olvir pale in the gills,
    I let the spray of ox-spears   *ox-spears*: drinking-horns
    foam over my beard.
    Your wits have gone, inviter
    of showers on to shields;
    now the rain of the high god   *rain*: i.e. of spears, perhaps of poetry
    starts pouring upon you.   (or vomit?)

Egil tossed away the horn, grabbed hold of his sword and drew it. It was dark in the doorway; he thrust the sword so deep into Bard's stomach that the point came out through his back. Bard fell down dead, blood pouring from the wound. Then Olvir dropped to the floor, spewing vomit. Egil ran out of the room. It was pitch-dark outside, and he dashed from the farm.

People left the room and saw Bard and Olvir lying on the floor together, and imagined at first that they had killed each other. Because it was dark, the king had a light brought over, and they could see that Olvir was lying unconscious in his vomit, but Bard had been killed, and the floor was awash with his blood.

The king asked where that huge man was who had drunk the most that night, and was told that he had gone out in front of Olvir.

'Search for him,' ordered the king, 'and bring him to me.'

A search was made for him around the farm, but he was nowhere to be found. When the king's men went into the fire-room where they had been eating that night, many of Olvir's men were lying there on the floor and others up against the wall of the house. They asked whether Egil had been there. They were told he had run in and taken his weapons, then gone back out.

Then they went into the main room and reported this to the

king, who ordered his men to act quickly and take all the ships that were on the island, 'and tomorrow when it is light we will comb the whole island and kill that man'.

45 | Egil went by night, heading for the place the ships were, but wherever he came to the beach, there were people. He kept on the move for the whole night, unable to find a ship anywhere.

When dawn began to break, he was on a promontory and could see an island off the shore, across a very long strait. He decided to take off his helmet and sword, and broke the head off his spear and threw the shaft out to sea, then wrapped his weapons in his cloak to make a bundle that he tied to his back. Then he leapt into the sea and swam without stopping until he reached the island, which is called Saudoy, a small island covered with low shrub. A great number of livestock were kept there, cows and sheep, from the king's farm on Atloy. On reaching the island Egil wrung out his clothes and made ready; it was daylight by then and the sun was up.

King Eirik had Atloy combed to look for Egil as soon as it was light. This was a lengthy task because it was a large island, and he was nowhere to be found.

Then the king sent parties out to other islands to look for him. It was late in the evening when twelve men went to Saudoy in a skiff to look for Egil and to take some livestock back with them to slaughter. Egil saw the ship approaching the island, and he lay down in the shrub to hide before the ship landed.

Nine men went ashore and split up into search parties of three each, leaving three men to guard the ship. When they went behind a hill which blocked their view of the ship, Egil stood up, his weapons at the ready. He went straight to the waterfront and along the beach. The men guarding the ship did not notice Egil until he was upon them. He killed one of them with a single blow. Another took to his heels and ran up a slope. Egil swung at him, chopping off his leg. The third leapt into the boat and pushed it out to sea, but Egil grabbed the moorings, pulled the boat back in and jumped into it. They did not exchange many blows before Egil killed him and threw him overboard. He took hold of the oars and rowed the boat away for the rest of the night and the following day, not stopping until he had reached Thorir the Hersir.

Olvir and his men were incapable of doing anything at first after the feast. When they started to feel better, they set off for home. The king allowed them to leave without recrimination.

The men who were stuck on Saudoy spent several nights there; they slaughtered animals to eat and built a big fire to cook them, on the part of the island that faced Atloy, and to serve as a beacon. When this was seen from Atloy, people rowed over to bring the survivors back. By then the king had left Atloy for another feast.

To return to Olvir, he arrived home before Egil, but Thorolf and Thorir were already there. Olvir told them the news about the killing of Bard and everything that had happened, but he knew nothing of Egil's whereabouts after that. Thorolf became very upset, and Arinbjorn too. They did not expect Egil to return. But in daylight the next morning, Egil was discovered lying in his bed. When he heard of this, Thorolf got up and went to see Egil, and asked how he had managed to escape or whether anything of note had happened on his travels. Then Egil spoke a verse:

11. Great in my deeds, I slipped
    away from the realm of the lord
    of Norway and Gunnhild
    – I do not boast overly –
    by sending three servants
    of that tree of the Valkyrie   *tree of the Valkyrie*: warrior, i.e. the king
    to the otherworld, to stay
    in Hel's high hall.   *Hel*: goddess of death

Arinbjorn applauded the deeds and said it was his father's duty to make terms with the king.

Thorir said people might well agree that Bard deserved to be killed.

'But you, Egil, have inherited your family's gift for caring too little about incurring the king's wrath, and that will be a great burden for most people to bear,' he said. 'But I will try to achieve a settlement between you and King Eirik.'

Thorir soon went to see the king, while Arinbjorn stayed at home and kept watch for himself and Egil, saying they should all meet the same fate. When Thorir saw the king he made an offer on Egil's behalf and proposed pledges for the judgement that the king would pass. King Eirik was so furious that it was virtually impossible to talk to him, and he said his father would be proved right when he had said that pledges could hardly be made on behalf of those kinsmen. He told Thorir to make sure that Egil did not stay in his realm for long.

'But for your sake, Thorir, I will accept money for the death of these men,' he said.

The king set the compensation for the men who had been killed at an amount that he saw fit, and they parted ways. Thorir went home then, and Thorolf and Egil spent the winter with him and Arinbjorn, and were treated well.

46 | In the spring, Thorolf and Egil equipped big longships and took on a crew to go raiding in the Baltic that summer. They won a huge amount of booty and fought many battles there, and the same summer they also went to Courland[35] where they lay offshore for a while. They offered the people there a fortnight's truce and traded with them, and when the truce was over they began plundering again. The Courlanders had gathered forces on land, but Thorolf and Egil raided various places that seemed most attractive.

One day they put in to an estuary with a large forest on the upland above it. They went ashore there and split up into parties of twelve men. They walked through the woodland and it was not far until the first settlement began, fairly sparse at first. The Vikings began plundering and killing people at once, and everyone fled from them. The settlements were separated by woods. Meeting no resistance, the raiders split up into smaller bands. Towards the end of the day, Thorolf had the horn sounded to call the men back, and they returned to the woods from wherever they were, since the only way to check whether they were all there was to go to the ships. When they took the count, Egil and his party had not returned. By then night was falling and they did not think there was any point in looking for him.

Egil had crossed a wood with twelve men and found great plains which were settled in many places. A large farm stood nearby them, not far from the wood, and they headed for it. When they reached it they ran inside, but found nobody there. They seized all the valuables they could take with them, but there were so many buildings to search that it took them a fairly long time. When they came out again and headed away from the farm, a large band of men had gathered between them and the wood, and was advancing upon them.

A high stockade extended from the farm to the wood. Egil said they should skirt it to prevent them being attacked from all sides, and his men did so. Egil led the way, with all of them so close together that no one could get between them. The Courlanders shot arrows at them but did not engage in hand-to-hand fighting. As they skirted the stockade, Egil and his men did not realize at first that there was another stockade on the other side of them, narrowing to a bend where they could not proceed any farther. The Courlanders pursued them into this pen. Some attacked them from the outside by lunging with their swords and spears through the fences, while others rendered them harmless by throwing blankets over their weapons. They suffered wounds and were captured, and all were tied up and led back to the farm.

The farm was owned by a powerful and wealthy man who had a grown-up son. They talked about what to do with the prisoners. The farmer advocated killing them one after the other, but his son said that since night was falling, they would not be able to enjoy torturing them, and asked him to wait until morning. The prisoners were thrown into one of the buildings, tightly bound. Egil was tied hand and foot against a post. Then the house was locked up tight, and the Courlanders went into the main room to eat, make merry and drink. Egil wriggled and pressed against the post until it came free of the floor. Then the post fell over. He slipped himself off it, loosened the binding on his hands with his teeth, and when his hands were free he untied his feet. Then he released his companions.

When they were all free, they looked around the building for the most suitable place to escape. The walls of the building were made of large logs, with flat timber panelling at one end. They rammed it, broke down the panelling and found themselves in another building, with timber walls as well.

Then they could hear voices coming from below. They searched around and found a trap-door in the floor, and opened it. Underneath it was a deep pit where they could hear voices. Egil asked who was there, and a man called Aki spoke to him. Egil asked him if he wanted to come out of the pit, and he said all of them certainly did. Egil and his men lowered the ropes they had been tied up with down into the pit, and hauled three men up.

Aki told them that these were his sons, and that they were Danes and had been captured the previous summer.

'I was well looked after during the winter,' he said. 'I was put in charge of tending the cattle for the farmers here, but the boys disliked being made to work as slaves. In the spring we decided to run away, but then we were caught and put in this pit.'

'You must be familiar with the layout of the buildings,' Egil said. 'Where's the best place to get out?'

Aki told them there was another panelled wall: 'Break it down, and you will be in the barn where you can walk out as you please.'

Egil and his men broke down the panelling, entered the barn and got out from there. It was pitch-dark. Their companions told them to run for the woods.

Egil said to Aki, 'If you are familiar with the houses around here, you must be able to show us some booty.'

Aki said there were plenty of valuables they could take, 'and a large loft where the farmer sleeps. There's no lack of weapons inside.'

Egil told them to show them the loft. When they went up the stairs they saw that the loft was open and there were lights inside, and servants were making the beds. Egil told some of his men to stay outside and make sure that no one escaped. He ran into the loft and snatched up some weapons there, for there was no lack of them, and they killed everyone who was inside. His men armed themselves fully. Aki went over to a hatch in the floorboards and opened it, saying that they should go down into the room below. They took a light and went down. The farmer's treasure-chests were kept there, with valuable articles and much silver, and they took all they could carry and left. Egil picked up a large chest and carried it under his arm, and they headed for the woods.

In the woods, Egil stopped and said, 'This is a poor and cowardly raid. We have stolen all the farmer's wealth without his knowing. Such shame will never befall us. Let's go back to the farm and let people know what has happened.'

Everyone tried to dissuade him, saying that they wanted to go to the ship. But Egil put down the chest, and dashed off towards the farm. When he reached it he could see servants leaving the fire-room, carrying trenchers into the main room. Egil saw a great fire in a fire-room with cauldrons on top of it. He went over to it. Large logs had been brought inside and the fire was made in the customary manner, by lighting the end of a log and letting it burn all the way down to the others. Egil grabbed the log, carried it over to the main room and thrust the burning end under the eaves and up into the rafters. Some pieces of wood lay in the yard, and he carried them to the door of the main room. The fire quickly kindled the lining of the roof. The first thing the people knew who were sitting there drinking was that the rafters were ablaze. They ran to the door but there was no easy escape there, because of both the piled wood blocking the door and Egil guarding it. He killed them in the doorway and just outside. It was only moments before the main room flared up and caved in. Everyone else was inside and trapped, while Egil went back to the woods and rejoined his companions. They went to the ship together. Egil claimed as his private booty the treasure-chest he had taken, which turned out to be full of silver.

Thorolf and the others were relieved when Egil came back to the ship, and they left when morning broke. Aki and his sons were in Egil's party. They all sailed to Denmark later that

summer and sat in ambush for merchant ships, robbing wherever they could.

47 | Harald Gormsson[36] had ascended to the throne of Den-
     | mark on the death of his father, King Gorm. Denmark was
in a state of war, and Vikings lay off its shores in large numbers.
Aki was familiar with both the sea and land there. Egil pressed
him to find out about places where large amounts of booty
could be taken.

When they reached Oresund, Aki told him there was a large
town called Lund on the shore where they could expect to find
some booty, but would probably encounter resistance from the
townspeople. The men were asked whether they should go
ashore and raid there, and there was much disagreement. Some
advocated mounting an attack, but others argued against it.
Then the question was put to the steersmen. Thorolf favoured
going ashore. Then Egil was asked his opinion, and he spoke a
verse:

12. Let us make our drawn swords glitter,
       you who stain wolf's teeth with blood;
       now that the fish of the valleys thrive,   *fish of the valleys*: snakes;
       let us perform brave deeds.   when they *thrive*: summer
       Each man in this band
       will set off for Lund apace,
       there before sunset we will
       make noisy clamour of spears.

Then Egil and his men made ready to go ashore and went
towards the town. When the townspeople became aware of the
threat, they marched to face Egil's men. A wooden fortress
surrounded the town, on which they posted men to defend
it. Then battle ensued. Egil entered the fortress first, and the
townspeople fled. Egil and his men inflicted heavy casualties,
plundered the town and set fire to it before leaving. Then they
returned to their ships.

48 | Thorolf took his men north of Halland,[37] and they moored
     | in a harbour when the weather hindered their journey, but
they did not raid there. Living just inland was an earl called
Arnfinn. When he learned that Vikings had landed, he sent men
to meet them and find out whether their mission was peaceful
or warlike.

When the messengers met Thorolf and told him their errand,
he said they had no need to raid and plunder in what was not a
rich country anyway.

The messengers returned to the earl and told him the outcome
of the meeting. When the earl heard that he did not need to
gather any forces, he rode down to meet the Vikings without
taking any men with him. They got on well together, and the
earl invited Thorolf to a feast with any men he wanted to bring
with him. Thorolf promised to come.

At the appointed time, the earl had some chargers sent down
to them. Both Thorolf and Egil went along, and took thirty men
with them. The earl welcomed them kindly when they arrived,
and they were shown into the main room. The ale was already
there and they were served with drink. They sat there until
night.

Before the tables were set up, the earl said that they should
cast lots to pair off the men and women who would drink
together, as far as numbers allowed, and the remainder would
drink by themselves. They all cast their lots into a cloth and the
earl picked them out. He had an attractive and nubile daughter
who drew lots with Egil to sit together for the evening. She
walked around, keeping herself amused, but Egil got up and
went to the place she had been sitting during the day. When
people took their seats, the earl's daughter went to her place.
She spoke a verse:

13.   What do you want my seat for?
      You have not often fed
      wolves with warm flesh;
      I'd rather stoke my own fire.
      This autumn you did not see ravens

screeching over chopped bodies,
you were not there when
razor-sharp blades clashed.

Egil took hold of her and sat her beside him, and spoke a verse:

14. I have wielded a blood-stained sword
    and howling spear; the bird
    of carrion followed me   *bird of carrion*: raven
    when the Vikings pressed forth;
    In fury we fought battles,
    fire swept through men's homes,
    we made bloody bodies
    slump dead by city gates.

They drank together that night and got on well together. It was a fine feast, and there was another the next day. Then the Vikings went to their ships. They left in friendship and exchanged gifts with the earl. Thorolf and Egil took their men to the Branno Islands, where Vikings used to lie in wait in those days for the many trading ships that sailed through them.

Aki and his sons went home to his farmlands. He was a wealthy man who owned many farms in Jutland. They left Thorolf and Egil on close terms, and each promised the other firm friendship.

When autumn arrived, Thorolf and Egil sailed north to Norway and put in at Fjordane, where they went to see Thorir the Hersir. He welcomed them warmly, and his son Arinbjorn even more so. Arinbjorn invited Egil to stay there for the winter, and he accepted gratefully.

But Thorir considered this a rather rash invitation when he heard about it.

'I do not know what King Eirik will think about it,' he said, 'because after Bard was killed, he said he did not want Egil in this country.'

'Father, you can easily use your influence with the king to stop him objecting to Egil's staying here. You can invite Thorolf, your kinsman by marriage, to be here, and Egil and I will both stay in the same place for the winter.'

From what Arinbjorn said, Thorir could see he intended to have his own way. The two of them invited Thorolf to stay for the winter, and he accepted the offer. Twelve men spent the winter there.

There were two brothers called Thorvald the Overbearing and Thorfinn the Strong, close relatives of Bjorn the Land-owner, and many who had been brought up with him. They were big, strong men, great fighters and assertive. They had gone with Bjorn on his Viking raids, and when he settled down the brothers joined Thorolf and went raiding with him. They sat in the prow of his ship, and when Egil took over command of his own ship, Thorfinn manned the prow. The brothers went everywhere with Thorolf and he favoured them above the rest of his crew. They joined his men that winter, and sat next to Thorolf and Egil at table. Thorolf sat in the high seat, sharing drink with Thorir, while Egil's drinking partner was Arinbjorn. Guests left their seats and took to the floor every time a toast was drunk.

In the autumn, Thorir the Hersir went to see King Eirik, who gave him a fine welcome. Thorir began by asking him not to take offence at the fact that Egil was staying with him for the winter.

The king answered favourably, saying that Thorir could have whatever he wanted from him, 'although things would be different if someone else had taken Egil in'.

But when Gunnhild heard what they were talking about, she said, 'I think that once again you are allowing yourself to be too easily persuaded and are quick to forget being wronged. You'll go on favouring Skallagrim's sons until they kill a few more of your close kinsmen. Even though you happen to think Bard's killing was insignificant, I don't.'

The king said, 'More than anyone else, Gunnhild, you doubt my ferocity, and you used to be fonder of Thorolf than you are now. But I will not go back on my word once I have given it to him and his brother.'

'Thorolf was welcome here until Egil spoiled things for him,'
she said. 'Now there is no difference between them.'

Thorir went home when he was ready, and told the brothers
what the king and queen had said.

49 | Gunnhild had two brothers called Eyvind Braggart and
     | Alf Askmann,[38] sons of Ozur Snout. They were big, power-
ful men and great fighters, and held in very high regard by King
Eirik and Gunnhild, although they were not popular with most
people. They were young at this time, but fully grown.

That spring, a huge sacrificial feast was arranged for the
summer at Gaular, where there was a fine main temple.[39] A
large party attended from the Fjordane, Fjaler and Sognefjord
provinces, most of them men of high birth. King Eirik went
there too.

Gunnhild said to her brothers, 'I want you to take advantage
of the crowd here and kill one of Skallagrim's sons, or preferably
both.'

They said they would do so.

Thorir the Hersir made ready for the journey. He called
Arinbjorn to talk to him.

'I am going to the sacrifice,' he said, 'and I don't want Egil to
go. I know about Gunnhild's conniving, Egil's impetuousness
and the king's severity, and we cannot keep an eye on all three
at once. But Egil will not be dissuaded from going unless you
stay behind too. Thorolf will be going with me, and their other
companions. Thorolf will make a sacrifice and seek good fortune
for himself and his brother.'

Arinbjorn told Egil afterwards that he would be staying at
home.

'The two of us will stay here,' he said.

Egil agreed.

Thorir and the others went to the sacrifice and a sizeable
crowd gathered there, drinking heavily. Thorolf followed Thorir
everywhere he went, and they were never separated, neither by
day nor by night.

Eyvind told Gunnhild he hadn't had a chance to get at Thorolf.

She ordered him to kill one of his men instead, 'rather than all of them escaping'.

One night the king had gone to bed, and so had Thorir and Thorolf, but Thorfinn and Thorvald were still up. Eyvind and Alf came and sat down with them and made merry, drinking from the same horn at first, then in pairs. Eyvind and Thorvald drank together from one horn, and Alf and Thorfinn from the other. As the night wore on they started cheating over the drinking, and a quarrel broke out that ended in abuse. Eyvind leapt to his feet, drew his short-sword and stabbed Thorvald, delivering a wound that was more than enough to kill him. Then the king's men and Thorir's men both leapt to their feet, but none of them was armed because they were in a sacred temple, and people broke up the fighting among those who were the most furious. Nothing else of note happened that night.

Because Eyvind had committed murder in a sacred place he was declared a defiler and had to go into outlawry at once. The king offered compensation for the man he had killed, but Thorolf and Thorfinn said they had never accepted compensation from anyone, refused the offer and left. Then Thorir, Thorolf and the rest went home.

King Eirik and Gunnhild sent Eyvind south to King Harald Gormsson in Denmark, because he had been banished from wherever Norwegian laws applied. The king welcomed him and his companions warmly. Eyvind had taken a big longship to Denmark with him and the king put him in charge of defending the land from Vikings. Eyvind was a great warrior.

The winter came to an end and spring arrived, and Thorolf and Egil made ready to go on Viking raids again. When they had prepared themselves they headed for the Baltic again, but on reaching Vik they sailed south past Jutland to plunder there. Afterwards they went to Frisia and stayed much of the summer there, then went back to Denmark.

One night when they were moored at the border between Denmark and Frisia, and were getting ready for bed, two men boarded Egil's ship and said they needed to talk to him. They were led in to see Egil.

The men said they had been sent by Aki the Wealthy to tell him that 'Eyvind Braggart is moored off the coast of Jutland and plans to ambush you when you come back from the south. He has gathered such a large force that you won't stand a chance if you confront all of it at once. Eyvind himself is in command of two light ships and is not far away.'

When he heard this news, Egil ordered his men to lift the awnings and not make any noise. They did so. At dawn they came upon Eyvind and his men where they were anchored. They attacked them with a volley of rocks and spears. Many of Eyvind's men were killed, but Eyvind himself jumped overboard and swam to land, along with some others who also escaped.

Egil and his men seized their ships, clothes and weapons, then returned to Thorolf. He asked Egil where he had been, and where he had got the ships they were sailing. Egil told him they had taken them from Eyvind Braggart. Then Egil spoke a verse:

15. A mighty fierce attack
     we made off Jutland's shores.
     He fought well, the Viking
     who guarded the Danish realm,
     until swift Eyvind Braggart
     and his men all bolted
     from their horse of the waves   *horse of the waves*: ship
     and swam off the eastern sand.

Thorolf said, 'I think what you have done will make it inadvisable for us to go to Norway this autumn.'

Egil said it was well for them to look for another place.

50 | In the days of King Harald Fair-hair of Norway, Alfred
   | the Great[40] reigned over England, the first of his kinsmen to be sole ruler there. His son Edward[41] succeeded him on the throne; he was the father of Athelstan the Victorious,[42] who fostered Hakon the Good.[43] At this time, Athelstan succeeded

his father on the throne. Edward had other sons, Athelstan's brothers.

After Athelstan's succession, some of the noblemen who had lost their realms to his family started to make war upon him, seizing the opportunity to claim them back when a young king was in control. These were British,[44] Scots and Irish. But King Athelstan mustered an army, and paid anyone who wanted to enter his service, English and foreign alike.

Thorolf and Egil sailed south past Saxony and Flanders, and heard that the king of England was in need of soldiers, and that there was hope of much booty there. They decided to go there with their men. In the autumn they set off and went to see King Athelstan. He welcomed them warmly and felt that their support would strengthen his forces greatly. In the course of their conversations he invited them to stay with him, enter his service and defend his country. It was agreed that they would become King Athelstan's men.

England had been Christian for a long time when this happened. King Athelstan was a devout Christian, and was called Athelstan the Faithful. The king asked Thorolf and Egil to take the sign of the cross, because that was a common custom then among both merchants and mercenaries who dealt with Christians. Anyone who had taken the sign of the cross could mix freely with both Christians and heathens, while keeping the faith that they pleased. Thorolf and Egil did so at the king's request, and both took the sign of the cross. Three hundred of their men entered the king's service.

51 | Olaf the Red[45] was the king of Scotland. He was Scottish on his father's side and Danish on his mother's, a descendant of Ragnar Shaggy-breeches.[46] He was a powerful man; the realm of Scotland was considered to be one-third of the size of England.

Northumbria was considered to be one-fifth of the English realm. It is the northernmost district, next to Scotland in the east, and had belonged to Danish kings in times of old. The main town is York. Northumbria belonged to King Athelstan, and he had appointed two earls to rule it, named Alfgeir and Godric. They stayed there to defend it against aggression by Scots and by Danes and Norwegians, who raided heavily and made a strong claim on the land, since the only people there of any standing were of Danish descent on their father's or mother's side, and there were many of each.

Two brothers called Hring and Adils ruled Britain.[47] They paid tribute to King Athelstan, and accordingly, when they went to battle with the king, they and their men were in the vanguard, with the king's standard-bearers. These brothers were great warriors, even though they were no longer young men.

Alfred the Great had deprived all the tributary kings of their rank and power. Those who had been kings or princes before were now titled earls. This arrangement prevailed throughout his lifetime and that of his son Edward, but when Athelstan ascended to the throne at an early age he was considered a less imposing figure and many people who had once served the king became disloyal.

52 | King Olaf of Scotland gathered a great army and went south to England, and on reaching Northumbria he began plundering. When the earls who ruled there heard this, they mustered troops and went to face the king. A great battle ensued when they met, which ended in a victory for King Olaf, while Godric was killed and Alfgeir fled, together with the majority of the troops that had accompanied them and managed to escape from the fighting. Since Alfgeir offered no resistance, King Olaf conquered the whole of Northumbria. Alfgeir went to meet King Athelstan and told him of his misfortunes.

Hearing that such a huge army had entered his land, Athelstan dispatched messengers at once, gathered forces and sent word to the earls and other leaders. The king set off straight away with the troops he mustered and went to face the Scots.

When word spread that King Olaf had won a battle and taken control of a large part of England, acquiring a much greater army than Athelstan, many powerful men joined him. Hring and Adils heard this when they had gathered a large force and joined his side, making an enormous army.

When King Athelstan heard all this, he met his chieftains and counsellors to ask what the best course of action would be, and gave everyone a full account of what he had heard about the deeds of the Scottish king and his large band of men. They were unanimous that Earl Alfgeir had done terribly and deserved to be stripped of his rank. A plan was decided whereby King Athelstan would go back to the south of England and move northwards across the whole country gathering troops, because they saw that it would be a slow process mustering forces on the scale they needed unless the king himself were to lead the army.

The king appointed Thorolf and Egil as leaders of the army that had rallied there. They were to be in charge of the forces that the Vikings had brought to the king; Alfgeir was still in control of his own troops. The king appointed other men to lead the other divisions as he saw fit. When Egil returned to his companions after the meeting, they asked him what news he had to report about the king of the Scots. He spoke a verse:

16. Olaf turned one earl in flight
     in a sharp encounter,
     and felled another; I have heard
     this warrior is hard to face.
     Godric went far astray
     on his path through the battlefield;
     the scourge of the English subdues
     half of Alfgeir's realm.

After that they sent messengers to King Olaf, saying that King Athelstan challenged him to a battle and proposed Wen Heath[48] by Wen Forest as a site; he wanted them to stop raiding his realm, and the victor of the battle should rule England. He proposed meeting in battle after one week, and that the first to arrive should wait one week for the other. It was a custom then that if a king had been challenged to a pitched battle, he incurred dishonour if he went on raiding before it had been fought. King Olaf responded by stopping his armies and ceasing his attacks until the appointed day for the battle. Then he moved his troops to Wen Heath.

There was a fortress north of the heath where King Olaf stayed and kept the greater part of his army, because beyond it lay a large stretch of countryside which he considered well suited for transporting provisions for his army. He sent his men up to the heath which had been appointed as the battlefield, to camp there and prepare themselves before the other army arrived. When they reached the place chosen for the battlefield, hazel rods had already been put up to mark where it would be fought. The site had to be chosen carefully, since it had to be level and big enough for large armies to gather. At the site of the battlefield there was a level moor with a river on one side and a large forest on the other.

King Athelstan's men had set up camp over a very long range at the narrowest point between the forest and river. Their tents stretched all the way from the forest to the river, and they had made camp so as to leave every third tent empty, with only a few men in each of the others.

When King Olaf's men arrived, Athelstan's troops had gathered at the front of the camp, preventing them from entering the area. Athelstan's troops said that their tents were so full of men that there was nowhere near enough room for them all. The tents were on such high ground that it was impossible for Olaf's men to see past them and tell whether they were closely pitched, so they assumed that this must be a great army.

King Olaf's men pitched their tents north of the hazel rods that marked out the battlefield, on a fairly steep slope. Every day, moreover, Athelstan's men said their king was either on his way then or had reached the fortress south of the moor. Troops joined them day and night.

Once the appointed time had passed, Athelstan's men sent messengers to King Olaf to tell him that their king was ready to do battle and had a great army with him, but that he wanted to avoid inflicting casualties on the scale that seemed likely. Instead, he told them to return to Scotland, offering to give them a shilling of silver for every plough in all his realm[49] as a pledge of friendship between them.

King Olaf began preparing his army for battle when the messengers arrived, and intended to set off. But when they had delivered their message, he called a halt for the day and discussed it with the leaders of his army. They were divided over what to do. Some were eager to accept the offer, claiming that it would earn them great renown to return after exacting such a payment from Athelstan. Others discouraged him, saying that Athelstan would offer much more the second time if they turned this gesture down. This was what they decided to do.

The messengers asked King Olaf for time to meet King Athelstan again and find out if he was prepared to pay more to keep the peace. They asked for a day's leave to ride home, another day to discuss the matter and a third to come back, and the king agreed. The messengers went home and returned on the third day as had been settled, to tell King Olaf that King Athelstan was prepared to repeat his earlier offer, with an extra payment to the troops of one shilling for every free-born man, a mark for every leader of twelve men or more, a mark of gold for every captain and five marks of gold for every earl.

Olaf had the offer put to his men, and once again some were against it and others were eager to accept. In the end the king pronounced that he would accept the offer on condition that King Athelstan would give him Northumbria too, with all the dues and tributes that went with it.

The messengers asked for another three days' leave, and also for some of Olaf's men to go with them to hear King Athelstan's reply about whether or not he would accept this option, saying that they expected he would let little or nothing stand in the way of achieving a settlement. King Olaf agreed, and sent his men to King Athelstan. The messengers rode together and met King Athelstan in the nearest fortress on the southern side of the moor.

King Olaf's men delivered their message and offer of a settlement. Athelstan's men also told him the offer they had made to King Olaf, adding that wise men had advised them to delay the battle until King Athelstan arrived.

King Athelstan made a quick decision on the matter, telling the messengers, 'Send word from me to King Olaf that I want to give him leave to return to Scotland with his troops and repay all the money which he wrongly took in this country. Let us then declare peace between our countries, and promise not to attack each other. In addition, King Olaf will swear allegiance to me, and rule Scotland in my name as my tributary king. Go back and tell him the way things stand.'

That same evening the messengers went back and reached King Olaf in the middle of the night. They woke him up and told him King Athelstan's reply at once. The king had his earls and other leaders called over, then had the messengers repeat the outcome of their mission and King Athelstan's reply. When they heard it they were unanimous that the next step would be to prepare for battle. The messengers added that Athelstan had a huge army and had arrived in the fortress where they had been that same day.

The Earl Adils said, 'What I told you is coming to pass, King: you will find the English are cunning. While we have spent so much time sitting here waiting, they have mustered all their forces, but their king was nowhere around when we arrived here. They have been gathering a huge army since we put up camp here. My advice now is that I ride to battle with my brother this very night, with our troops. There is a chance that they will not be on their guard now that they have heard their king is nearby with a great army. We will mount an attack on them, and when they flee they will be routed and prove all the less courageous to fight us afterwards.'

The king considered this a fine plan: 'We will make our army ready at daybreak and join you.'

After deciding on this plan of action, they called an end to their meeting.

53 | Earl Hring and his brother Adils prepared their army and set off southwards towards the moor the same night. At daybreak, Thorolf and Egil's guards saw the army approaching. Trumpets were sounded and the troops put on their armour, then formed into two columns. Earl Alfgeir commanded one of the columns with the standard at its head. In the column were

the troops he had taken with him, together with others who had joined them from the countryside. It was a much larger band than the one under Thorolf and Egil's command.

Thorolf was equipped with a broad, thick shield and a tough helmet on his head, and was girded with a sword which he called Long, a fine and trusty weapon. He carried a thrusting-spear in his hand. Its blade was two ells long and rectangular, tapering to a point at one end but thick at the other. The shaft measured only a hand's length below the long and thick socket which joined it to the blade, but it was exceptionally stout. There was an iron spike through the socket, and the shaft was completely clad with iron. Such spears were known as 'scrapers of mail'.

Egil was equipped like Thorolf, girded with a sword that he called Adder and had received in Courland, an outstanding weapon. Neither of them wore a coat of mail.

They raised the standard, which Thorfinn the Strong carried. All their troops had Viking shields and other Viking weaponry, and all the Vikings who were in the army were in their column. Thorolf and his men gathered near the wood, while Alfgeir's went along the riverside.

Realizing that they would not be able to take Thorolf by surprise, Earl Adils and his brother began to group into two columns as well, with two standards. Adils grouped his troops to face Earl Alfgeir, and Hring against the Vikings. Then battle began, and both sides marched forward bravely.

Earl Adils pressed forward until Alfgeir yielded ground. Then they advanced all the more bravely, and it was not long before Alfgeir fled. What happened to him was that he rode away south along the moor, with a band of men with him. He rode until he approached the fortress where the king was staying.

Then Earl Alfgeir said, 'I do not want to go to the town. We were showered with abuse the last time we returned to the king after suffering defeat at King Olaf's hands, and King Athelstan will not think our qualities have improved on this expedition. I won't expect him to show me any honour.'

Then he set off for the south of England and what happened on his journey was that he rode night and day until he and his men reached Earlsness[50] in the west. He took a ship over the channel to France, where one side of his family came from, and he never returned to England.

Adils pursued the fleeing troops a short way at first, then returned to the site of the battle and mounted an attack.

Seeing this, Thorolf swung round to face the earl and ordered his men to bring his banner there, keep on the alert and stay close together.

'We will edge our way towards the forest,' he said, 'and use it to cover us from the rear, so that they cannot attack us from all sides.'

They did so and skirted the forest. A tough battle ensued. Egil attacked Adils and they fought hard. Despite the considerable difference in numbers, more of Adils' men were killed.

Then Thorolf began fighting so furiously that he threw his shield over his back, grabbed his spear with both hands and charged forward, hacking and thrusting to either side. Men leapt out of the way all around, but he killed many of them. He cleared a path to Earl Hring's standard, and there was no holding him back. He killed Earl Hring's standard-bearer and chopped down the pole. Then he drove the spear through the earl's coat of mail, into his chest and through his body so that it came out between his shoulder blades, lifted him up on it above his own head and thrust the end into the ground. Everyone saw how the earl died on the spear, both his own men and his enemies. Then Thorolf drew his sword and hacked to either side, and his men attacked. Many British and Scots were killed then, and others turned and fled.

When Earl Adils saw his brother's death, the heavy casualties in his ranks and the men who were fleeing, he realized that the cause was lost. He turned to flee as well and ran for the forest, where he hid with his band. All the troops who had been with them fled too. They sustained heavy casualties and they scattered far and wide across the moor. Earl Adils had thrown down his standard and no one could tell whether it was he who was fleeing, or someone else. Night soon began to fall, and Thorolf and Egil returned to their camp just as King Athelstan arrived with all his army, and they put up their tents and settled down.

Shortly afterwards, King Olaf appeared with his army. They

put up their tents and settled for the night where their men had already made camp. King Olaf was told that both his earls, Hring and Adils, had been killed along with many other men.

54 | King Athelstan had settled for the night in the fortress mentioned earlier where he had heard about the battle on the moor. He and his whole army made ready at once and went north along the moor, where they heard clear accounts of the outcome of the battle. Thorolf and Egil went to meet the king, and he thanked them for their courage and the victory they had won, pledging them his total friendship. They remained there together for the night.

King Athelstan woke his men early the next morning. He spoke to his leaders and described how his troops were to be arranged. He ordered his band to lead the way, spearheaded by the finest fighters, and put Egil in command of it.

'Thorolf will stay with his men and some others that I will place there,' he said. 'This will be our second column and he will be in charge of it, because the Scots tend to break ranks, run back and forth and appear in different places. They often prove dangerous if you do not keep on the alert, but retreat if you confront them.'

Egil answered the king, 'I do not want to be separated from Thorolf in battle, but I think we should be assigned where we are needed the most and the fighting is the heaviest.'

Thorolf said, 'Let the king decide where he wants to assign us. We will support him as he wishes. I can take the place you have been assigned, if you want.'

Egil said, 'You can decide, but this is an arrangement I will live to regret.'

The men formed columns as the king had ordered and raised the standards. The king's column entered the plain in the direction of the river, and Thorolf's skirted the forest above it.

King Olaf saw that Athelstan had arranged his troops, and he began doing the same. He formed two columns as well, and moved his standard and the column that he commanded, to face King Athelstan and his men. Both armies were so big that it was

impossible to tell which was the larger. King Olaf's other column
moved closer to the forest to face the men who were under
Thorolf's command. It was led by Scottish earls and was very
large, mostly consisting of Scots.

Then the troops clashed and a great battle soon ensued.
Thorolf advanced bravely and had his standard carried along
the side of the forest, intending to approach the king's men from
their vulnerable side. He and his men were holding their shields
in front of them, using the forest as cover to their right. Thorolf
advanced so far that few of his men were in front of him, and
when he was least expecting it, Earl Adils and his men ran out
of the forest. Thorolf was stabbed with many spears at once
and died there beside the forest. Thorfinn, his standard-bearer,
retreated to where the troops were closer together, but Adils
attacked them and a mighty battle ensued. The Scots let out a
cry of victory when they had felled the leader.

When Egil heard their cry and saw Thorolf's standard being
withdrawn, he sensed that Thorolf could not be following it.
He then ran out between the columns, and as soon as he met his
men he found out what had happened. He urged them to show
great courage, and led the way. Holding his sword Adder, he
advanced bravely and chopped to either side, and killed many
men. Thorfinn carried the standard directly behind Egil, and the
rest of the men followed it. A fierce battle took place, and Egil
fought on until he came to Earl Adils. They exchanged a few
blows before Adils was killed, and many men around him too,
and when he died the troops he had led fled the field. Egil and
his men pursued them, killing everyone they could catch, and it
was pointless for anyone to ask for his life to be spared. The
Scottish earls did not remain very long when they saw their
companions fleeing, and ran away themselves.

Egil and his men headed for the king's column, came upon
them from their vulnerable side and soon inflicted heavy casualties. The formation broke up and disintegrated. Many of Olaf's
men fled, and the Vikings let out a cry of victory. When King
Athelstan sensed that King Olaf's column was giving way, he
urged his own men forward and had his standard brought
forward, launching such a fierce assault that they broke ranks

and suffered heavy losses. King Olaf was killed there, along with the majority of his men, because all those who fled were killed if they were caught. King Athelstan won a great victory there.

55 | King Athelstan left the scene of the battle and his men pursued those who had fled. He rode back to the fortress without stopping for the night until he reached it, while Egil pursued the fleeing troops for a long time, killing every one of them that he caught. Then he returned to the scene of the battle with his band of men and found his dead brother Thorolf. He picked up his body and washed it, then dressed the corpse according to custom. They dug a grave there and buried Thorolf in it with his full weaponry and armour. Egil clasped a gold ring on to each of his arms before he left him, then they piled rocks over the grave and sprinkled it with earth. Then Egil spoke a verse:

17. The slayer of the earl, unfearing,
    ventured bravely forth
    in the thunder god's din: *thunder god's din*: battle
    bold-hearted Thorolf fell.
    The ground will grow over
    my great brother near Wen;
    deep as my sorrow is
    I must keep it to myself.

    And he spoke another verse:

18. I piled body-mounds, west of where
    the poles marked the battlefield.
    With black Adder I smote Adils
    in a heavy shower of blows.
    The young Olaf made
    thunder of steel with the English;   *thunder of steel*: battle
    Hring entered the weapon-fray
    and the ravens did not starve.

Then Egil went with his band of men to see King Athelstan, and approached him where he was sitting and drinking. There was much revelry. And when the king saw Egil arrive, he gave an order to clear the lower bench for his men, and told Egil to sit in the high seat there, facing him.

Egil sat down and put his shield at his feet. He was wearing a helmet and laid his sword across his knees, and now and again he would draw it half-way out of the scabbard, then thrust it back in. He sat upright, but with his head bowed low. Egil had very distinctive features, with a wide forehead, bushy brows and a nose that was not long but extremely broad. His upper jaw was broad and long, and his chin and jawbones were exceptionally wide. With his thick neck and stout shoulders, he stood out from other men. When he was angry, his face grew harsh and fierce. He was well built and taller than other men, with thick wolf-grey hair, although he had gone bald at an early age. When he was sitting in this particular scene, he wrinkled one eyebrow right down on to his cheek and raised the other up to the roots of his hair. Egil had dark eyes and was swarthy. He refused to drink even when served, but just raised and lowered his eyebrows in turn.

King Athelstan was sitting in the high seat, with his sword laid across his knees too. And after they had been sitting there like that for a while, the king unsheathed his sword, took a fine, large ring from his arm and slipped it over the point of the sword, then stood up and walked across the floor and handed it over the fire to Egil. Egil stood up, drew his sword and walked out on to the floor. He put his sword through the ring and pulled it towards him, then went back to his place. The king sat down in his high seat. When Egil sat down, he drew the ring on to his arm, and his brow went back to normal. He put down his sword and helmet and took the drinking-horn that was served to him, and finished it. Then he spoke a verse:

19. The god of the armour hangs   *god of the armour*: warrior, king
     a jangling snare upon my clutch,   *jangling snare*: ring
     the gibbet of hunting-birds,   *gibbet of hunting-birds*: arm
     the stamping-ground of hawks.
     I raise the ring, the clasp that is worn
     on the shield-splitting arm,

on to my rod of the battle-storm,   *rod of the battle-storm*: sword
in praise of the feeder of ravens.   *feeder of ravens*: warrior, i.e.
                                       Athelstan

From then onwards, Egil drank his full share and spoke to the others.

Afterwards, the king had two chests brought in, carried by two men each. They were both full of silver.

The king said, 'These chests are yours, Egil. And if you go to Iceland, you will present this money to your father, which I am sending him as compensation for the death of his son. Share some of the money with Thorolf's kinsmen, those you regard as the best. Take compensation for your brother from me here, land or wealth, whichever you prefer, and if you wish to stay with me for longer I will grant you any honour and respect that you care to name yourself.'

Egil accepted the money and thanked the king for his gift and friendship. From then on he began to cheer up, and spoke a verse:

20. For sorrow my beetling brows
    drooped over my eyelids.
    Now I have found one who smoothed
    the wrinkles on my forehead:
    the king has pushed the cliffs   *cliffs*: eyebrows
    that gird my mask's ground,   *mask's ground*: face
    back above my eyes.
    He grants bracelets no quarter.

Afterwards the men who were thought likely to survive had their wounds dressed.

Egil remained with King Athelstan for the winter after Thorolf's death, and earned great respect from him. All the men who had been with the brothers and survived the battle stayed with him. Egil composed a drapa in praise of the king which includes the following verse:

21. The wager of battle who towers
    over the land, the royal progeny,
    has felled three kings; the realm

passes to the kin of Ella.   *Ella*: (probably) king of
Athelstan did other feats,   Northumbria, d. 867.
the high-born king subdues all.
This I swear, dispenser   *wave-fire*: gold; its *dispenser*:
of golden wave-fire.   generous man, king

This is the refrain in the drapa:

22. Even the highland deer's paths   *highland deer's paths*: Scotland
    belong to mighty Athelstan now.

As a reward for his poetry, Athelstan gave Egil two more gold rings weighing a mark each, along with an expensive cloak that the king himself had worn.

When spring came, Egil announced to the king that he intended to leave for Norway that summer and find out about the situation of Asgerd, 'who was my brother Thorolf's wife. They have amassed plenty of wealth, but I do not know whether any of their children are still alive. I must provide for them if they are alive, but shall inherit everything if Thorolf has died childless.'[51]

The king said, 'While it is your decision, of course, to leave here if you feel you have duties to attend to, Egil, I would prefer you to do otherwise; stay here permanently and accept anything you care to name.'

Egil thanked the king for this offer: 'I must leave immediately,' he said, 'as is my duty. But I am more likely than not to return to collect what you have promised me, when I can arrange it.'

The king invited him to do so. Then Egil made ready to leave with his men, although many remained behind with the king. Egil had a great longship with a hundred men or more on board. And when he was ready to set off and a fair wind got up, he put out to sea. He and King Athelstan parted in great friendship. He asked Egil to come back as quickly as he possibly could. Egil said he would do so.

Then Egil headed for Norway, and when he reached land he sailed straight to Fjordane. He was told that Thorir the Hersir had died and that his son Arinbjorn had succeeded to his titles and become one of the king's men. Egil went to meet Arinbjorn and was well received by him. Arinbjorn invited him to stay there, and Egil accepted the offer. He had his ship pulled up on the beach, and his men were given places to stay. Arinbjorn took Egil and eleven other men into his house, and he spent the winter with him.

56 | Berg-Onund, son of Thorgeir Thorn-foot, had married Bjorn the Landowner's daughter Gunnhild, and she was living with him at Ask. Asgerd, now Thorolf Skallagrimsson's widow, was staying with her kinsman Arinbjorn. She and Thorolf had a young daughter named Thordis, who was with her mother. Egil told Asgerd of Thorolf's death and offered to provide for her. Asgerd was very upset at the news but she answered Egil fittingly, and played the matter down.

As autumn progressed, Egil grew very melancholy and would often sit down with his head bowed into his cloak.

Once, Arinbjorn went to him and asked what was causing his melancholy – 'Even though you have suffered a great loss with your brother's death, the manly thing to do is bear it well. One man lives after another's death. What poetry have you been composing? Let me hear some.'

Egil told him this was his most recent verse:

23. The goddess of the arm where hawks perch,
    woman, must suffer my rudeness;
    when young I would easily dare
    to lift the sheer cliffs of my brow.
    Now I must conceal in my cloak
    the outcrop between my brows
    when she enters the poet's mind,
    head-dress of the rock-giant's earth.

goddess of the arm: woman

lift . . . my brow: i.e. look up

outcrop between my brows: nose

head-dress of the rock-giant's earth: woman (possibly also a play on As-gerd, which means 'God-fence' but its components can also be read as 'hill-head-dress')

Arinbjorn asked who this woman was that he was making love poems about – 'There seems to be a clue about her name concealed in the verse.'

Then Egil spoke this verse:

24. I seldom hide the name
    of my female relative
    in the drink of the giant's kin;   *drink of the giant's kin*: poetry
    sorrow wanes in sea-fire's fortress.   *sea-fire*: gold; its *fortress*: woman
    Some who stir the din
    of Valkyries' armour   *Valkyries' armour*: battle
    have poetic fingers that feel
    the essence of the war-god's wine.   *war-god*: Odin; his *wine*: poetry

'This is a case where the saying applies that you can tell anything to a friend,' said Egil. 'I will answer your question who the woman is that I make poems about. It is your kinswoman Asgerd, and I would like your support in arranging this marriage.'

Arinbjorn said he thought this was a fine idea, 'and I will certainly put in a word to bring the match about'.

Afterwards, Egil put his proposal to Asgerd, but she referred it for the advice of her father and her kinsman Arinbjorn. Then Arinbjorn discussed it with Asgerd, and she gave the same answer as before. Arinbjorn urged her to accept the offer of marriage. After that, Arinbjorn and Egil went to see Bjorn and Egil made a proposal to marry his daughter. Bjorn responded favourably, saying that it was up to Arinbjorn to decide. Arinbjorn favoured it strongly, so in the end they became betrothed, and their wedding was arranged to be held at Arinbjorn's house. When the appointed time came, a lavish feast was held there, and Egil took her for his wife. He remained in good spirits for the rest of the winter.

In the spring, Egil equipped a merchant ship to sail to Iceland. Arinbjorn had advised him not to stay in Norway while Queen Gunnhild held such power.

'She is very ill-disposed towards you,' Arinbjorn said, 'and it made things much worse when you ran into Eyvind off Jutland.'

When Egil was ready and a favourable wind got up, he sailed

out to sea and had an easy passage. He reached Iceland in the autumn and headed for Borgarfjord. He had been away for twelve years. Skallagrim was growing very old by then, and was delighted when Egil returned. Egil went to stay at Borg, taking with him Thorfinn the Strong and many of his men. They spent the winter with Skallagrim. Egil had an enormous amount of wealth, but it is not mentioned whether he ever shared the silver that King Athelstan had presented to him, either with Skallagrim or anyone else.

That winter, Thorfinn married Skallagrim's daughter Saeunn, and the following spring Skallagrim gave them a place to live at Langarfoss, and the land stretching inshore from the Leirulaek brook between the Langa and Alfta rivers, all the way up to the mountains. Thorfinn and Saeunn had a daughter named Thordis, who married Arngeir from Holm, the son of Bersi the Godless. Their son was Bjorn, Champion of the Hitardal people.[52]

Egil stayed with Skallagrim for several winters, and looked after the property and ran the farm just as much as Skallagrim did. Egil went balder than ever.

Then the district began to be settled in many places. Hromund, brother of Grim the Halogalander, was living at Thverarhlid with the crew of his ship. Hromund was the father of Gunnlaug, whose daughter, Thurid Dylla, was the mother of Illugi the Black.[53]

57 | One summer when Egil had been at Borg for many years, a ship arrived in Iceland from Norway, bringing the news that Bjorn the Landowner was dead. It was also reported that Bjorn's son-in-law, Berg-Onund, had taken all his wealth. He had taken all the valuables to his own home, and had put tenants on the farms and was collecting rent from them. He had also seized all the lands that Bjorn had owned.

When Egil learned of this, he asked in detail whether Berg-Onund would have done this on his own initiative, or with the backing of more powerful people. He was told that Onund was a good friend of King Eirik, and even closer to Queen Gunnhild.

Egil let the matter rest for the autumn. But at the end of winter and in early spring, Egil had the ship brought out that he owned and that had been standing in a shed at Langarfoss, equipped it to go to sea and gathered a crew. His wife Asgerd went on the journey, but Thorolf's daughter Thordis stayed behind. Egil put out to sea when he was ready, and nothing of note happened until he reached Norway. He went straight to see Arinbjorn at the first opportunity. Arinbjorn welcomed Egil and invited him to stay, which he accepted. Asgerd went there with him, along with several people.

Egil soon brought up the subject with Arinbjorn of collecting the property he laid claim to in that country.

'It does not look too promising,' Arinbjorn said. 'Berg-Onund is tough and troublesome, unfair and greedy, and now the king and queen are giving him much support. As you are aware, Gunnhild is your greatest enemy, and she will not urge Onund to settle up.'

Egil said, 'The king will allow me to win my lawful rights in this case, and with your support I won't hesitate about taking Onund to law.'

They decided that Egil should equip a boat, which he manned with a crew of almost twenty. They headed south for Hordaland, landed at Ask and went to the house to ask for Berg-Onund. Egil presented his case and demanded his share of Bjorn's inheritance from Onund, saying that both daughters had equal rights to inherit from Bjorn by law.

'Even if it seems to me that Asgerd might be considered of much higher birth than your wife Gunnhild,' he added.

'You've certainly got some nerve, Egil,' Onund snapped back. 'You've been outlawed by King Eirik, then you come back here to his country to pester his men. You can be sure that I have got the better of plenty of people like you, Egil, even when I have considered there to be much less reason than you with your claim on an inheritance for your wife, because everyone knows she's the daughter of a slave-woman.'

Onund delivered a long string of abuse.

When Egil saw that Onund was not prepared to make any

settlement, he summonsed him to appear at an assembly and to be judged according to laws of the Gula Assembly.[54]

Onund said, 'I'll be at the Gula Assembly, and if I have my way you won't be leaving there in one piece.'

Egil said he would risk going to the assembly, whatever happened – 'come what may of our dealings'.

Egil and his men went away, and when he returned home he told Arinbjorn about his journey and Onund's answers. Arinbjorn was furious at hearing his aunt Thora called a slave-woman.

Arinbjorn went to see King Eirik and put the matter to him.

The king took the matter quite badly, saying that Arinbjorn had taken Egil's side for a long time: 'It is for your sake that I have allowed him to stay in this country, but that will prove more difficult if you support him whenever he encroaches on my friends.'

Arinbjorn said, 'You should allow us to claim our rights in this case.'

The king was stubborn about the whole business, but Arinbjorn could tell that the queen was even more averse to it. Arinbjorn went back and said the outlook was quite bleak.

Winter passed and the time came round to attend the Gula Assembly. Arinbjorn took a large band of men with him, and Egil was among them. King Eirik was there too, and had a large band with him. Berg-Onund and his brothers were in the king's party, and had many men with them. When the time came to discuss the cases, both sides went to the place where the court was held, to present their testimonies. Onund was bragging.

The court was held on a flat plain, marked out by hazel poles with a rope around them. This was known as staking out a sanctuary. Inside the circle sat the court, twelve men from the Fjordane province, twelve from Sognefjord province and twelve from Hordaland province. These three dozen men were to rule on all the cases. Arinbjorn selected the members of the Fjordane court, and Thord from Aurland those from Sognefjord, and they were all on the same side.

Arinbjorn had taken a large band of men to the assembly, a

fully manned fast vessel and many small boats, skiffs and ferries owned by farmers. King Eirik had a large party there too, six or seven longships and many farmers.

Egil began his statement by demanding that the court rule in his favour against Onund. He recounted his grounds for claiming Bjorn Brynjolfsson's inheritance. He said that his wife Asgerd deserved to inherit from her father Bjorn, being descended entirely from landowners and ultimately of royal stock. He demanded that the court rule that Asgerd should inherit half of Bjorn's estate, both money and land.

When Egil finished his speech, Berg-Onund spoke.

'My wife Gunnhild is the daughter of Bjorn and Olof, Bjorn's lawful wife,' he said. 'Gunnhild is therefore Bjorn's legal heiress. I claimed ownership of everything Bjorn owned on the grounds that Bjorn had only one other daughter and she had no right to the inheritance. Her mother was captured and made a concubine without her kinsmen's approval, and taken from one country to another. And you, Egil, want to act as unreasonably and overbearingly here as you do everywhere else you go. But you do not stand to gain by it this time, for King Eirik and Queen Gunnhild have promised me that every case of mine in their realm will be ruled in my favour. I present irrefutable evidence to the king and queen and members of the court to prove that Thora of the Embroidered Hand, Asgerd's mother, was captured from her brother Thorir's home and on another occasion from Brynjolf's in Aurland. She travelled from one country to the next with Bjorn and some Vikings and outlaws who had been exiled by the king, and while she was away she became pregnant with Asgerd by Bjorn. It is astonishing that you, Egil, intend to ignore all King Eirik's rulings. For a start, you are here in this country after Eirik outlawed you, and what is more, even though you have married a slave-woman, you claim she has a right to an inheritance. I demand of the members of the court that they award me all of Bjorn's inheritance, and declare Asgerd a king's slave-woman, because she was begotten when her mother and father were under king's outlawry.'

Then Arinbjorn spoke: 'We will bring forth witnesses who will swear on oath that my father Thorir and Bjorn stated in their settlement that Asgerd, Bjorn and Thora's daughter, was deemed one of her father's heiresses, and also that you, King, granted him the right to live in this country,[55] as you know for yourself, and that everything was settled that had once prevented them from reaching an agreement.'

The king took a long time answering his speech.

Then Egil spoke a verse:

25. This man pinned with thorns claims   *thorns*: brooches
    that my wife, who bears my drinking-horn,
    is born of a slave-woman;
    Selfish Onund looks after himself.
    Spear-wielder, my brooch-goddess   *brooch-goddess*:
    is born to an inheritance.   woman, wife
    This can be sworn to, descendant
    of ancient kings: accept an oath.

Arinbjorn then had twelve worthy men testify that they had heard the terms of Thorir and Bjorn's settlement, and they all offered to swear an oath on it for the king and the court. The court wanted to take their oaths, if the king did not forbid it. The king replied that he would neither order it nor forbid it.

Then Queen Gunnhild spoke: 'How peculiar of you, King, to let this big man Egil run circles around you. Would you even raise an objection if he claimed the throne out of your hands? You might refuse to make any ruling in Onund's favour, but I will not tolerate Egil trampling over our friends and wrongly taking this money from Onund. Where are you now, Alf Askmann? Take your men to where the court is sitting and prevent this injustice from coming to pass.'

Askmann and his men ran to the court and cut the ropes where the sanctuary had been staked out, broke the hazel poles and drove the court away. Commotion broke out at the assembly; no one carried arms there.

Then Egil said, 'Can Berg-Onund hear me?'

'I'm listening,' he replied.

'I challenge you to a duel, here at the assembly. The victor will take all the property, the lands and the valuables, and you will be a figure of public scorn if you do not dare.'

Then King Eirik said, 'If you're looking for a fight, Egil, we can arrange one for you.'

Egil answered, 'I'm not prepared to fight the king's forces and be outnumbered, but I will not run away if I am granted a fight on equal terms. I will give you all the same treatment.'

Then Arinbjorn said, 'Let's leave, Egil. We've no business here for the time being.'

Arinbjorn went away, taking all his men with him.

Egil turned round and said in a loud voice, 'Testify to this, Arinbjorn, Thord and all who hear me now, landholders and men of law and common people, that I forbid that the lands once owned by Bjorn Brynjolfsson will be lived on, worked on and used for any purpose. This I forbid you, Berg-Onund, and all other men, foreign or native, of high or low birth, and anyone who does so I pronounce to have broken the laws of the land, incurred the wrath of the gods and violated the peace.'

After that, Egil left with Arinbjorn. They went to their ships, crossing a hill some distance away which prevented them from being seen in the assembly place.

When they reached the ships, Arinbjorn addressed his men: 'You are all aware how this assembly turned out. We failed to win our rights and the king is so furious that I expect him to deal out the harshest treatment to our men if he has the chance. I want everyone to board his ship and go home immediately. Let no man wait for any other.'

Then Arinbjorn boarded his ship and said to Egil, 'You board the boat that is tied to the seaward side of the longship and get away as quickly as possible. Travel by night if you can, not by day, and lie low, because the king will try to find a way to make your paths cross. Whatever may happen, come to me when all this is over.'

Egil did as Arinbjorn had told him. Thirty of them boarded the boat and rowed as fast as they could. It was an exceptionally fast craft. A large number of Arinbjorn's men rowed out of the harbour in boats and ferries, and the longship commanded by Arinbjorn went last, being the hardest to row. The boat that Egil was in soon went ahead of the others. Then Egil spoke a verse:

26. Thorn-foot's false heir ruined
     my claim to the inheritance.
     From him I earn only
     threats and hectoring,
     whenever I may repay his robbing
     my lands where oxen toil.
     We disputed great fields
     that serpents slumber on: gold.

King Eirik had heard Egil's departing words to the assembly, and was furious. But since everyone had gone to the assembly unarmed, he did not attack him there. He ordered his men to board their ships, and they did so.

When they reached the shore, the king arranged a meeting to describe his plan: 'We will take down the awnings from our ships and row after Arinbjorn and Egil. Then we will execute Egil and spare no one who takes his side.'

They boarded their ships, quickly made ready to put to sea and rowed to where Arinbjorn's ships had been moored, but they had already left by then. The king ordered his men to row after them through the northern part of the sound, and when he entered Sognefjord, Arinbjorn's men were rowing into the Saudungssund. He pursued them and caught up with Arinbjorn's ships in the sound. Drawing up beside them, they called out and the king asked if Egil was on board.

Arinbjorn replied, 'Egil is not here, as you will soon find out for yourself, my lord. The men on board are all known to you, and you won't find Egil below deck if you look there.'

The king asked Arinbjorn about Egil's most recent whereabouts. He replied that Egil was on board a boat with thirty men, rowing out to Steinssund.

Then the king ordered his men to row along the channels that were farthest inland, and try to cut Egil off. They did so.

There was a man from Oppland called Ketil the Slayer, a member of King Eirik's court. He navigated and steered the king's ship. Ketil was a big, handsome man and a relative of the king's. Many people said there was a close resemblance between them.

Egil had left his ship afloat and moved the cargo before he went to the assembly. After leaving Arinbjorn, he and his men rowed to Steinssund to their ship, and boarded it. The boat was left to float between ship and shore, with its rudder ready and the oars tied in place in the rowlocks.

The following morning, when day had scarcely broken, the guards noticed several ships rowing up to them, and when Egil woke up he got straight to his feet and ordered all his men to board the boat. He armed himself quickly, and so did all the others. Egil took the chests of silver that he had been given by King Athelstan and took with him everywhere. They boarded the boat and rowed on the shore side of the warship closest to land; it was King Eirik's.

Because all this happened so quickly and there was still little daylight, the ships sailed past each other. When they stood aft to aft Egil threw a spear, striking the helmsman, Ketil the Slayer, through the middle. King Eirik called out an order to his men to row after Egil. When the ships passed the merchant vessel, the king's men boarded it. All of Egil's men who had stayed behind there and not boarded the boat were killed, if the king's men caught them; some fled to land. Ten of Egil's men died there. Some of the ships rowed after Egil and others plundered the merchant vessel. They took all the valuables they found on board, then burned it.

The party pursuing Egil rowed vigorously, with two men on each oar. They had plenty of men on board, while Egil had a small crew of eighteen men on his boat, and the king's men began to catch them up. Inland from the island was a fairly shallow fording-point to another island. It was low tide. Egil and his men headed for the shallow channel, and the warships ran aground there and lost sight of them. Then the king turned back for the south, while Egil headed north to see Arinbjorn. He spoke a verse:

27. The mighty wielder of swords
     that flame in battle
     has felled ten of our men,
     but I acquitted myself,

when the stout branch wetted   *branch*: spear
with the war-goddess's wound-sea,   *wound-sea*: blood
dispatched by my hand, flew straight
between Ketil's curved ribs.

Egil went to see Arinbjorn and told him the news.

Arinbjorn replied that Egil could not have expected anything else from his dealings with King Eirik, 'But you will not lack for money, Egil. I will compensate you for your ship and give you another that will provide you with an easy passage to Iceland.'

Asgerd, Egil's wife, had stayed at Arinbjorn's house while they were at the assembly.

Arinbjorn gave Egil a very seaworthy ship and had it loaded with timber. Egil prepared the ship to put out to sea, and had almost thirty men with him again. He and Arinbjorn parted in great friendship, and Egil spoke a verse:

28. Let the gods banish the king,
     pay him for stealing my wealth,
     let him incur the wrath
     of Odin and the gods.
     Make the tyrant flee his lands,
     Frey and Njord; may Thor
     the land-god be angered at this foe,
     the defiler of his holy place.

58 | When Harald Fair-hair began to age he appointed his sons as rulers of Norway, and made Eirik king of them all. After he had been king of Norway for seventy years, Harald handed over the kingdom to Eirik. At that time, Gunnhild bore Eirik a son, whom Harald sprinkled with water and named after himself, adding that he should become king after his father if he lived long enough.[56] King Harald then withdrew to live a quieter life, mainly staying at Rogaland or Hordaland. Three years later, King Harald died at Rogaland, and was buried in a mound at Haugesund.

After his death, a great dispute developed between his sons, for the people of Vik took Olaf as their king, and the people of

Trondheim took Sigurd.[57] Eirik killed both of his brothers in battle at Tunsberg a year after Harald's death. He took his army eastwards from Hordaland to Oslo to fight his brothers the same summer that Egil and Berg-Onund clashed at the Gula Assembly and that the events just described took place.

Berg-Onund stayed at home on his farm while the king went on his expedition, since he felt wary of leaving it when Egil was still in the country. His brother Hadd was with him.

There was a man called Frodi, a relative and foster-son of King Eirik. He was a handsome man, young but well built. King Eirik left him behind to provide Berg-Onund with extra support. Frodi was staying at Aarstad, on the king's farm, and had a band of men there with him.

King Eirik and Gunnhild had a son called Rognvald. He was ten or eleven years old at this time, a promising and attractive lad. He was staying with Frodi when all this happened.

Before sailing off on his expedition, King Eirik declared Egil an outlaw throughout Norway, whom anyone might kill with impunity. Arinbjorn accompanied the king on his expedition, but before he left, Egil set sail for the fishing camp called Vitar which lies off Alden, well away from travel routes. There were fishermen there who were good sources for the latest news. When he heard that the king had declared him an outlaw, Egil spoke this verse:

29. Land spirit, the law-breaker
      has forced me to travel
      far and wide; his bride deceives
      the man who slew his brothers.
      Grim-tempered Gunnhild must pay
      for driving me from this land.
      In my youth, I was quick to conquer
      hesitation and avenge treachery.

The weather was calm, with a wind from the mountains at night and a sea breeze during the day. One night Egil and his men put out to sea, and the fishermen who had been appointed to spy on Egil's travels rowed to land. They reported that Egil had put out to sea and had left the country, and had the word passed on to Berg-Onund. When Onund heard this, he sent away all the men he had been keeping as a safeguard there. Then he rowed to Aarstad and invited Frodi to stay with him, telling him that he had plenty of ale there. Frodi went with him and took several men along. They held a fine feast there and made merry, with nothing to fear.

Prince Rognvald had a small warship with six oars on either side and painted above the plumbline. He always had the ten or twelve men on board who followed him everywhere. And when Frodi left, Rognvald took the boat and twelve of them rowed out to Herdla. The king owned a large farm there, run by a man called Beard-Thorir; Rognvald had been fostered there when he was younger. Thorir welcomed the prince and provided plenty to drink.

Egil sailed out to sea at night, as written earlier, and the next morning the wind dropped and it grew calm. They let the ship drift before the wind for a few nights.

Then, when the sea breeze got up, Egil said to his crew, 'Now we will sail to land, because it is impossible to tell where we would make land if a gale came in from the sea. Most places here are fairly hostile.'

The crew said Egil should decide where they went. Then they hoisted sail and sailed to the fishing camp at Herdla. Finding a good place to anchor, they put up the awnings and moored there for the night. On their ship they had a small boat, which Egil boarded with two men. He rowed over to Herdla by cover of night, and sent a man on to the island to ask for news.

When he returned, he reported that Eirik's son Rognvald was at a farm there with his men: 'They were sitting drinking. I met one of the farmhands who was blind drunk, and he said they didn't plan to drink any less than was being drunk at Berg-Onund's house, where Frodi was with four of his men.'

Apart from Frodi and his men, he said, the only people there were those who lived on the farm.

Then Egil rowed back to his ship and told his men to get up and take their weapons. They did so. They anchored the ship, and Egil left twelve men to guard it, then got into the smaller boat. There were eighteen of them in all, and they rowed through the sounds. They timed their landing to reach Fenring at night and put in at a concealed cove there.

Then Egil said, 'Now I want to go up on to the island and see what I can find out. Wait for me here.'

Egil had his customary weapons, a helmet and shield, and was girded with a sword and carried a halberd in his hand. He went up on to the island and along the side of a wood, wearing a long hood over his helmet. He arrived at a place where there were several young lads with big sheepdogs. Once they had started talking, he asked where they were from and why they were there with such huge dogs.

'You must be pretty stupid,' they answered. 'Haven't you heard about the bear that's roaming around the island, causing all sorts of damage and killing people and animals? A reward's being offered for catching it. Here at Ask, we stay up every night watching over our flocks that are kept in these pens. Why are you going around armed at night, anyway?'

'I'm afraid of the bear too,' Egil replied, 'and not many people seem to go around unarmed at the moment. The bear has been chasing me for much of the night. Look, it's over at the edge of the wood. Is everyone at the farm asleep?'

One lad said that Berg-Onund and Frodi would still be up drinking – 'They sit up all night.'

'Tell them where the bear is,' said Egil. 'I must hurry back home.'

He walked away while the boy ran back to the farm and into the room where they were drinking. By that time, all but three of them had gone to sleep: Onund, Frodi and Hadd. The boy told them where the bear was, and they took their weapons that were hanging there and ran straight outside and into the woods. A strip of land with patches of bushes jutted out from the woods. The boy told them that the bear was in the bushes, and when they saw the branches moving, they assumed that the bear was there. Berg-Onund told Hadd and Frodi to get between the bushes and the main part of the wood, to prevent the bear from reaching it.

Berg-Onund ran up to the shrubs. He was wearing a helmet, carried a shield in one hand and a spear in the other, and was girded with a sword. But it was Egil, not a bear, that was hiding in the shrubs, and when he saw Berg-Onund he drew his sword. There was a strap on the hilt which he pulled over his hand to let the sword hang there. Taking his spear, he rushed towards Berg-Onund. When Berg-Onund saw this he quickened his pace and put the shield in front of him, and before they clashed they threw their spears at each other. Egil darted his shield out to block the spear, at such an angle that the spear glanced off and stuck into the ground. His own spear struck the middle of Onund's shield and sank in so deep that it stuck there, making it heavy for Onund to hold. Then Egil quickly grabbed the hilt of his sword. Onund began to draw his sword, but had only pulled it half-way out of its sheath by the time Egil ran him through with his sword. Onund recoiled at the blow, but Egil drew his sword back swiftly and struck at Onund, almost chopping his head off. Then Egil took his spear out of the shield.

Hadd and Frodi ran over to Berg-Onund when they saw he had been felled. Egil turned to face them. He lunged at Frodi with his spear, piercing his shield and plunging it so deep into his chest that the point came out through his back. He fell over backwards dead on the spot. Then Egil took his sword and set on Hadd, and they exchanged a few blows before Hadd was killed.

The boys came over, and Egil said to them, 'Stand guard over your master Onund and his companions and make sure that the animals or birds do not eat their carcasses.'

Egil proceeded on his way and had not gone far when his men came from the opposite direction. There were eleven of them, and six others were guarding the ship. They asked what he had been doing. He spoke a verse:

30. Too long I was short-changed
    by that tree of the glowing den   *tree*: man
    of the heather-fjord's fish;   *heather-fjord*: earth; its
    I guarded my wealth better once,   *fish*: serpent that guards
    until I dealt out mortal wounds   gold
    to Berg-Onund, Hadd and Frodi too.
    Odin's wife, the earth,
    I clad in a cloak of blood.

Then Egil said, 'Let us go back to the farm and acquit ourselves like true warriors: kill everyone we can catch and take all the valuables we can carry.'

They went to the farmhouse and stormed it, killing fifteen or sixteen men. Some ran away and escaped. They took all the valuables and destroyed what they could not take with them. They drove the cattle down to the shore and slaughtered them, filled their boat, then proceeded on their way, rowing out through the sounds.

Egil was so furious that no one dared talk to him. He was sitting at the helm of the boat.

When they headed out into the fjord, Prince Rognvald and his twelve men rowed into their path in the painted warship. They had heard that Egil's boat was near the fishing camp at Herdla, and wanted to spy on his whereabouts for Onund. Egil recognized the warship as soon as he saw it. He steered straight for it and rammed its side with the prow of his own boat. The warship gave such a jolt that the sea flooded over one side and filled it. Egil leapt aboard, clutched his halberd and urged his men to let no one on the ship escape alive. Meeting no resistance, they did just that: everyone on the ship was killed, and none escaped. Rognvald and his men died there, thirteen of them in all. Egil and his men rowed to the island of Herdla. Then Egil spoke a verse:

31. We fought; I paid no heed
     that my violent deeds might be repaid.
     My lightning sword I daubed with the blood
     of warlike Eirik and Gunnhild's son.
     Thirteen men fell there,
     pines of the sea's golden moon,   *sea's ... moon*:
     on a single ship; the bringer   gold; its *pines*
     of battle is hard at work.   (trees): men

When Egil and his men reached Herdla they ran straight up to the farmhouse, fully armed. Seeing them, Thorir and his people ran away from the farm at once, and everyone capable of escaping did so, men and women alike. Egil and his men took all the valuables they could find, then went to their ship. It was not long until a favourable wind got up from the land, and they made ready to sail. When their sails were hoisted, Egil went back on to the island.

He took a hazel pole in his hand and went to the edge of a rock facing inland. Then he took a horse's head and put it on the end of the pole.

Afterwards he made an invocation, saying, 'Here I set up this scorn-pole and turn its scorn upon King Eirik and Queen Gunnhild' – then turned the horse's head to face land – 'and I turn its scorn upon the nature spirits that inhabit this land, sending them all astray so that none of them will find its resting-place by chance or design until they have driven King Eirik and Gunnhild from this land.'

Then he thrust the pole into a cleft in the rock and left it to stand there. He turned the head towards the land and carved the whole invocation in runes on the pole.

After that, Egil went to his ship. They hoisted the sail and put out to sea. The wind began to get up and a strong, favourable wind came. The ship raced along, and Egil spoke this verse:

32. With its chisel of snow, the headwind,
    scourge of the mast, mightily
    hones its file by the prow
    on the path that my sea-bull treads.   *sea-bull*: ship
    In gusts of wind, that chillful
    destroyer of timber planes down   *destroyer of timber*: wave,
    the planks before the head   imagined as a file
    of my sea-king's swan.   *sea-king's swan*: ship

After that they sailed out to sea and had a smooth passage, making land in Iceland in Borgarfjord. Egil headed for harbour there and brought his cargo ashore. He went home to Borg, while his crew found other quarters to stay in. By this time Skallagrim was old and fragile with age, so Egil took charge of the property and maintaining the farm.

59 | There was a man called Thorgeir Lamb. He was married
   | to Thordis, who was the daughter of Yngvar and the sister
of Bera, Egil's mother. Thorgeir lived inland from Alftanes, at
Lambastadir, and had come to Iceland with Yngvar. He was
wealthy and well respected. His son, Thord, had inherited
Lambastadir from his father and was living there when Egil
came to Iceland.

That autumn, some time before winter, Thord rode over to
Borg to meet his kinsman Egil and invite him to a feast. He had
brewed some ale at home. Egil promised to go along and the
time was set for a week later. When this came around, he made
ready to go, and his wife, Asgerd, with him. They were ten or
twelve in all.

And when Egil was ready, Skallagrim came out with him,
embraced him before he mounted his horse and said, 'You seem
to be taking your time about paying me the money that King
Athelstan sent me, Egil. How do you intend to dispose of it?'

Egil said, 'Are you very short of money, Father? I wasn't
aware. I will let you have silver as soon as I know that you need
it, but I know you have kept a chest or two aside, full of silver.'

'You seem to think we have already divided our money
equably,' said Skallagrim. 'So you won't mind if I do as I please
with what I have put aside.'

Egil said, 'Don't pretend you need to ask my permission,
because you will do as you please, whatever I say.'

Then Egil rode off to Lambastadir. He was given a warm and
friendly welcome and was to stay there for the next three nights.

The same evening that Egil left home, Skallagrim had his
horse saddled, then rode away from home when everyone else
went to bed. He was carrying a fairly large chest on his knees,
and had an iron cauldron under his arm when he left. People
have claimed ever since that he put either or both of them in the
Krumskelda Marsh, with a great slab of stone on top.

Skallagrim came home in the middle of the night, went to his
bed and lay down, still wearing his clothes. At daybreak next
morning, when everybody was getting dressed, Skallagrim was
dead, sitting on the edge of his bed, and so stiff that they could

neither straighten him out nor lift him no matter how hard they tried.

A horse was saddled quickly and the rider set off at full pelt all the way to Lambastadir. He went straight to see Egil and told him the news. Egil took his weapons and clothes and rode back to Borg that evening. He dismounted, entered the house and went to an alcove in the fire-room where there was a door through to the room in which were the benches where people sat and slept. Egil went through to the bench and stood behind Skallagrim, taking him by the shoulders and tugging him backwards. He laid him down on the bench and closed his nostrils, eyes and mouth. Then he ordered the men to take spades and break down the south wall. When this had been done, Egil took hold of him by the head and shoulders, and the others by his legs. They carried him like this right across the house and out through where the wall had been broken down. They carried him out to Naustanes without stopping and covered his body up for the night. In the morning, at high tide, Skallagrim's body was put in a ship and they rowed with it out to Digranes. Egil had a mound made on the edge of the promontory, where Skallagrim was laid to rest with his horse and weapons and tools. It is not mentioned whether any money was put into his tomb.[58]

Egil inherited his father's lands and valuables, and ran the farm. Thordis, Asgerd's daughter by Thorolf, was with him there.

60 | King Eirik ruled Norway for one year after the death of his father, before another of King Harald's sons, Hakon, arrived in Norway from England, where he had been fostered by King Athelstan. This was the same summer that Egil Skallagrimsson went to Iceland. Hakon went north to Trondheim, and was accepted as king there. That winter, he and Eirik were joint kings of Norway. The following spring, they both gathered armies, and Hakon's was by far the more numerous. Eirik saw that he had no option but to flee the country, and left with his wife, Gunnhild, and their children.

Arinbjorn the Hersir was King Eirik's foster-brother, and foster-father to his children. King Eirik was fondest of him among all his landholders, and had made him the chieftain of all the Fjordane province. Arinbjorn left the country with the king, and they began by crossing over to the Orkneys. There the king gave his daughter Ragnhild in marriage to Earl Arnfinn.[59] Then he travelled south with all his men to Scotland and raided there, and from there he continued southwards to England and raided there as well.

When King Athelstan heard this he gathered a great force and went to face Eirik. When they met, an agreement was settled whereby King Athelstan would appoint Eirik to rule Northumbria and defend his kingdom from the Scots and Irish. King Athelstan had made Scotland a tributary kingdom after the death of King Olaf, but the people there were invariably disloyal to him. King Eirik generally stayed in York.

It is said that Gunnhild had a magic rite performed to curse Egil Skallagrimsson from ever finding peace in Iceland until she had seen him. That summer, after Hakon and Eirik had met and disputed the control of Norway, an embargo was placed on all travel from that country, so no ships sailed for Iceland then, and there was no news from Norway.

Egil Skallagrimsson remained on his farm. In his second year at Borg after Skallagrim's death, Egil grew restless and became increasingly melancholy as the winter progressed. When summer came, Egil announced that he was going to prepare his ship to sail abroad. He took on a crew, planning to sail to England. There were thirty men on board. Asgerd would remain behind to look after the farm, while Egil planned to go to see King Athelstan and collect what he had promised when they parted.

Egil was slow in getting ready, and by the time he put to sea it was too late for favourable winds, with autumn and bad weather approaching. They sailed north of Orkney. Egil did not want to stop there, since he assumed King Eirik was ruling the islands.[60] They sailed southwards along the coast of Scotland in a heavy storm and crosswinds, but managed to tack and head south of Scotland to the north of England. In the evening, when it began to get dark, the storm intensified. Before they knew it, the waves were breaking on shoals both on their seaward side and ahead of them, so the only course of action was to make for land. They did so, running their ship aground in the mouth of the Humber. All the men were saved and most of their possessions, but the ship was smashed to pieces.

When they met people to talk to, they heard something that Egil thought rather ominous: King Eirik Blood-axe and Gunnhild were there, rulers of the kingdom, and he was staying not far away in York. He also heard that Arinbjorn the Hersir was with the king and on good terms with him.

After he had found out all this news, Egil made his plans. He did not feel he had much chance of getting away even if he were to try to hide and keep under cover all the way back out of Eirik's kingdom. Anyone who saw him would recognize him. Considering it unmanly to be caught fleeing like that, he steeled himself and decided the very night that they arrived to get a horse and ride to York. He arrived in the evening and rode straight into town. He was wearing a long hood over his helmet, and was fully armed.

Egil asked where Arinbjorn's house was in the town; he was told, and rode to it. When he reached the house, he dismounted and spoke to someone who told him that Arinbjorn was sitting at table.

Egil said, 'I would like you to go into the hall, my good man, and ask Arinbjorn whether he would prefer to talk to Egil Skallagrimsson indoors or outside.'

The man said, 'It's not much bother for me to do that.'

He went into the hall and said in a loud voice, 'There's a man outside, as huge as a troll. He asked me to come in and ask whether you would prefer to talk to Egil Skallagrimsson indoors or outside.'

Arinbjorn replied, 'Go and ask him to wait outside. He won't need to wait for long.'

He did as Arinbjorn said, went out and told Egil what he had said.

Arinbjorn ordered the tables to be cleared, then went outside with all the people from his household. He greeted Egil and asked him why he had come.

Egil gave him a brief account of the highlights of his journey
– 'And now you will decide what I should do, if you want to
help me in any way.'

'Did you meet anyone in town who may have recognized you
before you came to the house?' asked Arinbjorn.

'No one,' said Egil.

'Then take up your arms, men,' said Arinbjorn.

They did so. And when Egil, Arinbjorn and all his men were
armed, they went to the king's residence. When they reached
the hall, Arinbjorn knocked on the door and asked to be let in,
after identifying himself. The guards opened the door at once.
The king was sitting at table.

Arinbjorn said twelve men would go inside, and nominated
Egil and ten others.

'Egil, now you must go and offer the king your head and
embrace his foot.[61] I will present your case to him.'

Then they went inside. Arinbjorn went up to the king and
greeted him. The king welcomed him and asked what he wanted.

Arinbjorn said, 'I have brought someone here who has travelled a long way to visit you and wants to make a reconciliation
with you. It is a great honour for you, my lord, when your
enemies come to see you voluntarily from other countries, feeling that they cannot live with your wrath even in your absence.
Please treat this man nobly. Make fair reconciliation with him
for the great honour he has shown you by crossing many great
seas and treacherous paths far from his home. He had no motivation to make the journey other than goodwill towards you,
because he could well spare himself from your anger in Iceland.'

Then the king looked around and saw over the heads of the
other men that Egil was standing there. The king recognized
him at once, glared at him and said, 'Why are you so bold as to
dare to come to see me, Egil? We parted on such bad terms the
last time that you had no hope of my sparing your life.'

Then Egil went up to the table and took the king's foot in his
hand. He spoke a verse:

33. I have travelled on the sea-god's steed   *sea-god's steed*: ship
     a long and turbulent wave-path

to visit the one who sits
in command of the English land.
In great boldness, the shaker   *shaker of the*
of the wound-flaming sword   *wound-flaming sword*:
has met the mainstay   warrior (Egil)
of King Harald's line.

King Eirik said, 'I have no need to enumerate all the wrongs
you have done. They are so great and so numerous that any one
of them would suffice to warrant your never leaving here alive.
You cannot expect anything but to die here. You should have
known in advance that you would not be granted any reconciliation with me.'

Gunnhild said, 'Why not have Egil killed at once? Don't you
remember, King, what Egil has done to you: killed your friends
and kinsmen and even your own son, and heaped scorn upon
your own person. Where would anyone dare to treat royalty in
such a way?'

'If Egil has spoken badly of the king,' Arinbjorn said, 'he can
make recompense with words of praise that will live for ever.'

Gunnhild said, 'We do not want to hear his praise. Have Egil
taken outside and executed, King. I neither want to hear his
words nor see him.'

Then Arinbjorn replied, 'The king will not be urged to do all
your scornful biddings. He will not have Egil killed by night,
because killing at night is murder.'

The king said, 'Let it be as you ask, Arinbjorn: Egil will live
tonight. Take him home with you and bring him back to me in
the morning.'

Arinbjorn thanked the king for his words: 'I hope that Egil's
affairs will take a turn for the better in future, my lord. But
much as Egil may have wronged you, you should consider the
losses he has suffered at the hands of your kinsmen. Your father
King Harald had his uncle Thorolf, a fine man, put to death
solely on the grounds of slander by evil men. You broke the
law against Egil yourself, King, in favour of Berg-Onund, and
moreover you wanted him put to death, and you killed his men
and stole all his wealth. And then you declared him an outlaw

and drove him out of the country. Egil is not the sort of man to stand being provoked. Every case should be judged in light of the circumstances,' Arinbjorn said. 'I will take Egil home to my house now.'

This was done. When the two men reached the house they went up to one of the garrets to talk things over.

Arinbjorn said, 'The king was furious, but his temper seemed to calm down a little towards the end. Fortune alone will determine what comes of this. I know that Gunnhild will do her utmost to spoil things for you. My advice is for you to stay awake all night and make a poem in praise of King Eirik. I feel a drapa of twenty stanzas would be appropriate, and you could deliver it when we go to see the king tomorrow. Your kinsman Bragi[62] did that when he incurred the wrath of King Bjorn of Sweden: he spent the whole night composing a drapa of twenty stanzas in his praise, and kept his head as a reward. We might be fortunate enough in our dealings with the king for this to make a reconciliation between you and him.'

Egil said, 'I will follow the advice you offer, but I would never have imagined I would ever make a poem in praise of King Eirik.'

Arinbjorn asked him to try, then went off to his men. They sat up drinking until the middle of the night. Arinbjorn and the others went off to their sleeping quarters, and before he got undressed, he went up to the garret to Egil and asked how the poem was coming along.

Egil said he hadn't composed a thing: 'A swallow has been sitting at the window twittering all night, and I haven't had a moment's peace.'

Arinbjorn went out through the door that led to the roof. He sat down near the attic window where the bird had been sitting, and saw a shape-shifter in the form of a bird leaving the other side of the house. Arinbjorn sat there all night, until daybreak. Once Arinbjorn was there, Egil composed the whole poem and memorized it, so that he could recite it to him when he met him the next morning. Then they kept watch until it was time to meet the king.

61 | King Eirik went to table as usual with a lot of people.
| When Arinbjorn noticed this, he took all his men, fully
armed, to the hall when the king was sitting down to dine.
Arinbjorn asked to be let in to the hall and was allowed to enter.
He and Egil went in, with half their men. The other half waited
outside the door.

Arinbjorn greeted the king, who welcomed him.

'Egil is here, my lord,' he said. 'He has not tried to escape
during the night. We would like to know what his lot will be. I
expect you to show us favour. I have acted as you deserve,
sparing nothing in word and deed to enhance your renown. I
have relinquished all the possessions and kinsmen and friends
that I had in Norway to follow you, while all your other landholders turned their backs on you. I feel you deserved this from
me, because you have treated me outstandingly in many ways.'

Then Gunnhild said, 'Stop going on about that, Arinbjorn.
You have treated King Eirik well in many ways, and he has
rewarded you in full. You owe much more to the king than to
Egil. You cannot ask for Egil to be sent away from King Eirik
unpunished, after all the wrongs he has done him.'

Arinbjorn said, 'If you and Gunnhild have decided for yourselves, King, that Egil will not be granted any reconciliation
here, the noble course of action is to allow him a week's grace
to get away, since he came here of his own accord and expected
a peaceful reception. After that, may your dealings follow their
own course.'

Gunnhild replied, 'I can tell from all this that you are more
loyal to Egil than to King Eirik, Arinbjorn. If Egil is given a
week to ride away from here in peace, he will have time to reach
King Athelstan. And Eirik can't ignore the fact that every king
is more powerful than himself now, even though not long ago
King Eirik would have seemed unlikely to lack the will and
character to take vengeance for what he has suffered from the
likes of Egil.'

'No one will think Eirik any the greater for killing a foreign
farmer's son who has given himself into his hands,' said
Arinbjorn. 'If it is reputation that he is seeking, I can help him

make this episode truly memorable, because Egil and I intend to stand by each other. Everyone will have to face the two of us together. The king will pay a dear price for Egil's life by killing us all, me and my men as well. I would have expected more from you than to choose to see me dead rather than to grant me the life of one man when I ask you for it.'

Then the king said, 'You are staking a great deal to help Egil, Arinbjorn. I am reluctant to cause harm to you if it should come to this, that you prefer to lose your own life than to see him killed. But Egil has done me plenty of wrong, whatever I may decide to do with him.'

When the king had finished speaking, Egil went before him and delivered his poem, reciting it in a loud voice, and everyone fell silent at once:

1. West over water I fared,
    bearing poetry's waves to the shore   *waves*: i.e. the mead of poetry
    of the war-god's heart;   *war-god*: Odin, also the god
    my course was set.   of poetry
    I launched my oaken craft
    at the breaking of ice,
    loaded my cargo of praise
    aboard my ship aft.

2. The warrior welcomed me,
    to him my praise is due.
    I carry Odin's mead
    to England's meadows.
    The leader I laud,
    sing surely his praise;
    I ask to be heard,
    an ode I can devise.

3. Consider, lord –
    well it will befit –
    how I recite
    if my poem is heard.
    Most men have learned
    of the king's battle deeds

and the war-god saw
corpses strewn on the field.

4.   The clash of swords roared
     on the edge of shields,
     battle grew around the king,
     fierce he ventured forth.
     The blood-river raced,
     the din was heard then
     of metal showered in battle,
     the most in that land.

5.   The web of spears
     did not stray from their course
     above the king's
     bright rows of shields.
     The shore groaned,
     pounded by the flood
     of blood, resounded
     under the banners' march.

6.   In the mud men lay
     when spears rained down.
     Eirik that day
     won great renown.

7.   Still I will tell
     if you pay me heed,
     more I have heard
     of those famous deeds.
     Wounds grew the more
     when the king stepped in,
     swords smashed
     on the shields' black rims.

8.   Swords clashed, battle-sun   *battle-sun, whetstone's saddle*:
     and whetstone's saddle;   sword
     the wound-digger bit
     with its venomous point.
     I heard they were felled,

Odin's forest of oaks,   *forest of oaks*: men
by scabbard-icicles   *scabbard-icicles*: swords
in the play of iron.

9.   Blades made play
     and swords bore down.
     Eirik that day
     won great renown.

10. Ravens flocked
     to the reddened sword,
     spears plucked lives
     and gory shafts sped.
     The scourge of Scots
     fed the wolves that trolls ride,   *wolves*: (in myth seen as ridden by
     Loki's daughter, Hel,   trollwomen)
     trod the eagle's food.   *eagle's food*: corpses

11. Battle-cranes swooped
     over heaps of dead,
     wound-birds did not want
     for blood to gulp.
     The wolf gobbled flesh,
     the raven daubed
     the prow of its beak
     in waves of red.

12. The troll's wolfish steed   *troll's . . . steed*: wolf
     met a match for its greed.
     Eirik fed flesh
     to the wolf afresh.

13. The battle-maiden keeps
     the swordsman awake
     when the ship's wall
     of shields breaks.
     Shafts sang
     and points stung,
     flaxen strings shot
     arrows from bows.

14. Flying spears bit,
    the peace was rent;
    wolves took heart
    at the taut elm bow.
    The war-wise king fended
    a deadly blow,
    the yew-bow twanged
    in the battle's fray.

15. Like bees, arrows flew
    from his drawn bow of yew.
    Eirik fed flesh
    to the wolf afresh.

16. Yet more I desire
    that men realize
    his generous nature;
    I urge on my praise.
    He throws gold river-flame   *river-flame*: gold
    but holds his lands
    in his horn-gripping hand,
    he is worthy of praise.

17. By the fistful he gives
    the fire of the arm.   *fire of the arm*: gold
    Never sparing rings' lives   *never sparing rings' lives*: i.e.
    he gives riches no rest,   throwing them away, being generous
    hands gold out like sand
    from the hawk's coast.   *hawk's coast*: wrist
    Fleets take cheer
    from the grindings of dwarfs.   *grindings of dwarfs*: gold

18. The maker of war
    sheds beds for spears   *beds for spears*: shields
    from his gold-laden arm,
    he spreads brooches afar.
    I speak from the heart:
    Everywhere he is grand,
    Eirik's feats were heard
    on the east-lying shore.

19. King, bear in mind
    how my ode is wrought,
    I take delight
    in the hearing I gained.
    Through my lips I stirred
    from the depths of my heart
    Odin's sea of verse
    about the craftsman of war.

20. I bore the king's praise
    into the silent void,
    my words I tailor
    to the company.
    From the seat of my laughter   *seat of my laughter*: mind
    I lauded the warrior
    and it came to pass
    that most understood.

62 | King Eirik sat upright and glared at Egil while he was
     reciting the poem. When it was over, the king said, 'The
poem was well delivered.[63] Arinbjorn, I have thought about the
outcome of my dealings with Egil. You have presented Egil's
case so fervently that you were even prepared to enter into
conflict with me. For your sake, I will do as you have asked and
let Egil leave, safe and unharmed. You, Egil, will arrange things
so that the moment you leave this room, neither I nor my sons
will ever set eyes upon you again. Never cross my path nor my
men's. I am letting you keep your head for the time being. Since
you put yourself into my hands, I do not want to commit a
base deed against you. But you can be sure that this is not a
reconciliation with me or my sons, nor any of my kinsmen who
wants to seek justice.'

Then Egil spoke a verse:

34. Ugly as my head may be,
    the cliff my helmet rests upon,
    I am not loath
    to accept it from the king.

Where is the man who ever
received a finer gift
from a noble-minded
son of a great ruler?   *great ruler*: King Harald Fair-hair

Arinbjorn thanked the king eloquently for the honour and
friendship he had shown him. Then Arinbjorn and Egil rode
back to his house. Arinbjorn had horses made ready for his
men, then with one hundred of them, all fully armed, he rode
off with Egil. Arinbjorn rode with the party until they reached
King Athelstan, who welcomed them. The king invited Egil to
stay with him for as long as he wished and be in great honour,
and asked how he had got on with King Eirik.

Then Egil spoke a verse:

35. That niggard with justice, maker
    of blood-waves for ravens,
    let Egil keep his black-browed eyes;
    my relative's courage availed me much.
    Now as before I rule
    the noble seat that my helmet,
    the sea-lord's hat, is heir to,   *sea-lord's hat*: cliff
    in spite of the wound-dispenser. *wound-dispenser*: warrior (king)

When they parted ways, Egil gave Arinbjorn the two gold
rings weighing a mark each that King Athelstan had given him,
while Arinbjorn gave Egil a sword called Dragvandil (Slicer).
Arinbjorn had been given it by Egil's brother Thorolf. Before
him, Skallagrim had been given it by Egil's uncle Thorolf, who
had received it from Grim Hairy-cheeks,[64] the son of Ketil
Haeng. Ketil had owned the sword and used it in duels, and it
was exceedingly sharp. Egil and Arinbjorn parted in the greatest
friendship. Arinbjorn returned to King Eirik in York, where
Egil's companions and crew were left in peace to trade their
cargo under his protection. As the winter progressed, they went
south to meet Egil.

63 | There was a landholder in Norway called Eirik the All-
     wise, who was married to Thora, Thorir's daughter and
Arinbjorn's sister. He owned land in Vik, in the east, and was
very wealthy, distinguished and wise of mind. Their son,
Thorstein, had been brought up at Arinbjorn's home, and
although still young he was fully developed. He had gone west
to England with Arinbjorn.

The same autumn that Egil went to England, word arrived
from Norway that Eirik the All-wise had died and the royal
agents had seized his inheritance in the king's name. When
Arinbjorn and Thorstein heard this news, they decided that
Thorstein should go to Norway to claim his inheritance.

As spring drew on and people who planned to sail abroad
began to make their ships ready, Thorstein went south to
London to see King Athelstan. He presented the king with
tokens and a message from Arinbjorn, and also gave a message
to Egil asking him to propose that the king should use his
influence with his foster-son Hakon to help Thorstein win
back his inheritance and property in Norway. King Athelstan
needed little persuasion, saying that he knew Arinbjorn as a fine
person.

Then Egil went to speak to King Athelstan and told him of
his plans.

'I want to go over to Norway this summer,' he said, 'to collect
the property that King Eirik and Berg-Onund robbed me of.
Berg-Onund's brother, Atli the Short, has it in his possession
now. I know I would win justice in the matter with a message
from you to back me up.'

The king said that it was up to Egil to decide where he went,
'But I would greatly prefer it if you stayed with me to defend
my kingdom and command my armies. I shall grant you great
revenues.'

Egil said, 'This is a very attractive offer, and I accept it rather
than refuse it. But first I must go to Iceland to collect my wife
and the wealth I own there.'

King Athelstan gave Egil a good merchant vessel, and a cargo
to go with it. The bulk of it was wheat and honey, and there

was greater wealth still in other goods. When Egil was preparing his ship for the voyage, Arinbjorn's kinsman Thorstein joined his crew. Thorstein was the son of Eirik, as mentioned before, but was later known as Thora's son. When they were ready they all sailed away. King Athelstan and Egil parted in great friendship.

Egil and his crew had a smooth journey, made land in Norway at Vik in the east and headed all the way in to Oslo fjord. Thorstein owned a farm in the uplands there, stretching all the way to the province of Raumarike. When Thorstein reached land, he laid a claim to his inheritance against the king's agents who had occupied his farm. Many people helped Thorstein, and charges were brought. Thorstein had many kinsmen of high birth. In the end the matter was referred to the king for a ruling, and Thorstein took over safeguarding the property his father had owned.

Egil spent the winter with Thorstein, and there were twelve of them there in all. Wheat and honey were brought to his house, there was much celebration during that winter and Thorstein lived grandly with plenty of provisions.

64 | Hakon, King Athelstan's foster-son, was ruling Norway at this time, as described earlier. The king spent that winter in Trondheim in the north.

As the winter wore on, Thorstein set off on his journey, accompanied by Egil. They had almost thirty men with them. When they had made their preparations, they went first to Oppland, then north over the Dovrefjell Mountains to Trondheim, where they went to see King Hakon. They delivered their messages to the king. Thorstein described the whole matter and produced witnesses to the fact that he owned the entire inheritance he had claimed. The king took the matter favourably, allowing Thorstein to recover his property and thereby become one of the king's landholders, as his father had been.

Egil went to see King Hakon and presented his own case, along with a message and tokens from King Athelstan. He enumerated the property once owned by Bjorn the Landowner, in the form of both land and money, and claimed half of it for himself and his wife, Asgerd. Supporting his case with witnesses and oaths, he said that he had presented the case to King Eirik as well, adding that he had not been given justice because of Eirik's severity and Gunnhild's incitements. Egil recounted the whole episode that had taken place at the Gula Assembly, and asked the king to grant him justice in the matter.

King Hakon answered, 'I have heard that my brother Eirik and his wife, Gunnhild, both think you have thrown a stone that was too heavy for you in your dealings with them, Egil. I think you ought to be quite contented if I do not involve myself in this matter, even though Eirik and I did not have the good fortune to agree with each other.'

Egil replied, 'You cannot keep quiet about such a great matter, King, because everyone in this country, native and foreign, must obey your orders. I have been told that you are establishing a code of law and rights for every man in this country, and I am certain that you will allow me to secure these rights like anybody else. I consider myself a match for Atli the Short in both strength and kinsmen here. As far as my dealings with King Eirik are concerned, I can tell you that I went to see him and when we parted he told me to go in peace wherever I wanted. I will offer you my allegiance and service, Lord. I know that you have men here with you who do not look any more fearsome in battle than I am. I have an intuition that it will not be very long before you cross paths with King Eirik again, if you both live to see the day. I would not be surprised if the time comes when you feel Gunnhild has rather too many ambitious sons.'

'You will not enter my service, Egil,' said the king. 'You and your kinsmen have carved too deep a breach in my family for you to be able to settle down in this country. Go out to Iceland and look after your inheritance from your father there. You will not suffer harm at the hands of myself or my kinsmen there, but you can expect my family to remain the most powerful in this country for the rest of your days. For King Athelstan's sake, however, you will be left in peace here and win justice and your rights, because I know how fond King Athelstan is of you.'

Egil thanked the king for his words and asked to be given tokens of proof to show to Thord at Aurland or his other landholders in Sognefjord and Hordaland. The king said he would do so.

65 | Once they had finished their business with the king, Thorstein and Egil made preparations for their journey. They set off. On their way south over Dovrefjell, Egil said he wanted to go up to Romsdal and then back south along the coast.

'I want to finish my business in Sognefjord and Hordaland, because I want to make my ship ready to leave for Iceland this summer,' he said.

Thorstein told him to go his way as he pleased. He and Egil parted, and Thorstein went south through Dalene and all the way to his lands. He produced the king's tokens and gave his message to the agents to hand over all the possessions that they had seized and Thorstein had laid claim to.

Egil went on his way with eleven men. Arriving in Romsdal, they arranged transport; then they went south to More. Nothing happened on their journey until they reached Hod Island and stayed at a farm there called Blindheim. It was a fine farm and a landholder called Fridgeir lived there. He was a young man and had recently received his inheritance from his father. His mother was Gyda, the sister of Arinbjorn the Hersir, a fine and determined woman. She ran the farm with her son Fridgeir, and they lived in style. Egil and his men were well received there. In the evening, Egil sat next to Fridgeir, with Egil's companions farther down the table. There was plenty of drinking and a splendid feast.

Gyda, the lady of the house, went to talk to Egil that night. She asked about her brother Arinbjorn and other kinsmen and friends of hers who had gone to England with him, and Egil answered her questions. She asked Egil whether anything noteworthy had happened on his travels, and he gave her a straightforward account. Then he spoke a verse:

36. I could not stand the ugly
    land-claimer's wrath;
    no cuckoo will alight knowing
    that the squawking eagle prowls.
    There, as before, I benefited
    from the bear of the hearth-seat.   *bear*: *Arinbjorn* means
    No one need give up who boasts   'hearth-bear'
    such a loyal helper on his travels.

Egil was in good spirits that evening, but Fridgeir and the people on the farm were fairly subdued. Egil saw a beautiful and well-dressed girl there, and was told she was Fridgeir's sister. She was unhappy and wept all the evening, which the visitors thought was peculiar.

They spent the night there. The next morning there was a gale and the seas were too heavy for sailing; they needed a ship to take them from the island. Fridgeir and Gyda went to talk to Egil, inviting him to stay there with his companions until the weather was good enough to sail away, and offering him any transport he needed. Egil accepted and they spent three nights there weather-bound, amid great celebrations. After that the wind calmed down. Egil and his men got up early that morning and made their preparations to leave, then went off to eat and were served with ale, and they sat at table for a while. Then they took their cloaks, and Egil stood up, thanked the farmer and his mother for what they had provided and went outside. Fridgeir and Gyda accompanied them on their way, until she took her son aside and whispered something to him.

While he stood and waited, Egil asked the girl, 'What are you crying about? I have never seen you happy for a moment.'

Unable to answer, she cried all the more.

Fridgeir answered his mother in a loud voice, 'I don't want to ask them to do that. They're ready to leave now.'

Then Gyda went up to Egil and said, 'I will tell you what is going on here. There is a man called Ljot the Pale, a berserk and a dueller who is very much loathed. He came here and asked for my daughter's hand in marriage, but we turned him down on the spot. So he challenged my son Fridgeir to a duel. He'll be coming to fight him at Valdero Island tomorrow. I'd like you to go to the site of the duel with Fridgeir, Egil. If Arinbjorn were here, we would prove that we do not put up with overbearing behaviour from such a man as Ljot.'

'For the sake of your brother Arinbjorn it is my duty to make this journey with Fridgeir,' answered Egil, 'if he thinks I can help him in any way.'

'That is noble of you,' Gyda said. 'Let us go into the main room and spend the day here together.'

Egil and his men went into the main room and started drinking. They sat there all day, and in the evening Fridgeir's friends who were to accompany him arrived and there was a great gathering and feast that night.

The next day, Fridgeir prepared himself to set off, with a large band of men. Egil was with them. It was good weather for sailing, and they set off and reached Valdero Island. There was a fine field a short way from the shore where the duel was to be held. Stones had been arranged in a circle to mark out the site.

Ljot arrived with his men and got ready for the duel. He had a shield and a sword. Ljot was a huge, strong man. And when he entered the arena, a berserk fury came over him and he started howling menacingly and biting at his shield. Fridgeir was not a big, strong man, but slim and handsome and unaccustomed to fighting. Seeing Ljot, Egil spoke a verse:

37. Fridgeir is not fit to fight a duel
     with a maker of Valkyries' showers   *Valkyries' showers*: battle
     who bites his shield's rim
     and invokes the gods
     – we'll ban the man from the maiden.
     That awful character throws
     fated glances at us; men,
     let us go to the duelling-place.

Ljot saw Egil standing there and, hearing his words, spoke to him: 'Come here into the arena, big man, and fight me if you are so eager to do so. Let us test our strength. It will be a much more even fight than with Fridgeir, because I do not imagine I will grow in stature by taking his life.'

Then Egil spoke a verse:

38.   It is not right to refuse
      Ljot his little request.
      I will sport with the pale man
      with my armour-prodder.
      Prepare for a fight, I give him
      no hope of mercy.
      Man, we must make shields
      skirmish on this island.

   After that, Egil made ready for his duel with Ljot. He held the
shield he always carried and was girded with his sword Adder
and held his other sword called Slicer in his hand. When he
entered the arena marked out for the duel, Ljot was still not
ready. Egil shook his sword and spoke this verse:

39.   Let polished hilt-wands clash,
      strike shields with brands,   *brands*: i.e. swords
      test our swords' shine on shields,
      redden them with blood.
      Hack Ljot's life away,
      play the pale man foul,
      silence the troublemaker
      with iron, feed eagle flesh.

   Then Ljot entered the arena and they went for each other.
Egil struck at Ljot, who parried with his shield, but Egil dealt
such a succession of blows that Ljot was unable to strike back.
Every time Ljot yielded ground to give himself room to deliver
a blow, Egil followed him just as quickly, striking furiously.
Ljot went outside the circle of stones and all over the field. The
fight went on like this at first, until Ljot asked to rest, and Egil
granted him that. They stopped to rest, and Egil spoke this
verse:

40.   The thruster of spear-burners   *spear-burners*: swords
      seems to back off from my force,
      the ill-fated wealth-snatcher
      fears my fierce onslaught.

The spear-dewed stave falters   *spear-dew*: blood; its *stave*:
and fails to strike.   warrior
He who asks for doom is sent
roaming by old bald-head.

According to the laws of duelling in those days, a man who challenged someone for anything and won would collect the stake, but if he lost he would pay a sum that had been determined beforehand. If he was killed in the duel, he would forfeit all his property and his slayer would inherit it. The laws also said that if a foreigner died with no heirs in that country, his inheritance would pass to the king.

Egil told Ljot to get ready – 'I want us to finish this duel now.'

Then Egil ran at him and struck at him. He dealt such a blow that Ljot stumbled and dropped his shield. Egil struck Ljot above the knee, chopping off his leg. Ljot dropped dead on the spot.

Egil went over to Fridgeir and the others, and was thanked kindly for his deed. Then Egil spoke a verse:

41. The feeder of wolves fell,   *feeder of wolves*: warrior
     worker of evil deeds.
     The poet chopped Ljot's leg off,
     I brought Fridgeir peace.   *Fridgeir* means 'peace-spear'
     I do not ask a reward
     from the splasher of gold for that.   *splasher of gold*: generous man
     The spears' din was fun enough,   *spears' din*: battle, fight
     the fight with the pale man.

Most people did not mourn Ljot's death, because he had been such a troublemaker. He was Swedish[65] and had no kinsmen in Norway, but had gone there and grown wealthy by duelling. After challenging many worthy men to duels, he had killed them and claimed their farms and lands, and had great wealth in both property and money.

Egil went home with Fridgeir after the duel. He stayed there for a while before going south to More. Egil and Fridgeir parted in great friendship, and Egil asked him to claim the land that Ljot had owned. Then Egil went on his way and arrived in

Fjordane. From there, he went to Sognefjord to meet Thord at Aurland, who gave him a good welcome. Egil stated his business and King Hakon's message, and Thord responded favourably to what he said, promising his assistance in the matter. Egil stayed with Thord for much of the spring.

66 | Egil made his journey south to Hordaland, taking a row-boat and thirty men on board. One day they arrived at Ask on Fenring. Egil took twenty men up to the farm with him, and left ten to guard the ship. Atli the Short was there with several men. Egil had him called out, with a message saying that Egil Skallagrimsson had a matter to attend to with him. Atli took his weapons; so did all the men who were fit to fight, and they went outside.

'I am told you have been keeping the money that belongs by rights to me and my wife, Asgerd,' Egil said. 'You have heard it mentioned that I claimed an inheritance from Bjorn the Land-owner that your brother Berg-Onund withheld from me. Now I have come to collect this property, the lands and money, and demand that you relinquish it and make it over to me at once.'

Atli replied, 'We've been hearing for a long time that you are overbearing, Egil, and now I'm being given a taste of this myself, if you intend to claim the money from me that King Eirik awarded to my brother Onund. King Eirik's word was law in this country then. I thought you would have come here to offer me compensation for killing my brothers and plundering the property here at Ask. I can answer your case if you intend to pursue the matter, but I cannot give any answers here.'

'I will offer you what I offered Onund,' Egil replied. 'To have the case settled according to the laws of the Gula Assembly. I think the claim for your brothers became void because of their acts, when they deprived me of justice and my rights and seized my property. I have permission from the king to seek redress by law. I will summons you before the Gula Assembly and have a ruling made on the case.'

'I'll go to the Gula Assembly,' said Atli, 'and we can discuss it there.'

Then Egil and his companions left. He went north to Sogne-fjord and in to Aurland, where he stayed with his kinsman Thord until the Gula Assembly.

When people arrived for the assembly, Egil was there too. Atli the Short had also arrived. They began stating their cases, presenting them to the men who were to rule upon them. Egil lodged a claim for the money, while Atli defended himself with the sworn testimony of twelve witnesses that he did not have Egil's property in his keeping.

When Atli went to the court with his witnesses, Egil went up to him with his own men and said that he would not accept his oath in place of his money: 'I offer you a different type of justice, a duel here at the assembly, staking the money for the winner to take.'

What Egil said was law too, under the ancient custom that every man had the right to challenge another to a duel, whether to prosecute a case or defend it.

Atli said he would not refuse a duel with Egil – 'You took the words right out of my mouth. I have plenty of grounds for taking vengeance on you. You have killed my two brothers, and I would be a long way from achieving justice if I chose to hand over my money to you in defiance of the law, instead of taking up your offer of a fight.'

Egil and Atli shook hands to confirm their duel for the stake of the lands they had been disputing.

After that they prepared themselves for the duel. Egil came forward wearing a helmet on his head and carrying a shield in front of him, with a halberd in his hand and his sword Slicer tied to his right hand. It was the custom among duellers to have their swords at hand to have them ready when they wanted them, instead of needing to draw them during the fight. Atli was equipped in the same way as Egil. He was strong and courageous, an experienced dueller, and skilled in the magic arts.

Then a huge old bull was brought out, known as the sacrificial bull, for the victor to slaughter. Sometimes there was one bull, and sometimes each of the duellers brought his own.

When they were ready for the duel, they ran at each other and began by throwing their spears. Neither stuck in the shields;

the spears both fell to the ground. Then they both grabbed their
swords, closed in and exchanged blows. Atli did not yield. They
struck hard and fast, and their shields soon began to split. When
Atli's shield was split right through, he tossed it away, took his
sword in both hands and hacked away with all his might. Egil
struck him a blow on the shoulder, but his sword did not bite.
He dealt a second and third blow, finding places to strike because
Atli had no protection. Egil wielded his sword with all his might,
but it would not bite wherever he struck him.

Egil saw that this was pointless, because his own shield was
splitting through by then. He threw down his sword and shield,
ran for Atli and grabbed him with his hands. By his greater
strength, Egil pushed Atli over backwards, then sprawled over
him and bit through his throat. Atli died on the spot. Egil rushed
to his feet and ran over to the sacrificial bull, took it by the
nostrils with one hand and by the horns with the other, and
swung it over on to its back, breaking its neck. Then Egil went
over to his companions. He spoke this verse:

42.   Black Slicer did not bite
      the shield when I brandished it.
      Atli the Short kept blunting
      its edge with his magic.
      I used my strength against
      that sword-wielding braggart,
      my teeth removed that peril.
      Thus I vanquished the beast.

Then Egil acquired all the lands he had fought over and
had claimed as his wife Asgerd's inheritance from her father.
Nothing else of note is said to have happened at the assembly.
Egil went first to Sognefjord to make arrangements for the
property that he had won the title to, and stayed there well into
the spring. Then he set off east for Vik with his companions,
went to see Thorstein and stayed with him for a while.

67 | Egil prepared his ship that summer and put to sea when
    | he was ready. He headed for Iceland and had a smooth
crossing, sailing in to Borgarfjord and landing his ship close to
his farm. He had the cargo carried home, then drew the ship up
on the beach. Egil spent that winter on his farm. He had taken
great riches to Iceland with him and was now very wealthy, and
he ran his farm lavishly.

Egil was not the type to interfere in other people's affairs, and
generally did not act aggressively in Iceland. Nevertheless, no
one dared to meddle in his affairs. Egil then spent a good number
of years on his farm.

Egil and Asgerd had children whose names were these: Bodvar
was their first son, and Gunnar the second, and their daughters
were Thorgerd and Bera. Their youngest was Thorstein. All
Egil's children were promising and intelligent. Thorgerd was the
eldest of Egil's children, followed by Bera.

68 | Egil received word from Norway that Eirik Blood-axe had
    | been killed on a Viking raid in Britain, Gunnhild and
their sons had gone to Denmark and all the men who had
accompanied them had left England. Arinbjorn had gone back
to Norway. He had been granted the lands and revenues he had
previously had and was on very friendly terms with King Hakon,
so Egil thought it was a desirable prospect to go to Norway once
more. Word also arrived that King Athelstan had died and
England was being ruled by his brother Edmund.[66]

Egil began preparing his ship and gathering a crew. Onund
Sjoni, the son of Ani from Anabrekka, joined them. He was well
built and the strongest man in his district. Not everyone agreed
that he was not a shape-shifter. Onund had often travelled to
other countries. He was somewhat older than Egil, and they had
long been good friends.

When Egil was ready, he put to sea, and they had a smooth
voyage, arriving half-way up the Norwegian coast. When they
sighted land they headed for Fjordane. On land, they heard the

news that Arinbjorn was at home on his farm. Egil took his ship there and docked close to Arinbjorn's farm.

Then Egil went to see Arinbjorn, and they greeted each other with great warmth. Arinbjorn invited Egil to stay with him, along with any of his companions as he pleased. Egil accepted the offer and had his ship drawn up and found places for the crew to stay; he and eleven others went to stay with Arinbjorn. He had had a very ornate sail made for a longship and gave it to Arinbjorn, together with other fitting gifts. Egil spent the winter there in great comfort, but also made a trip south to Sognefjord to his lands and stayed there for a considerable time before returning north to Fjordane.

Arinbjorn held a great Yule feast to which he invited his friends and neighbours from the district. It was a splendid feast and well attended. He gave Egil a customary Yuletide gift, a silk gown with ornate gold embroidery and gold buttons all the way down the front, which was cut especially to fit Egil's frame. He also gave him a complete set of clothes, cut from English cloth in many colours. Arinbjorn gave all manner of tokens of friendship at Yuletide to the people who visited him, since he was exceptionally generous and firm of character.

Then Egil made a verse:

43. From kindness alone
       that noble man gave the poet
       a silk gown with gold buttons;
       I will never have a better friend.
       Selfless Arinbjorn has earned
       the stature of a king
       – or more. A long time will pass
       before his like is born again.

69 | After the Yuletide feast, Egil grew so depressed that he did not speak a word. Noticing this, Arinbjorn spoke to him and asked why he was so depressed.

'I want you to tell me whether you are ill or if there is some other reason,' he said, 'so that we might find a remedy.'

Egil said, 'I'm not suffering from an ailment. I'm just very anxious about how to claim the property I won when I killed Ljot the Pale up north in More. I have heard that the king's agents have seized all the property and claimed it in the king's name. I would like your assistance in recovering it.'

'I don't think there's a law in this country that prevents you from acquiring that property,' said Arinbjorn, 'but it seems to have been put in very secure hands. The king's palace is an easy place to enter but hard to leave. I have had a lot of trouble claiming debts from those overbearing characters, even when I enjoyed much closer confidence with the king – but my friendship with King Hakon is only recent. But I must do as the old saying has it: "Tend the oak if you want to live under it."'

'I am interested in putting to the test,' replied Egil, 'whether the law is on our side. Maybe the king will grant me what is mine by rights here, because I am told he is a just man and abides by the laws he himself has established in this country. I have more than half a mind to go and see the king and put the matter to him.'

Arinbjorn said he did not feel eager to do so – 'I don't expect there's much chance of reconciling your temper and rashness with the king's disposition and severity, because I don't think he is a friend of yours or feels any reason to be, either. I'd prefer we drop the matter and not bring it up again. But if you really want, Egil, I will go to see the king and put the matter to him.'

Egil expressed his thanks and gratitude and was eager to try that course. At this time, Hakon was in Rogaland, but he sometimes stayed in Hordaland instead, so it was not difficult to go to see him. This was shortly after the two men's conversation.

Arinbjorn made preparations for his journey, and explained to everyone that he was going to see the king. He manned a twenty-seater rowboat that he owned, with men from his household, but Egil remained behind at Arinbjorn's wish. Once he was ready, Arinbjorn set off and had a smooth journey. He met King Hakon and was given a good welcome.

After he had been there for a short while, he stated his errand to the king, telling him that Egil Skallagrimsson was in the country and laid claim to all the money once owned by Ljot the Pale.

'I have been told that the law is in Egil's favour, King, but that your agents have taken the money and claimed it in your name. I beseech you to grant justice to Egil.'

After a long pause the king answered him: 'I do not know why you are presenting such a claim on Egil's behalf. He came to see me once, and I told him I did not want him staying in this country for reasons that you are well aware of. Egil has no need to make such a claim to me, as he did to my brother Eirik. And I will tell you one thing, Arinbjorn: you may only stay in this country on condition that you do not value foreigners more highly than myself or my words. I know your loyalty lies with your foster-son, my nephew Harald Eiriksson. The best course for you would be to go abroad to stay with him and his brothers, because I have a strong suspicion that men like you will prove unreliable if a confrontation arises between me and Eirik's sons.'

Since the king was absolutely firm, Arinbjorn realized it was futile to argue about the matter further, and made preparations to go home. The king was rather angry and abrupt to Arinbjorn after he found out the reason for his visit. Nor was it in Arinbjorn's character to humble himself before the king. They parted at this point.

Arinbjorn returned home and told Egil how his errand had turned out.

'I will not be asking the king's favour over such matters again,' he added.

Egil was very sullen at this news, feeling he had lost a great amount of money that was his by rights.

A few days later, when Arinbjorn was in his room early one morning and there were not many people about, he had Egil called in to him.

When he arrived, Arinbjorn opened a chest and handed over forty marks of silver to him, with the words, 'I'm paying you this money for the lands owned by Ljot the Pale, Egil. It seems fair to me to let you have this reward from my kinsman Fridgeir and myself for saving his life from Ljot. I know you did it as a favour to me and it's my duty to make sure that you are not deprived of what is yours by law.'

Egil accepted the money and thanked Arinbjorn. He regained his good spirits.

70 | Arinbjorn spent the winter on his lands, and the following spring he announced that he wanted to go on some Viking raids. He owned a good selection of ships and prepared three longships for the journey that spring, all of them large, and took a crew of three hundred with him. The ship he went on was well manned with people from his household and many local farmers' sons. Egil joined him at the helm of one of the ships, taking many of the band of men he had brought with him from Iceland. Egil sent the merchant ship he had brought from Iceland on to Vik, where he took on men to guard its cargo. Arinbjorn and Egil sailed their longships south along the coast, heading with their men for Saxony, where they stayed during the summer and won great wealth. When autumn arrived they went north on more raids, and moored their ships off Frisia.

One night when the weather was calm they anchored in a large estuary, since there were few places to harbour there, and the tide was far out. On shore were great rolling plains, with a forest a short distance away. It had been raining heavily and the fields were wet.

Then they set off for land, leaving one-third of the men behind to guard the ships. They went along the riverbank, with the forest on their other side, and soon came across a village where a lot of farmers lived. All the villagers ran for their lives when they noticed the raiders, and the Vikings set off in pursuit. Then they found another village, and a third. Everyone who was able to do so fled from them. The land was flat, with great plains. Ditches had been dug in many places and were full of water. These were meant to separate the fields and meadows, but in some places there were bridges for crossing over, made of logs with planks on the floor. All the villagers fled to the forest.

Once the Vikings had ventured quite deep inland, the Frisians mustered forces in the woods, and when there were more than three hundred of them they set off to confront the Vikings and fight them. A fierce battle ensued, and in the end the Frisians fled and the Vikings chased after them. The fleeing villagers spread out in all directions, and so did their pursuers. Eventually they all split up into groups of a few men.

With a few men of his own, Egil set off in hot pursuit after a large group. The Frisians reached a ditch and crossed it, then took the bridge away. When Egil arrived with his men on the other side, he took a run up and leapt over, but it was too far for the others, and none of them tried. Seeing this, the Frisians attacked Egil, and he defended himself. Eleven of them attacked him, but eventually he killed them all. After that, Egil put the bridge back in place and crossed over the ditch again, to find that all his men had gone back to the ships. He was near the forest then, so he skirted it on his way back to the ship to provide himself with cover if he needed it.

The Vikings took a great deal of plunder inland and cattle as well. When they reached their ships, some of them slaughtered the cattle or took their booty out to the ships, while the others formed a wall of shields in front of them, because a large band of Frisians had come back down to the shore and they were firing arrows at them. Then the Frisians received more support. And when Egil reached the shore and saw what was going on, he ran towards the crowd at full pelt with his halberd in front of him and his shield thrown over his back. As he lunged out with his halberd, everyone jumped back and cleared the way for him through the column. Then he headed down towards his men, who had given him up for dead.

They went back to their ships and sailed off to Denmark. When they reached Limfjord and anchored off Hals, Arinbjorn called a meeting with his men to tell them about his plans.

'I'm going to meet Eirik's sons,' he said, 'and I'll take anyone with me who wants to come. I have heard that the brothers are here in Denmark with great armies. They go raiding in the summer but stay in Denmark during the winter. If anyone would prefer to go back to Norway instead of coming with me, I will give my permission. It seems advisable for you to go back to

Norway, Egil, and then set straight off back to Iceland when we part.'

The men switched ships, and those who wanted to go back to Norway joined Egil. Many more chose to go with Arinbjorn. Egil and Arinbjorn parted with kindness and friendship. Arinbjorn went to see Eirik's sons, and they joined the army of Harald Grey-cloak, his foster-son, and stayed with him for the rest of their lives.

Egil went north to Vik and entered Oslo fjord. The merchant ship was there that he had sent south that spring, together with its cargo and crew.

Thorstein, Thora's son, went to see Egil and invited him to stay for the winter, along with any of his men that he chose. Egil accepted the offer and had his ships drawn up and the cargo put into storage. Some of the men who had been with him stayed, while others returned to their homes in the north. Egil stayed with Thorstein; ten or twelve of them were there in all. He spent the winter there amid great celebrations.

71 | King Harald Fair-hair had brought Norway under his rule as far east as Varmland.[67] The first person to control Varmland was Olaf Wood-carver, father of Halfdan White-leg, who was the first of his family to become king of Norway. King Harald was directly descended from him and all the line had ruled Varmland, collecting tribute there and appointing men to govern it.

In King Harald's old age, Varmland was governed by Earl Arnvid. As was the case in many places, the tribute proved more difficult to collect then than when Harald was younger, now that his sons were disputing control of Norway. There was little supervision of the more remote tributary lands.

Once King Hakon ruled in peace, he sought to re-establish his rule throughout the lands that his father had reigned over. King Hakon sent a band of twelve men east to Varmland. After collecting tribute from the earl, they were going through Eideskog Forest when they were ambushed by robbers and all were killed. The same happened to other men that King Hakon sent to Varmland: they were killed and the money went missing. Some people claimed Earl Arnvid was sending his own men to ambush the king's men and bring the money back to him.

So while King Hakon was staying in Trondheim, he sent a third party there. They were told to go east to Vik and see Thorstein, Thora's son, with an ultimatum ordering him to go to Varmland and collect the tribute for the king, or be banished from the realm. By then, the king had heard that Thorstein's uncle Arinbjorn was in Denmark with Eirik's sons, and also that they had a large army there and went raiding during the summers. King Hakon did not feel that any of them could be trusted, because he expected hostilities from Eirik's sons if they ever acquired a large enough force to rebel against him. He dealt out the same treatment to all Arinbjorn's kinsmen, relatives by marriage and friends: he banished many of them and issued others with ultimatums. Thorstein was told this distrust was the main reason that the king issued the ultimatum to him.

The messenger who brought the command from the king was a widely travelled man. He had spent long periods in Denmark and Sweden and was familiar with the routes and knew all about the people there too. He had also been all over Norway. When he had presented Thorstein Thoruson with the order, Thorstein told Egil about the messengers' errand and asked how he should respond.

'It seems obvious to me that the king wants you out of the country like the rest of Arinbjorn's family,' said Egil. 'It's a dangerous mission for a man of your standing. I advise you to call the king's messengers in to talk to you, and I'll be there when you do. Then we'll see what happens.'

Thorstein did as Egil said, and brought them in to talk to him. The messengers gave a straight account of the reason for their visit, and of the king's order that Thorstein should either undertake the journey or else be made an outlaw.

Then Egil said, 'I can see what lies behind this business of yours. If Thorstein doesn't want to go on the mission, you will go and collect the tribute yourselves.'

The messengers said that he had guessed correctly.

'Thorstein will not be going on this mission,' Egil declared. 'A man of his standing is not obliged to undertake such a paltry voyage. On the other hand, Thorstein will do his duty to follow the king in Norway and abroad if the king demands it of him. If you want to take some of Thorstein's men with you on the mission he will grant you that, along with anything you ask him to provide for the journey.'

The messengers discussed the offer among themselves and agreed to it, provided Egil would join them.

'The king hates him and would be pleased with our mission if we could arrange to have him killed,' they said. 'Then he can drive Thorstein out of the country too if he sees fit.'

Then they told Thorstein that they wouldn't mind the plan if Egil went with them and Thorstein stayed behind.

'Let it be done, then,' said Egil. 'I will take Thorstein's place on the mission. How many men do you think you need to take from here?'

'There are eight of us,' they said, 'and we would like four more from here, to make twelve.'

Egil said this would be done.

Onund Sjoni and some of Egil's men had gone down to the sea to see about their ships and the cargo they had put in storage that autumn, and had not returned yet. Egil thought that was a great setback, because the king's men were impatient about going on the journey and did not want to wait.

72 | Egil and the three men who were going with him made preparations for their journey. They took horses and sleighs, and so did the king's men. There had been heavy snows which had altered all the routes that could be taken. Once they were ready they set off and drove inland. On their way to Eid it snowed so much one night that it was impossible to make out where the trails were. The next day they made slow progress, because they kept sinking into the snowdrifts whenever they left the trail.

In the course of the day they paused to rest their horses near a wooded ridge.

'The trail forks here,' they told Egil. 'The farmer who lives beneath the ridge is named Arnald and he's a friend of ours. We will go and stay with him, and you should go up on the ridge. When you get there you'll soon see a big farm where you are sure of a place to stay. A very wealthy man called Armod Beard lives there. We will meet up again early tomorrow morning and go to Eideskog in the evening. A farmer lives there, a good man called Thorfinn.'

Then they parted. Egil and his men went up on the ridge. As for the king's men, as soon as they were out of Egil's sight, they put on skis they had brought with them, then went back as fast as they could. Travelling day and night, they went to Oppland and north from there across Dovrefjell, and did not stop until they reached King Hakon and told him about how things had gone.

Egil and his companions crossed the ridge that evening and lost their way at once in the heavy snows. Their horses repeatedly sank down into drifts and had to be pulled out. There were rocky slopes and brushwood which were difficult to negotiate. The horses caused them a long delay, and it was extremely hard going on foot too. Exhausted, they made their way down from the ridge at last, saw a big farm and headed for it.

When they arrived in the fields in front of the farmhouse, they saw Armod and his men standing outside. They exchanged greetings and asked each other if there was any news. When he heard that these men were envoys from the king, Armod invited them to stay, and they accepted. Armod's farmhands took their horses and baggage, while the farmer invited Egil and his men to go in to the main room, and they did so. Armod gave Egil a seat on the lower bench and seated his companions farther down the table. They spoke at length about their tough journey that night, and the people who lived there were astonished that they had made it at all, saying that the ridge could not even be crossed when it was free of snow.

'Don't you think the best thing I can provide you with now is to lay the tables and give you a meal for the night, and then you can go to bed?' asked Armod. 'You'll get the best night's rest that way.'

'That would be fine,' said Egil.

Then Armod had the tables laid for them, and large bowls of curds were brought in. Armod gave the impression he was upset at not having any ale to serve them. Because Egil and his men were so thirsty after their ordeal, they picked up the bowls and gulped down the curds, Egil much more than the others. No other food was served.

Many people were living and working on the farm. The farmer's wife sat on a cross-bench with some other women beside her. Their daughter, aged ten or eleven, was on the floor. The wife called over to her, and whispered in her ear. Then the girl went round to where Egil was sitting at the table. She spoke this verse:

44. My mother sent me
    to talk to you
    and bring Egil word
    to keep on his guard.
    The maid of the ale-horn
    said treat your stomach
    as if you expect
    to be served something better.

Armod slapped the girl and told her to keep quiet – 'You're always saying things at the worst of times.'

The girl went away, and Egil put down the bowl of curds, which was almost empty. Then the bowls were taken away and the men of the household went to their seats as well. Tables were laid across the whole room and the food was spread out on them. Choice food was served to Egil and his men, and everyone else.

Then the ale was brought in, an exceptionally strong brew. Each man was given a horn to drink from, and the host made a special point of letting Egil and his men drink as much as possible. Egil drank incessantly for a long time at first, and when his companions became incapacitated, he drank what they could not finish as well. This continued until the tables were cleared.

Everyone became very drunk, and for every toast that Armod drank he said, 'I drink this to your health, Egil.'

The men of the household drank to his companions' health, with the same words. A man was given the job of keeping Egil and his companions served with one toast after another, and he urged them to drink it up at once. Egil told his companions they should not drink any more, and he drank theirs for them too when there was no way to avoid it.

Egil started to feel that he would not be able to go on like this. He stood up and walked across the floor to where Armod was sitting, seized him by the shoulders and thrust him up against a wall-post. Then Egil spewed a torrent of vomit that gushed all over Armod's face, filling his eyes and nostrils and mouth and pouring down his beard and chest. Armod was close to choking, and when he managed to let out his breath, a jet of vomit gushed out with it. All Armod's men who were there said that Egil had done a base and despicable deed by not going outside when he needed to vomit, but had made a spectacle of himself in the drinking-room instead.

Egil said, 'Don't blame me for following the master of the house's example. He's spewing his guts up just as much as I am.'

Then Egil went over to his place, sat down and asked for a drink. Then he blared out this verse:

45. With my cheeks' swell I repaid
     the compliment you served.
     I had heavy cause to venture
     my steps across the floor.
     Many guests thank favours
     with sweeter-flavoured rewards.
     But we meet rarely. Armod's beard
     is awash with dregs of ale.

Armod leapt to his feet and ran out, but Egil asked for more to drink. The farmer's wife told the man who had been pouring out the drinks all evening to keep serving them so they would not lack drink for as long as they wanted. He took a large horn, filled it and carried it over to Egil. Egil quaffed the drink, then spoke this verse:

46. Drink every toast down,
      though the rider of the waves   *rider of the waves*: seaman
      brings brimful horns often
      to the shaper of verse.
      I will leave no drop
      of malt-sea, even if the maker   *malt-sea*: ale
      of sword-play brings me
      horns until morning.

Egil went on drinking for some time, polishing off every
drinking-horn that was brought to him, but there was not much
merry-making in the room even though a few other men were
still drinking. Then Egil and his companions stood up and took
their weapons from the wall where they had hung them, went
to the barn where their horses were being kept, lay down in the
straw and slept the night there.

73 | Egil got up at daybreak the next morning. He and his
     | companions prepared to leave, and when they were ready
they went back to the farm to look for Armod. When they
found the chamber where Armod was sleeping with his wife and
daughter, Egil flung the door open and went over to his bed. He
drew his sword, seized Armod by the beard with his other hand
and tugged him over to the side of the bed. Armod's wife and
daughter both jumped up and implored Egil not to kill him.

Egil said he would spare him for their sake – 'That is the fair
thing to do, but if he were worth the bother I would kill him.'

Then he spoke a verse:

47. His wife and daughter aid
      the foul-mouthed man
      who twines arms with rings.   *twines arms with rings*: i.e. is
      I do not fear this battle-maker.   generous; a conventional image used
      You will not feel deserving   ironically
      of such dealings from the poet
      for that drink you served him.
      Let us be gone far on our way.

Then Egil cut off Armod's beard close to the chin, and gouged
out one of his eyes with his finger, leaving it hanging on his
cheek. After that, Egil went off to his companions.

They went on their way and arrived at Thorfinn's farm early
in the morning. He lived in Eideskog. Egil and his men asked
for breakfast and somewhere to rest their horses. Thorfinn
granted them that, and Egil and his men went into the main
room.

Egil asked Thorfinn if he knew anything about his companions.

'We arranged to meet here,' he said.

Thorfinn replied, 'Six men came by here some time before
daybreak, all heavily armed.'

One of Thorfinn's farmhands added, 'I went out to gather
timber in the night and came across six men who were going
somewhere. They were Armod's farmhands and it was well
before daybreak. I don't know whether these were the same six
you mentioned.'

Thorfinn said the men he met had been travelling later than
when the farmhand brought the cartload of timber back.

When Egil and his men sat down to eat, he saw a sick woman
lying on the cross-bench. Egil asked Thorfinn who the woman
was and why she was in such a poor state.

Thorfinn said she was his daughter Helga – 'She has been
weak for a long time.'

She was suffering from a wasting sickness, and could not sleep
at night because of some kind of a delirium.

'Has anyone tried to find out the cause of her illness?' Egil
asked.

'We had some runes carved,' said Thorfinn. 'The son of a
farmer who lives close by did it, and since then she's been much
worse. Do you know any remedy, Egil?'

Egil said, 'It might not do any harm if I try something.'

When Egil had eaten his fill he went to where the woman was
lying and spoke to her. He ordered them to lift her out of her
bed and place clean sheets underneath her, and this was done.
Then he examined the bed she had been lying in, and found a
whalebone with runes carved on it. After reading the runes, Egil

shaved them off and scraped them into the fire. He burned the whalebone and had her bedclothes aired. Then Egil spoke a verse:

48. No man should carve runes
     unless he can read them well;
     many a man goes astray
     around those dark letters.
     On the whalebone I saw
     ten secret letters carved,
     from them the linden tree   *linden tree*: woman
     took her long harm.

Egil cut some runes and placed them under the pillow of the bed where she was lying. She felt as if she were waking from a deep sleep, and she said she was well again, but still very weak. But her father and mother were overjoyed. Thorfinn offered Egil all the provisions he thought he needed.

74 | Egil told his companions that he wanted to continue on his journey and not wait any longer. Thorfinn offered to accompany Egil through the forest with his son Helgi, who was a brave lad. They told him they were certain Armod Beard had sent the six men to waylay them in the forest, and that there were likely to be more ambushes if the first failed. Thorfinn and three others offered to go with them. Then Egil spoke a verse:

49. You know if I take four men,
     six will not manage to swap
     bloody blows of the battle-god's
     shield-piercer with me.   *battle-god's shield-piercer*: sword
     And if I have eight men,
     no twelve will strike fear
     into the dark-browed man's heart
     when the swords clash.

Thorfinn and his men decided to go to the forest with Egil, so there were eight of them in all. When they came to the ambush

they saw some people there. Armod's six farmhands were lying
in ambush, but when they saw eight men approaching, they did
not think they had any chance against them, and stole away to
the forest. When Egil and his men reached the spot where the
spies had been, they could tell that danger was lurking. Egil told
Thorfinn and his men to go back, but they wanted to go on. Egil
refused and insisted that they go home, so in the end they did.
They set off for home again, while Egil and his three men
continued their journey.

As the day wore on, Egil and his men noticed six men in the
woods, and guessed that they were Armod's farmhands. The
spies jumped out and attacked them, but Egil fought back.
When they clashed, Egil killed two of the attackers and the rest
ran back into the forest.

Then Egil and his men proceeded on their way, and nothing
else happened until they emerged from the forest and spent the
night on a nearby farm with a farmer named Alf, who was
nicknamed Alf the Wealthy. He was an old, wealthy man, but
so unsociable that he could only bear having a few people
working for him on the farm. Egil received a warm welcome
there, and Alf was talkative to him. Egil asked him many things,
and he answered them all. They talked mainly about the earl
and the envoys of the king of Norway who had gone out to the
east to collect tribute. From what Alf said, he was no friend of
the earl's.

75 | Early the next morning, Egil and his companions prepared
     | to leave. As a parting gift, Egil gave Alf a fur coat which
he accepted thankfully.

'I can have it made into a fur cape,'[68] he said, as he invited
Egil to visit him again on his way back.

They parted good friends, and Egil continued on his way. In
the evening he reached Earl Arnvid's company and was well
received there. He and his companions were given seats next to
the head of the table.

After staying there for the night, Egil and his companions told
the earl of their errand and the king's message, saying he wanted

all the tribute from Varmland that had gone unpaid since Arnvid was appointed to rule there.

The earl told them he had already paid all the tribute to the king's envoys: 'I don't know what they did with it after that, whether they handed it over to the king or ran away with it to another country. Since you are carrying genuine tokens to prove the king sent you, I will pay all the tribute he is entitled to and hand it over to you. But I won't be held responsible for the way you look after it.'

Egil and his men stayed there for some while, and before they left, the earl paid the tribute over to them. Some of it was in silver and the rest in furs.

After Egil and his men had made their preparations to leave, they set off.

When they parted, Egil told the earl, 'We will give the king the tribute we have received from you, but you ought to realize that this is much less money than the king lays claim to here. And that's not counting the fact that he feels you should pay compensation for the lives of his envoys, because people are saying you had them killed.'

The earl said this rumour was untrue, and they parted.

Once Egil had left, the earl called in two brothers, both of them named Ulf.

He said to them, 'That big man, Egil, who was around here for a while – I think it will cause us a lot of trouble if he makes it back to the king. I can imagine the impression he will give about me to the king, judging from the accusations he threw around here about executing the king's men. You go after them and kill them all to stop them spreading such slander to the king. My advice is to ambush them in Eideskog. Take enough men with you, to be sure that none of them gets away and that you do not suffer any injuries at their hands.'

The brothers got ready to leave, taking thirty men with them. They entered the forest, where they were familiar with every trail, and kept watch for Egil's movements.

There were two routes through the forest. The shorter one involved crossing a ridge that had steep slopes and a narrow track over the top. The other route was to go round the ridge where there were large marshes, covered by felled logs to cross by, with a single track over them too. Fifteen men sat in ambush on each route.

76 | Egil proceeded until he reached Alf's farm, where he stayed for the night and was well looked after. The next morning he got up before daybreak and prepared to leave. Alf came over to them when they were having breakfast.

'You're making an early start, Egil,' he said. 'But I wouldn't advise you to rush your journey. Be careful, because I expect people to be waiting in ambush for you in the forest. I do not have any men who would be any help to send with you, but I want to invite you to stay here with me until I can tell you it's safe to go through the forest.'

'It's nothing but nonsense to claim that we will be ambushed,' Egil replied. 'I will go on my way as I planned.'

Egil and his men made preparations to leave, but Alf tried to discourage him and told him to come back if he noticed tracks on the path, saying that no one had come back through the forest from the east since Egil went there, 'unless the people that I expect will be looking for you have been there'.

'How many of them do you think there are, assuming what you say is right?' asked Egil. 'We're not at their mercy, even if they outnumber us by a few men.'

'I went over near the forest with my farmhands,' said Alf, 'and we came across human tracks that extended into the forest. There must have been a lot of them together. If you don't believe what I'm saying, go there yourself and take a look at the tracks, but come back here if you think what I've told you is right.'

Egil went on his way, and when the party reached the road through the forest, they saw tracks left by both men and horses. Egil's companions said they wanted to turn back.

'We will go on,' Egil said. 'It doesn't surprise me that people have been travelling through Eideskog, because it's the route everyone takes.'

They set off again and the tracks continued, many of them,

until they reached a fork in the road where the tracks also split up into two equal groups.

'It looks as though Alf may have been telling the truth,' said Egil. 'Let us be prepared to expect an encounter.'

Egil and his men took off their cloaks and all their loose clothing, and put them on the sleighs. He had taken along a long bast rope in his sleigh, since it was the custom on longer journeys to have a spare rope in case the reins needed mending. Then he took a huge slab of rock and placed it against his chest and stomach, then strapped it tight with the rope, winding it around his body all the way up to his shoulders.

Eideskog is heavily wooded right up to the settlements on either side of it, but deep inside it are bushes and brushwood, and in some places no trees at all.

Egil and his men took the shorter route that lay over the ridge. They were all carrying shields and wearing helmets, and had axes and spears as well. Egil led the way. The ridge was wooded at its foot, but the slopes up to the bluff were bare of trees.

When they were on the bluff, seven men leapt out of the trees and up the cliff after them, shooting arrows at them. Egil and his men turned around and blocked the whole path. Other men came down at them from the top of the ridge and threw rocks at them from above, which was much more dangerous.

Egil told them, 'You go and seek shelter at the foot of the bluff and protect yourselves as best you can, while I take a look on top.'

They did so. And when Egil reached the top of the bluff, there were eight men waiting there, who all attacked him at once. Without describing the blows, their clash ended with Egil killing them all. Then he went up to the edge of the bluff and hurled down rocks that were impossible to fend off. Three of the Varmlanders were left dead, while four escaped into the forest, hurt and bruised.

After that, Egil and his men returned to their horses and continued until they had crossed the ridge. The Varmlanders who had escaped tipped off their companions who were by the marshes. They headed along the lower path and emerged on the track in front of Egil and his men.

One of the brothers who were both named Ulf said to his men, 'Now we have to devise a scheme and arrange things to prevent them running away. The route here skirts the ridge, and there's a cliff above it where the marsh extends up to it. The path there is no wider than a single track. Some of us should go around the ridge and face them if they try to move forwards, and the rest should hide here in the forest and jump out behind them when they come past. We will make sure that no one gets away.'

They did as Ulf said. Ulf went around the cliff, taking ten men with him.

Egil and his men went on their way, unaware of this plan until they reached the single track, where they were attacked from behind by nine armed men. When Egil and his men fought back and defended themselves, others rushed up who had been in front of the ridge. Seeing this, Egil turned to face them. In a few quick blows he killed some of them, and the rest retreated to where the ground was more level. Egil pursued them. Ulf died there, and in the end Egil killed eleven men by himself. Then he pressed on to where his companions were holding eight men at bay on the path. Men were wounded on both sides. When Egil arrived, the Varmlanders fled at once into the nearby forest. Five of them escaped, all severely wounded, and three were killed on the spot.

Egil received many wounds, but none of them serious. They went on their way, and Egil tended his companions' wounds, none of which was fatal. Then they got on to their sleighs and rode for the rest of the day.

The Varmlanders who managed to escape took their horses and struggled back from the forest to the settlement in the east, where their wounds were tended to. There they got some men to go and see the earl and tell him about their misfortunes.

They reported that both brothers named Ulf were dead, and twenty-five men in all: 'Only five escaped with their lives, all of them wounded or injured.'

The earl asked about Egil and his men.

'We have no idea how many of them were wounded,' they replied. 'They attacked us with great bravery. When there were eight of us and four of them, we fled. Five of us made it to the forest and the other three died, and as far as we could see, Egil and his men hadn't taken a scratch.'

The earl said their expedition had turned out in the worst possible way.

'I could have put up with you suffering heavy losses if you had killed the Norwegians,' he said, 'but now when they go west of the forest and tell this news to the king of Norway we can expect the harshest treatment imaginable from him.'

77 | Egil continued his journey until he emerged on the western side of the forest. He and his men went to Thorfinn at night and were warmly welcomed. Egil and his companions had their wounds dressed there, and they stayed for several nights. By then, Thorfinn's daughter Helga was back on her feet, cured of her ailment, and she and everybody else thanked Egil for that. The travellers rested their horses at the farm as well.

The man who had carved runes for Helga lived close by. It transpired that he had asked for her hand in marriage, but Thorfinn had refused him. Then the farmer's son had tried to seduce her, but she did not want him. After that he pretended to carve love runes to her, but did not know how to, and what he carved had caused sickness instead.

When Egil was ready to leave, Thorfinn and his sons accompanied him along the trail. There were ten or twelve of them in all. They travelled together all day as a precaution against Armod and his men. When word spread that Egil and his men had fought against overwhelming odds and won, Armod realized there was no hope that he might be able to put up a fight against him, so he stayed at home with all his men. Egil and Thorfinn exchanged gifts when they parted, and promised each other friendship.

Then Egil and his men continued on their way and nothing happened on the journey until they reached Thorstein. Their wounds had healed by then. Egil stayed there until spring. Thorstein sent envoys to King Hakon to deliver the tribute that Egil had collected in Varmland, and when they saw the king and handed it over, they told him what had happened on the expedition. The king realized then that his suspicions were true and Earl Arnvid had killed the two teams of envoys that he had sent to the east. The king told Thorstein he would be allowed to stay in Norway and be reconciled with him. Then the envoys went home. When they returned, they told him that the king was pleased with the expedition and had promised Thorstein reconciliation and friendship.

King Hakon travelled to Vik in the summer, and east from there to Varmland with a large army. Earl Arnvid fled from him, while the king exacted heavy levies from the farmers he considered to have wronged him, as reported by the collectors of the tribute. He appointed another earl and took hostages from him and the farmers.

On this voyage King Hakon travelled widely in Vastergotland and brought it under his rule, as is described in his saga and mentioned in the poems that have been composed about him.[69] It is also said that he went to Denmark and raided many places. He disabled twelve Danish ships with just two of his own, granted his nephew Tryggvi Olafsson the title of king and made him ruler of Vik in the east.

Egil made his trading vessel ready and took on a crew, and as a parting gift he gave Thorstein the longship he had brought from Denmark that autumn. Thorstein presented Egil with fine gifts, and they promised each other great friendship. Egil sent messengers to his kinsman Thord at Aurland, granting him authority to manage the lands Egil owned in Sognefjord and Hordaland and asking him to sell them if buyers could be found.

When Egil and his men were ready to make their journey and a fair wind got up, they sailed out of Vik and along the coast of Norway, then out to sea for Iceland. They had a fairly smooth journey and arrived in Borgarfjord. Egil took his ship along the fjord to anchor it close to his farm, then had his cargo taken home and the ship pulled up. Egil went home to his farm, and everyone was pleased to see him. He stayed there for the winter.

78 | By the time Egil returned from this voyage, the district was completely settled. All the original settlers had died by then, and their sons or grandsons were living in the district.

Ketil Gufa (Steam) came to Iceland when it was by and large settled. He spent the first winter at Gufuskalar on Rosmhvalanes. Ketil had sailed over from Ireland, and brought many Irish slaves with him. Since all the land on Rosmhvalanes was settled by that time, Ketil moved away to Nes and spent his second winter at Gufunes, but found nowhere to make his home. Then he went into Borgarfjord and stayed for the third winter at the place now called Gufuskalar, keeping his ship on the river Gufua, which comes down from the mountains there.

Thord Lambason was living at Lambastadir then. He was married and had a son named Lambi, who was fully grown by this time and big and strong for his age. In the summer when everyone rode off to the Thing, Lambi did so too. By then, Ketil had moved west to Breidafjord to look for a place to live.

Ketil's slaves ran away and came upon Thord at Lambastadir by night. They set fire to the houses, burning Thord and all his farmhands inside, broke into his sheds and brought all the cattle and goods outside. They rounded up the horses, loaded the booty on to them and rode out to Alftanes.

That morning around sunrise, Lambi returned home, having seen the flames during the night. There were several men with him. He rode off at once to search for the slaves, and people from other farms joined him. When the slaves saw they were being pursued, they discarded their booty and headed for shelter. Some ran to Myrar, and others towards the sea until they reached a fjord.

Lambi and his men pursued them and killed the slave named Kori at the place now known as Koranes. Skorri, Thormod and Svart dived into the sea and swam away from land. Lambi and his men looked around for some boats and rowed after them. They found Skorri on Skorrey Island, where they killed him, then rowed out to the skerry where they killed Thormod, which has been called Thormodssker (Thormod's skerry) ever since.

They caught other slaves at places that are also named after them now.

Lambi lived at Lambastadir after this, and became a worthy farmer. He was a man of great might, but not a troublemaker.

Ketil Gufa went west to Breidafjord and settled in Thorskafjord. Gufudal valley and Gufufjord are named after him. He married Yr, the daughter of Geirmund Dark-skin,[70] and they had a son called Vali.

There was a man named Grim, the son of Sverting, and he lived at Mosfell at the foot of the moor called Heidi. He was wealthy and of good family. His half-sister was Rannveig, wife of Thorodd the Godi from Olfus, and their son was Skafti the Lawspeaker.[71] Grim also became Lawspeaker later. He asked to marry Egil's niece and foster-daughter Thordis, the daughter of Thorolf. Egil loved Thordis no less dearly than his own children; she was a very attractive woman. Since Egil knew that Grim was a man of good birth and this was a good match, the marriage was settled. When Thordis married Grim, Egil handed over the inheritance her father had left to her. She went to Grim's farm and they lived at Mosfell for a long time.

79 | There was a man named Olaf, the son of Hoskuld and grandson of Koll of Dalir. His mother Melkorka was the daughter of King Myrkjartan of Ireland. Olaf lived at Hjardarholt in Laxardal,[72] in the valleys of Breidafjord. He was very wealthy, one of the most handsome men in Iceland at the time, and very firm-minded.

Olaf asked to marry Egil's daughter Thorgerd, who was a very fine woman, wise, rather strong-tempered, but usually quiet. Egil knew from Olaf's background that this was a splendid offer of marriage, and so she married him and went to live with him at Hjardarholt. Their children were Kjartan, Thorberg, Halldor, Steindor, Thurid, Thorbjorg and Bergthora, who became the wife of Thorhall Oddason the Godi. Thorbjorg was married first to Asgeir Knattarson and later to Vermund Thorgrimsson. Thurid married Gudmund, son of Solmund, and their sons were Hall and Killer-Bardi.

Ozur, the son of Eyvind and brother of Thorodd from Olfus, married Egil's daughter Bera.

By this time, Egil's son Bodvar was grown up. He was exceptionally promising and handsome, big and strong like Egil and Thorolf at his age. Egil loved him dearly, and Bodvar was likewise very attached to his father.

One summer there was a ship moored on Hvita and a large market was held there. Egil had bought a lot of timber and arranged for it to be shipped back to his farm. The men of his household went out to fetch it from Hvita on an eight-oared vessel that Egil owned. On this occasion Bodvar had asked to go with them, and they allowed him to. He went down to Vellir with the farmhands, and there were six of them on the eight-oared ship. When they were ready to put to sea, high tide was in the afternoon, and since they had to wait for it they did not set out until late in the evening. A wild south-westerly gale got up, against the current of the tide, and the sea grew very rough in the fjord, as often happens. In the end their ship sank beneath them, and they were all lost at sea. The following day the bodies were washed up. Bodvar's body came ashore at Einarsnes, and some of the others farther south where the ship drifted to land, too; it was found washed ashore at Reykjarhamar.

Egil heard the news that day and rode off immediately to search for the bodies. He found Bodvar's body, picked it up and put it across his knees, then rode with it out to Digranes to Skallagrim's burial mound. He opened the mound and laid Bodvar inside by Skallagrim's side. The mound was closed again, which took until sunset. After that, Egil rode back to Borg, and when he got home he went straight to his normal sleeping-place in his bed-closet, lay down and locked the door. No one dared to ask to speak to him.

It is said that when Bodvar was buried, Egil was wearing tight-fitting hose and a tight red fustian tunic laced at the sides. People say that he became so swollen that his tunic and hose burst off his body.

Later that day, Egil kept his bed-closet locked, and took neither food nor drink. He lay there that day, and the following night. No one dared to speak to him.

On the third day, when it was daylight, Asgerd sent a messenger off on horseback. He galloped westwards to Hjardarholt and when he arrived in mid-afternoon he told Thorgerd the whole story. He also gave her a message from Asgerd asking her to come to Borg as quickly as possible.

Thorgerd had a horse saddled at once and set off with two men. They rode that evening and into the night until they reached Borg. Thorgerd went straight into the fire-room. Asgerd greeted her and asked whether they had eaten their evening meal.

Thorgerd replied in a loud voice, 'I have had no evening meal, nor will I do so until I go to join Freyja[73]. I know no better course of action than my father's. I do not want to live after my father and brother are dead.'

She went to the door to Egil's bed-closet and called out, 'Father, open the door, I want both of us to go the same way.'

Egil unfastened the door. Thorgerd walked in to the bed-closet and closed the door again. Then she lay down in another bed there.

Then Egil said, 'You do well, my daughter, in wanting to follow your father. You have shown great love for me. How can I be expected to want to live with such great sorrow?'

Then they were silent for a while.

Then Egil said, 'What are you doing, my daughter? Are you chewing something?'

'I'm chewing dulse,'[74] she replied, 'because I think it will make me feel worse. Otherwise I expect I will live too long.'

'Is it bad for you?' asked Egil.

'Very bad,' said Thorgerd. 'Do you want some?'

'What difference does it make?' he said.

A little later she called out for some water to drink, and she was brought something to drink.

Then Egil said, 'That happens if you eat dulse, it makes you even thirstier.'

'Would you like a drink, Father?' she asked.

She passed him the animal horn and he took a great draught.

Then Thorgerd said, 'We've been tricked. This is milk.'

Egil bit a lump from the horn, as much as he could get his teeth into, then threw the horn away.

Then Thorgerd said, 'What will we do now? Our plan has failed. Now I want us to stay alive, Father, long enough for you to compose a poem in Bodvar's memory and I will carve it on to a rune-stick. Then we can die if we want to. I doubt whether your son Thorstein would ever compose a poem for Bodvar, and it is unseemly if his memory is not honoured, because I do not expect us to be sitting there at the feast when it is.'

Egil said it was unlikely that he would be able to compose a poem even if he attempted to.

'But I will try,' he said.

Another of Egil's sons, called Gunnar, had died shortly before. Then Egil composed this poem:

1. My tongue is sluggish
    for me to move,
    my poem's scales
    ponderous to raise.
    The god's prize   *god's prize*: poetry. The dwarfs
    is beyond my grasp,   made the mead of poetry from the
    tough to drag out   blood of a wise man, and a giant
    from my mind's haunts.   held them to ransom for it. Odin
                                   was given a drink of the mead by
2. Since heavy sobbing   the giantess who guarded it, then
    is the cause –   flew back to the gods and spat it
    how hard to pour forth   out for them.
    from the mind's root
    the prize that Frigg's   *Frigg's progeny*: the gods; their
    progeny found,   *prize . . . borne . . . from the world
    borne of old   *of giants*: poetry
    from the world of giants,

3. unflawed, which Bragi   *Bragi*: god of poetry
    inspired with life
    on the craft
    of the watcher-dwarf.
    Blood surges   *Blood*: sea, made from the blood
    from the giant's wounded neck, of a giant; also the mead of poetry.

crashes on the death-dwarf's
boathouse door.

> *boathouse door*: rocks, cliffs; also
> the gates of Hel (i.e. loss hinders
> Egil's verse-making).

4. My stock
    stands on the brink,
    pounded as plane-trees
    on the forest's rim,
    no man is glad
    who carries the bones
    of his dead kinsman
    out of the bed.

5. Yet I will
    first recount
    my father's death
    and mother's loss,
    carry from my word-shrine
    the timber that I build
    my poem from,
    leafed with language.

6. Harsh was the rift
    that the wave hewed
    in the wall
    of my father's kin;
    I know it stands
    unfilled and open,
    my son's breach
    that the sea wrought.

7. The sea-goddess
    has ruffled me,
    stripped me bare
    of my loved ones:
    the ocean severed
    my family's bonds,
    the tight knot
    that ties me down.

8. If by sword I might
   avenge that deed,
   the brewer of waves   *brewer of waves*: sea-god
   would meet his end;
   smite the wind's brother   *wind's brother*: sea
   that dashes the bay,
   do battle against
   the sea-god's wife.

9. Yet I felt
   I lacked the might
   to seek justice against
   the killer of ships,   *killer of ships*: sea
   for it is clear
   to all eyes,
   how an old man
   lacks helpers.

10. The sea has robbed
    me of much,
    my kinsmen's deaths
    are harsh to tell,
    after the shield
    of my family
    retreated down
    the god's joyful road.   *road*: i.e. to death

11. Myself I know
    that in my son
    grew the makings
    of a worthy man,
    had that shield-tree   *shield-tree*: man, warrior
    reached manhood,
    then earned the claim   *earned the claim of war's arms*: become a
    of war's arms.   warrior; or be claimed (in death) by the
                                      war-god

12. Always he prized
    his father's words
    highest of all, though

the world said otherwise.
He shored me up,
defended me,
lent my strength
the most support.

13. My lack of brothers
    often enters my thoughts
    where the winds
    of moon-bears rage,
    I think of the other
    as the battle grows,
    scout around
    and wonder

moon-bears: giants; their *winds*: thoughts
(this image occurs elsewhere, but its
original justification (myth?) is now lost).
the other: Thorolf?

14. which other valiant
    warrior stands
    by my side
    in the peril;
    I often need him
    when facing foes.
    When friends dwindle
    I am wary to soar.

15. It is rare to find
    one to trust
    amongst men who dwell
    beneath Odin's gallows,
    for the dark-minded
    destroyer of kin
    swaps his brother's
    death for treasure.

Odin's gallows: the tree of life
(Yggdrasil) where Odin sacrificed
himself to himself in order to gain
wisdom

16. I often feel
    when the ruler of wealth
    . . .

[defective verse]

17. It is also said
    that no one regains
    his son's worth

without bearing
another offspring
that other men
hold in esteem
as his brother's match.

18. I do not relish
the company of men
though each of them might
live in peace with me:
my wife's son
has come in search
of friendship
to One-Eye's hall.   *One-Eye*: Odin; his *hall*: Valhalla

19. But the lord of the sea,
brewer of storms,
seems to oppose me,
his mind set.
I cannot hold
my head upright,
the ground of my face,
my thoughts' steed

20. ever since the raging
surf of heat   *surf of heat*: fever
snatched from the world
that son of mine
whom I knew
to shun disgrace,
avoid words
of ill repute.

21. I remember still
when the Gauts' friend   *Gauts' friend*: Odin
raised high
to the gods' world
the ash that grew
from my stock,

the tree bearing
my wife's kin.

22. I was in league
with the lord of spears,   *lord of spears*: Odin
pledged myself loyal
to believe in him,
before he broke off
his friendship with me,
the guardian of chariots,
architect of victory.

23. I do not worship
Vilir's brother,   *Vilir*: one of Odin's two brothers who
guardian of the gods,   were minor deities
through my own longing,
though in good ways too
the friend of wisdom
has granted me
redress for affliction.

24. He who does battle   *hell-wolf*: Fenrir, the wolf that kills
and tackles the hell-wolf   Odin in the Doom of the Gods
gave me the craft   *craft*: poetry
that is beyond reproach,
and the nature
that I could reveal
those who plotted against me
as my true enemies.

25. Now my course is tough:
Death, close sister
of Odin's enemy,   *sister of Odin's enemy*: Death (Hel)
stands on the ness: was the sister of the wolf Fenrir,
with resolution   whom Odin fought; their father was
and without remorse   Loki, the treacherous god
I will gladly
await my own.

Egil began to recover his spirits as he proceeded to compose
the poem, and when it was finished, he delivered it to Asgerd

and Thorgerd and his farmhands, left his bed and sat down in the high seat. He called the poem The Loss of My Sons. After that, Egil held a funeral feast according to ancient custom. When Thorgerd went home, Egil presented her with parting gifts.

80 | Egil lived at Borg for a long time and grew to an old age. He is not said to have been involved in disputes with anyone in Iceland. Nor is anything told about him duelling or killing anyone after he settled down in Iceland.

People also say that Egil did not leave Iceland after the incidents that were described earlier, the main reason being that he could not stay in Norway because of the wrongs that the king felt he had done him, as narrated before. Egil lived lavishly, for he did not lack the means to do so, and he had the temperament as well.

King Hakon, King Athelstan's foster-son, ruled Norway for a long while. In Hakon's later years, King Eirik's sons went to Norway and disputed the control of the realm with him. They fought several battles and Hakon invariably won. Their last battle was in Hordaland, at Stord in Fitjar. King Hakon won the battle, but was fatally wounded, and Eirik's sons took over the kingdom afterwards.

Arinbjorn the Hersir was with Eirik's son Harald, and became his counsellor and was granted great revenues by him. He was in charge of his forces and defences. Arinbjorn was an outstanding and victorious warrior. He lived on the revenues from the Fjordane province.

Egil Skallagrimsson received word that there was a new king in Norway and that Arinbjorn had returned to his lands there and was held in high respect. Then Egil composed a poem in Arinbjorn's praise and sent it to him in Norway, and this is the beginning of it:

1.   I am quick to sing
     a noble man's praises.
     but stumble for words
     about misers;
     freely I speak

        of a king's deeds,
        but stay silent
        about the people's lies.

2.   Replete with taunts
        for bearers of lies,
        I sing the favours
        of my friends;
        I have visited many
        seats of mild kings,
        with the ingenuous
        intent of a poet.

3.   Once I had
        incurred the wrath
        of a mighty king
        of Yngling's line;   *Yngling*: ancestor of the kings of
        I drew a bold hat   Norway
        over my black hair,
        paid a visit
        to the war-lord

4.   where that mighty
        maker of men
        ruled the land from beneath
        his helmet of terror;
        In York
        the king reigned,
        rigid of mind,
        over rainy shores.

5.   The shining glare
        from Eirik's brow
        was not safe to behold
        nor free from terror;
        when the moons
        of that tyrant's face   *moons of . . . face*: eyes
        shone, serpent-like,
        with their awesome glow.

6. Yet I ventured
    my poem to the king,
    the bed-prize that Odin   *bed-prize . . . slithered*: Odin stole
    had slithered to claim,   the mead of poetry after entering
    his frothing horn   the giantess Gunnlod's chamber in
    passed around   the guise of a serpent; *frothing*
    to quench   *horn*: mead of poetry
    all men's ears.

7. No one praised
    the beauty of the prize
    my poetry earned
    in that lavish house
    when I accepted from the king
    in reward for my verse
    my own sable head
    to stand my hat on.

8. My head I won
    and with it the two
    dark jewels   *jewels*: i.e. eyes
    of my beetling brow,
    and the mouth
    that had delivered
    my head's ransom
    at the king's knee.

9. A field of teeth there
    and my tongue I took back,
    and my flapping ears
    endowed with sound;
    such a gift
    was prized higher
    than earning gold
    from a famous king.

10. By my side, better
    than every other
    spreader of treasure,

       stood my loyal friend
       whom I truly trusted,
       growing in stature
       with his every deed.

11.   Arinbjorn,
       paragon of men,
       who lifted me alone
       above the king's anger:
       the king's friend,
       who never told untruth
       in the warlike
       ruler's hall.

12.   And ...   [defective verse]
       ... the pillar,
       glorifier
       of my deeds,
       which ...
       ...
       ... the scourge
       of Halfdan's line.

13.   I would be deemed
       a thief from my friend
       and unfulfilling
       of Odin's horn,
       unworthy of praise
       and a breaker of oaths
       if I omitted
       to repay his favour.

14.   Now it is clear
       where to present
       my praise of the mighty
       leader of men
       before the people,
       to their many eyes,
       the tortuous path
       that my verse treads.

15. The stuff of my praise
    is easily smoothed
    by my voice's plane
    for my friend,
    Thorir's kinsman,
    for double, triple
    choices lie
    upon my tongue.

16. First I will name –
    as most men know
    and is ever borne
    to people's ears –
    how generous
    he always seemed,
    the bear whose land
    the birch fears.

land the birch fears: fire, hearth; the
name *Arinbjorn* means 'hearth-bear'

17. All people
    watch in marvel
    how he sates
    men with riches;
    Frey and Njord
    have endowed
    rock-bear
    with wealth's force.

18. Endless wealth
    flows to the hands
    of the chosen son
    of Hroald's line
    his friends ride
    from far around
    where the world lies beneath
    the sky's cup of winds.

19. Crowned from ear
    to ear like a king
    he owned

a drawn line,   [defective and cryptic verse, a conjectural
dear to the gods   reading. *drawn line*: the sword Dragvandil,
with his flock of men,   'Slicer'?]
friend of the sacred
and pillar of the poor.

20. His deeds will
     outlast most men's
     even those who are
     blessed with wealth;
     givers' houses are
     few and far between,
     a legion's spears   *a legion's spears need many shafts*: it is not
     need many shafts.   easy to tend to every man's problem

21. No man went
     to the longboat   *longboat*: house
     where Arinbjorn's
     bed lay at rest
     led by mockery
     or bitter words,
     or his spear's
     grip empty.   *spear's grip*: hands

22. The man in Fjordane
     shows money no love:
     he banishes rings
     that drip like fruit,   *drip like fruit*: Draupnir, Odin's ring,
     defies the ring-clad   dripped eight identical rings every ninth
     verse-brew's thief,   night; *verse-brew's thief*: Odin, who stole
     hacks treasures in half, the mead of poetry
     imperils brooches.

23. The acre
     of his ample life
     was much sown
     with the seeds of peace.
     . . .   [defective verse]

24. It would be unjust
    if that spreader of wealth
    had cast overboard
    on to the course
    where the sea-god's steeds   *sea-god's steeds*: ships; their *course*:
    trample and race   sea
    the many favours
    he has done for me.

25. I awoke early
    to heap my words;
    as a servant of speech
    I did my morning's work.
    I have piled a mound
    of praise that long
    will stand without crumbling
    in poetry's field.

81 | There was a man named Einar, the son of Helgi Ottarsson
   | and the great-grandson of Bjorn the Easterner who settled
in Breidafjord. Einar was the brother of Osvif the Wise. Even at
an early age, Einar was large and strong and a man of great
accomplishments. He began composing poetry when he was
young and was fond of learning.

One summer at the Althing, Einar went to Egil Skallagrimsson's booth and they began talking. The conversation
soon turned to poetry and they both took great delight in the
discussion.

After that, Einar made a habit of talking to Egil and a great
friendship developed between them. Einar had just come back
from a voyage abroad. Egil asked Einar about recent news and
his friends in Norway, and also about the men he regarded as
his enemies. He also often asked about the leading men there.
Einar asked in return about Egil's voyages and exploits; Egil
enjoyed talking about them and they got on well together. Einar
asked Egil to tell him where his toughest ordeal had been, and
Egil spoke a verse:

50. I fought alone with eight,
     and twice with eleven.
     I fed the wolf with corpses,
     killed them all myself.
     Fiercely we swapped
     blades that shiver through shields.   *blades that shiver through*
     From the tree of my arm   *shields*: swords
     I tossed the plated fire of death.   *plated fire of death*: sword

Egil and Einar promised each other friendship when they
parted. Einar spent a long time in other countries with men of
rank. He was generous but usually had scant means, and he was
a firm character and a noble man. He was one of Earl Hakon
Sigurdarson's men.

At that time there was much unrest in Norway. Earl Hakon
was at war with Eirik's sons and many people fled the country.
King Harald Eiriksson died in Denmark, at Hals in Limfjord,
when he was betrayed. He fought against Harald, the son of
Canute, who was called Gold-Harald, and against Earl Hakon.

Arinbjorn the Hersir died with Harald Eiriksson in that battle.
When Egil heard of Arinbjorn's death, he composed this verse:

51. Their numbers are dwindling, the famous
     warriors who met with weapons
     and spread gifts like the gold of day.
     Where will I find generous men,
     who beyond the sea that, nailed with islands,
     girds the earth, showered snows of silver
     on to my hands where hawks perch,
     in return for my words of praise?

The poet Einar Helgason was nicknamed Skalaglamm (Bowl-
rattle). He composed a drapa about Earl Hakon called Lack of
Gold, which was very long. For a long time the earl was angry
with Einar and refused to listen to it. Then Einar spoke a verse:

52. I made mead for the battle-father   *mead*: poetry; *battle-father*:
     while everyone slept, about the noble   Odin, god of poetry and
     warrior who rules the lands –   battle
     and now I regret it.

>I think that the spreader of treasure,
>the renowned leader, considers few
>poets worse than me; I was
>too eager to come to see him.

And he spoke another verse:

53. Let us seek to meet the earl who dares
>to make meals for the wolf with his sword,
>adorn the ship's oar-sides
>with ornate victory shields;
>the warrior who swings his sword
>like a serpent inflicting wounds
>will not turn his hand
>to rebuff me when I find him.

The earl did not want Einar to leave then, but listened to his poem and afterwards gave him as a reward a shield, which was an outstanding treasure. It was adorned with legends, and between the carvings it was overlaid with gold and embossed with jewels. Then Einar went to Iceland to stay with his brother Osvif.

In the autumn, Einar rode over to Borg and stayed there. Egil was not at home, having gone north, but was expected shortly. Einar stayed three nights waiting for him; it was not the custom to stay more than three nights on a visit. Einar then prepared to leave, and when he was ready to go he went to Egil's bed and hung up his precious shield there, and told the people of the household that it was a present for Egil.

After that, Einar rode away, and Egil came home the same day. When he went to his bed he saw the shield and asked who owned such a treasure. He was told that Einar Skalaglamm had been there and given him the shield as a present.

Then Egil said, 'That scoundrel! Does he expect me to stay awake making a poem about his shield? Fetch my horse, I will ride after him and kill him.'

Then he was told that Einar had ridden away early that morning – 'He will have reached Dalir by now.'

Then Egil made a drapa, which begins with this verse:

54. It is time to light up with praise
     the bright bulwark I was given.   *bright bulwark*: shield
     The sender of generosity's message
     reached me at my home.
     I will steer the reins well
     of the sea-king's horse,   *sea-king's horse*: ship
     my dwarf's ship of verse.   *dwarf's ship*: poetry
     Listen to my words.

Egil and Einar remained friends all their lives. It is said of the
fate of the shield that Egil took it with him when he went north
to Vidimyri with Thorkel Gunnvaldsson, who was going to
fetch his bride there, and Bjorn the Red's sons Scarf and Helgi.
The shield was dilapidated by then; it had been thrown into a
tub of whey. Afterwards Egil had the fittings taken off, and there
were twelve ounces of gold in the overlays.

82 | Thorstein, Egil's son, was a very handsome man when he
    | grew up, with fair hair and a fair complexion. He was tall
and strong, although not on his father's scale. Thorstein was a
wise and peaceful man, a model of modesty and self-control.
Egil was not very fond of him. Thorstein, in turn, did not show
his father much affection, but Asgerd and Thorstein were very
close. By this time, Egil was growing very old.

One summer, Thorstein rode to the Althing, while Egil stayed
at home. Before Thorstein left home, he and Asgerd decided to
take Arinbjorn's gift, the silk cloak, out of Egil's chest, and
Thorstein wore it to the Thing. It was so long that it dragged
along the ground and the hem got dirty during the procession
to the Law Rock. When he returned home, Asgerd put the gown
back where it had come from. Much later, when Egil opened
his chest, he discovered that the gown was ruined, and asked
Asgerd what the explanation was. She told him the truth, and
Egil spoke a verse:

55. I had little need of an heir
     to use my inheritance.
     My son has betrayed me

in my lifetime, I call that treachery.

The horseman of the sea	*horseman of the sea*:
could well have waited	seafarer, man
for other sea-skiers	*sea-skiers*: seafarers
to pile rocks over me.	

Thorstein married Jofrid, the daughter of Gunnar Hlifarson. Her mother was Helga, who was the daughter of Olaf Feilan and sister of Thord Bellower. Jofrid had previously been married to Thorodd, son of Tungu-Odd.

Shortly after this, Asgerd died. Then Egil gave up his farm and handed it over to Thorstein, and went south to Mosfell to his son-in-law Grim, because he was fondest of his step-daughter Thordis of all the people who were alive.

One summer a ship arrived in Leiruvog, with a man called Thormod at the helm. He was Norwegian and lived on the farm of Thora's son Thorstein the Hersir. He brought with him a shield that Thorstein had sent to Egil Skallagrimsson, a fine piece of work. Thormod gave Egil the shield and he accepted it with thanks. Later that winter, Egil composed a drapa in honour of the shield he had been given, which he called the Drapa of the Shield. It begins with the verse:

56.   Hear, king's subject, my fountain
      of praise from long-haired Odin,
      the guardian of sacrificial fire:
      may men pledge silence.

My words of praise, my seed sown	*seed sown from the eagle's*
from the eagle's mouth, will often	*mouth*: poetry, stolen by
be heard in Hordaland, O guider	Odin in the guise of an eagle
of the wave-cliffs' raven.	*wave-cliffs' raven*: ship

Egil's son Thorstein lived at Borg. He had two sons outside wedlock, Hrifla and Hrafn, and ten children with Jofrid after they were married. One of their daughters was Helga the Fair, whose love Hrafn the Poet and Gunnlaug Serpent-tongue contested.[75] Grim was their oldest son, followed by Skuli, Thorgeir, Kollsvein, Hjorleif, Halli, Egil and Thord. They had another daughter named Thora, who married Thormod

Kleppjarnsson. A great family is descended from Thorstein's children, including many great men. Everyone descended from Skallagrim is said to belong to the Myrar clan.

83 | Onund Sjoni was living at Anabrekka when Egil lived at Borg. His wife was Thorgerd, the daughter of Bjarni the Stout from Snaefellsstrond. Their children were Steinar, and Dalla, who married Ogmund Galtason and had two sons named Thorgils and Kormak. When Onund grew old and began to go blind, he handed over his farm to his son Steinar. The two of them were very wealthy. Steinar was exceedingly large and strong, an ugly man, stooping, with long legs but a short trunk. He was a great troublemaker, overbearing, difficult to deal with and ruthless, and very quarrelsome.

When Egil's son Thorstein was living at Borg, he and Steinar did not get along. South of the Hafslaek Brook is a marsh called Stakksmyri which is submerged in winter, but in spring when the ice has thawed it is such good pasture for cows that it was considered worth a whole haystack. Hafslaek had marked the boundary between farms since early times. During the spring, Steinar's cattle grazed heavily on Stakksmyri when they were driven out from Hafslaek. Thorstein's farmhands complained, but Steinar paid no heed to them, and there the matter rested for the first summer.

The following spring, Steinar continued to graze his cattle there. Thorstein talked calmly to him about it and asked him to graze his cattle within the old boundaries. Steinar replied that cattle would always go wherever they pleased. He spoke quite forcefully on the matter, and they exchanged harsh words. Then Thorstein had the cattle driven back over the brook. When Steinar realized this, he sent his slave Grani to watch over the cattle at Stakksmyri, and he stayed there every day. This was towards the end of summer, and all the pasture south of Hafslaek was completely grazed.

One day Thorstein went up on to a rock to take a look around and, seeing where Steinar's cattle were heading, he went out to the marsh. It was late in the day. He could see that the cattle had gone a long way up the tract between the hills. Thorstein ran out to the meadows, and when Grani saw this, he drove the cattle as hard as he could back to the milking-pens. Thorstein went after them and met Grani at the gate to the farm. Thorstein killed him there, and the spot at the hayfield wall has been called Granahlid (Grani's Gate) ever since. Thorstein pulled down the wall to cover his body,[76] then went back to Borg. The women found Grani lying there when they went out to the milking-pens, and returned to the farmhouse to tell Steinar what had happened. Steinar buried him up in the hills, then appointed another slave, whose name is not mentioned, to go with the cattle. Thorstein pretended to ignore the grazing cattle for the rest of the summer.

Early in the winter, Steinar went out to Snaefellsstrond and spent some time there. He saw a slave named Thrand there, a very large and strong man. Steinar offered a high price to buy the slave; his owner valued him at three marks of silver, which was twice the value of an ordinary slave. The deal was made and he took Thrand home with him.

When they returned home, Steinar said to Thrand, 'It so happens that I want you to do some work for me, but all the jobs have been shared out already. I want to ask you to do a job which will not be very difficult for you. You will watch over my cattle. I think it is important that they are grazed well, and I want you to rely solely on your own judgement about where the best pasture is on the marsh. I'm a poor judge of character if you don't turn out to have the courage or strength to stand up to any of Thorstein's farmhands.'

Steinar gave Thrand a big axe, its blade measuring almost one ell and razor-sharp.

'From the look of you, I can't tell how highly you would think of the fact that Thorstein is a godi, if the two of you met face to face,' Steinar added.

Thrand answered, 'I don't owe Thorstein any loyalty, but I think I realize what the job is you're asking me to do. You don't reckon you have much to lose in me. But when Thorstein and I put our strength to the test, whichever of us wins will be a worthy victor.'

Then Thrand started tending the cattle. Although he had not been there long, Thrand realized where Steinar had sent his cattle, and he sat watching over them in Stakksmyri.

When Thorstein noticed this, he sent one of his farmhands to see Thrand and tell him where the boundary between his land and Steinar's lay. The farmhand met Thrand and gave him the message to keep his cattle on the other side, since they were on Thorstein Egilsson's side.

'I don't care whose land they are on,' said Thrand. 'I will keep the cattle where I think the best pasture is.'

They parted, and the farmhand went home and told Thorstein what the slave had replied. Thorstein let the matter rest, and Thrand started watching over the cattle day and night.

84 | One morning Thorstein got up at sunrise and went up to the top of a rock. Seeing where Steinar's cattle were, he walked over to the marsh until he reached them. A wooded cliff overlooks Hafslaek, and Thrand was sleeping barefoot on the top of it. Thorstein went up to the top of the cliff, carrying an axe which was not very large, and no other weapon. He prodded Thrand with the shaft of the axe and ordered him to wake up. Thrand leapt to his feet, grabbed his axe with both hands and raised it. He asked Thorstein what he wanted.

Thorstein said, 'I want to tell you that this is my land, and your pasture is on the other side of the brook. I'm not surprised you don't realize where the boundaries lie here.'

'I don't care whose land it is,' Thrand replied. 'I will let the cattle be where they prefer.'

'I'd rather be in charge of my own land than leave that to Steinar's slaves,' said Thorstein.

'You're more stupid than I thought, Thorstein, if you want to risk your honour by seeking a place to sleep for the night under my axe,' said Thrand. 'I'd guess I have twice your strength, and I don't lack courage either. And I'm better armed than you.'

Thorstein said, 'That's a risk I'm prepared to take if you don't do anything about the cattle grazing. I trust there's as much difference between our fortunes as there is between our claims in this matter.'

Thrand said, 'Now you'll find out whether I'm scared of your threats, Thorstein.'

Then Thrand sat down to tie his shoe, and Thorstein raised his axe high in the air and struck him on the neck, so that his head fell on to his chest. Thorstein piled some rocks over his body to cover it up and went back home to Borg.

That day Steinar's cattle were late coming back. When there seemed to be no hope left of them returning, Steinar took his horse and saddled it. He rode south to Borg, fully armed, and spoke to some people when he arrived. He asked about Thorstein and was told he was indoors. Steinar told them he wanted Thorstein to come outside to attend to some business. When Thorstein heard this, he picked up his weapons and went to the door. Then he asked Steinar what he wanted.

'Did you kill my slave Thrand?' Steinar asked.

'That's right,' said Thorstein. 'You don't need to imagine that anyone else did.'

'I can see you're set on defending your land with a firm hand, since you've killed two of my slaves,' replied Steinar. 'But I don't consider that much of a feat. If you're so determined to defend your land bravely, I can give you a much more worthy option. From now on I won't rely on anyone else to look after my cattle, and you can rest assured that they'll remain on your land both day and night.'

'It so happened that last summer I killed the slave you sent to graze the cattle on my land,' said Thorstein. 'Then I let you have all the pasture you wanted right up until winter. Now I have killed another of your slaves for the same reason I killed the first one. You can have all the pasture you want for the coming summer, but after that, if you graze your cattle on my land and send men to drive your cattle here, I will kill every single one who herds them, even if it is you yourself. I will go on doing this every summer for as long as you keep on grazing them there.'

Then Steinar rode off back to Brekka and on to Stafaholt shortly afterwards. A godi called Einar lived there. Steinar asked for his support and offered to pay him for it.

Einar said, 'My support will make little difference to you unless other men of standing back you up in this matter.'

After that Steinar rode up to Reykjadal to see Tungu-Odd, asked him for support and offered to pay him for it. Odd took the money and promised his support in helping Steinar to secure his rights against Thorstein. Then Steinar rode home.

That spring Odd and Einar went with Steinar to Borg to announce their summons, taking a large band of men with them. Steinar summonsed Thorstein for killing his slaves and demanded a penalty of lesser outlawry for each of them, which was the punishment for killing a man's slaves unless compensation was paid before the third sunrise.[77] Double lesser outlawry was considered equal to full outlawry.

Thorstein brought no counter-charges, but sent some men off to Nes shortly afterwards. They went to Grim at Mosfell and told him the news. Egil showed little interest, but asked secretly in detail about Thorstein's dealings with Steinar and about the men who had supported Steinar in the case. Then the messengers went back home, and Thorstein was pleased with their journey.

Thorstein Egilsson took a very large party to the Spring Assembly and arrived the night before everybody else. They pitched tents over their booths, and so did his Thingmen who had booths there. When they had set everything up, Thorstein sent word to his supporters to build great walls for a booth, which he then covered with a much larger tent than all the others there. No men were in that booth.

Steinar rode to the assembly with very many men. Tungu-Odd was in charge of a large band of his own men, and Einar from Stafaholt also brought a large party. They pitched their tents over their booths. It was a very well-attended assembly. When the cases were presented, Thorstein made no offer of a settlement on his own behalf, and told anyone who tried to arrange one that he would wait to hear the ruling, since he set little store by Steinar's charges of killing his slaves after all they had done to deserve it. Steinar made a great show about his case, claiming that his charges were valid and that he had ample support to win his rights, and was very aggressive about the whole matter.

The same day all the men went to the Assembly Slope to plead against the charges before they went before the courts in the evening. Thorstein was there with his party. He had the most influence over the conduct of proceedings there, just as Egil had done when he was a godi and chieftain. Both sides were fully armed.

From the assembly, a band of men was seen riding alongside the river Gljufura, their shields glinting. They rode into the assembly led by a large man wearing a black cloak and gilded helmet and carrying a shield decorated with gold by his side. In his hand he held a barbed spear with its socket embossed with gold, and he was girded with a sword. Egil Skallagrimsson had arrived with eighty men, all armed for battle. It was an elite band of men, for Egil had brought along the finest farmers' sons from the south side of Nes, those whom he considered most warlike. Egil rode with his party over to the booth where Thorstein had already pitched tents which were standing empty. They dismounted from their horses.

When Thorstein recognized his father, he went up to him with all his men and welcomed him warmly. Egil and his men had all the gear they had brought with them carried into the booth, and drove the horses out to graze. Once this was done, Egil and Thorstein went up the Assembly Slope with all their men and sat down in their usual places.

Then Egil stood up and said in a loud voice, 'Is Onund Sjoni here on the slope?'

Onund said he was, 'And I am pleased that you have come, Egil. It will make a great contribution towards solving this dispute.'

Egil asked, 'Are you responsible for the charges your son Steinar has brought against my son Thorstein and the forces he has gathered to have Thorstein declared an outlaw?'

'Their quarrel is none of my doing,' said Onund. 'I have spent a lot of words telling Steinar to make a reconciliation with Thorstein, because I have always been reluctant to bring any dishonour upon your son Thorstein. The reason is our lifelong friendship, Egil, ever since we were brought up here together.'

'It will soon emerge,' said Egil, 'whether you are speaking earnest or empty words, although I consider the latter less likely.

I remember the days when neither of us could have imagined that we would quarrel with each other or need to restrain our sons from committing such folly as I hear is in the offing now. It seems advisable to me, for as long as we live and witness their dispute, that we should take charge of the matter ourselves and settle it, without letting Tungu-Odd and Einar pit our sons against each other like horses at a fight. They can find a better way to earn their living than involving themselves in this.'

Onund stood up and said, 'What you say is right, Egil. It is unfitting for us to attend an assembly where our sons are quarrelling. We will never incur the shame of being so weak in character that we cannot reconcile them. Steinar, I want you to grant me charge of this case and allow me to pursue it as I please.'

'I don't know whether I want to drop my case,' said Steinar, 'after seeking the support of great men. I want to settle the matter immediately to Odd and Einar's satisfaction.'

Then Odd and Steinar conferred, and Odd said, 'I will grant you the support I promised you, Steinar, to win your rights or a settlement that you are prepared to accept. It will be largely your responsibility if Egil rules on the matter.'

Then Onund said, 'I don't want to leave the matter up to Odd's tongue to decide, for he has neither treated me well nor badly. But Egil has done many fine things for me. I trust him better than other people, and I will have my own way now. You will be better off not having to tackle all of us. I have made the decisions on our behalf until now, and that's the way it will stay.'

'You are very insistent about it, Father,' said Steinar, 'but I expect we will regret it later.'

Then Steinar handed over charge of the case to Onund, who was to prosecute or settle, as the law stipulated.

Once Onund had taken charge of the case, he went to see Thorstein and Egil.

Onund said, 'I will leave it up to you to rule and judge here, Egil, just as you please, because I trust you most to decide on these matters of mine and all others.'

Then Onund and Thorstein shook hands and named

witnesses, adding that Egil Skallagrimsson alone should rule on the case at that assembly as he saw fit, without reservations, and so the matter ended. Everyone went back to the booths. Thorstein had three oxen brought to Egil's booth and had them slaughtered to provide him with a feast at the assembly.

When Tungu-Odd and Steinar returned to their booths, Odd said, 'You and your father have decided how your case will be concluded, Steinar. Now I am free of all obligation to grant you the support that I promised you, because we agreed that I should help you to pursue your case or bring it to a conclusion that you found favourable, however Egil's settlement turns out.'

Steinar told Odd he had supported him well and nobly, and that they would be closer friends than before.

'I declare that you are free of all your earlier obligations to me,' he said.

That evening the courts met, and nothing eventful is said to have happened then.

85 | Egil Skallagrimsson went to the Assembly Slope the following day together with Thorstein and all their men. Onund and Steinar were there too, and Tungu-Odd and Einar.

When everyone had stated their cases, Egil stood up and asked, 'Are Steinar and his father Onund here and able to hear what I am saying?'

Onund said they were there.

'Then I will pronounce the settlement between Steinar and Thorstein: I will begin my statement with my father Grim's arrival in Iceland, when he took all the land in Myrar and around the district and made his home at Borg. He designated that land for his farm, but gave his friends the outlying lands which they settled later. He gave Ani a place to live at Anabrekka, where Onund and Steinar have lived until now. We all know, Steinar, where the boundary lies between Borg and Anabrekka: the brook at Hafslaek separates them. It was not by accident that you grazed your cattle on Thorstein's land, Steinar, and seized his property, expecting him to be such a disgrace to his family that he would let you get away with robbing him. You are well aware, Steinar and Onund, that Ani accepted that land from my father Grim. When Thorstein killed two of your slaves, it is obvious to everyone that they fell by their own doing and do not qualify for compensation; even if they were free men, they would be considered criminals and thereby not qualify for compensation. Yet since you, Steinar, planned to rob my son Thorstein of his land, which he took over with my approval and I had inherited from my father, you will forfeit your land at Anabrekka and be paid nothing for it. Furthermore, you will not make your home or accept lodging in this district on the south side of the river Langa, and leave Anabrekka before the end of the Moving Days, and be rightfully killed by Thorstein or any man who is ready to grant Thorstein his assistance after that time if you refuse to leave or to abide by any of these stipulations I have made towards you.'

When Egil sat down, Thorstein named witnesses to his settlement.

Then Onund Sjoni said, 'Everyone will agree, Egil, that the settlement you have made and delivered here is unjust. For my part, I have made every effort to prevent the trouble between them, but from now on I will not restrain myself from any inconvenience I can cause to Thorstein.'

'On the contrary,' said Egil, 'I expect you and your son's lot to worsen, the longer that our quarrel lasts. I would have thought you realized, Onund, that I have always held my own against people like you and your son. And Odd and Einar, who were so interested in this matter, have received the honour they deserve from it.'

86 | Thorgeir Blund, Egil's nephew, was at the assembly and had supported Thorstein strongly in the case. He asked Egil and Thorstein to grant him some land in Myrar; he had been living on the south side of Hvita, below the lake called Blundsvatn (Snooze Lake). Egil took his request well, and Thorstein urged his father to let him move there. They gave Thorgeir Anabrekka to live in, while Steinar moved his home to

the other side of Langa and settled at Leirulaek. Egil rode off home to Nes, and he and his son parted on warm terms.

There was a man named Iri who was a member of Thorstein's household, very swift of foot and exceptionally sharp-sighted. Although he was a foreigner and a freedman, he was in charge of watching over Thorstein's sheep, which mainly involved rounding up the sheep that were unsuitable for milking, and driving them up to the mountains in spring and rounding them up again for penning in autumn. After the Moving Days, Thorstein had the sheep rounded up which had been left behind in the spring and planned to drive them up in the mountains. Iri was in the fold, but Thorstein and his farmhands, eight of them altogether, rode off to the mountains.

Thorstein built a fence right across Grisartunga between Langavatn and Gljufura and sent a number of men to work on it in the spring. After inspecting his farmhands' work, he rode home, and as he was passing the site of the assembly, Iri came running up from the opposite direction and said he wanted to talk to him in private. Thorstein told his companions to ride ahead while they talked.

Iri told Thorstein that they had been up to Einkunnir earlier that day to keep an eye on the sheep.

'And in the woods above the winter track,' he said, 'I saw the glint of twelve spears and several shields.'

Thorstein answered in a loud enough voice for his companions to hear him clearly: 'Why does he want to see me so badly that I can't even ride home? Olvald must know that I'm unlikely to refuse to speak to him when he's ill.'

Iri ran up the mountain as fast as he could.

Then Thorstein said to his companions, 'I want to make a detour and ride south to Olvaldsstadir. Olvald sent me word asking me to meet him. He'll think I owe him at least that for the ox he gave me last autumn, to go and see him when he thinks it's important.'

After that, Thorstein and his men rode south across the marshland above Stangarholt, then south to Gufa and along the riding path that skirts the river. On their way down from Vatn they saw a large number of bulls on the south side of the river, and a man there with them. It was Olvald's farmhand. Thorstein asked him if everybody was well, and he said that they all were, and Olvald was in the woods chopping timber.

'Then go and tell him to go to Borg if he has any business with me,' said Thorstein. 'I will ride home now.'

And then he did that.

Later, word went around that Steinar Sjonason had been lying in wait on Einkunnir with eleven men that same day. Thorstein pretended not to know, and everything remained quiet afterwards.

87 | There was a man named Thorgeir, a kinsman and close friend of Thorstein's. At that time he was living at Alftanes. Thorgeir was in the habit of holding a feast every autumn. He went to see Thorstein Egilsson to invite him. Thorstein accepted the invitation, and Thorgeir went back home.

On the appointed day, Thorstein made his preparations for the journey; this was four weeks before winter. A Norwegian and two of his farmhands went with him. Thorstein had a ten-year-old son named Grim who went with them too, so that there were five of them when they rode out to Foss to cross Langa, then straight on to the river Aurridaa.

On the other side of the river was a long and narrow wood through which the path lay, and meadows west of the trees, belonging to several farms. Steinar, Onund and their farmhands were working there. When they recognized Thorstein they ran for their weapons and set off in pursuit. And when Thorstein saw Steinar chasing them, he and his men rode from Langaholt towards a high, narrow hill which was nearby. Thorstein and his men dismounted and set off up the hill, and he told the boy Grim to stay clear of their encounter and go into the woods. When Steinar and the others reached the hill, they attacked Thorstein and his men and a battle ensued. There were six grown men on Steinar's side, as well as his ten-year-old son. People from nearby farms who were working in the meadows saw the two sides clash and ran over to separate them. By the time the fight was broken up, both of Thorstein's farmhands had been killed. One of Steinar's farmhands was dead and some of the others wounded.

After the battle had been broken up, Thorstein went to look for Grim. They found him severely wounded, with Steinar's son lying dead beside him.

As Thorstein jumped on his horse, Steinar called out to him, 'Are you running away now, Thorstein the White?'

Thorstein replied, 'You'll run further before the week is past.'

Then Thorstein and his men rode over the marshland, taking Grim with them. When they reached the hillock that stands there, the boy died. They buried him on the hillock, and it was called Grimsholt afterwards; the hill where they had fought is called Orustuhvol (Battle Hill).

That evening, Thorstein rode out to Alftanes as he had planned, stayed at the feast for three days and then prepared to go back home. People offered to accompany him, but he refused, and set off with the Norwegian.

Steinar rode out towards the shore on the day that he knew he could expect Thorstein to be riding home. He sat down on the sand banks that start below Lambastadir, and was armed with a sword called Skrymir, an outstanding weapon. He stood on the bank with his sword drawn, his eyes focused on Thorstein whom he saw riding along the edge of the sands.

Lambi, who lived at Lambastadir, saw what Steinar was doing. He set off from home and down to the sand bank, and when he reached Steinar he grabbed his arms from behind. Steinar tried to shake him off, but Lambi held him tight, and they struggled down from the bank and on to level ground just as Thorstein and his companion rode past along the track below. Steinar had ridden his horse there and had tethered it; the horse freed itself and galloped off along the shore. This surprised Thorstein and his companion when they saw it, because they had not noticed Steinar's movements. Not seeing Thorstein ride past, Steinar worked his way back to the sand bank, and when they reached the edge Lambi caught him off his guard and pushed him off it. He tumbled on to the sands, Lambi ran home and when Steinar got to his feet he chased after him. When Lambi reached the door of his house he ran inside and slammed it. Steinar swung a blow at him, but his sword stuck tight in the rafters. That was the end of their dealings, and Steinar went home.

The day after Thorstein came back home he sent his farmhand off to Leirulaek to tell Steinar to move house beyond Borgarhraun and be gone by the next evening with everything he had, or he would take advantage of his greater power, 'and if I do, then you won't have the chance to leave'.

Steinar moved out to the coast at Snaefellsstrond and set up a farm at the place called Ellidi, and that was the end of his dealings with Thorstein Egilsson.

Thorgeir Blund lived at Anabrekka and quarrelled with Thorstein about everything he could.

On one occasion when Egil and Thorstein met they talked at great length about their kinsman Thorgeir Blund and agreed entirely about him. Then Egil spoke this verse:

57.   In the past I pulled the land
      out of Steinar's hands with words
      thinking I was working
      in Thorgeir's favour.
      My sister's son failed me,
      gave me golden promises,
      yet Snooze, to my astonishment,
      could not refrain from causing harm.

Thorgeir Blund left Anabrekka and went south to Flokadal, because even though he was prepared to back down, Thorstein refused to have anything to do with him.

Thorstein was a straightforward, just and unimposing man, yet stood firm if others imposed on him and proved a tough opponent when challenged. He and Tungu-Odd were on cold terms after Steinar's case.

Odd was the chieftain of Borgarfjord on the south side of Hvita then. He was the godi of the temple to which everyone living south of Skardsheidi paid tribute.

88 | Egil Skallagrimsson lived a long life, but in his old age he grew very frail, and both his hearing and sight failed. He also suffered from very stiff legs. Egil was living at Mosfell with Grim and Thordis then.

One day Egil was walking outdoors alongside the wall when he stumbled and fell.

Some women saw this, laughed at him and said, 'You're completely finished, Egil, now that you fall over of your own accord.'

Grim replied, 'Women made less fun of us when we were younger. And I expect they find little of value in our womanizing now.'

Egil said that things had reached that pass, and he spoke a verse:

58. My head bobs like a bridled horse
    it plunges baldly into woe.
    my middle leg both droops and drips
    while both my ears are dry.

Egil went completely blind. One winter day when the weather was cold, he went to warm himself by the fire. The cook said it was astonishing for a man who had been as great as Egil to lie around under people's feet and stop them going about their work.

'Don't grudge me that I warm myself through by the fire,' said Egil. 'We should make room for each other.'

'Stand up,' she said, 'and go off to your bed and leave us to get on with our work.'

Egil stood up, went off to his bed and spoke this verse:

59. Blind I wandered to sit by the fire,
    asked the flame-maiden for peace;
    such affliction I bear on the border
    where my eyebrows cross.
    Once when the land-rich king
    took pleasure in my words
    he granted me the hoard
    that giants warded, gold.

Another time Egil went over to the fire to keep warm, and someone asked him if his legs were cold and told him not to stretch them out too close to the fire.

'I will do that,' said Egil, 'but I don't find it easy to control my legs now that I cannot see. Being blind is dismal.'

Then Egil spoke a verse:

60. Time seems long in passing
        as I lie alone,
        a senile old man
        on the downy bed.
        My legs are two
        frigid widows,
        those women
        need some flame.

This was at the start of Earl Hakon the Powerful's reign.[78] Egil Skallagrimsson was in his eighties then and still active apart from his blindness.

In the summer, when everyone was preparing to ride to the Thing, Egil asked Grim to ride there with him. Grim was reluctant.

When Grim spoke to Thordis, he told her what Egil had asked of him.

'I want you to find out what lies behind this request of his,' he said.

Thordis went to see her kinsman Egil, who by that time had no greater pleasure in life than talking to her.

When she saw him she asked, 'Is it true that you want to ride to the Thing, kinsman? I'd like you to tell me what you're planning.'

'I will tell you what I've been thinking,' he said. 'I want to go to the Thing with the two chests full of English silver that King Athelstan gave to me. I'm going to have the chests carried to the Law Rock when the crowd there is at its biggest. Then I'll toss the silver at them and I'll be very much surprised if they all share it out fairly amongst themselves. I expect there'll be plenty of pushing and shoving. It might even end with the whole Thing breaking out in a brawl.'

Thordis said, 'That sounds like a brilliant plan. It will live for as long as people live in Iceland.'

Then Thordis went to talk to Grim and tell him about Egil's plan.

'He must never be allowed to get away with such a mad scheme,' said Grim.

When Egil brought up the subject of riding to the Thing with Grim he would have none of it, so Egil stayed at home while the Thing was held. He was displeased and wore a rather grumpy look.

The cattle at Mosfell were kept in a shieling, and Thordis stayed there while the Thing took place.

One evening when everyone was going to bed at Mosfell, Egil called in two of Grim's slaves.

He told them to fetch him a horse, 'because I want to go to bathe in the pool'.

When he was ready he went out, taking his chests of silver with him. He mounted the horse, crossed the hayfields to the slope that begins there and disappeared.

In the morning, when all the people got up, they saw Egil wandering around on the hill east of the farm, leading a horse behind him. They went over to him and brought him home.

But neither the slaves nor the chests of treasure ever returned, and there are many theories about where Egil hid his treasure. East of the farm is a gully leading down from the mountain. It has been noticed that English coins have been found in the gully when the river recedes after floods caused by sudden thaws. Some people believe Egil must have hidden his treasure there. Then there are large and exceptionally deep marshes below the hayfields at Mosfell, and it is claimed that Egil threw his treasure into them. On the south side of the rivers are hot springs with big pits nearby, where some people believe Egil must have hidden his treasure, because a will-o'-the-wisp[79] is often seen there. Egil himself said he had killed Grim's slaves and hidden his treasure somewhere, but he never told a single person where it was.

In the autumn Egil caught the illness that eventually led to his death. When he died, Grim had his body dressed in fine clothes and taken over to Tjaldanes, where a mound was made that Egil was buried in, along with his weapons and clothes.

89 | Grim from Mosfell was baptized when Christianity was made the law in Iceland and he had a church built at Mosfell. It is said that Thordis had Egil's bones moved to the church. This is supported by the fact that when a cemetery was dug, after the church that Grim had had built at Hrisbru was taken down and set up at Mosfell, human bones were found under the site of the altar. They were much larger than normal human bones, and on the basis of old accounts people are certain they must have belonged to Egil.

Skafti Thorarinsson the Priest, a wise man, was there at the time. He picked up Egil's skull and put it on the wall of the churchyard. The skull was astonishingly large and even more incredible for its weight. It was all ridged on the outside, like a scallop shell.[80] Curious to test its thickness, Skafti took a fair-sized hand-axe in one hand and struck the skull with it as hard as he could, to try to break it. A white mark was left where he struck the skull, but it neither dented nor cracked. This goes to prove that such a skull would not have been easy for weak men to damage when it was covered with hair and skin. Egil's bones were buried by the edge of the churchyard at Mosfell.

90 | Thorstein, Egil's son, was baptized when Christianity came to Iceland and he had a church built at Borg. He was a devout and orderly man. He grew to an old age, died of illness and was buried at Borg in the church he had had built there.

A great family is descended from Thorstein which includes many prominent men and poets. Thorstein's descendants belong to the Myrar clan, as do all other descendants of Skallagrim. For a long time it was a family trait to be strong and war-like, and some members were men of great wisdom. It was a family of contrasts. Some of the best-looking people ever known in Iceland belonged to it, such as Thorstein Egilsson, his nephew Kjartan Olafsson, Hall Gudmundarson and Thorstein's daughter Helga the Fair, whose love Gunnlaug Serpent-tongue and Hrafn the Poet contested. But most members of the Myrar clan were exceptionally ugly.

Of Thorstein's sons, Thorgeir was the strongest but Skuli was the greatest. He lived at Borg after his father's day and spent a long time on Viking raids. He was at the stem of Earl Eirik's ship Iron-prow in the battle where King Olaf Tryggvason was killed.[81] Skuli fought seven battles on his Viking raids and was considered to be outstandingly resolute and brave. He went to Iceland afterwards and farmed at Borg, where he lived until his old age, and many people are descended from him. And here this saga ends.

Notes

1. *Bjalfi*: Lit. animal skin, possibly linked to the shape-shifting family trait.
2. *Half-troll*: i.e. the offspring of a troll and a human being.
3. *Haeng*: Lit. a male salmon or the hook on its lower jaw; the nickname may suggest that Ketil had a drooping lower lip.
4. *Kari from Berle*: Also features in *The Saga of King Harald Fair-hair* in Snorri Sturluson's *Heimskringla*.
5. *landholder*: The holder of seigneurial rights to land owned by the king, ranking next to an earl in social status.
6. *Tangle-hair*: According to tradition, King Harald's nickname refers to his oath to his betrothed, Gytha, that he would not have his hair cut until he had subdued all of Norway, as related in *The Saga of King Harald Fair-hair*. Once Harald became sole ruler of Norway, however, Earl Rognvald of More gave him the new nickname 'Fair-hair'. King Harald Fair-hair ruled in Norway for almost sixty years, from *c.* 875–932. The main emigration from Norway to Iceland took place during his reign and is often attributed to his tyranny. Several sagas of the Icelanders begin at this point in history.
7. *Earl Rognvald*: Earl of More, a fairly prominent character in *Heimskringla* and *The Saga of the Orkney Islanders*. He was the ancestor of the earls of Rouen and Orkney.
8. *wedding*: The peremptory wedding that Bjorgolf decides upon here does not follow the formal legal procedure of a betrothal at which the prospective bride's father and the groom settle the bride-price and announce the date of the wedding feast. While Bjorgulf pays a nominal sum, the marriage does not fulfil other legal provisions; Hildirid's disputed marital status later proves crucial in Thorolf Skallagrimsson's claim to inherit from Brynjolf. The same argument, in fact, is used against Egil when he tries to claim rights to land in Norway (see chapter 57).

9. *an ounce of gold*: Approximately 25 grams, the equivalent to one mark of silver.

10. *the right to collect tribute and trade in Finnmark*: Collecting taxes from and trading with the people of Finnmark – apparently a much larger area than the modern-day part of northern Scandinavia that goes by this name – was a lucrative privilege held by landowners in Halogaland, later assumed by the king of Norway.

11. *bench opposite his high seat*: The highest seat of honour after the king.

12. *Havsfjord in Rogaland, in the greatest battle King Harald ever fought*: Although this battle, fought about 885, clinched Harald's bid for the crown of all Norway, the precise site is uncertain.

13. *Kylfing people*: One of the peoples living in the Russia of the Saga Age, i.e. what is modern-day western Russia and the Ukraine.

14. *Kven people*: According to *Egil's Saga*, these people lived in the Baltic basin south of Finnmark but north and west of what was then Finland. However, other accounts locate their territory much farther east and south, close to the Caspian Sea.

15. *Karelians*: Apparently from roughly the same place as modern-day Karelia, between Finland and Russia.

16. *Hising*: An island in the mouth of the river Gota.

17. *Eyvind the Plagiarist*: Court poet to King Hakon the Good (King Athelstan's foster-son), to whom he composed a eulogy. Whether his nickname was justified or merely a jealous slight cannot be established.

18. *Ingolf and Hjorleif*: Ingolf Arnarson, the first settler of Iceland (who made his home in Reykjavík), and his sworn brother Hjorleif Hrodmundarson.

19. *Orm the Strong*: Renowned for his trials of strength, as recounted in *The Tale of Orm the Strong*.

20. *Veturlidi the Poet*: Known from *Njal's Saga* and *The Saga of Christianity*. He was killed for composing a lampoon about the first Christian missionary in Iceland, Thorbrand the Priest.

21. *Ofeig Grettir*: Half-brother of Grettir Asmundarson the Strong's grandfather, Thorgrim Grey-head. He occurs in *The Saga of Grettir the Strong* and *The Book of Settlements*. The name Grettir means snake or serpent (lit. 'face-puller').

22. *coal-biter*: A stereotypical 'male Cinderella' figure who unpromisingly lounges around in the fire-room in youth, only to stand up one day and perform mighty deeds to prove his worth.

23. *Guttorm . . . the son of Sigurd Hart*: A major character in *The Saga of Harald Fair-hair*.

24. *Grim*: Son of Thorir. Also known from *The Book of Settlements* and *The Saga of the People of Vatnsdal*, where (as in *Egil's Saga* too) he is called Grim the Halogalander, after his home district.

25. *Olaf Feilan*: Grandson of Aud the Deep-minded, the matriarch in *The Saga of the People of Laxardal*. His nick-name, Feilan, is probably an Icelandic form of the Irish name *Faelan*, meaning 'wolf cub'.

26. *bog-iron*: A precious resource in the Viking Age. Found in peat bogs with mountain streams, it was used to make weapons and tools. Charcoal is used in the smelting process, hence Skallagrim's decision to move the forge closer to woodland.

27. *Mousa*: One of the Shetland Islands, where an Iron Age broch tower still stands today to a height of over 40 feet.

28. *Eirik, Harald's son*: King Eirik Blood-axe was the favourite son of Harald Fair-hair and earned his nickname for his ruthless elimination of many of his (half-)brothers. Together with his devious queen, Gunnhild, Eirik was ejected from Norway and ruled in York until his death in battle in 954.

29. *Permia*: The area around the White Sea, prized for products including furs and walrus ivory. Effectively beyond the boundaries of the civilized world, it serves as an apt place of origin for Gunnhild, who is versed in the magic arts. She is known not only from the sagas of kings, but also from *Njal's Saga* and *The Saga of the People of Laxardal*.

30. *Ketil Blund*: Also appears in *Hen-Thorir's Saga*.

31. *Brak*: An implement for stretching skin; her nickname possibly derives from her job on the farm.

32. *they jumped in a boat*: i.e. the boat used on ocean-going vessels for rowing ashore or between ships.

33. *King Olaf*: King Olaf the Quiet of Norway (reigned 1067–93).

34. *disir*: dís, pl. dísir, appear to have been high-ranking female guardian spirits that watched over farms, families and, occasionally, individuals. They have certain traits in common with fetches and Valkyries, but were seen as being much more powerful, almost like minor local deities, since a sacrifice was made to them during the Winter Nights every year.

35. *Courland*: The area of the Baltic roughly approximating to modern-day Latvia.

36. *Harald Gormsson*: King of Denmark (c. 940–86). His father, King Gorm the Old, ruled Jutland and died c. 950.

37. *Halland*: Part of modern-day Skane in Sweden, for centuries part of the Danish realm.

38. *Askmann*: Seafarer, from *ask-* (lit. ash), a kenning for 'ship'. Alf
    Askmann and Eyvind are mentioned in *Heimskringla*, and Eyvind
    features in other kings' sagas as well.

39. *main temple*: Where people from far and wide would attend the
    most important feasts of the year.

40. *Alfred the Great*: Ruled Wessex from 871–99.

41. *Edward*: King Edward 'The Elder', son of Alfred the Great. Ruled
    Wessex from 899–924.

42. *Athelstan the Victorious*: King Athelstan, son of Edward the
    Elder. Brought Mercia and Northumberland under his rule and
    became the first monarch of all England (924–39).

43. *Hakon the Good*: King Hakon, Athelstan's foster-son. Reigned
    in Norway from *c.* 934–60. One of the numerous sons of Harald
    Fair-hair, he was fostered as a boy by King Athelstan in England.

44. *British*: i.e. Welsh and possibly other native peoples.

45. *Olaf the Red*: No king of Scotland by this name is mentioned in
    Old English sources, although they refer to King Anlaf (a variant
    form of the name) of Northumberland, who was heavily defeated
    by Athelstan at the battle of Brunanburh in 937.

46. *Ragnar Shaggy-breeches*: A semi-legendary Viking leader, hero
    of one of the legendary sagas.

47. *Britain*: i.e. Wales and neighbouring territories.

48. *Wen Heath*: The site of this battle has not been satisfactorily
    identified. The place-names may echo, deliberately or not, those
    in Permia where Thorolf made another heroic stand in battle by
    the river Dvina. In Icelandic Wen and Dvina are both *Vín(a)*.

49. *a shilling of silver for every plough in all his realm*: cf. the 'plough
    tax', levied per strip of land which could be worked with a single
    plough.

50. *Earlsness*: Unidentified, apparently in Wales.

51. *inherit everything if Thorolf has died childless*: According to the
    ancient 'Grey Goose' legal code, the relatives rather than the
    widow inherited from a dead man. The children were first in
    succession, then the father, then the brother.

52. *Bjorn, Champion of the Hitardal people*: Eponymous hero of a
    saga, who also appears in *The Saga of St Olaf the Holy*.

53. *Thurid Dylla* and *Illugi the Black*: Grandparents of Gunnlaug,
    the hero of *The Saga of Gunnlaug Serpent-tongue*. The nickname
    Dylla is the name of a weed, perennial sowthistle.

54. *Gula Assembly*: One of the four law-making assemblies in medi-
    eval Norway.

55. *granted him the right to live in this country*: Bjorn had been

outlawed, but when the king allowed him to return to Norway all of his privileges were restored.

56. *Gunnhild bore Eirik a son, whom Harald ... named after himself*: This child grew up to be King Harald Grey-cloak. Pre-eminent among the sons of Eirik Blood-axe and Gunnhild, Harald Grey-cloak ruled Norway from 960–75 after defeating King Hakon, Athelstan's foster-son, at the Battle of Fitjar.

57. *After his death ... the people of Trondheim took Sigurd*: The dispute between Eirik's sons is recounted in detail in *Heimskringla* (chapters 92–8).

58. *Egil went through to the bench ... put into his tomb*: Egil approaches Skallagrim from behind in order to avoid his gaze until he has closed his nostrils, eyes and mouth as a precaution against the 'evil eye'. The fact that Skallagrim was a shape-shifter and had died in disagreement with Egil may have exacerbated the risk of his returning to haunt the farm. Although breaking down the wall to remove him may have been more practical given Skallagrim's huge frame and the fact that rigor mortis appears to have set in, it could equally be a deliberate way of not showing him the door back in to the farm before he was buried. The description of the contents of Skallagrim's mound is consistent with archaeological findings, but the ironic aside that 'It is not mentioned whether any money was put into his tomb' seems to suggest that Egil's strong miserly streak got the better of his religion.

59. *Earl Arnfinn*: Son of Thorfinn Skull-splitter, Earl of Orkney, also mentioned in *Heimskringla* and *The Saga of the People of Orkney*.

60. *assumed King Eirik was ruling the islands*: Orkney was ruled (or at least claimed) by earls in the name of the king of Norway, but here Egil is apparently unaware that Eirik had been driven out of his realm to York.

61. *embrace his foot*: A sign of humility towards both secular and spiritual leaders.

62. *Bragi*: Bragi Broddason (eighth century), court poet to Ragnar Shaggy-breeches and considered the 'father' of the *dróttkvætt* metre in which the verses in the sagas are composed.

63. *The poem was well delivered*: This peculiar retort after hearing a masterfully wrought eulogy to oneself has invited the conclusion that Eirik did not in fact understand a word of it. Certainly the poem's outrageous hyperbole – in contrast to the ingenuous

soul-searching of Egil's other two long poems – might suggest that it was composed at least partly tongue-in-cheek.

64. *Grim Hairy-cheeks*: Eponymous hero of one of the legendary sagas.

65. *Swedish*: Sweden often features as the home of troublemakers of almost superhuman strength, cf. Glam in *The Saga of Grettir the Strong*, Skjold in *Njal's Saga* and the berserks in *The Saga of the People of Eyri*.

66. *Edmund*: King Edmund, son of Edward the Elder and Athelstan's half-brother, ruled England from 940–46.

67. *Varmland*: District in Norway, now part of Sweden.

68. *I can have it made into a fur cape*: Presumably a reference to Egil's huge size: worn by an ordinary man, his half-length coat would almost have touched the ground.

69. *in his saga and . . . the poems . . . about him*: Hakon's conquest of Vastergotland is described in *Heimskringla* (chapters 99–102), which cites poetry by Guttorm Sindri.

70. *Geirmund Dark-skin*: Features in *The Saga of Grettir the Strong*, *Half's Saga* and *The Book of Settlements*, and a tale about him is included in *The Saga of the Sturlungs*.

71. *Skafti the Lawspeaker*: Skafti Thoroddsson was Lawspeaker from 1004–1030 and appears in many sagas.

72. *Laxardal*: The marriage of Egil's daughter Thorgerd is also described in *The Saga of the People of Laxardal*.

73. *until I go to join Freyja*: Join the goddess, by dying.

74. *dulse*: Edible seaweed.

75. *whose love Hrafn the Poet and Gunnlaug Serpent-tongue contested*: As described in *The Saga of Gunnlaug Serpent-tongue*.

76. *to cover his body*: According to the 'Grey Goose' legal code, failure to cover up a corpse and protect it from being eaten by animals and birds was punishable by outlawry.

77. *unless compensation was paid before the third sunrise*: According to 'Grey Goose', the deadline for paying compensation for a slave was a fortnight.

78. *Hakon the Powerful's reign*: Earl Hakon Sigurdarson ruled Norway from 975–95. He gained a reputation for political brilliance, as well as a famous victory against the mighty Jomsvikings, and for paganism and lechery.

79. *will-o'-the-wisp*: Icelandic *haugaeldur* (lit. 'grave mound-fire'), considered in folklore to mark the spot where gold or silver are buried.

80. *ridged on the outside, like a scallop shell*: This and other charac-
    teristics of Egil's skull have been interpreted as symptoms of
    Paget's disease. See Jesse L. Byock's study in Further Reading.
81. *the battle where King Olaf Tryggvason was killed*: A dramatic
    sea battle off the island of Svold in the Baltic Sea in 1000. Despite
    a short reign (*c.* 995–1000), King Olaf Tryggvason presided over
    the Christianization of Norway and Iceland.

Maps

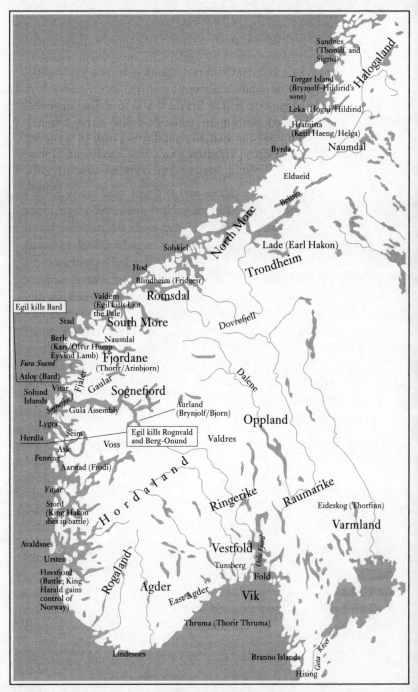

Sandnes
(Thorolf and
Sigrid)

Torgar Island
(Brynjolf–Hildirid's
sons)

Leka (Hogni/Hildirid)

Hrafnista
(Ketil Haeng/Helga)

Byrda

Naumdal

Eldueid

Halogaland

North More

Lade (Earl Hakon)

Beitsto

Solskjel

Trondheim

Hod

Blindheim (Fridgeir)

Valdero
(Egil kills Ljot
the Pale)

Egil kills Bard

Stad

Romsdal

South More

Dovrefjell

Berle
(Kari/Olvir Hump)
Eyvind Lamb)

Naustdal

Fjordane

Fura Sound

Atloy (Bard)

Vitar

Fialer

Thorir/Arinbjorn)

Gaular

Solund
Islands

Sognefjord

Sognefjord

Gula Assembly

Aurland
(Brynjolf/Bjorn)

Dalene

Oppland

Lygra

Seim

Herdla

Ask

Fenring

Aarstad (Frodi)

Voss

Egil kills Rognvald
and Berg-Onund

Valdres

Fitjar

Stord
(King Hakon
dies in battle)

Hordaland

Ringerike

Raumarike

Eideskog (Thorfinn)

Varmland

Avaldsnes

Ursten

Havsfjord
(Battle; King
Harald gains
control of
Norway)

Rogaland

Agder

Vestfold

Tunsberg

East Agder

Fold

Vik

Oslo fjord

Thruma (Thorir Thruma)

Lindesnes

Branno Islands

Hising

Gota River

Norway

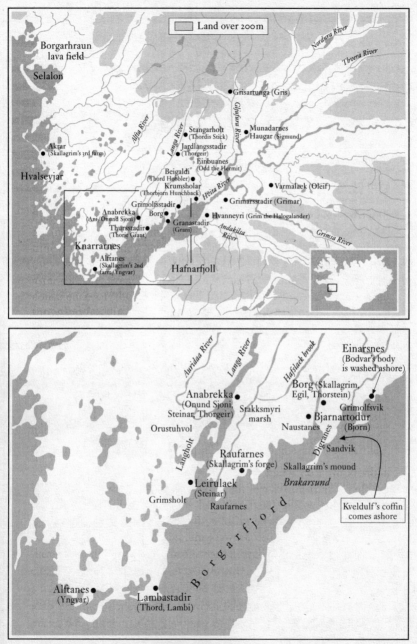

Borgarfjord (Iceland)

Egil's Ancestors and Family

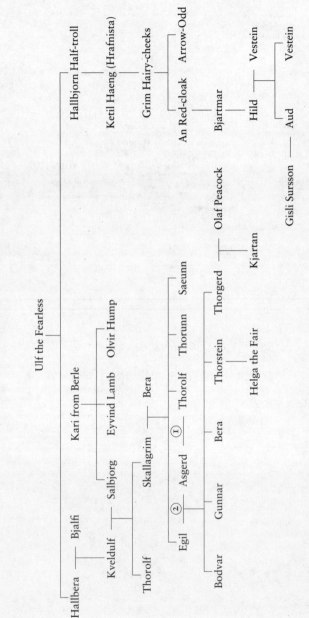

Chronology

It is impossible to establish any precise chronology for the sagas, which are largely fictionalized reconstructions of events written down in a society in which the precision of modern time-reckoning was unnecessary. Nonetheless; on the basis of broad chronological consistency, precise references to time intervals between events, and known and datable persons and events, scholars have managed to reconstruct a fairly plausible timeframe for many of them. *Egil's Saga*, however, poses many difficulties in this respect. It is impossible to reconcile the inner time span of the saga with known historical events.

In the following table the aim is to give a chronological overview of Egil's life rather than attempt to fit all of the events in the saga into a chronological framework. The dates are anchored to events in the history of the kings of Norway and England which the saga uses as points of reference for its chronology. For example, the saga mentions three events – the battle in which Eirik killed his brothers, Hakon's arrival in Norway, and Egil's dispute with Atli the Short at Gulathing – as all taking place in the same summer. Eirik then flees to England the following year. English sources record that Eirik ruled Northumbria from *c.* 947 to 954. That date does not fit with the saga's claim that Egil's last journey abroad (some years after his meeting with Eirik in York) took place around the time when Edmund became king of England; that is, between 940 and 946. According to the accepted chronology based on Norse sources, Hakon is believed to have taken power in parts of Norway in 934. That date fits better the inner chronology of *Egil's Saga* and has therefore been adopted as a key date in the table below. The inner time of the saga, however, is not always consistent – for instance, it is difficult to account for the activities of Thorolf and Egil for all of the twelve years Egil is said to have been abroad for the first time. A close reading of the saga gives one the impression that the duration of the whole journey was closer to six years. All dates are approximate. The story of the saga appears in bold, while Scandinavian and English history is given in italics.

Settlement of Iceland, mainly from Norway, begins	*c.* 870
Battle of Havsfjord (Harald Fair-hair takes control of Norway)	*c.* 885–900
Birth of Egil	902
Egil's first journey abroad (with Thorolf)	915–27
Athelstan becomes King of Wessex (later first king of England)	924
The Battle at Wen Heath: Thorolf killed	925
Egil marries Asgerd	926
Establishment of the Althing	*c.* 930
Egil's second journey abroad	933–4
Dispute at the Gula Assembly	934
King Hakon takes power in Norway	934/5
Egil's third journey abroad	936–8
Egil meets King Eirik at York	936
Battle of Brunanburh	937
Egil kills Atli the Short	938
Death of King Athelstan	939
Egil's fourth journey abroad	945–7
Journey to Varmland (winter)	946–7
Eirik Blood-axe accepted as King of Northumbria	947/8
King Eirik driven out of Northumbria	954
Battle of Stord: King Hakon dies of his wounds. Harald Grey-cloak and the other sons of Eirik take power in Norway	*c.* 960
Egil composes 'Ode to Arinbjorn'	962
Division of Iceland into Quarters	*c.* 965
Battle of Limfjord: death of King Harald Grey-cloak. **Arinbjorn killed fighting for King Harald Grey-cloak.** *Earl Hakon Sigurdarson takes control of Norway*	975
Death of Egil	985
Scandinavians discover Greenland	985/6
Christianity accepted in Iceland	999 or 1000
Battle of Svold: death of King Olaf Tryggvason of Norway	*c.* 1000
Íslendingabók (The Book of Icelanders) written by Ari the Wise	*c.* 1122–33
First kings' sagas compiled	*c.* 1150
Snorri Sturluson born	1179
First Sagas of Icelanders compiled	*c.* 1220
Heimskringla compiled by Snorri Sturluson	*c.* 1230–40

Snorri Sturluson dies   1241
End of the Icelandic commonwealth   1262
Codex Regius of the Eddic poems compiled   *c.* 1270
Oldest surviving manuscripts of *Egil's Saga* (now only
   fragments) written   1250–1300
The Möðruvallabók codex of the sagas compiled   mid-14th century

Social and Political Structure

The notion of kinship is central to the sense of honour and duty in the sagas, and thereby to their action. Kinship essentially involves a sense of belonging not unlike that underlying the Celtic clan systems. The Icelandic word for 'kin' or 'clan' (*ætt*) is cognate with other words meaning 'to own' and 'direction' – the notion could be described as a 'social compass'.

Establishing kinship is one of the justifications for the long genealogies, which tend to strike non-Icelandic readers as idiosyncratic detours, and also for the preludes in Norway before the main saga action begins. Members of the modern nuclear family or close relatives are only part of the picture, since kinsmen are all those who are linked through a common ancestor – preferably one of high birth and high repute – as far back as five or six generations or even more.

Marriage ties, sworn brotherhood and other bonds could create conflicting loyalties with respect to the duty of revenge, of course, as we see in many sagas, but by the same token they could serve as instruments for resolving such vendettas. A strict order stipulated who was to take revenge within the fairly immediate family, with a 'multiplier effect' if those seeking vengeance were killed in the process. The obligation to take revenge was inherited, just like wealth, property and claims.

Patriarchy was the order of the day, although notable exceptions are found. Likewise, the physical duty of revenge devolved only upon males, but women were often responsible for instigating it, either by urging a husband or brother to action with slurs about their cowardice or by bringing up their sons with a vengeful sense of purpose and even supplying them with old weapons that had become family heirlooms.

Iceland was unique among European societies in the tenth to thirteenth centuries in two respects in particular: it had no king and no executive power to follow through the pronouncements of its highly sophisticated legislative and judicial institutions. The lack of executive power meant that there was no means for preventing men from taking the law into their own hands. This gave rise to many memorable conflicts recorded in the sagas, but also led to the gradual disintegration of the Commonwealth in the thirteenth century.

The Althing served not only as a general or national assembly (which is what its name means), but also as the main festival and social gathering of the year, where people exchanged stories and news and renewed acquaintances with old friends and relatives. Originally it was inaugurated (with a pagan ceremony) by the leading godi or chieftain (*allsherjargoði*) who was a descendant of the first settler Ingolf Arnarson, in the tenth week of summer. Early in the eleventh century the opening day was changed to the Thursday of the eleventh week of summer (June 18–24). Legislative authority at the Althing was in the hands of the Law Council, while there were two levels of judiciary, the Quarter Courts and the Fifth Court.

The Law Council was originally comprised of the 36 godis, along with two thingmen for each, and the Lawspeaker, who was the highest authority in the Commonwealth, elected by the Law Council for a term of three years. It was the duty of the Lawspeaker to recite the entire procedures of the assembly and one-third of the laws of the country every year. He presided over the meetings of the Law Council and ruled on points of legal interpretation.

Quarter Courts, established at the Althing around 965, evolved from earlier regional Spring Assemblies, probably panels of nine men, which had dealt with cases involving people from the same quarter. Three new godords (the office of a godi) were created in the north when the Quarter Courts were set up. The godis appointed 36 men to the Quarter Court and their decisions had to be unanimous.

Around 1005, a Fifth Court was established as a kind of court of appeal to hear cases which were unresolved by the Quarter Courts. The godis appointed 48 members to the Fifth Court and the two sides in each case were allowed to reject six each. A simple majority among the remaining 36 then decided the outcome and lots were drawn in the event of a tie. With the creation of the Fifth Court, the number of godis was increased correspondingly, and with their two thingmen each and the Lawspeaker, the Law Council was then comprised of 145 people in all.

Legal disputes feature prominently in the Sagas of Icelanders and the prosecution and defence of a case followed clearly defined procedures. Cases were prepared locally some time before the Thing and could be dismissed there if they were technically flawed. Preparation generally took one of two forms. A panel of 'neighbours' could be called, comprising five or nine people who lived near the scene of the incident or the home of the accused, to testify to what had happened. Alternatively, a party could go to the home of the accused to summons him during the Summons Days, two weeks before the Spring Assembly, but three or four weeks before the Althing.

The accused generally did not attend the Thing, but was defended by someone else, who called witnesses and was entitled to disqualify members of the panel. Panels did not testify to the details and facts of the case in the modern sense, but determined whether the incident had taken place. The case was then summed up and a ruling passed on it by the Quarter Court.

Penalties depended upon the seriousness of the case and took the form of either monetary compensation or outlawry. Lesser outlawry lasted for three years, while full outlawry meant that a man must not be 'fed or helped on his way' and was tantamount to a death sentence. A confiscation court would seize the belongings of a person outlawed for three years or life. Cases were often settled without going through the complex court procedure, either by arbitration, a ruling from a third party who was accepted by both sides, or by self-judgement by either of the parties involved in the case. Duelling was another method for settling disputes, but was formally banned in Iceland in 1006.

The Farm

The farm (*bær*) was a basic social and economic unit in Iceland. Although farms varied in size, there was presumably only one building on a 'farm' at the time of settlement, an all-purpose building known as a hall or farmhouse (*skáli*) or longhouse (*langhús*), constructed on the model of the farmhouses the settlers had inhabited in Norway. Over time, additional rooms and/or wings were often added to the original construction.

The Icelandic farmhouse shown in the illustrations is based on information provided by the excavations at Stong (Stöng) in the Thjorsardal valley in the south of Iceland. Stong is regarded as having been an average-sized farm by Icelandic standards. The settlement was abandoned as a result of the devastating ash-fall from the great eruption of Hekla in 1104.

The illustrations are intended to help readers visualize the farm, and understand the specialized vocabulary used to describe it. Many of these terms can be found in the Glossary.

The plan of the farmstead (Figure 1) shows an overall layout of a typical farm. It is based on measurements carried out by the archaeologist Daniel Bruun, but it should be stressed that the layout of these farms was far from fixed. Nonetheless, the plan indicates the common positioning of the haystack wall/yard (*stakkgarður*) in the often-mentioned hayfield (*tún*). The hayfield wall (*túngarður*) surrounds the farm and its hayfield.

Also placed outside the main farm are the animal sheds. With the exception of a cow shed, no barns or other animal sheds came to light at Stong, but these must have existed as they did on most farms. Sometimes they were attached to the farmhouse, but more often were independent constructions some distance away from the building. Sheep sheds, in particular, tended to be built farther away from the hall, and closer to the meadows used for grazing.

The smithy is also separate (for safety reasons), and the same often

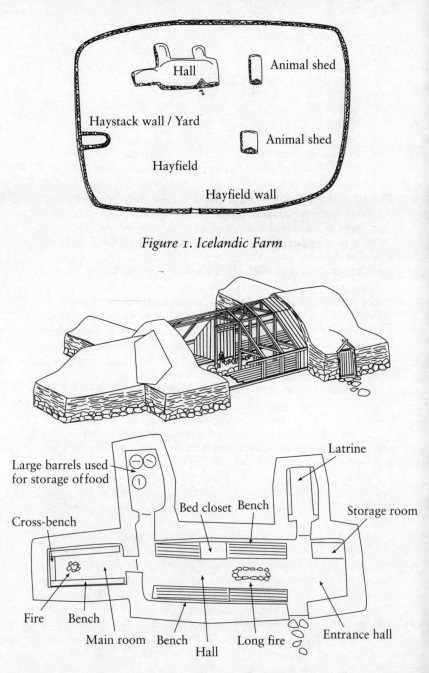

Figure 1. Icelandic Farm

Figures 2 and 3. The Farmhouse at Stong

Labels in Figure 1:
Hall
Animal shed
Haystack wall / Yard
Animal shed
Hayfield
Hayfield wall

Labels in Figure 3:
Large barrels used for storage of food
Latrine
Cross-bench
Bed closet Bench
Storage room
Fire Bench
Main room Bench Hall Long fire Entrance hall

appears to have applied to the fire-room/fire hall (*eldhús/eldaskáli*). The latter was essentially a form of specialized kitchen. It was not only used for cooking, but was also the site of other daily household activities carried out around the fire. Indeed, sometimes the term *eldhús* seems to refer not to a separate building, but to the farmhouse, instead of the word 'hall', stressing the presence of the fire and warmth in the living quarters.

Figure 2 is a cross-section of the hall at Stong, giving an idea of the way the buildings were constructed. The framework was timber. The main weight of the roof rested on beams, which, in turn, were supported by pillars on either side of the hall. The high-seat pillars (*öndvegissúlur*) that some settlers brought with them from Norway might have been related to the pillars placed on either side of the high seat (*hásæti*). The outer walls of most farms in Iceland were constructed of a thick layer of turf and stone, which served to insulate the building. The smoke from the main fire was usually let out through a vent in the roof, but the living quarters would still have been rather smoke-ridden.

Figure 3 depicts the layout of the farmhouse excavated at Stong. The purpose of the area, here marked 'latrine', is uncertain, but this role makes sense on the basis of the layout of the room, and the description given in *The Tale of Thorstein Shiver*, for example. For information about the bed-closet, see the Glossary.

Glossary

Althing *alþingi*: General assembly. See 'Social and Political Structure'.

Assembly *þing*: See 'Social and Political Structure'.

ball game *knattleikur*: A game played with a hard ball and a bat, possibly similar to the Gaelic game known as hurling which is still played in Scotland and Ireland, only with two players instead of two teams. The rules are uncertain, but the object appears to be to knock the ball over the opponent's goal line. A common motif in the sagas; quarrels over ball games often lead to lasting and fatal conflicts.

bed-closet *hvílugólf, lokrekkja, lokhvíla, lokrekkjugólf*: A private sleeping area used for the heads of better-off households. The closet was usually partitioned off from the rest of the house and had a door that was secured from the inside.

berserk *berserkur*: A warrior who could assume extraordinary strength during a kind of induced trance in battle which made him apparently immune to the effect of blows from weapons. In his *Heimskringla* (History of the Kings of Norway), Snorri Sturluson attributes this power to a blessing by Odin, the chief god of the pagan pantheon: 'Odin knew how to make his enemies in battle blind or deaf or full of fear and their weapons would bite no more than sticks, while his own men went without armour and were as crazed as dogs or wolves, biting at their shields and as strong as bears or bulls. They killed people, but were impervious to both fire and iron. This is called "going beserk".' By the time of the sagas, berserks had lost all religious dignity and tended to be cast in the role of brutal but simple-minded villains; when heroes dispatch them, there is usually little regret and a great deal of local relief.

booth *búð*: A temporary dwelling used by those who attended the various assemblies. Structurally, it seems to have involved permanent walls which were covered by a tent-like roof, probably made from cloth.

bride-price *mundur*: In formal terms, this was the amount that the prospective husband's family gave to the prospective wife's family at the wedding and became the personal property of the wife.

compensation *manngjöld, bœtur*: Penalties imposed by the courts were of three main kinds: awards of compensation in cash; sentences of lesser outlawry, which could be lessened or dropped by the payment of compensation; and sentences of full outlawry with no chance of being moderated. In certain cases a man's right to immediate vengeance was recognized, but for many offences compensation was the fixed legal penalty and the injured party had little choice but to accept the settlement offered by the court, an arbitrator or a man who had been given the right to self-judgement (*sjálfdœmi*). It was certainly legal to put pressure on the guilty party to pay. Neither court verdicts nor legislation, nor even the constitutional arrangements, had any coercive power behind them other than the free initiative of individual chieftains with their armed following.

cross-bench *pallur, þverpallur*: A raised platform or bench at the inner end of the main room, where women were usually seated.

directions *austur/vestur/norður/suður* (east/west/north/south): These directional terms are used in a very wide sense in the sagas; they are largely dependent on context and cannot always be trusted to reflect compass directions. Internationally, 'the east' generally refers to the countries to the east and south-east of Iceland, and although 'easterner' usually refers to a Norwegian, it can also apply to a Swede (especially since the concept of nationality was still not entirely clear when the sagas were being written) and might even be used for a person who has picked up Russian habits. 'The west' or to 'go west' tends to refer to Ireland and what are now the British Isles, but might refer to lands farther afield; the point of orientation is west of Norway. When confined to Iceland, directional terms sometimes refer to the quarter to which a person is travelling, e.g. a man going to the Althing from the east of the country might be said to be going 'south' rather than 'west', and a person going home to the West Fjords from the Althing is said to be going 'west' rather than 'north'.

drapa *drápa*: A heroic, laudatory poem, usually in the complicated metre preferred by the Icelandic poets. Such poems were in fashion between the tenth and thirteenth centuries. They were usually composed in honour of kings, earls and other prominent men, living or dead. Occasionally they were addressed to a loved one or made in praise of pagan or Christian religious figures. A *drapa* usually consisted of three parts: an introduction, a middle section including one or more refrains, and a conclusion. It was usually clearly distinguished from the *flokk*, which tended to be shorter, less lauda-tory and without refrains.

duel *hólmganga*: Used for a formally organized duel, literally meaning 'going to the island'. This is probably because the area prescribed for the fight formed a small 'island' with clearly defined boundaries which separated the action from the outside world; it might also refer to the fact that small islands were originally favoured sites for duels. The rules included that the two duellists slashed at each other alternately, the seconds protecting the principal fighters with shields. Shields hacked to pieces could be replaced by up to three shields on each side. If blood was shed, the fight could be ended and the wounded man could buy himself off with a ransom of three marks of silver, either on the spot or later. The rules are stated in detail in chapter 10 of *Kormak's Saga*: 'The duelling laws had it that the cloak was to be five ells square, with loops at the corners, and pegs had to be put down there of the kind that had a head at one end. They were called tarses, and he who made the preparations was to approach the tarses in such a way that he could see the sky between his legs while grasping his ear lobes with the invocation that has since been used again in the sacrifice known as the tarse-sacrifice. There were to be three spaces marked out all round the cloak, each a foot in breadth, and outside the marked spaces there should be four strings, named hazel poles; what you had was a hazel-poled stretch of ground, when that was done. You were supposed to have three shields, but when they were used up, you were to go onto the cloak, even if you had withdrawn from it before, and from then on you were supposed to protect yourself with weapons. He who was challenged had to strike. If one of the two was wounded in such a way that blood fell onto the cloak, there was no obligation to continue fighting. If someone stepped with just one foot outside the hazel poles, he was said to be retreating, or to be running if he did so with both. There would be a man to hold the shield for each one of the two fighting. He who was the more wounded of the two was to release himself by paying duel ransom, to the tune of three marks of silver.' The duel was formally banned by law in Iceland in 1006, six years after the Icelanders had accepted Christianity.

earl *jarl*: A title generally restricted to men of high rank in northern countries (though not in Iceland), who could be independent rulers or subordinate to a king. The title could be inherited or it could be conferred by a king on a prominent supporter or leader of military forces. The Earls of Lade who appear in a number of sagas and tales ruled large sections of northern Norway (and often many southerly areas as well) for several centuries. Another prominent, almost independent, earldom was that of Orkney and Shetland.

east *austur*: See 'directions'.

fire-room *eldaskáli*: In literal terms, this was a room or special building (as perhaps at Jarlshof in Shetland) containing a fire, and its primary function was that of a kitchen. Such a definition, however, would be too limited, since the fire-room was also used for eating, working and sleeping. Indeed, in many cases the word *eldaskáli* seems to have been synonymous with the word *skáli* meaning the hall of a farm.

follower *hirðmaður*: A member of the inner circle of followers that surrounded the Scandinavian kings, a sworn king's man.

foster- *fóstur-, fóstri, fóstra*: Children during the saga period were often brought up by foster-parents, who received either payment or support in return from the real parents. Being fostered was therefore somewhat different from being adopted: it was essentially a legal agreement and, more importantly, a form of alliance. Nonetheless, emotionally, and in some cases legally, fostered children were seen as being part of the family circle. Relationships and loyalties between foster-kindred could become very strong. It should be noted that the expressions *fóstri/fóstra* were also used for people who had the function of looking after, bringing up and teaching the children on the farm.

freed slave *lausingi, leysingi*: A slave could be set or bought free and thus acquired the general status of a free man, although this status was low, since if he/she died with no heir, his/her inheritance would return to the original owner. The children of freed slaves, however, were completely free.

full outlawry *skóggangur*: Outlawry for life. One of the terms applied to a man sentenced to full outlawry was *skógarmaður*, which literally means 'forest man', even though in Iceland there was scant possibility of his taking refuge in a forest. Full outlawry simply meant banishment from civilized society, whether the local district, the province or the whole country. It also meant the confiscation of the outlaw's property to pay the prosecutor, cover debts and sometimes provide an allowance for the dependants he had left behind. A full outlaw was to be neither fed nor offered shelter. According to one legal codex from Norway it was 'as if he were dead'. He had lost all goods and all rights. Wherever he went he could be killed without any legal redress. His children became illegitimate and his body was to be buried in unconsecrated ground.

games *leikar*: *Leikur* (sing.) in Icelandic contained the same breadth of meaning as 'game' in English. The games meetings described in the sagas would probably have included a whole range of 'play' activities. Essentially, they involved men's sports such as wrestling, ball games, 'skin-throwing games', 'scraper games' and horse-fights. Games of this kind took place whenever people came together and seem to have formed a regular feature of assemblies and other gatherings (including the Althing) and religious festivals such as the Winter Nights. Sometimes prominent men invited people together specifically to take part in games.

giant *jötunn, risi*: According to Nordic mythology, the giants (*jötnar*) had existed from the dawn of time. In many ways they can be seen as the personification of the more powerful natural elements and the enemies of the gods and mankind. The original belief was that they lived in the distant north and east in a place called Jotunheim ('the world of the giants'), where they were eternally planning the eventual overthrow of the gods. The final battle between the giants and the gods, Ragnarok ('the fate of the gods'), would mark the end of the world. The original giants were regarded as clever and devious and had an even greater knowledge of the world and the future than that which was available to Odin. *Risi* is a later coinage, when old beliefs were fading and the ancient giants were merging into the troll figure, which was also losing its original characteristics; it refers primarily to the physical size of these beings, which live in the mountains on the borders of civilization.

godi *goði*: This word was little known outside Iceland in early Christian times and seems to refer to a particularly Icelandic concept. A godi was a local chieftain who had legal and administrative responsibilities in Iceland. The name seems to have originally meant 'priest' or at least a person having a special relationship with gods or supernatural powers, and thus shows an early connection between religious and secular power. As time went on, however, the chief function of a godi came to be secular. The first godis were chosen from the leading families who settled Iceland in *c*.870–930. See 'Social and Political Structure'.

halberd *atgeir*: *Atgeir* is translated as 'halberd', which it seems to have resembled even though no specimens of this combination of spear and axe have been found in archaeological excavations in Iceland.

hall *skáli*: *Skáli* was used both for large halls such as those used by kings and for the main farmhouse on the typical Icelandic farm.

hand *spönn*: A measurement, originally the width of a man's hand (approximately 16–17 cm).

hayfield *tún*: An enclosed field for hay cultivation close to or surrounding a farm house. This was the only 'cultivated' part of a farm and produced the best hay. Other hay, generally of lesser quality, came from the meadows which could be a good distance from the farm itself.

hayfield wall *túngarður*: A wall of stones surrounding the hayfield in order to protect it from grazing livestock.

hersir *hersir*: A local leader in western and northern Norway; his rank was hereditary. Originally the hersirs were probably those who took command when the men of the district were called to arms.

high seat *öndvegi*: The central section of one bench in the hall (at the inner end or in the middle of the 'senior' side, to the right as one entered) was the rightful high seat of the owner of the farm. Even though it is usually referred to in English as the 'high seat', this position was not necessarily higher in elevation, only in honour. Opposite the owner sat the guest of honour.

hundred *hundrað*: A 'long hundred' or 120. The expression, however, rarely refers to an accurate number, but to a generalized 'round' figure.

knorr *knörr*: An ocean-going cargo vessel.

Law Rock *Lögberg*: The raised spot at the Althing at Thingvellir where the Lawspeaker may have recited the law code and where public announcements and speeches were made. See also 'Social and Political Structure'.

Lawspeaker *lögsögumaður*, *lögmaður*: means literally 'the man who recites the law', referring to the time before the advent of writing when the Lawspeaker had to learn the law by heart and recite one-third of it every year, perhaps at the Law Rock. If he was unsure about the text, he had to consult a team of five or more 'lawmen' (*lögmenn*) who knew the law well. The Lawspeaker presided over the assembly at the Althing and was responsible for the preservation and clarification of legal tradition. He could exert influence, as in the case about whether the Icelanders should accept Christianity, but should not be regarded as having ruled the country. See also 'Social and Political Structure'.

lesser outlawry *fjörbaugsgarður*: Differed from full or greater outlawry in that the lesser outlaw was only banished from society for three years. Furthermore, his land was not confiscated and money was put aside to support his family. This made it possible for him to return later and continue a normal life. *Fjörbaugsgarður* means literally 'life-ring enclosure'. 'Life-ring' refers to the silver ring that the outlaw originally had to pay the godi in order to spare his life.

(This was later fixed at a value of one mark.) 'Enclosure' refers to three sacrosanct homes no more than one day's journey from each other where the outlaw was permitted to stay while he arranged passage out of Iceland. He was allowed limited movement along the tracks directly joining these farms and *en route* to the ship which would take him abroad. Anywhere else the outlaw was fair game and could be killed without redress. He had to leave the country and begin his sentence within the space of three summers after the verdict, but once abroad regained normal rights.

longship *langskip*: The largest warship.

magic rite *seiður*: The exact nature of magic ritual or *seiður* is somewhat obscure. It appears that it was originally only practised by women. Even though there are several accounts of males who performed this rite (including the god Odin), they are almost always looked down upon as having engaged in an 'effeminate' activity. The magic rite seems to have had two main purposes: a spell to influence people or the elements (as in *Egil's Saga*, chapter 60) and a means of finding out about the future. There are evidently certain parallels between *seiður* and shamanistic rituals like those carried out by the Lapps and Native Americans. However, the magic rite referred to in *Egil's Saga* is performed by Gunnhild off-stage, as it were, and seems to be more of a narrative device to explain Egil's restlessness.

main room *stofa*: A room off the hall of a farmhouse.

mark *mörk*: A measurement of weight, eight ounces, approximately 214 grams.

Moving Days *fardagar*: Four successive days in the seventh week of 'summer' (in May) during which householders in Iceland could change their abode.

nature spirit *vættur*: There were various kinds of nature spirits that the Icelanders (and other Scandinavians) believed in and sometimes gave sacrifices to. There are early references to elves (*álfar*) in mainland Scandinavia. Like their modern-day equivalents, the 'hidden people' (an expression used in both Norway and Iceland) were of human size. Even closer to nature were the guardian spirits (*landvættir*) which inhabited the landscape. The welfare of the inhabitants of the country depended on their welfare and support, as can be seen in *Egil's Saga* (chapter 58) when Egil raises a scorn-pole facing the guardian spirits of Norway. According to the earliest Icelandic law, Ulfljot's Law, people approaching Iceland by sea had to remove the dragon-heads from the prows of their ships to avoid frightening the guardian spirits.

north *norður*: See 'directions'.

ounce *eyrir* (pl. *aurar*): A unit of weight, varying slightly through time, but roughly 27 grams. Eight ounces were equal to one mark.

outlawry *útlegð, skóggangur, fjörbaugsgarður*: Two of the Icelandic words, *útlegð*, literally meaning 'lying or sleeping outside', and *skóggangur*, 'forest-walking', stress the idea of the outlaw having been ejected from the safe boundaries of civilized society and being forced to live in the wild alongside the animals and nature spirits, little better than an animal himself. The word *útlagi* ('outlaw') is closely related to *útlegð*, but has also taken on the additional meaning of 'outside the law', which for early Scandinavians was synonymous with 'lying outside society'. Law was what made society. See also 'full outlawry' and 'lesser outlawry'.

runes *rúnir*: A system of writing native to Scandinavia, England and areas on the Continent where Germanic languages were spoken. Runes predated the introduction of the Roman alphabet among Scandinavians (the earliest runic inscriptions are dated to the second century AD), but runic writing continued to be used alongside Roman throughout the Middle Ages. There is scattered evidence – archaeological, runological and literary – for the magical use of runes, although it remains uncertain whether the magic power was considered to be vested in the runes themselves or in the words they form.

sacrifice, sacrificial feast *blót*: There is great uncertainty about the nature of pagan worship and cult-activities in Scandinavia, and just as the theology and mythology of the Nordic peoples seem to have varied according to area, it is highly questionable whether any standardized rules of ritual practice ever existed there. It should also be remembered that the population of Iceland came from all over Scandinavia as well as from Ireland and the islands off Scotland. Religion was very much an individual matter and practices varied. The few references to sacrifices in the sagas are somewhat vague, but these sometimes seem to have involved the ritual slaughter of animals.

scorn-pole *níðstöng*: In the sagas, *níð* (scorn) is used both of mockery (especially lampoons) and physical representations to deliver a public insult, such as wooden figures in some compromising sexual position. In *Egil's Saga* (chapter 58) the scorn-pole with a horse's head on a stick has a purpose more akin to voodoo: to place a curse on the king.

shape-shifter *hamrammur* (adj): Closely associated with the berserks, those who were *hamrammir* (pl.) were believed to change their shape at night or in times of stress or leave their bodies (which appeared asleep) and take the physical form of wild animals. There are again faint associations with shamanistic activities and figures known in folklore throughout the world, such as the werewolf. The transformation was not necessarily intentional. See introduction, pp. xxi.

shieling *sel*: A roughly constructed hut in the highland grazing pastures away from the farm, where shepherds and cowherds lived during the summer. Milking and the preparation of various dairy products took place here, as did other important farm activities like the collection of peat and charcoal burning (depending on the surroundings). This arrangement was well known throughout the Scandinavian countries from the earliest times.

slave *þrœll*: Slavery was quite an important aspect of Viking Age trade. A large number of slaves were taken from the Baltic nations and the western European countries that were raided and invaded by Scandinavians between the eighth and eleventh centuries. In addition, the Scandinavians had few scruples against taking slaves from the other Nordic countries. Judging from their names and appearance, a large number of the slaves mentioned in the sagas seem to have come from Ireland and Scotland. Stereotypically they are presented as being stupid and lazy. By law, slaves had hardly any rights at all and they and their families could only gain freedom if their owners chose to free them or somebody else bought their freedom: see 'freed slave'. In the Icelandic Commonwealth a slave who was wounded was entitled to one-third of the compensation money; the rest went to his owner.

south *suður*: See 'directions'.

Spring Assembly *vorþing*: The local assembly, held each spring. These were the first regular assemblies to be held in Iceland. Held at 13 sites and lasting four to seven days between 7–27 May, they were jointly supervised by three godis. The Spring Assembly had a dual legal and economic function. It consisted of a court of 36 men, twelve appointed by each of the godis, where local legal actions were heard, while major cases and those which could not be resolved locally were sent on to the Althing. In its other function it was a forum for settling debts, deciding prices and the like. Godis probably used the Spring Assembly to urge their followers to ride to the Althing; those who remained behind paid the costs of those who went. See 'Social and Political Structure'.

sprinkled with water *vatni ausinn*: Even before the arrival of Christianity, the Scandinavians practised a naming ceremony clearly similar to that involved in the modern-day 'christening'. The action of sprinkling a child with water and naming it meant that the child was initiated into society. After this ceremony, a child could not be taken out to die of exposure (a common practice in pagan times).

temple *hof*: In spite of the elaborate description of the 'temple' at Hofstadir (lit. 'Temple Place') in chapter 4 of *The Saga of the People of Eyri*, and other temples mentioned in the sagas, there is no certainty that buildings erected for the sole purpose of pagan worship ever existed in Iceland or the other Scandinavian countries. To date, no such building has been found in archaeological excavations. In all likelihood, pagan rituals and sacrifices took place outdoors or in a specified area in certain large farmhouses belonging to priests, where the idols of the gods would also have been kept.

Thing *alþingi*: See 'Althing' and 'Spring Assembly'.

thingman/men *þingmaður/þingmenn*: Every free man and landowner was required to serve as a thingman ('assembly man') by aligning himself with a godi. He would either accompany the godi to assemblies and other functions or pay a tax supposed to cover the godi's costs of attending them. See 'Social and Political Structure'.

troll *tröll*: Trolls in the minds of the Icelanders were not the huge, stupid figures that we read about in later Scandinavian wonder-tales and legends. At the time of the sagas they were essentially evil nature spirits, a little like large dark elves. It is only in later times that they come to blend with the image of the Scandinavian giants.

Viking *víkingur*: Normally has an unfavourable sense in the sagas of Icelanders, referring to violent seafaring raiders, especially of the pagan period. It can also denote general bullies and villains.

west *vestur*: See 'directions'.

Index